False Reckoning

Joe Moore

Published by Kimber Moore & Associates, 2023.

FALSE RECKONING

First edition. August 24, 2023.

ISBN: 978-0645913019

Written by Joe Moore.

Table of Contents

To Janice

Acknowledgements

. . . .

For her in-depth editing, encouragement and thoughtful observations on so many revisions Linda Godfrey.

. . . .

For their inspiration, opinions and reassurance, Al Ruskin, George Manojlovic, Bob Gray, Kathryn Barton, and Jim Soorley.

. . . .

Illustrated by Michelle Moore.

I'm not one of them.

'You've got a lot of problems Minister,' agreed Mick Darby. 'But, I'm not one of them.'

'Yet.' The Attorney-General said. Darby had interrupted her litany of problems. He'd had the temerity to suggest she distance her office from her Pastor.

The Attorney-General and the Intelligence Assessment chief had been meeting every ten days or so now for months. At the PM's insistence the Attorney-General was to dull the independence of the Intelligence Committee. And, at his boss's insistence, Darby was to hone its edge.

'Yet?' They were still to get each other's measure.

'I don't see you as a problem Mick,' said the Attorney-General. She leant forward, elbows on the desk, right hand nestled in her left, thumbs to her chin. 'As we work more together, well, some boundary issues are sure to crop up. Unavoidable.' She opened her hands, fingers spread. 'But you've trampled one.' She put her hands flat on the desk, 'I wouldn't have thought your role as Intelligence Assessment chief would go to personal attacks on my faith. Perhaps I misread your job description?'

He wasn't answering this question.

'No, I thought not,' she said, smiled, turned her left-hand palm up, 'we'll find a solution I'm sure.'

'I'll say it again. We are yet to receive any security clearance paperwork for Hudson and Phoebe Lang from Asher Ministries,' said Darby.

'Pastor. Pastor Phoebe,' corrected the Attorney-General.

She smoothed an already immaculate skirt, brushed an imaginary hair from her forehead, squared her shoulders and rested her elbows on the desk, hands together again. 'That's because they are not a risk. Not involved in any security issues, fraud nor corruption. Many Australians are happy to confuse thrills with news, and a left-wing media is keen to amplify any sensation about the right. I would have assumed that beneath you.'

Darby leaned forward, suit sleeves riding up, exposing bespoke cufflinks, 'without a clearance, they're to be escorted at all times in Parliament House and government offices, it doesn't matter what their titles are. They visit the House frequently, so a pass would make it easier for everyone.'

'I agree. But...'

Darby sat back, annoyed, security clearance errands beneath him.

'No need for any security paperwork,' said the Attorney-General, 'they have both signed confidentiality agreements, witnessed by me. Passes, issued by me.'

'Confidentiality agreements? I'm sure,' said Darby, 'that would ease any discomfort.'

'It was Hudson's idea.' Missing the sarcasm. 'He thought that a confidentiality agreement made more sense than a security clearance. He is gearing up the next phase of remote monitoring of people in aged care; commercial-in-confidence, confidentiality, a much better fit than a clearance. After all, Mick, I doubt he was ever a terrorist.'

'You worship at Asher Ministries, Hudson and Phoebe share the leadership; Phoebe is your pastor...'

'Not just mine, the PM's too, and Phoebe leads the Parliamentary Choir, multi-party, you know. The choir is open to the public service too, something to think about?'

'Not sure my voice would want to be heard there,' said Mick. 'So, Hudson and Phoebe must be seen to be and actually be, above and beyond. It has to mean cleared, security cleared, above and beyond.'

'I drafted the confidentiality agreements.'

Mick interrupted. 'Minister, do I need to explain the difference between a confidentiality agreement and a security clearance, to you?'

She sat back, elbows resting on the arms of her chair, leather, ergonomic, 'they are above and beyond. All right?'

'But not security cleared!'

Darby opened his brown leather folio, empty save for a single piece of newspaper, and the smell of new leather.

'From an admirer Mick?'

'One you admire,' said Darby, putting the paper on the desk between them, facing the Attorney-General. The clipping was from a magazine for senior Australians and featured the beaming Minister for Aged Care under the headline "Robots for Seniors".

'Well, they've captured his personality,' said the Attorney-General. 'I suggest you take it up with him, he's got oversight of the Commonwealth's spend on aged care.'

'Him,' said Darby, his fingers on the paper, 'he's quoted on the cost savings, his only interest reported here.'

'His only interest, other than promotion; and the savings will be so far into the future, they'll not materialise.'

'So, saving money in aged care,' said Darby, 'that's down to him. Minister, he's an economist working with a scientist; technology and cost savings, that's all they can see. Why not consider a working group to review the wider issues? In the nursing homes, residents interacting mainly with robots, minimal human contact, other than visitors?'

'Are you worried about moral issues?' She shrugged. 'Moral issues covered. We can leave that to the Langs can't we? Seems to me that a church is well placed to consider moral issues, and out of that we can look at any legal implications. At implementation.'

Have to hand it to her thought Darby, but not willing to let it go.

'The detect and alert devices and the sensors in the current trial,' said Darby, 'were designed and made in Australia. What of phase two, outsourced? China?' He tapped the magazine clipping. 'We do have an interest in where they are made.'

'Slave labour part of your remit now?'

'Technology. And who may have access to the data collected and stored. Phase two is a security issue. Part of your remit.' Mick had a near photographic memory, could see the words dancing across the page of the magazine clipping. 'Socially assisted robots, Bluetooth enabled,' said Mick, seeking confirmation in the Attorney-General's face, 'integrating facial recognition and DNA of older people with location,' maybe over-reading her even expression, 'add Zoom or Skype for audio and video recording. Unregulated, yeah. We're interested.'

'The trial is working perfectly. Although,' she continued, 'the next phase is much more intrusive and designed to include older people needing acute care, so more intensive monitoring. Is that what you're worried about?'

'You visit your mother?'

The Attorney General nodded. 'Every Sunday when I'm in Canberra. She's in Asher House Reid, a new build, "salt and pepper" they call it, nursing homes sprinkled around the community.'

She thinks her mother's a fucking condiment. 'She's on Facebook?' he asked, 'you message her with WhatsApp. Have you thought the bracelet she wears might sync with these apps? Be good to know it's not possible, wouldn't it?'

'Do you think it is being done now?' She asked Mick. One shoe, balanced on her toes, dropped as she jerked, leaned across the desk.

'I'd want to be sure it's not done,' said Mick, and decided to go back to the start. 'What we'd want to do is security checks, and, before the next phase, review the specs and the contract. This is not a simple Purchase Order. It also makes sense to review the complaints against Asher House nursing homes.'

The Attorney General opened her laptop, typed rapidly.

'The complaints,' Darby continued, 'cover tax free status, the traineeship scheme, quality of care, neglect, staffing ratios, access to medical staff. Get some distance, some independence between this office,' he paused looked about him, 'and nursing homes run with people whose beliefs you share.'

She picked up her cup and saucer in one hand, the other turned the screen towards Darby. The teaspoon slipped, Darby caught it, put it back. 'Thanks', she said, 'now, look, Mick, you're overreacting. Asher House, Hudson Lang, the Board of Asher Ministries, they dealt with the complaints. All the complaints were directed back to Asher House to address. They have come back stating the concerns raised had already been addressed. Nothing more for us to do.'

'Asher House was the sole provider in the trial phase and based on those results; remote monitoring is to be rolled out. Think about this, federal government funding of nursing homes owned and run by a wealthy church counting the Prime Minister, the Attorney-General, other senior government ministers as members. You want to see that as a headline in the national papers?' He said; resisting the urge to slap the clipping, to startle her.

The Attorney-General sunk into the leather, hands to the chair's arms.

'There'll be public concerns about privacy. Thrills? Sensation? Be much easier to deal with that if you know there's nothing to hide,' said Darby.

'Nothing to hide?' Raising her voice, the Attorney General continued, leaning across her desk, 'Ian Sturgess, the Aged Care Chief Scientist, personally, has oversight of the clinical trial; I thought you said you're not one of my problems! The people running

Asher House are beyond reproach. Their work needs to be respected. Now, if there's nothing else.'

Mick Darby continued sitting, hands resting in his lap, thought to pass the time he might count the dust motes caught in the afternoon sun. The Attorney-General crossed her legs, one shoe slipped off, she put her foot to the ground wriggled it back into the shoe. Soon, thought Darby; anytime now. He glanced around the room; took in the photos, all taken with people more famous people than her, for this was Canberra, so, an aspirational office.

Suddenly he wanted to protect her.

'Minister,' he said, 'there are a couple of things you don't want conflated...'

'I think you might mean inflated?'

He turned away from her, afraid he'd lose it. Had a sudden memory of a boy he'd saved from drowning. The kid had nearly drowned him as the teenage Darby struggled to shore. Later at the hospital a nurse had told him many drown fighting their rescuer. He realised he'd go down with her.

'Nursing homes run by Asher Ministries, federal funding. Nursing homes with sole access to expensive technology trials; again, federal funds.'

'Look, I know what you're going to say,' she interrupted.

But not what I mean thought Darby. 'Hudson and Phoebe,' he said, 'personal friends of Cabinet members, oh, who, decide federal funds. Hudson and Phoebe roam the corridors of Parliament House with their tithing app. You, you need them to have security clearances.'

She checked her watch. 'You are not my last appointment.'

'Purchase Order? Security clearances? Working party?'

She stood and came around her desk, escorted Darby to her door. 'I'll consider it, in due course, the trial has a month to go, there's more to do after that concludes; so, we're two months away.' They shook hands.

'I've a window tomorrow,' she said. Darby thought it would not be a Johari.

Darby thanked her for her time, and about to open the door, was beaten to it by the Attorney-General's EA.

'Goodbye Mr Darby,' she said, dismissing him, 'Minister, your next appointment is here. She was a little early, but she's been wonderful about it.'

Darby nodded at the EA, nodded again at the woman who got out of the chair, oddly placed beside the EA's workstation. Dr. Pastor, Phoebe Lang, smiled at Darby, who wondered what the two of them had been looking at on screen.

An aviary of parrots.

A Commonwealth car was no stranger to Canberra's most exclusive suburbs. Like residents of exclusive suburbs, the world over, Yarralumla owners were equipped with gauges forensically attuned to evidence of stature; mere wealth, a given. Being collected by a Commonwealth car, especially the armoured luxury used for the Attorney-General, now, that was clout. Yarralumla residents, twitching behind partly drawn curtains, were not surprised to see the vehicle draw up to the expansive courtyard of the Lang mansion.

The Attorney-General had sent the car to pick up Phoebe Lang. The two of them were to visit an Asher House nursing home. Phoebe had talked the minister into the visit a week earlier; 'you have a couple of hours free next Wednesday, come with me,' Phoebe had said, 'these people are inspiring; wealth, health and faith, they have had it all, now calmly waiting their turn to claim victory with Jesus.'

The Prime Minister and the Attorney-General had discussed the visit, 'best to diarise it as a facilities tour, relate it to the complaints you have referred back to Asher House,' the PM said. 'Phoebe is an excellent candidate for the upcoming Senate vacancy. NSW is set to nominate her. She's popular, good with people and we need one more vote to wind back Ethics Australia's powers, make some changes there, other places. Phoebe has her heart set on it. I doubt she'll raise the vacancy, but you need to support her.'

The car was back at the Attorney-General's offices with Phoebe, it was time to leave. 'I'm never quite sure what to wear when I'm with Phoebe,' she confided to her Chief of Staff, 'I feel I'm either overdressed or underdressed.'

'Never Goldilocks,' said Molly, 'maybe you could call her and check before you meet?'

'And tell her about the boy I like while I'm at it,' she said.

Molly Lavandar rolled her eyes, 'has it occurred to you that Phoebe Lang may feel that she's the one ill-dressed to hang out with the Attorney-General? You are the most powerful woman in government, other than the PM, of course; what you wear sets the tone, not your Pastor. The flats with your Zampatti suit? Perfect.'

'Molly thanks, you always know what to say. Something Mick Darby mentioned has been on my mind,' she said, 'he was quite excited about robots in aged care. Anything I should know? I felt out of my depth a little when he rattled on about them being socially assisted.'

'Socially assistive,' corrected Molly, 'the robots are socially assistive. It's early stages, very risky. They've only tested prototypes, only over six months at best.' Then Molly served an ace, 'the Aged Care Minister is very keen, sees them as just the sexy new thing he needs.'

'Him,' snorted the Attorney General, 'he sees himself as the sexy new thing everybody needs! You see the project failing?'

'If it gets that far. You'd have to approve it,' said Molly.

'Tell me more.'

'Robots talking to people, interacting; just a few moral, ethical, even psychological hurdles don't you think? You'd have to approve the legal end. What if older people trust what the robot says more than their carers, nurses, doctors even. The robot's programmed to suggest a change in medication...some legal implications there. The media will eat it alive, and anyone who touches the idea.'

'Now,' said the A-G, allowing herself a discreet smile, 'that would be awkward.'

• • • •

P hoebe sat in the back of the Commonwealth car, closed her phone when the driver opened the door to admit the Attorney-General.

'I'm blessed,' said Phoebe, 'thanks for arranging the driver for me.'

'Oh, no bother, I thought it would make it easier for both of us.'

'Good to see you dressed for performance then, I wasn't sure I'd mentioned it last week.'

The Attorney-General was sure it hadn't been mentioned at all; Phoebe's so busy, she thought to herself.

'Oh this,' she said sweeping her hand along her thigh, 'this is just...' And, remembering Molly's gentle admonition, stopped talking, gently squeezed Phoebe's wrist. 'I am looking forward to this, and not going to Reid to see my mother.'

'We are praying to Jesus, so her spiritual channels may be unblocked. She'll be ready to claim victory with Jesus. We have no end, no beginning,' said Phoebe, 'sure, our bodies end; but your mother, she doesn't end.'

'Bless,' she said, 'it's a great comfort,' withdrawing her hand, resting it in her lap; Phoebe commanded the centre armrest.

Phoebe was ready for activity, all Camilla'd up in a silk pantsuit, the softest of white chunky leather sneakers, striking rather than tasteful, to the Attorney-General's more conservative eye, like an aviary of parrots on the move she thought.

They were on their way to Asher House Ainslie; even with the address in his sat nav the driver nearly missed it, so carefully orchestrated with the Ainslie streetscape was the tenure blind build.

Phoebe's EA greeted them as they walked through the Gate into Asher House Ainslie. 'I've got a staff of three,' Phoebe had confided on the drive, neglecting to mention one was a stylist, another a social media acolyte; the third, who greeted them was her EA, organiser, researcher.

'While Pastor Phoebe will do some spiritual work with our friends,' said the EA, 'some of the carers will show you around, I'm sure they'll be able to answer any questions you may have.'

'Some of our friends can be a bit difficult with those unknown to them,' said the carer standing with Phoebe's EA, 'some are yet to gain the insight of what they're meant to bring through as they age, struggling to learn to get out of themselves, they can get a bit worked up. That's why Pastor Phoebe, and the other pastors are such an important part of our ministry here.'

The carers chatted to the Minister as they guided her around the sanitised, durable, and easy-to-clean Asher House Ainslie; the only uneasy-to-clean surfaces here would be residents' skin. Aircon a soft hum, faint murmur of voices puzzled her.

'So,' explained the carer, 'coming along to Pastor Phoebe's session is a choice which some are yet to make, those more consumed with what suits them. They prefer to stay in their rooms, and we broadcast the Pastor's sermon to them, that's what you can hear. May we show you the gardens? Our naturopathic healing uses all the herbs organically grown here.'

The Minister spoke to an older woman in a kimono, sitting in the garden, 'Do you have a favourite plant?' She asked sitting down beside her.

The older woman looked at her, said, 'blue...'

The carer interrupted, 'blue, it's unusual, a rare colour for flowers,' she looked around her, 'but there are none here. Not that colour.'

The older woman persisted, 'I had my daughter bring forget-me-nots from her place, but I don't see them.'

The carer took the lady's elbow, helped her up and away from the Minister, 'you're always in the garden aren't you love?'

The Minister wondered if her mother now enjoyed the luxury of finishing her own sentence. Were things done to her, for her, with her or by her? Did her mother have a preposition of choice, did her carers bother? She shrugged, 'do they all like the garden?'

'Really, our naturopath is not so keen on having the friends here in the garden, she grows herbs and some flowers for her treatments; but some of them calm down in here.'

Phoebe was winding up; twenty minutes here was long enough for her, and probably for the friends if she thought about them.

'Friends. My friends. Friends of Jesus. Allow me to finish up with two reminders of his love for you. I know the best tablets are from Moses; Jesus enabled doctors too, so bless them, and you and I, you, and I; we pray, we believe health for each other, and take your tablets! Remember, Moses asked 'why me?', still, he took the tablets. So, for you, why me? Well, some of your prayers will be answered through the work of doctors.' Phoebe had been alerted to residents, friends, refusing their medication, sedatives mostly. Faith and tranquilizers, Phoebe spoke both tongues.

Her second reminder, her final words, were about money. 'Before you claim your final victory with Jesus you still have the opportunity to let others emerge through you, to allow others to live victoriously. Give Jesus first place in this,' she opened her arms, 'carers will help you with the app.' The carer crew moved as one to arm devices and cross check tithes.

'So, you wanted to know more about the bracelets, some wear anklets, their choice,' said Phoebe, 'let's take a look at one.' Phoebe led the Attorney-General to a table at which a few friends were sitting, they each greeted Phoebe, 'bless you Pastor.'

'We'd be blessed if you could tell us a little about your bracelets,' said Phoebe. They found out the bracelets were no bother at all, they hadn't caused them any problems wearing them and they had managed not to set off any alarms. They wore them all the time as they had heard what had happened to a friend at another place who had the bracelet but didn't wear it.

'Should we try one out Phoebe, leave a fridge door open?'

'Oh no,' said Phoebe, 'you'd have the first responders here in a flash, and we'd be fined for a false alarm! How would that look on your desk? Oh, joke right,' laughed Phoebe.

The Attorney-General was not sure whether she was joking. She would like to see the system in action, 'would you mind if I had a closer look?'

Phoebe nodded her head to the carer standing just beside the group, 'I'm sure there are some packs in the office?'

'I'll be right back,' said the carer.

Phoebe and the minister moved away from the group, followed the carer.

'It would be best if these remain sealed,' said the carer presenting the clean, smooth blue box, the words 'detect and alert' in black, embossed on the lid. She opened it. 'You can see the bracelet, and the sensors for the appliances. This pack is to be activated for a new friend we're onboarding later this afternoon.' The carer handed over a USB too, 'this holds a short video demonstrating how our system helps our friends retain their independence, for longer. The systems monitor friends' use of appliances; they detect a problem and alert the call. It's such a comfort to relatives too.'

They were guided out of Asher House, the carers and their charges had all moved to recreation areas, uplifting music playing softly.

Settled into the back of the Commonwealth car, Phoebe tweeted a picture of the Attorney-General in deep conversation with a group of older residents of Asher House, 'she knows who she is', read the caption. By the time the car was out of Ainslie the tweet had nearly five hundred likes.

'You sure are popular, 'said Phoebe, 'I'm so blessed you came. Now, I can't wait to get home and change, shower,' she said, 'and have this silk,' she swept her hands down, over but not touching her thighs, 'I need to get it hand washed.'

Square that circle.

Mick Darby was twelve when his mother hit him for the first, and the last time. She called to him from the kitchen as he crashed through the back door, 'how was school today? Don't let the door bang, the spring's busted.'

'OK,' he said, and speaking the universal language of the soon-to-be teen, 'starving.'

'There's nothing to eat. You'll have to wait for your tea,' she said, 'your father's pay's late again. And tea is only an apple and a piece of bread, it's all we have for the four of us,' she said continuing with the washing up.

Mick made sure he closed the back door, slouched into the kitchen. Dirty plates, cups and saucers, saucepans and cutlery were to the left of the sink, breadboard left to dry standing up behind the taps to rest against the windowsill. As his mother finished washing a plate, a cup, she put it in the drying rack to the right of the sink, carefully, she didn't want to chip the crockery. She was the only one in the house left-handed, but his father and Mick dare not alter her regime. His mother had been home with his granny all day, like every other day, Mick wondered why there was so much washing up to do?

'Father Vincent was here, so your grandma and I won't be needing any tea tonight. So, there's tea for you and your father.'

Mick Darby knew what he had to do. From each pay envelope his father handed five dollars to his mother who would fold it and keep it in the collection's envelope for Sunday Mass. Darby figured if the priest had come for a free lunch, then the priest could afford to buy their tea. He returned from the corner shop with four meat pies, a loaf of bread, tin of jam, strawberry his mother's favourite, biscuits for his granny.

His mother cried when he returned, hit him once, and told him to go back to the shop and get the money back, 'just wait til your father gets home,' he heard as he fled. His father heard the story, gave Mick a slap, a light one, which together with his tousling of Mick's hair sent a message of male solidarity.

• • • •

Mick graduated from police recruit training six years later and was posted to an inner-city Brisbane station. His father retired that year and took his wife on a Mary Rossi spiritual tour of the holy sites of Italy. The tour included an audience with the Pope, and a tour of the Vatican. It was the trip of their lifetime.

Mick met them at the airport when his parents landed back in Brisbane six weeks later. His parents were very quiet in the car, Mick put it down to jet lag.

When they got home, he retrieved their bags, while his mother put the kettle on.

The three of them sat at the kitchen table over a cup of tea. Mick asked about the tour and got nothing, not even one-word answers, not even from his mother. His father finished his tea, sat back, and said, 'you know Mick, I wish we'd never gone, your mother's the same.'

It turned out that the tour of the Vatican had ruined their trip. Now both of them talked, 'we only saw a fraction of what's there Mick,' said his mother, 'it broke our hearts.'

Years of doing without so that money could be on the collection plate every Sunday, additional money when the missions came to their suburban church, extra collections for the Holy Father in Rome. To then, at age sixty-five, to see the Aladdin's Cave of the church, riches beyond their imagination. It was too much. They never spoke of the trip again, never went to church again.

'Lose my faith?' His father spat the answer to his elder brother's question, 'mate, I threw it away.'

A month later the local parish priest was moved. Mick's mother said he was transferred to 'remove him from temptation'. The gossip mill, from which his mother never strayed far, spoke of anonymous phone calls to the Bishop, hinted at an affair. Mick's father told him that 'sometimes God needs a helping hand to set things right. Mick,' he advised him, 'no doubt you'll find in your career that justice also sometimes needs a helping hand to reckon things, set things right.'

Mick took his dad's advice. When he saw the blatant corruption of some of his colleagues, his bosses, the money made from not seeing, the framing of innocent men and women, 'well, at least they were innocent of the crimes for which they were framed,' he said, struggling with the syntax better to impress counsel, he lent a 'helping hand.' He informed on corrupt colleagues to a police integrity inquiry, even giving the inquiry a 'helping hand' where the evidence against police or suspects wasn't strong enough. It's how he began to see himself.

. . . .

Now, in his mid-forties Mick Darby was with the Intelligence Committee. The government's response to more complex security challenges was to create more security agencies. The agencies had so far joined battle with each other and only occasionally with security threats. A small group of high-ranking professional intelligence officers formed the Committee out of their despair with government. The irony of the name undetected. The worn oxymoron belied its official status, unchecked power, but, limited funds.

'Unchecked?' Mick interrupted his boss.

'Unchecked? Yeah, last time I looked, means don't get caught. Now funds; short, limited, not much of. So don't break anything of ours. Right?'

Mick read aloud, '...matters pertaining to...assessment ....intelligence ...Boss, the schedule, is there more to this?' He held the document up.

'I expect you'll let me know if there is,' said his boss, 'anything not covered by Intelligence Assessment? Fill in the blanks Mick, join the dots, your secret power.'

The Committee concentrated on those few critical, cross-agency security briefs too important to be left to those who bickered. For some time now Mick Darby's sole focus was countering the capture of federal government by the religious right. He and his team hid behind the title of Intelligence Assessment.

Mick had reached almost to the summit of what he viewed privately as the Department of the Helping Hand. The current Attorney-General had restricted the powers of oversight committees to review security policy not operations. Members of parliament, senior advisors, and bureaucrats met; lunched heavily, pored over abstruse policy capability frameworks, argued about the application of style guides and legal citation guidelines, and congratulated themselves on their contribution to keeping their country safe. It was a con. Bowing to some public pressure, parliamentary oversight committees had doubled in number at the same time as their facility to hold security services to account for anything other than poor grammar shrivelled.

It was a circle to be squared; increased security threats, competing security agencies granted more powers which they had not the funds to exercise, governed by watered-down regulations, badgered by politicians, but not held to account. It suited Darby. He and his team, and other Intelligence Committee teams were free to act with no operational accountability to government. He knew it couldn't last so he was always in a hurry. Darby wore silver cufflinks; round with an open square inscribed inside the circle. His colleagues thought it was of Celtic design.

Darby was challenged by how the conservative government and the religious right intersected internal security. The result was a kind of bilingualism; where the government spoke the language of strengthening security, and in the same sentence slipped into another language: freedom, curbing security powers. His response to his confusion was paranoia. Asher Ministries, because of their infiltration of government, was a weekly agenda piece.

'Security and freedom,' said Mick, 'we're dealing with a government, illiterate and cynical, in both those languages,' ending his explanation to his lead team.

'Maybe it's what they mean by speaking in tongues,' said one.

'Hmm,' said Mick, 'I know there's little to report, but I want to keep Asher Ministries on our agenda,' Mick said, introducing the item. 'Complaints about their aged care services to the Attorney General have all been referred back to Asher House to resolve. What else do we have? Updates?'

'Lawsuits,' said one of the team, 'you mentioned the complaints, of the ones we know about, four are anonymous. Lawyers acting for Asher Ministries have threatened litigation against the other complainants unless they withdraw. Freedom of Information requests have been lodged to get the names of the four anonymous complainants, and the word is the Asher lawyers will get access.'

'Anonymous complainants? They'll find out who they are? Do we know who's ruling on that?' Mick asked.

'Minister for Aged Care.'

'Asher Ministries' member?'

'Yeah. Coincidence.'

'Do we have any other coincidences?' Mick asked. 'What have you got?' Darby said to an investigator who'd nodded.

'I've been digging around the complaints. They're all different, that's unusual. Usually, providers get complaints about a common item; medication, falls, or neglect typically. It's rare for one provider to get a bunch of different complaints.'

'There's one bloke, wants to talk to someone about his complaint,' said another of the team.'

'Make it quick, I'm on a roll here,' said the operator who'd been interrupted.

'Bloke says his father was billed for the bracelets and sensor kit, but Asher House reckons he never had one, the bill was a mistake. Only the son reckons he has photos of his old man wearing it.'

'Forget it,' said Darby, 'we're not interested in the bracelets, or any of that detect and alert piece. Seems legit. So,' he turned to the guy on a roll, 'rare for providers to get different complaints?'

'Yeah. Asher House is the exception, each complaint is about a different feature of service, for example, staffing levels, food quality, medication error, falls, access to medical practitioner, money. These are only the complaints lodged externally. We have no records of complaints made directly to any of the Asher House facilities, internally. Doesn't mean there aren't any.'

'Thing is,' said Mick, 'no matter what we think, the A-G's handling these the way they should be handled, first thing to do is refer the complainant to the service provider. She's done that.'

There were two more pieces of information. One of the team reported that next-of-kin of Asher House residents had been emailed by Hudson and Phoebe Lang, global pastors and directors of Asher Ministries, owner of Asher House. The email had assured them their relatives were blessed to live in Asher House, were provided the highest level of care, asked for donations, and, reminded of the confidentiality clauses signed on admission agreements.

'I thought this might be interesting,' said one of Darby's lead team, 'it's less than a minute, a bit loud.'

The screen along the back wall of the meeting room burst into life, with the sound muted the light was an assault, even the guy who knew it was coming winced. A sombre Phoebe Lang appeared in the radiant circle of one powerful spotlight; suited, tanned, coiffed.

'Friends, friends,' opening her arms wide, 'who among us has not been misunderstood? Who among us doesn't know how it feels to be misunderstood? Some of us have our loved ones in our nursing homes, calmly waiting for Jesus to reveal himself. Their vulnerability naked, they are being misunderstood! The evil one, you know who he is,' drawing loud shouts from the crowd, 'telling false and shameful stories of the care your loved ones receive from us.' Some in the crowd wailed now as Phoebe confessed to not understanding how people could spread mischief about the wonderful carers looking after our loved ones in Asher House.

'We will not run from these mischief makers.' The crowd roared approval. 'Like David, we will attack this Goliath threatening your loved ones.' The crowd now warlike, feet stamping. The stamping stopped and Hudson joined Phoebe in the spotlight.

'Friends,' said Hudson, 'do not be distracted, we are in need of you now. Now it falls to giving, help us join battle with Goliath...'

The segment finished, Darby looked around the room, 'David and Goliath,' he shook his head, 'so, what's taking shape here? Anything? What do we do? Any of this change anything?'

'What about chasing up who is leaking the information? It's a serious breach of security if it's coming from inside.'

'Forget it,' said Darby, 'it's a distraction right now. For all we know it's just the local backbencher playing local member. Put your mind at ease and call him. Going after the leaks gets in the way of going after Asher Ministries. And, it'll get noticed. You'd have to talk to people, that'd attract attention. Remember, we're just driving desks for now. We'll find the leaks by going hard on Asher, information about the source of the leaks will emerge the more we investigate Asher Ministries. The Langs are up in arms about it. The pollies are shouting about it. We will find the source eventually, then we can decide if it's important.'

'Just pollies being pollies,' said one. 'Happy-clappers are always thin-skinned.'

The group agreed no changes in the priority attached to Asher Ministries, it stayed on the agenda and attracted no additional resources.

Mick was left in the meeting room alone with Alex Briggs, his offsider, rolling a Ford/Holden coin across his knuckles. They leaned back in their chairs, carefully. The office furniture was at best unreliable, hastily assembled from the warehouses of ex-government goods which didn't sell at auction, mismatched, worn, not to be trusted.

'Mick,' said Alex, 'I don't get the interest in Asher.' He nodded towards the door, 'bloke had it right. It's just business as usual, isn't it?'

'Mate, I'm not so sure. Might be nothing in it. The Langs are a divisive couple, so you'd expect naïve loving and naïve loathing.'

'Which is what we've got,' said Alex.

'Which is what we've got,' said Mick. 'The A-G warned me off, told me the Langs had signed confidentiality agreements and so don't need to have security passes for Parliament House.'

'Our guys won't let them in. What should I tell them?'

'Treat the Langs the same as everyone else without a security pass. They need to be signed in and escorted. I'll email Parliament House security so they can quote me as authorising it,' Mick said.

'How about we do the background security checks anyway?' Alex risked a grin, unsure of the relationship Darby had with the A-G.

Darby nodded.

'One more thing,' said Alex. 'I know you're not keen on pursuing "detect and alert", but the language has changed, makes me suspicious.'

'How so?'

'Well, when they started it was a pilot project. Now it's talked about as phase one, with a phase two planned. I've got rumours coming from Aged Care about their interest in further phases. Maybe it was never a trial or a pilot, maybe it was always about the later phases. The name, Ian Sturgess, Chief Scientist, pops up as well. Phase one was tested only in Asher Ministries' places. Aged Care and Asher Ministries acting together again?'

'What do you think we should do?' asked Mick.

'To change from calling it a pilot to phase one, there must be more money. More money from the department, maybe through Sturgess, into the Asher nursing homes, from there to the Langs. We need to find and track that money.'

'So, phase one is legit, a way to get into the next phase, caring robots? That may be one of the reasons they're so pissed about the leaks. Nice work mate.'

'Robots,' said Alex, 'what's this about robots? Security, complaints, sensors, I get all that, but robots? Where'd that come from?'

Mick leaned forward, 'Hudson Lang, has a plan to bring them into aged care homes, nursing homes.' He read from a sheet of paper, 'socially assistive robots, surveillance robots.'

'Mick, where's the evidence for that? Hudson as a hustler, yes. Cyber crim, mate.'

'Mate, I'm telling it as it is. I know it. He gets these things into aged care, old people get attached to them, as bad as your kids with their phones. And then what, picture this old lady, the robot talks to her, wakes her up, reminds her to take her pills; she trusts it, sees it every day, her kids on Mother's Day. Then, bingo, her best friend the robot suggests she change her will.'

'Mick,' said Alex throwing wide his arms.

'That bloke Sturgess, scientist with the sensors, he's behind it, that's the second phase. Very clever, first phase, benign. Second phase, malign.'

Alex sat, leaned back, his chair warned him not to go too far. 'Sturgess?' he said.

'Get your blokes to hack him at home and at work, I want the specs for those robots. Now, can you broaden the search for the money, they'll have to secure funds for phase two?'

'It'll be a stretch,' said Alex, 'but you've freed up guys from the leaks and now we can leave that first phase alone?'

'For now,' said Darby thumbing his phone, 'I'll get you an email to get the security checks started.'

'Do I need that?'

'Yes,' said Mick, 'best to have it authorised, you never know.'

Detect and alert.

The lead up to the detect and alert monitoring research had begun a few months earlier by Nigel Blakeley. Ian Sturgess had met him in the bar of the Kurrajong Hotel in Canberra. Nigel made sure they got on well.

A week later, after a long day for Ian at Senate Estimates; he had spent all day there waiting to not be called, they met again. A fake English pub in Kingston. Nigel explained that a business partner of his was doing government procurement. Procurement of major government IT contracts in aged care was outsourced to this consultant.

'Hang on – are you seriously telling me that a consultant – not a public servant – has a contract to procure services and equipment, technology?'

'Not a consultant,' said Blakeley. 'It's a company, Polonius, does IT procurement. Not for everything, just special projects, speed things up. You know what it's like, you want a printer, a phone, a laptop for a new researcher starting. You have to order it before you start recruiting, and that takes long enough!'

Ian nodded, 'so slow,' he added, 'speed of a glacier.' He'd had to lease laptops for two of his staff, disguising the payments as lab equipment maintenance.

'It's just an expansion of outsourcing,' Nigel said, 'part of the government agenda to get more value for the public dollar, get the best expertise there is around procurement. You only need look at some of the fuckups in Defence, Centrelink, and Tax to understand that the private sector does procurement better than the public service – leave public servants to do what they do best – play to their strengths. Polonius is efficient, pays those who deal with it very well, and still saves the Commonwealth money.'

Ian pushed back weakly – like putting your thumb to a steak cooked rare on a barbecue, resistance soft. 'I've never heard of government procurement outsourced to a consultant. Surprised they could even think of it'.

'Ian, mate, you've done the courses on how we're wired to reject new ideas, biased. You're allowing your mind to hijack you with one word here. What about Prime Contractors, it's just the same – different scale that's all. There's not been a parliamentary inquiry into Primes has there? Into the private sector mismanaging government money? No! But there's a room full of inquiries and reports of investigations into government buying gone wrong. Ian, democracy doesn't buy excellence, it buys compromise. The Minister gets it, Secretary gets it...'

Ian felt fogged in, like flying into a Canberra winter. Thoughts were trying to land only to veer off and try again. Fog induced by alcohol and Blakeley's bullshit.

A moment of clarity.

'Why are we having this conversation? What do you want from me?'

'Well, it's not what I want from you', said Blakeley. 'It's what you want, for yourself. Not for tonight mate, let's get you an Uber, back to that small flat you have here because all your money's in the house at Dalmeny. Pity, after all the years of diligent service, that medal...still, let me get this.' Blakely handed over a card to the server, nodded and said, 'tap's OK.'

• • • •

A week later Ian called Blakeley, they met over coffee and Ian invited him to Dalmeny. Hope you like fishing he'd said to Blakeley, who'd rather watch Question Time in slow motion, said he loved it, but his fishing gear was still in Brisbane. Ian had more than enough gear for him. Of course you do thought Blakeley.

Blakeley arrived the next day, too late for Ian to cook anything, they ate at the Bowling Club and walked back up the hill. Up early the next morning to fish with another bloke who had the boat. Usually Ian used a fishing kayak, but Blakeley wasn't up for that.

Back at Ian's after a few hours fishing and nothing to show for it, they shared a kilo of king prawns and a bottle of white. And got to the point.

Ian wanted to finish the Dalmeny house as designed, and to move out of Queanbeyan, into a better suburb. Blakeley said there was no cap, it would all happen gradually. He would provide instructions on how to account for a change in circumstances.

Blakeley asked Ian, 'You get some cash, what's the first thing you'd do?'

'How much?'

'Forget how much – cash in hand, what's the first thing? Who would you tell first?'

'That's easy,' said Ian. 'My plumber! The bathroom. You saw it this morning – having to stand in that kid's plastic swimming pool so the floor doesn't get wet, the walls don't get wet. It's nearly enough to stop me coming down here.'

Ian's rebuild had begun, thought Blakeley – on a drip feed. Blakeley handed Ian a flash drive. 'What you've got here,' said Blakeley, 'this will save the lives of older people, and cut the costs of caring for them. Detect and alert, that's how it works; detect when something is wrong and alert a carer to go and fix it.'

They read it over together, a proposal to implement the first phase of remote monitoring of seniors in aged care, combining electronic sensors with an electronic bracelet, or anklet.

Ian fidgeted, tapped a pencil, saw a phase two with more intrusive e-monitoring and socially assistive robots in nursing homes. He'd recruit doctoral students, saw a whole field of research, guided by technology developments, and research on the social acceptability of the technology - would seniors talk to robots? How would they feel about video?

Ian would have to approve the remote monitoring proposal, socialise the innovation through Health, and get the Purchase Order to Polonius, who would handle procurement. Ian just had to get it to Polonius.

'Hang on,' Ian was confused, 'Polonius? How does that work again?'

'Mate – here's how I see it; you might have a better idea. You get your research team to rewrite this,' he pointed to the screen, 'as your idea, approve it as head of the research committee. Then it goes to Polonius, as they do IT procurement for Aged Care. Then Polonius buys the gear. Any improvements on that?'

'That's it? This is perfectly legit, great innovation, practical too – I've got a research team looking at Artificial Intelligence in aged care, way down the track before anything practical comes out of that. Is there a catch?'

'If you find one, let me know. Keep the research group going, and why not distribute this proposal to a small team to prepare the paperwork. Put someone you trust to it, label it commercial-in-confidence. Keep an eye on it, like you'd do with any other project mate - just business as usual.

'What about your business,' asked Sturgess, 'what do you do? I thought you worked for Polonius, but you don't do you?'

'No mate, they just buy stuff. I'm with ElderTech. We're a bit like a think-tank. Bunch of people from everywhere, interested in using technology to help people age safely, with dignity. We research ideas, get the evidence, introduce advances to people like you; innovative, scientific, keen to make a difference. No fuss. We're like chips in your laptop, no-one knows the name of the chip company.'

'How do you make money?'

'We're in for the long haul, relationships. If our clients value what we bring we hope they'll advocate for us, take us into new opportunities. Long-term also means patents, royalties, licensing agreements; where there's no government conflict.'

· · · ·

The purchase order for sensor equipment and the monitoring bracelets was raised with Polonius, exempt from the procurement rules; therefore, exempt from government oversight.

Nigel canvassed providers for interest in the trial. The most promising phone call was with Hudson Lang of Asher Ministries. They agreed to meet over lunch at a quiet Canberra restaurant. Asher Ministries provided a suite of services to seniors living at home, in retirement homes and to those in nursing homes. Hudson was interested.

First to the Boat House, Nigel waited at the bar, watched Phoebe and Hudson walk through the carpark into the restaurant. Phoebe was all business, black suit over a white shirt, silk. High heels: he wondered if one heel was a little higher than the other, the way her hips swayed, at odds with the no-nonsense tailoring. Hudson wore a suit over a collarless shirt, silk too, white. They walked together, hand in hand and although he took small steps, Phoebe seemed to be rushing.

Escorted to their table, they all ordered the set lunch, eager to get to the point.

Hudson explained that Phoebe was the more recognised face and voice of Asher Ministries. Hudson, as the empire grew, was more across their aged care business, Asher House. They were on the lookout for innovation in service delivery, wanted to realise in looking after "our most vulnerable" what they had achieved with music.

Hudson and Phoebe looked at Nigel, sitting opposite. Their starters arrived and Hudson asked Nigel about the sensors project, 'you didn't give away much over the phone.' Nigel felt flattered at the undivided attention of the Langs. He was aware too of the many glances at their table, all admiring. He knew they weren't for him; unremarkable looking Nigel sort of snuck up on people, if he was noticed at all. The Langs arrived with a marching band.

So, Nigel struggled to keep his explanation low-key, fed them boring details of the sensors fitted to domestic appliances, bracelets and anklets, a call centre. He took out of his coat pocket a smooth blue box about the size of a cigarette packet.

'Go ahead,' he said putting it on the table in front of Phoebe, 'open it.'

He knew the packaging was vital; he'd had the box designed, inside and out, inspired by the packaging of an iPhone; smooth, luxurious, perfect. Nestled in the perfectly fitted mould were four black sensors the size of a one-dollar coin, and a bracelet, elegant, thin. A tiny battery tucked under a clear plastic tab.

The packaging worked. Hudson and Phoebe were in. Nigel could tell from the way they immediately began to talk about themselves.

'The presentation is perfect,' said Phoebe, 'our music is packaged the same way, not boxes, but the imagery, lighting, footage; all speaks to the presentation. We've done to music what Aldi did to food and wine. Go to the best producers and interest them in developing their artisanal craft in your brand. We do that.'

'You would never believe some of the writers of our songs,' said Hudson. 'It doesn't add to their fame, but it certainly swells their revenue. Some of them also convert to worship with us – it's nice, not mandatory. Just in case you wanted to know.'

'And the link to seniors here?'

'Let me finish,' said Hudson, not used to being interrupted. Teachers, preachers, academics, politicians, thought Nigel, they just keep talking, ignorant of their impact on audiences.

'Of course,' said Nigel.

'So, aged care, another human delivered service, expensive; even with using trainees and volunteers. Lower cost is what we want, I've replaced some staff with cleaning robots, only get cleaners in once a week for the stuff robots can't do yet, cheaper. Artificial Intelligence could replace most other staff; virtual assistants not nurses, time activated, programmed voice reminders to take medicine.'

'We're not quite there yet,' said Nigel, 'could be for phase two though. Our next update will be GPS tracking and stickers instead of magnets. Stickers for any surface. Not finalised yet, but included as part of this package. The GPS means you can track dementia patients, anyone who goes missing really.'

Hudson drummed the table with index fingers, 'hear what I'm saying Nigel; no people, they'll be just on call, in a glass box, marked 'in case of emergency break glass', a little hammer underneath. Again, reducing variation in care quality. That's what I want. Discrepancy is not part of God's plan.'

'I've never met anyone like you two,' said Nigel, 'how did you two get together?' Nigel, looking to slow the conversation as their mains arrived.

Hudson and Phoebe shared a look and a quiet giggle, getting ready to talk about their favourite subject. Nigel was more interested in Phoebe's story.

'I suppose I was dropping out of my medieval literature degree at Sydney Uni,' she said, 'I was bored. All the time. Bored in my tiny flat, bored at work, I was a research assistant doing some translating from Olde English, and bored studying. I was walking home one afternoon through Darlington and saw a sign over a church. It read, "Boredom is God's invitation to come inside". So, I went in, and God was revealed to me. I went to a bible study course the next week and met Hudson there.'

Nigel, relaxed, couldn't help himself, 'and the real story Phoebe?'

'Well, the real story? The real story,' she said, 'is that you're going home earlier than expected after a lunch cut short. You'll be letting your partner know you let a deal slip away.'

'OK,' said Nigel arms out wide, not daring a smile, 'tell me what to do.'

'So,' said Hudson, 'the cost?'

'Nothing. The gear, the training,' said Nigel, 'the observations, all funded by the research.'

'Who pays for the time the staff need to be trained on the technology?' queried Phoebe.

'OK,' said Nigel, 'the research will pay overtime if staff have to be trained outside normal hours, or we'll pay for replacement staff to cover the shifts. Your choice.'

'Exclusive.' Phoebe snapped, worked up now, 'I want all the research conducted only in Asher House nursing homes. No control group. All of our facilities need to be covered.'

'Well,' said Nigel, 'there's some competition to be in on the ground floor, including first option on the second phase. So, in consideration for working with ElderTech? Meeting your terms?'

'Consideration? I like that,' said Hudson.

'You know,' said Phoebe, 'if we're going to work together, you need to treat us with respect. We tell only the real story. Don't you ever doubt me. Now, if you're running away from something. Something in your past? Someone? You must stop running. Now is the time to reach out for Jesus.'

Nigel doubted that.

'Of course,' said Hudson, 'you may not be ready just now. Just one more thing though Nigel, what's in this for us?'

'If I reassure you on this,' said Nigel, 'does that mean we have a deal?'

'Put it this way,' said Hudson, 'if we are satisfied with your answer and you had a MOU prepared, we'd sign it now.'

'I'll email you an MOU when we're done, phone's in the car. Let me go over a few points,' said Nigel, happier now the talking wasn't about him, 'it's a clinical trial to flesh out the benefits, the advantages. The real customer in aged care is next of kin; we ran some sensitivity workshops, they're much more satisfied with the detect and alert technology, trust it more than supervision by night staff.'

'Right,' said Phoebe, 'next of kin, rellos,' she shook her head, 'cost us a lot of money with their demands.'

'Here's what happens,' Nigel said, 'when next of kin are comfortable that their relatives, loved ones, whatever, are not neglected, they post positive stories on social media, number of their visits drops, number of questions drops, number of complaints drop. It means you can get on with running the business. You need fewer staff on at night. Halve your night shift roster.'

'Halve staff costs? Just at night? Why not the other two shifts?'

'Hudson,' said Phoebe, 'don't bore the man, that's something we can look at.'

'One final detail,' said Nigel, 'Ian Sturgess is the research director you'll be dealing with. He's the Chief Scientist, Aged Care and he's funding the research. He's not to know of our consideration. These are his contact details. He'll be delighted by your call.'

The three of them sat back in their chairs, laughed, raised their coffee cups.

'You in?' Asked Nigel.

'We're in,' said Hudson and Phoebe.

They shook hands, deal done; Nigel had recorded it.

Break and enter.

Mick Darby never went into his house without thinking about his long career breaking and entering. Hotel rooms, motel rooms, B & Bs, apartments, flats, duplexes, bungalows, McMansions, farm houses, garden sheds, greenhouses, offices, gyms, building sites, garages, restaurants. Not always unseen, not always unnoticed, but uncaught. He broke in not to leave with anything, but to leave something. As he entered his house he always wondered if someone had done to him what he'd done unto another. Planted a single sheet of paper, a cd, a DVD, a usb, photo, money, drugs, film roll, mike, hair. Something which he would not want in his house, which didn't belong, and which would interest forensics. Something to wrench doubt and anxiety from a case. If you carried a secret which when revealed would trip the first domino in a sequence ending with the ruin of everything you cherish - Mick Darby would find it, unearth it, worry at it like a tongue over a chipped tooth, then use it. If you didn't have such a secret, and who doesn't, more likely he couldn't find it, Mick would provide.

Years ago Mick had given up on counter surveillance; threads across doorways, needles in door jambs, matches which fell to the ground when a door or window was breeched, memorising vehicle licence plates in his street, checking for bugs even. He had his place swept once a week, at irregular times, but he figured it was just about keeping anyone with a motive to bug on their toes.

Darby's defence against being fitted up was to collect and secret secrets of those who could harm him. The higher the rungs of the ladder he'd climbed the fewer who could harm him; the same fewer could protect him, or join him. He had something, enough, on his chosen few.

These days Mick Darby committed few crimes. He'd worked on national intelligence and security now for five years; finding and sifting secrets of politicians, political advisors, senior public servants, captains of industry and less well-camouflaged extremists. There was little call here for his fitting-up skills, this mob did it for him, called it backgrounding.

Still, as he unlocked his door, he remembered, and he was wary. His wariness wore off only when he left the house. He never called it home. Home to Mick Darby was the space between his ears. The last frontier. Alone, Darby wandered all over this territory, confident on familiar paths, stumbling on the unfamiliar, something unexpected or seen anew. Most nights he found himself on familiar ground. Memories. He'd been taught to compartmentalise once upon a time. He buried a few in the place he called the back forty, a place he never went to willingly; but they called him often in the night. Asking, always asking.

Mick saw himself talking to voices he couldn't place, with faces he couldn't see, shapes shapeless in half light. He'd begin by answering a different question. Standard practice, control. Narcissism 101.

'How many lives would have been lost, Mick, if you hadn't lent a helping hand?'

Tormentors would lull Mick. Play with him, play with his euphemism. Let him think he'd gotten away with it again.

It ended the same way. Always a question.

A gentle question, informal, innocent, friendly, a lure to confide, to begin with; descending to threat.

'Day of reckoning Mick. Given it much thought? Never mind what side of history old mate. What side of the ledger? There's a question for you. Try playing both sides of that?'

'I never,' said Mick Darby, half awake, half asleep. Fully awake now, free of the dream. He threw the covers back, sat up, legs over the side of the bed. Only in my dreams do I answer the question asked he thought, shrugged, scratched his head. Showered, he dressed for the day, ground coffee and lit the gas under an old moka pot. He ate a handful of nuts while he waited for his espresso. Mick poured coffee, and sat at the kitchen table, reached for the envelope he'd dropped there the night before.

· · · ·

H and delivered to his office early yesterday morning, the envelope had been scanned, opened, contents biosecurity scanned, logged, photographed, re-enveloped and taken to Micks' office.

Mick had opened the envelope to take out a white card. He took it straight to his boss.

'Mick, I very rarely tell you what to do. Saves me having to sack you for insubordination, mutiny. And on a good day you do get a result. The Lang's thing,' he glanced at the invitation, 'you'll be there.'

Mick countered with, 'We're investigating Asher Ministries, directors, the Langs. You've just signed off a joint op with Ethics Australia. I can't be seen having lunch with them, it compromises our investigation. Maybe that's what they want? Have you thought this through?'

'Maybe you should have thought of that earlier, or were you seeking answers here?' His boss turned over a sheet of paper on his desk, picture of Mick Darby clearly at an Asher Ministries' service. Darby sat back, ran a hand over one cheek. 'Never mind how I got it mate; I've got it and you're going. Don't forget to say "amen" on your way out.'

Hiba.

Hiba started with the form after the music finished, the end of the Asher Ministries' service. She must have looked a little unsure because a good-looking young guy in black ripped jeans, torso tightly crammed into a sparkling white T shirt, sat beside her. He reminded her of the perpetually cheery nuisances in the City Centre, selling subscriptions to charities to help koalas, to free laboratory animals, whatever. They were even more annoying as she never had any spare money. The buoyancy from the hour of music, dancing and even the preaching started to fade.

'You look like you need a hand?'

'I'm OK so far, but bank details? Why would they want that?'

'Don't worry about that, just skip it, and the next one too. Hey, just to make sure use my pencil and draw a red line though that, I guess they use the same form for donors too. Oh – so you're interested in caring for those less fortunate, wow yeah, I can definitely see that,' he said, holding her gaze, not uncomfortably.

They had coffee afterwards where she met an exuberant group of people around her age who planned to meet up later in the week.

Over the next few days, a series of texts about opportunities to gain a formal qualification while volunteering as a carer for seniors were sent to her phone. Two included a ten second video featuring a carer reading a book to an older lady, and a carer playing with the cutest grandchild.

Her reply, together with the thick red lines on her 'bio sheet' meant she got an email asking her two questions. Out of ten, where ten is the highest score, how important was it to her to care for seniors, and, again out of ten, how confident was she about learning the carer skills required? She emailed straight away and the next day the serious recruitment started by phone, and after the Sunday worship, in person.

She was so happy, taken seriously at last, accepted as a trainee in aged care, with Asher House Cook, a not-for-profit nursing home. Asher House was owned and run by Asher Ministries, offering their aging members a last chance to increase their material, hence, spiritual wealth. Of course, God's way to ensure your material wealth lived on after you, celebrating God's blessing on you, was to bequeath it to Asher Ministries.

Most of the training was OJT, on-the-job; task books to complete, hours to be recorded and some workshops. She even had a place to stay, a share house with three other trainees. The four of them got on well, studied bible together with a bigger group once a week, walked to the centre together, gossiped together.

She confided to one of the housemates she found some of the subjects in the traineeship unusual, there were a lot of hours devoted to singing lessons, music accompaniment, the theology of aged care and bible studies. The actual care of the old folk was OJT, skills on moving them safely, helping to them out of bed, feeding, cleaning up after their 'accidents'. Some 'show and tell' sessions run by the more senior carers, then practice under observation and after performing to satisfaction, she had the run of the ward. She didn't baulk at anything and was soon giving injections, changing drips, cleaning cannulas, nasal ones first and then injection cannulas. They were told to leave the sensors and the bracelets, anklets alone, only the researchers were permitted to touch them.

After taking her obs, proud she was learning the language, Hiba looked for the older woman's chart to update the records. It hadn't fallen behind or under the bed, not covered by bedclothes. She wrote the numbers and the time on her palm and headed for the office. Unusually, there was no-one in the office and she quickly found the woman's records. They were clipped to the front of a clipboard thick with paperwork. She updated her obs and flipping over the page was surprised to find the woman had been seen twice in the last two days by the centre's GP, had been to hydrotherapy. She hadn't noticed and she was on at the times indicated. She left the records where they were, and answered a call from another of her friends, she would have preferred to call them patients as she thought of herself as in the medical field, but friends was the language of the centre.

She mentioned the records not being with the patient to her supervisor at shift handover, was firmly told they were hung over the friend's bed or wheelchair if they were out of bed. She knew enough to understand that repeating the centre's policy didn't answer a question; but her shift finished, and she was soon caught up in the walk back to the share house.

'You've got the keys, Nigella.'

They were all laughing, as soon as her colleagues realised she could cook they called her Nigella, one of them able to mimic that sultry voice, all of them word perfect as they commented on her preparation, cooking, plating, and presentation. Hiba enjoyed the nickname, the attention, felt comfortable with them. Friends, music, bible study she could understand, a job she loved, her money going to a good cause, never had Hiba felt so safe, accepted.

As she retrieved the keys from her backpack one of her housemates asked, 'what are you writing on your hands for?'

'A note for myself from the centre, I was called away, and didn't want to forget these numbers.'

She quickly made a note on her iPhone about the odd records and went into the kitchen, to the prep and the banter.

Rose.

Has hero was never out of his sight until today when he'd left his toy with his new friend. His new friend was ninety-four years old and lived in Asher House Cook with twenty-three others of similar age and varying degrees of fragility. The four-year-old boy's hero was Batman, he took it with him to his day care centre trip to the aged care home, part of a new initiative called the Full Circle program. When she picked him up later his mum asked him about the trip.

'I have a new friend called – I forget – but she's my friend, she loves me. I gave her my Batman.'

He had so many Batmen, Batmans...what is the plural of a superhero, the boy's mother thought, he won't miss one.

As Rose was put back to bed after tea that night the carer found a tiny black and yellow figure with a small plastic cape, and a small black plastic sword.

'These are dangerous to have around you Rose, where did they come from? I'll get rid of them for you.'

'Don't you fucking touch them!' snarled Rose, who was promptly sedated for the night in fear of her becoming unmanageable.

The next morning a slightly groggy Rose found Batman and tried to snap the tiny sword into the even tinier hand, and gave up; tried to fit the cape, same result. She'd have to wait until someone came by and ask for help.

'Rose, I didn't take you for a superhero fan', Hiba teased.

'Well, I do like a man with superpowers, but I'd prefer him a little bigger and to not wear a cape. I do have a new friend though; he came with that school group yesterday and gave me his toy. It's more than a toy though, isn't it? What is a toy to a small boy? I'll tell you what a toy is to a small boy', said Rose. 'It's a friend, a companion on wild adventures, someone with whom one shares heroic stories and feats of bravery, a co-conspirator in plots against one's parents. So, he didn't give me a toy, really, did he?'

'No', said Hiba, entranced.

'Do you know what he gave me?' asked Rose. 'He gave me a reason to make a cake.'

. . . .

'Hey – you have a Batman too Rose, I can see it!' cried the four-year-old a week later.

'Yes, and do you remember, of course you do. You're four, you left Batman here to look after me last week.'

'Batman's good at looking after people. He's my favourite.'

'Well,' said Rose, 'he did such a good job and he helped me in the kitchen to make a surprise.'

'Where's the surprise?'

'I'll ring my bell and Hiba will bring it out,'Hiba, who'd confided her nickname to Rose that morning as they made a Batman cake, brought it out, complete with yellow and black icing, and a printed list of the ingredients in case of allergies.

The day care staff checked the list, pronounced the cake safe to eat, despite the colour scheme resembling a radioactive warning. Maybe there's something in this Full Circle program after all, the day care director thought as she posted photos of the day to Story Park. Cake, kids, and old people, smiling, laughing, Batman in a different place in each photo.

Rose's new friend pestered his mother to take him to see Rose on the weekend. Two hours later she pulled into the carpark at Rose's home, 'Yes, that's right Mum, this is where she lives.'

She rang a bell, they were not allowed in, told by a uniform it wasn't visiting hours. She explained; the uniform listed visiting hours. The mother reasoned, heard the hours again, raised her voice, so did the uniform. When the mother noticed her four-year-old was not beside her, she cried out.

The boy's face appeared around a partially open door, 'I found Rose, Mum.'

Showing a rare moment of wisdom, the uniform found some errant paperwork to be shuffled into order.

'Rose, I'm not coming for a sleepover.'

'Just as well young man, there's barely room for me and Batman.'

The two women chatted; the young mother opened her phone to show Rose the pictures of them all with the cake.

'These are lovely photos, you know I moved Batman around, and wondered if anyone noticed.'

'Well, he did,' they both laughed, 'Rose you've not been hungry today?', indicating the untouched meal, unopened plastic container of fruit salad, plastic cutlery still wrapped in the serviette.

'Oh, I'm hungry, just with my hand,' she brought it out from under the bed covers, 'the cannula had come out during the night and when the nurse cleaned it and fixed it, she also bandaged my fingers too, so I've not been able to open anything. They get so busy, and some of the others need more help than me, so I was waiting until someone came along.'

'Let me help if you want to eat now?'

The uniform came along as she buttered Rose's bread, muttered something about 'as long as you're being useful you can stay', and vanished. Batman and the boy sat quietly, eating one of his snacks. They left halfway through visiting hours, there were no other cars in the carpark, maybe there's another car park the mother thought, not believing it for a minute.

That night she and her husband talked about having Rose to lunch next Sunday.

'The food Rose had today is pretty ordinary. I'm sure it's good enough, hardly something to look forward to though. Home cooked meal, sparkling company, a Batman or two. Who could resist?'

She'd call in during the week on her way to work, see Rose and if she wanted to, make all the arrangements.No doubt there'd be paperwork.

· · · ·

To everyone's surprise lunch with Rose was the highlight of their week. Rose revealed she was an historian. 'When I started studying history; I was told that history brings people alive, now I rather think that people bring history alive.'

'Sunday lunch is not a time for history though,' said Rose, 'it's a time for amusement and maybe another small glass of that red wine?'

The boy's father fetched her wine and as he walked around beside her to pour it, she slipped forward in the chair, asleep. He gently sat her up and propped her up with cushions from the lounge on the chair beside her. As he plumped a cushion under her shoulder a bracelet slipped out of her cardigan pocket and fell to the floor.

His wife googled Rose Peters and found her Wikipedia entry, read bits aloud. 'Rose Peters PhD, dux of her school, university medal, captained the university debating team, Rhodes scholar, arrested during the Springboks tour.'

He said, 'and now she's asleep in our lounge room.'

'Don't worry, I don't think she'll be too much trouble today.'

'I'm not asleep,' said Rose, 'and what are all these fucking cushions doing around me?'

'Rose said "'fuck'", said the four-year-old.

'It's a grown-up word,' said his mother, 'Rose is a grown-up, you're not, so, we don't want you to use grown-up words.'

'I can use four-year-old words?'

'That's a perfect explanation, 'said Rose, 'I must remember that for when I'm next told to not swear.'

'We should do this again,' said her husband when they were home from taking Rose back. He suggested she invite her uncle too.

'Look,' he said, 'I know he's not your uncle, some distant rello. But Mick's good fun, been a while since we've seen him, and if Rose is boring, then, it's still a good lunch, right?'

So, she invited him.

'Nothing high powered, not even interesting, nothing like you're used to, no intrigue Mick,' she'd said, 'just us, and an older lady we met a few weeks ago.'

· · · ·

An early morning phone call threatened their plan.

'Hello, hello, hello...,' Rose's voice, tiny and hesitant.

'Yes Rose, what time would you like us to be there?'

'Well, it's just that...just like my daughter. She's in Canberra and wants to take me out to lunch. Journalist, so it'll be some place fancy, and I won't like it, they'll have wooden floors and I can't hear anything clearly where there's wooden floors, but she is my daughter.'

'Rose, she's here? Marcia? That's wonderful, would you like to bring her along to lunch with you? It's no bother, and we'd love to meet her, you've told us so much about her.'

Mick was a little early and his distant relation had a chance to explain there'd be an extra one for the meal, a journalist, she hoped he didn't mind. She quizzed him about his family in the way reserved for distant rellos. Mick didn't mind, he knew little, had even less interest.

'Do you see anything of Harriet, Mick, now you're here in Canberra? Catch up with her? I saw her on the News a while ago, she's aged well.'

'We're at some work meetings together.'

'And her..?'

'Paul,' said Mick, 'he's doing well. They love him at the School of Music.'

'Of course, it's none of my business I know, but we're family, and it's been, what, ten years now, more? We've been here in this house for a little longer,' she kept on talking, 'took out a few walls, opened the place up.'

'Ever thought about switching these two paintings,' said Mick pointing to water colours, one a beach scene, the other a desert, 'maybe the darker blue in your curtains would highlight the beach sky.'

'Art? Since when have you been bothered with art?'

'I'm developing a bit of an interest,' said Mick, 'you know, in my spare time.'

'Does this interest have a name?'

The doorbell rang, 'that'll be Rose and her daughter.'

It turned out to be just Rose, who was embarrassed, 'Marcia's going to be late, a deadline to meet. She said not to wait, I hope that's all right. I'm so sorry.'

Lunch was a little quieter than usual, flat after the build-up of meeting Rose's daughter. When she did arrive they left them together, talked about them.

'Do you know much about Marcia?' said Mick, 'what does she write about?'

'Environmental stuff mainly, quite the go-getter, surprised you haven't heard of her.'

Rose joined them, relaxed, and soon fell asleep. Marcia joined them, her urgent phone call over, 'I was just about to ask if I could charge my phone here,' she said, 'but, I've interrupted your afternoon so much already.' She put the phone in her bag.

More wine was poured, the flowers Mick had brought admired, Marcia entertained them with a few stories about the stories behind the printed ones. Mick and the four-year-old assembled the Batman, a gift from Mick. The superhero action figure fired a projectile which Mick caught to a round of applause, waking Rose.

'Rose, your bracelet,' said Mick getting up, 'it was on the floor.'

'It's so unsuitable', said Rose, 'not my style at all.'

'Oh, I don't know,' said Mick.

'Are you flirting with me young man?'

'Oh Mum,' said Marcia.

Mick held the bracelet, turned it over, worked the clasp; 'how come it doesn't suit you?'

'You know,' she said, 'it's not that it doesn't suit me. It's just that all my jewellery reminds me of the choices I made; to get married, to have Marcia, to take a gift from my husband on my birthday. This,' she took the bracelet from Mick, 'reminds me of choices I can make no longer. Reminds me,' she held it up, 'that I'm not free to choose. I have to wear it. I don't like it. My friends at Asher House and I never wear them if we can get away with it. It's supposed to let me know if the microwave is left open, but I don't even have a microwave.'

Mick raised his eyebrows and thought. Rose. Asher House. Unusable bracelet. He reached for it, ran his finger along the sides, felt it for the weight.

Marcia took it, 'here Mum,' she said and fastened the bracelet on her mother's wrist.

'How about I ask them about it when we take Mum back, and I'll let you know what they say.'

Hudson Lang.

She had named her baby after her favourite film star. The father disappeared; her father disowned her, neither she nor her father lived to find out that her favourite star was gay, which would have made her crime worse. With her newborn she caught the train to Sydney, moving in with an aunt in Leichhardt. Her father's sister had not caught the same bitter religious bug as her brother and welcomed her and baby Hudson. Her one-bedroom terrace was in the middle of a row of five, all with growing families. 'Baby Hudson' grew up speaking Italian and English and to spend his time after school at his mates' dad's motor scooter garage, watching, learning, and developing a passion for speed.

After his mother died when he was seven, her aunt looked after him. His aunt aged quickly and as she aged, she dropped out of her local church and sought to be 'born again'. She became a minor celebrity in one of the early Pentecostal communities, in those days devoid of celebrities, riding pillion behind Hudson on his 1968 Moto Guzzi. She maintained she couldn't hear the Holy Spirit with a helmet on, so when they were clipped by a truck running a red light she died instantly. Hudson survived with some injuries. He later revealed that the moment she died her spirit entered his and he could speak in tongues. It was recorded in his medical notes that the ambos, nurses and doctors thought he was babbling as he lay unconscious.

Hudson came back from hospital to his aunt's house in Leichhardt a wealthy young man. The house was his, as well as the other properties his aunt had in Balmain, Rozelle, and Petersham. Soon outgrowing the local charismatics, he bought a new bike and toured Australian Pentecostal churches preaching his conversion, raising money, healing, laying on his hands and baptising babies. Along the way he acquired the honorific, Pastor, and came to believe his wealth was a result of his and his aunt's sharing of the gospel, rather than his badgering of her to change her will. She'd wanted to leave him the house in Leichhardt, all the rest to a suite of bible study groups, silent orders of nuns and an American televangelist. His leading her out of those valleys of darkness was another tribute to his silky tongue, God given.

He met Phoebe at a bible college retreat in Mt Victoria, and they married a year later in the Covenant Evangelical Church in Toowoomba. They spent their honeymoon travelling Queensland campaigning for far-right political candidates. Hudson and Phoebe returned to Leichhardt; living well from donations, preaching, leading bible study groups, training others in leading bible study groups, renewal weekends, retreats and conferences. He put in his ten thousand hours. By 2000 they registered their own denomination, Asher Ministries, as a not-for profit charity and sold Hudson's inherited house in Petersham to their new church – their first worship centre.

The empire was revealed. As the empire grew; more people, more tithes, more centres, more preaching, the regulations of everyday life intruded into Hudson's and Phoebe's grand plans. Except now they had something to defend; local government officials wanted more clarification about the proposed centre's impact on local environments. The charitable not-for-profit status of some of their financial entities was challenged, along with media stories decrying their beliefs as the re-emergence of the happy-clappy church music of the early seventies.

'When Jesus was under pressure he fought back,' reasoned Hudson. 'Either with a wise saying, or having a temple destroyed, or embarrassing critics. So, we need to answer the question is there more for us, do we have already all the goodness of God?'

'There can never be enough of the goodness of God! That's what the message of Mary of Magdalene is all about. Let's get moving faster on finishing our centre in Canberra too.' Phoebe stood and stretched, moved to the window, 'I had an interesting chat with our youth leader's mother. Excited, gushy even; just won preselection for a safe Liberal seat, so going to Canberra. She loves my Magdalene Gospel, our message to strengthen women in our church and dare the others to come around.'

'Canberra?' Hudson asked her.

'Well, I think we've outgrown this,' she said, flicking her right hand at the window overlooking Petersham railway yards, 'don't you?'

Spice posts.

'Can't believe they cancelled my mother's pleasure.' Teased the invitation to outrage on Facebook, where the RSVP options are like, comment, share, emojis. It posted early in the morning on the page for 'Friends of Asher, Not'. Not the official, moderated and administered Asher House group, from which members of the Friends of Asher had been blocked for any critical comment.

The Facebook flurry turned into a storm while Phoebe neared the end of her preaching, keeping an eye out for the discreet signal that Hudson was ready to come on and ask for cash. She was preaching to the next-of-kin of Asher House residents. There had been some disquiet about the number of deaths in Asher Houses. Phoebe and Hudson had agreed to preach a timely reminder of Jesus' plan. Plus, an excellent opportunity to donate, and to sell the eternal value of bequests.

'This Saturday, for our friends in Asher House, from Ainslie' she stretched her left arm, 'to Weston,' extending her right, 'we pray hard to understand how the will of Jesus occasionally works through doctors. As our friends get closer to their great victory with Jesus, sometimes the doctor seems more powerful than Jesus. I know we want to pray to Saint Lazarus, he's our favourite saint when those we love pass.'

The crowd chanted 'Lazarus, Lazarus, Lazarus.'

Phoebe opened her arms, let them fall to her side, silence. 'You know,' she confided, 'you buy a book, you wanna know how it ends, read the last page. That's it, spend twenty-five bucks, read one page, you know how it ends. But, the book of life, only Jesus know how it ends, you get to the last page when he's ready. Let's remind ourselves, life is a near-death experience.'

She had stilled the crowd. 'But, I know,' Phoebe raised her voice, stopped moving. 'I know this,' she said, 'many of those prayers, many of our prayers,' she paused, 'will be answered in Heaven. Don't worry,' lifting her voice again, 'All. Prayers. Are. Answered.'

She got the sign; the lights focused on her dimmed as did the applause, the cheering, the crying. Hudson appeared beside her.

It's a Pavlovian moment, thought Mick Darby, who had gone along to see for himself what Phoebe was about. Hudson only has to appear on stage for the punters to thumb their phones to the iTithe app, ready to answer the hustler's call for cash. Darby looked around him; wondered if these people thought positively a hundred percent of the time, or would any impure, negative, normal thoughts creep in. Were any of them ever stumped to write three good things a day? Three? He sometimes felt lucky to get one good thing a week. He shook his head, money and religion.

He slipped away and was surprised to see a TV van outside the carpark, security blocking its entry. Luckily, I walked, and left through a side gate as worshippers streamed out of the centre. Some of the crowd chattered as messages lit and burped their phones alerting them to new Facebook posts.

The woman whose pleasure had been cancelled was now an early morning celebrity. The invitation issued by her daughter, was eagerly RSVP'd. Hundreds of likes, tens of comments; mostly questions and emojis.

The next post offered more emotion, even less detail; 'such ageism'. More questions, likes and emojis. Crescendo alert.

A new post. 'Asher House confiscated my mother's dildo.' Capital letters. Facebook kicked off. Hundreds of shares now added to the likes and comments. The post was twittered, instagramed and upvoted on Reddit as Phoebe and Hudson sang, preached, and solicited; unaware. Canberra media waited; fuming in the cold, denied by Asher security.

· · · ·

Phoebe's social media assistant scrolled thorough the site and briefed Phoebe and Hudson as they were bundled into their car and driven home. More media waited there. Hudson called security and his lawyers. He stalked the front rooms of their house, snatched the blinds away to mutter at the mob, blinked at the flashes. Police arrived, not sure why they had to be there. Hudson told the police to get rid of the crowd. 'No law's being broken sir; we'll just stay here for a while.' Police mingled with journalists, a club meeting, sharing thoughts on where to hunt for the confiscated item.

Hudson fired up the computer linked to security cameras installed along the front of the house. Downloaded and printed images of faces from when the crowd had assembled earlier that morning. He rushed out to the police officer nearest the front door, shoved the printouts at her, 'arrest these bastards,' he shouted. The officer thanked him, and Hudson, bewildered, found himself back inside his house.

'This is not helpful Hudson,' said Phoebe, 'let the lawyers deal with it. Now, we need to say something.'

Phoebe rehearsed her comment. She enlisted Hudson to ring around to solicit public messages of support from their contacts. 'Keep a list of those who decline too,' said Phoebe.

'Asher House,' said Phoebe, 'venerates the dignity and discretion of all God's people. Asher Houses, our residents, we call friends. We respect their right to privacy in the more intimate moments of their lives. Unlike their children. Some of whom value their parents' privacy by the number of likes they get for spicy posts. Pray for them; because it's about them, not us, not their parents.'

Phoebe relied on deflecting attention, and the stunted half-life of social media themes. By midday, whatever the fuss was about, was over; really, who wanted to talk about it.

Mick Darby had a longer attention span. He put an officer to work monitoring social media for Asher Ministries, Asher House. He was soon rewarded by Facebook avengers.

Hudson's ringing around resuscitated the story. A reactionary ex-minister praised Phoebe's stance on Twitter and was later interviewed by a conservative radio jock. Rumours circulated on Facebook and Reddit threatening litigation. The ABC carried an interview with an academic whose field of expertise was intimacy and ageing. During this, stories about inquiries conducted by the Attorney-General on Asher Ministries and Asher House appeared on social media.

During the night, the news migrated to the mainstream. Reports featured hastily arranged responses from aged care experts, probity specialists, tax lawyers and a photograph of the Attorney-General and Dr Phoebe Lang, in a Commonwealth car. The Minister for Aged Care was quoted as 'having every confidence in the high quality of service provided by Asher Houses.'

Over breakfast, Hudson and Phoebe sat with the papers, old school, heaped on the table.

'Before we look at these,' said Phoebe putting her hand to the heap, 'we need to go over the videos from yesterday's service.'

'Oh, you're right,' said Hudson, 'with yesterday's bullshit I forgot about them.'

Every service had cameras aimed at the audience. Hudson and Phoebe reviewed two selections of footage of every service they ran. Phoebe studied the greeters as people entered; counted the number of people not greeted, tallied the numbers, used the data to adjust greeter training. Hudson studied the manual tithing, followed the buckets as they moved throughout the lines, made sure no-one took money out.

Phoebe froze an image, called out to Hudson,' you need to see this.'

'What've you got?' he said sliding over. She angled her laptop so he could see the screen.

'This man here. It's Mick Darby. I recognise him from the Attorney-General's office, he's some kind of fed.'

'A cop?'

'No, I don't know. Maybe not a cop, federal security something though. He's in her diary a lot.'

'What's he doing here?' Hudson smudged the screen. 'Sneaking around our service? Spying on us? Following us?' Hudson stood, spilling coffee, 'bastards, policing our worship! We'll follow him,' he took two steps, rushed back to the table, snatched his phone.

'To call whom,' said Phoebe.

'Whom?' said Hudson, unused to the word, 'I'll get him followed, find out where he lives, find out more about him.'

'Hudson,' said Phoebe, 'sit back down, let me pour you more coffee. You don't need to do that. No need to follow him. He came to us,' she flicked her laptop, 'he'll come to us again.'

'How?' said Hudson, sitting beside her.

'We'll invite him.'

'Brilliant Phoebe. Brilliant.' He put his arm around her, kissed her.

'I know,' she said. 'Now, the greeters are done. The money?'

'Done, no problems there.'

'OK, the papers,' said Phoebe, 'I'll take these, and you can enjoy these,' as she dumped a pile in his lap.

They skimmed. Hudson calmed. 'These are tales of fancy,' he said, 'we have dealt with them. These, these nobodies,' he flicked the paper with the back of his hand, 'daring to tell us not to live the life Jesus has set for us.'

'Hudson,' said Phoebe reaching for his hand, 'we need to look, take this seriously.'

'Phoebe,' he said, 'among all this bullshit, donations are up. Yesterday was our highest-grossing day, ever; ever,' he repeated. 'I'm not including what we made during the service, the money poured in after this crap,' another blow to the paper, 'was on-line.'

Phoebe put her glasses on. She used them privately and not to read; she was short-sighted. Without them on stage she couldn't see. Hudson still found it disconcerting that she put her glasses on to look at him, took them off to read. He chuckled, 'those glasses.'

'What do you think we should do?'

'Well, I was up most of the night thinking this through. This journalist, Marcia Kiernan, of course we'll sue. We also have to get your friends in Parliament to step up, show up for us. And the thing is I have this vision of using this to lead our people out of these falsehoods. We do this.'

'Show them the way?'

'Show them the way? People are desperate for us to be victorious over the enemy. We redeem them,' said Hudson, agitated, fidgeting, he leaned towards Phoebe, 'we announce today we are opening a new Asher House to meet the demand; we ask for pledges; investments in making the dreams of older Australians to live in dignity, come true.' Hudson stood, 'we show how to fight the enemy.'

'Where do you want to do that?'

'That land we bought years ago in Belconnen,' said Hudson, 'we have eleven hectares there, we have it in a holding company. We sell that land to Asher House, it's the right time to sell.'

'It's the right time to pray,' said Phoebe.

'Don't stray,' said Mick to Alex as he got out of the car.
'Not planning on spending the night then boss?'
'I could tell you weren't listening,' said Mick.

Darby was met at the entrance to the Lang mansion by an eager twentysomething, a smiling bodybuilder in a black suit standing two metres behind her. His name thumbed on her tablet, she handed him to another advertisement for a wellness magazine who led him through the front door, through a square lobby walled with photos of the Langs with celebrities, narrowing to a two metre wide corridor, outside to a huge patio with a copse of gas heaters standing triffid like. Matched groups of men and women surged gently away from and back towards the heat, missing not a beat of small talk; nannies, schools, real estate, obscure vineyards, beach houses. All the while marking the movements of Hudson and Phoebe. Ranking the quality of their interactions with other guests. Smug about a quick handshake, anxious about a hug.

Darby stood to one side, watched, idly quartered the group which, since it was the start of the event fitted into predictable pockets, like with like. It was only towards the end of Canberra get-togethers you saw sworn enemies in close, whispered conversations. More people arrived and the gentle surges opened, swallowed, quickly got the new comers in step.

A knot of guests untangled Hudson and Phoebe, freed them to be embraced by those closest. Darby clocked the chair of Asher Ministries look up and stepped towards him. Frank Riccini, olive skin, heavily wrinkled, grey hair brushed back, light on his feet. Men saw Frank, moved and ushered others out of his way; hitching their pants, shooting their cuffs, resisting the urge to wipe their shoes on their calves, their women discretely brushing stray hair, fluff or dandruff from their partner's shoulders. Darby battled the temptations.

'Frank Riccini,' he offered his hand, 'forgive me,' said Frank, 'is it Michael or Mike Darby?'

'Mick, it's always been Mick, thank you Frank, except to my mother.'

'Yes,' said Frank, 'Francis for my mother. Traditionalists. You and I though, we had to adapt,' he gestured to the gathering, 'we assimilate or perish.'

'This is an impressive gathering,' said Mick.

'You fit in here easily,' said Frank, 'you'll know everyone, I won't need to introduce you?'

'I'll be fine,' said Mick, 'well assimilated,' he raised his glass of water to Frank, a toast, 'like you.'

'Wasn't always so, for some it's still difficult, Irish and Italians, we shouldn't forget, we lose more than our mother's name for us when we integrate. I am pleased to meet you,' said Frank, holding Mick's eye before turning to be embraced by the President of the Conservative party.

Darby moved easily away through the crowd of fifty or so with more arriving. Not a torn fingernail, unperfumed body, unplucked eyebrow, unwhitened tooth, uncultivated voice breeched his senses.

Mick walked to his boss, whispered in his ear, 'here by invite or edict?'

'Mick, so good to see you. No, like you mate, my own free will.'

Mick nodded, grinned, took a glass of water from the tray of a passing acolyte, handed over his empty.

His boss turned to Mick and said, 'the time we've used up, the people we've used up, you and I Mick. Hunting treachery, betrayal, deceit; hunting it and exposing it. Look around,' he swept the crowd with his hand holding his glass, 'what do you see?'

'Our failures,' said Mick.

'Think of it as a work in progress,' said his boss. 'Minister,' he turned and shook hands, 'an unexpected pleasure.'

'I am a little surprised to see you both,' said the Minister for Aged Care. 'May I ask? Work or worship?' smiling, mouth only.

'Oh, wouldn't be dead for quids,' said Darby's boss, 'was only saying to Mick just now.'

A hand appeared on the Minister's stiffened shoulder, 'introduce us,' said Phoebe Lang, turning to face Mick Darby.

'I don't know that they have names,' said the Minister, 'they're with Intelligence.'

'Stanford,' she looked from one to the other, paused, 'Binet I presume.'

'Is faith intelligent, do you think?' asked Phoebe.

'Well,' said Mick looking around, 'it's certainly rewarding.'

'Do you think if I were to ring a bell announcing lunch,' asked Phoebe, 'they would rush off to different ends of the terrace?'

Darby and his boss laughed with Phoebe who linked arms with them, started walking and said, 'gentlemen, shall we show them how it's done?'

Phoebe was soon separated from her escorts. All round them her guests were moving, gently ushered by Asher acolytes from the marble terrace down a short lane of potted figs. Under the transparent roof an orangery. Empty and smelling of citrus. Darby's unkind thought that it was sprayed minutes earlier. As the crowd saw the laden trestle tables the pace quickened. A bell did ring. Darby laughed. The crowd halted. Grace began. Hudson's deep voice came from all sides, wrapped itself around the conservatory.

• • • •

From rich food and boring conversation Darby escaped to the toilet. He was guided there and lost his guide on the way back. He opened a door into room with no furniture and walls busy with paintings, drawings, tapestries. Jostled together, frames butted up against each other, all oblongs and squares, of all sizes, almost crazy paving on a wall.

He was not alone. He turned around and reached for Hudson Lang's outstretched hand as they walked towards each other.

'What are you thinking?' asked Hudson.

Darby told him.

'Bloody expensive crazy paving,' said Hudson, 'be the finest Italian marble, hand cut by descendants of Michelangelo, rowed to Australia in open boats, hand carried to Canberra. That's how bloody expensive,' he laughed, slapping Darby on the shoulder, 'crazy! I'll give you crazy.' Hudson took a step back, confronted Darby, 'which one cost me the most?'

'I thought they'd all be gifts.'

'What?' Hudson's chin went up, he threw a hand out to his right, 'from this lot,' his eyes narrowed. He stepped close to Mick, took his elbow and turned him to the far wall, 'let me take you through these, see what you like?'

I may yet be saved thought Darby, both Langs have laid their hands on me today. Darby relaxed, and distracted. His current lady. An art specialist, he hoped he remembered her lessons on art. They'd met months ago at a money laundering conference. She'd tried to seduce him to investigate stolen art. She was unsuccessful, he was not. They were infrequent guests at each other's places, she travelled incessantly and Mick worked.

Hudson stopped them a metre away from that part of the wall covered by four paintings, oils on canvas, abstract landscapes, pastel, vague.

Darby took a step back, it didn't help, 'how do you get the sense of one painting when they're so close together?' he asked.

'Phoebe turns out all the lights and uses a miners lamp,' said Lang. 'So, which one, or none of them? Take me to one you like.'

Darby looked at Hudson, both men quite still.

'You're a guest in my home,' said Hudson, 'at least show me the respect of answering my fucking question.'

'These four,' Mick lifted his right hand, thumb to the four oil paintings, 'I find them desolate, bleak. I think the artist struggled to find anything uplifting, struggled to find beauty saw there was none, couldn't brush over the despair.'

'Sometimes,' Hudson looked to the paintings and back to Mick, 'sometimes I come here to look at only these four, the struggle as you say. They remind me of my calling.'

'Your calling?' Mick whispered.

'Calling' said Hudson, 'looks like there's a lot here beyond your understanding.' He smiled, a rabid Doberman would look kinder, put an arm around Darby's shoulder and said, 'let's join the others, we've had enough art for one day.'

. . . .

'You going back to the office?'

'Yes,' said Darby to his boss, 'Alex will be around the corner, can we give you a lift?'

'Thanks.'

Alex wasn't around the corner, he pulled up just behind them, 'must have a sixth sense,' muttered Darby.

Alex was out, had both back doors open.

'Where the fuck did you get to?'

'Didn't realise you'd miss me, Boss,' said Darby, 'I found myself in a room stuffed with artwork, Hudson and I had a quiet chat.'

'Thought so, a few minutes after you went inside, he jumped up like a bee'd stung his arse. Next thing I know, maybe ten minutes, the pair of you come out together. Caused quite a fuss, you two arm in arm.'

'He can put on a show. Just before he opened the door, he gestured me to go first, then the bastard took my arm. Best of mates.'

'Relax everyone, nothing to fear here?'

'Exactly,' said Mick, 'Plus a train smash of a reminder of what we're up against. Thanks for arranging my invitation.'

'Ha! Not at all, good you enjoyed it, may not be another.'

Alex parked underground and the three men made their way up to the lifts, through the half-full carpark of well-used cars. Out of the lift, a pale grey room, quiet noise of keystrokes, phone conversations, smelling of coffee, pizza and chips.

In his office Darby phoned Rome.

'Wondered where you were,' she said.

'Studying art, I've discovered I'm a good student.'

'Always room for improvement,' she laughed, 'and your homework?'

'Coming along nicely.'

'That's what I was afraid of,' more laughter, 'art on a Sunday?'

'Hudson and Phoebe Lang's soiree, found myself in their private art gallery.'

'Seriously? I'd love to get in there, heard so much about it, a few stories.'

He told her what he thought of it, the crazy paving.

'It's called a gallery wall Mick. My assessment is that more training is required. You know I started looking at the Langs and their art in Sydney before they moved to Canberra. The investigation went nowhere, petered out, I was sent to London. I heard they'd lost interest in art.'

'Well, they rediscovered their interest, with interest. Hudson has the value of every square metre of those four gallery walls calculated.'

'How so?'

'He rattled off the numbers. He adds the price he paid for each piece of work hanging on a wall, divides that total by the square metres. He told me that every few months he recalculates based on estimates of what the pieces'd fetch at auction.'

'I have never heard of that! Never known of anyone to do that. He's got a head for art, the dealers would see him coming. What does he quote you for a wall?'

'Not that easily, Miss. The room's a rectangle, say ten by seven metres. I reckon three and a half metres high. So, the two bigger walls weigh in at thirty five square metres. Let's start there?'

'Doors hung with art too?'

'Part of the thirty five.'

'Hundred and twenty grand.'

'Close. Hundred and forty eight is the most expensive wall. Hudson's number,' he waggled his hand, 'ish, artish.'

'Artish is right. What're the works like?'

'I couldn't concentrate. Everything jammed together. Even when I stood back, like you suggested, I saw three or four. Up close to focus on one, way too close. What was the interest back in Sydney?'

'Money laundering. It was easy then, buy art from a dealer at a low price. Fire sale or some such bullshit. Make up the price with dirty money under the table. Wait a few months and the pieces are sold on through another dealer for the right money. You get your cheque, cash it. Your money's washed. The Langs were buying and selling so much in a very short time, they were noticed. Suddenly they stopped. That's as far as it went, then London.'

'Thanks. Plans for the day?'

'Oh, you know, Rome in August, no-one around except Americans and Germans. I'm going to the office. I'll be back in a week. Ciao.'

'Chow? What's that a Roman word for lunch?'

'Philistine, I'm hanging up.'

Darby hung up, smiled, and cleared his desk of everything except a tablet. This one had no WIFI, no Bluetooth, he knew it offered some protection.

He'd be briefing his boss late tonight. For that he'd prepare a case to run a joint operation with Ethics Australia investigating Asher Ministries. Harriet Cooper ran the federal anti-corruption agency with a team of skilled corruption investigators; Darby's team had a broader range of expertise; intelligence analysis, forensic accounting, tracking and tracing people. Plus, he didn't have to report operational details to a parliamentary oversight committee, whereas Harriet did. A joint operation would avoid scrutiny, and give him resources.

He'd need approval, budget, and resources. His argument was thin. Spreading the costs, using Harriet's budget would help. Operations were generally approved when there was much more solid evidence than he had against Asher Ministries. The problem was their connections. Once this started...he thought and poured a small scotch. He left the opened bottle on his desk, conversation starter for his boss.

Circle of virtue.

Mick Darby called his lead team together. They got to the meeting room joking, laughing, teasing, 'well it's not the first time some prick's gone missing in Canberra, is it?'

'Don't bother,' he said.

'As the actress said to the Bishop,' as this was from one of his more sombre operators Mick thought he'd give them a few more minutes to sort themselves and poured himself another coffee.

'Want to get our facts straight on Asher Ministries. What do we have?' he counted off on his fingers. 'We have the complaints against various Asher Houses, now a security check has brought issues of probity around money, and there are the leaks to the press. Let's just go around the room?'

'Security clearances, Hudson and Phoebe Lang, work in progress' said Alex, 'police checks, nothing. Though there are threats and violence from some of their associates to people who oppose them. We started looking at money. Asher Ministries, Asher Houses, accounts in the Lang name. What have we got?' Alex looked around the room, he'd shifted the team's attention from devices to him, 'we've got a Canberra winter. Money dressed in layers. We've not got them all, the mansion they live in is owned by an Asher Ministries' company. They don't own their cars and we don't know yet who does. Clearly they have money, we don't where it is stashed yet.'

'OK,' said Mick, and gave short background to why he'd tasked Alex with clearance checks. 'I need us to look at finances more broadly too, keep on these layers. Can we check out the Lang's art collection, who insures it, who pays the insurance. And let's get someone on the company structures; Asher Ministries, Asher Houses, company reports, balance sheets, tax returns, directors.'

'I stepped back further into Asher Houses,' said another officer, 'aged care is a highly regulated industry, every part of it has a set

63

of rules and a governance authority. For example, traineeships have an external audit authority, care quality must be reported quarterly, it's own complaints agency. When I searched the regulators; CEOs, Commissioners, senior officials are all Asher Ministries members.'

'Great', said Mick, 'and again, any comparison data, how do their reports differ from other providers?'

'Asher Houses use a private benchmarking company to do their care audits, Asher Ministries registered the trust which owns the benchmarking firm.'

'A real circle of virtue,' said one.

Darby figured the circle was less virtue and more self-interest. He said, 'and complaints about Asher Ministries or Asher Houses really don't get beyond Asher. Even when concerns do get to a regulator; the complaints are referred to Asher to resolve, and Asher reports back that the complaints have been resolved. No further action required. Now, I wanna know if this happens with any other provider, any other company in aged care?'

'Let's move on,' he said. 'Can I have your thoughts on these stories?' Mick thumbed his device and the screen on the back wall lit with images of the Asher House complaints coverage. They got nowhere useful.

'Let's talk to the journalists,' said a team member, 'they often have more than they publish.'

'Looks like same old,' said another, 'people complain to the Attorney-General, she refers complaints to Asher, and they come back saying it's all sweet. No further action required.'

'Could be their theme song,' said one.

'That's it for now. Thanks for coming in,' said Mick. 'After I meet with the Attorney-General let's get together. Let's keep at it and let's keep this to ourselves. Desktop research only for now. No interviews with these characters. Verify it all. Identify any witnesses, paperwork, can we get a timeline, build a theory about what we think's going on here? Alex will coordinate that.'

'Mick,' said one of the team. 'I've never been inside an old people's home.'

'Well, you've a while to go yet,' said one of her colleagues.

'What are you thinking?' Mick said, cutting across the laughs.

'If we went into one of the Asher Houses, say we go in as ACT Health? Have a look around, see for ourselves, get a feel for the place.'

'Find the missing dildo...'

Laughter.

'Why ACT Health?' Alex asked.

'Because their CEO is not a fan of Asher Ministries, I think he'll help us out. Any other way we go there we're sprung. ACT Health though, they've been shut out of Asher House because Asher is Commonwealth funded; they've not been shut out of any other provider though. So, he's pissed off, so is his exec. If he's up for it, we'd get away with it. Be useful to know more about what we're dealing with.'

'Mick,' said Alex, 'I'm in, I know him well enough to ask.'

'OK,' said Mick, 'agreed.' He looked at the officer who made the call, 'why don't you go with Alex to Health, let me know the arrangements for Asher House when it's sorted. Good call, thank you.'

Team members drifted away. Mick took Alex aside, 'mate, when you've got the OK, let's get one of Harriet's officers to go along too. She's working on Asher; it'll be useful for us both to do this.'

'Sure,' said Alex, 'Look at these two, they seem absorbed in something.' He nodded towards two of the team who had settled at their workstations.

Mick shook his head. 'It's late, I'll hear about in the morning."

Alex went up to the two who'd stayed behind. He heard one of them say, 'wouldn't mind your thoughts on the money angle, mate. Can't get my head around it.'

'Need something?'

'If we were talking paper money grandpa; but, bitcoin, crypto, we're good thanks!'

'You won't need me for that,' Alex said, laughing. 'Leave you to it.'

They pulled chairs together, connected a laptop to a big screen monitor, scrolled pages of financials.

'So, Hudson Lang right, let's say he has no assets. How's he pay for shopping? Goes out to lunch, cash, credit card? Phoebe pays? Same deal, right? They go to Coles; how do they pay for stuff? Clothes? Petrol?'

'OK; let's do petrol first, maybe a fuel card, with their car regos? Can we find that?'

'You know, if they live in a house rent free, house provided by their employer. Taxable right, fringe benefit? I'll check for that while you do the petrol sniffing,' he said, skating his chair back to his workstation.

'Shit,' he said, 'they put some thought into this, their cars are leased by a holding company.'

'By them?' He poked his head over the workstation, peered at his colleague's big screen, 'or by someone else? Another company I bet.'

'Not there yet mate.'

Alex found Mick waiting for him at the lift, hand keeping the door from closing.

'Alex,' said Mick, beckoning Alex into the lift, door hissing behind them, 'the robot material from Sturgess? Surprised it wasn't top of your list.'

'Mick,' Alex shrugged, 'all we could find is a proposal from Sturgess for money to fund a literature review of assistive riobots, and a study tour, travel budget.'

'That's it,' said Mick, 'get your best people on that did you? To find out that a scientist wants to read fucking books. Get it done again!' He stabbed C1, again and again.

The Attorney General.

The Minister was unimpressed and keen to show it. Her displeasure was infectious, flowed from her like ripples in a pond. Not quite like ripples in a pond where the strongest ripples are closest to the source. In a meeting of a Minister, ministerial advisors, political staffers, and public servants the effect of the Minister's displeasure is more keenly observed on the faces of those furthest from the Minister. The lesser ranks arranged at the periphery of the Minister's pond frown the hardest. The reverse ripple effect.Will they ever learn, wondered Mick.

Mick Darby decided to look a little concerned and caught the Minister's eye.

'Mick?'

'A few informal observations Minister if I may.'

'Thanks,' said the Minister, adding, 'Mick is with the Intelligence Committee, leaking may be a security risk.'

'Thank you', Mick continued, 'public officials, political staffers, parliamentarians improperly using, maybe peddling, information gained from their position - that's what we're talking about.'

Mick's use of 'informal' was noted by the Chief of Staff, she raised an eyebrow. He was signalling that he expected no actions for him coming out of the meeting, this was just a conversation.

The Minister was pissed at the leaking of government information about Asher Ministries. She argued that the leaking went beyond the usual antipathy between government factions. Asher Ministries counted her among its faithful, along with the Prime Minister, senior ministers, opposition members and assorted bureaucrats. Not every parliamentarian was enamoured of Dr Phoebe and Hudson Lang so there was some antagonism and clamouring about undue influence. Rumours that Phoebe had ambitions to enter the Senate hadn't helped.

The meeting canvassed whether the leaking breached security. Fifteen complaints about Asher Ministries' traineeship scheme, some aged care facilities, and the classifying of some of the financial entities as charities had been assessed by her office. Her chief investigators had contacted Asher Ministries who assured them the matters had already been dealt with. No complaints were upheld, the entities retained their charitable status, traineeships continued, aged care services unchanged. Files closed; job done.

Until the media reports and rumours of a whitewash began. Within hours the complainants and the journalist had been threatened by Asher Ministries' lawyers. Still the stories and details of some of the cases were blogged, blogs were reported by mainstream media, amplifying the complaints.

'Maybe it's early to call; you may want to talk it through some more. My final observation is to talk it through with a broader group. I don't want to know how many of you are Asher Ministries' members. That's not my business,' Darby said, 'I do know this, if there is a call for an investigation into the leaks about Asher Ministries only by members of Asher Ministries...you want to consider a non-partisan referral. The big question here is leaking government information; from this, the chief law-maker's office.The lesser question is the leaks are about Asher.'

The advisors and staffers heard Darby in silence, the Attorney-General thumbed her phone; one of her more junior advisors, maybe emboldened by what he saw as his minister's indifference to Darby's observations, spoke up. 'I would have thought the bigger issue here is the attempt to libel Asher Ministries.'

'Quite,' said the Attorney-General. 'We received complaints about Asher Ministries. Our assessment was they were best left with Asher Ministries to resolve. Their advice was that the matters have been dealt with. So, our actions, entirely appropriate.'

Her staff nodded their heads in unison, she continued. 'I want to know if the leaks about the complaints came from this office. Asher Ministries is doing an internal inquiry on the remote chance the leaks came from there. The question is how do we investigate these leaks? Let's do it internally. Get that journalist in.'

'Now,' she turned, 'I'm so pleased you could spare us your valuable time and thoughts, Mick.'

Her acolytes beamed at him, Molly Lavandar rolled her eyes. Darby thought she had the voice of a sat nav when she wanted something, calculated one stun grenade for the room would probably do it.

'If we can't get the right answer from this journo,' she checked her device, 'Marcia Kiernan. I can refer her to you?'

For a public service medal or rendition? thought Darby; but said, 'yes Minister.'

'Good,' she said smiling, 'I want this closed yesterday. Anything else?'

'Related matter,' said Molly, 'the Aged Care Commission has investigated grievances against Asher Ministries and Asher House. Their investigations are complete, and they sent their reports to Ethics Australia for their expert review of their grievance investigation procedures.'

'Why would they do that?' asked a staffer.

'What part of expert review do you not understand?' Molly glared at the staffer. Molly wanted it known there were more grievances about Asher Ministries. 'The Commissioner wanted to make sure she wasn't being intemperate,' said Molly, 'or too lenient on Asher. These are contested issues; we may decide to do the same right?'

'Can I ask why Harriet Cooper,' said a party staffer looking up from his phone, 'Commissioner of Ethics Australia isn't here? Along with Mr Darby's observations, it'd be useful to have her thoughts on the leak, I'd have thought?'

'Chief Commissioner,' said the Attorney-General, 'precisely; national security, public safety and anti-corruption; three peas in a pod. That's why Ethics Australia should be less independent from this office, then the commissioner would attend, like Mick Darby does.'

The meeting finished, the mood a little perky, even the juniors recognised a boss lowering the boom. As iPads were closed, phones skimmed and thumbed furiously, Molly Lavandar escorted Mick through the door.

'Didn't take you for an Asher fan,' said Molly.

'What do you take me for?' said Mick.

'Well, I'd like to take you for a drink...soon, there's more to this.'

'Like?' said Darby.

'Well, for one thing, she's not paying enough attention to the aged care robotics research.'

Track your Prayer.

Phoebe Lang was onstage. Harsh lights in her face, worshippers she couldn't see, thousands of phone screens waving at her. Despite the discreet makeup she sweated down her forehead, nose, neck; relaxed about it though as there were strict directives forbidding closeups on stage. The opening musical of the prayer medley was finished, the musicians in darkness, they didn't need to see her cues now.

'Please,' she implored, 'please take a seat. You can all be seated.'

Long pause, swapped the mic to the right hand, brought both hands together wrapped around the base of the microphone, praying over it. Head up slowly; took a step, two, towards the faithful, looking at blocks of the audience as the lights lit up from the front to the back, making her eye contact match the sequence in which the arena was lit. How many times had she practised this?

'How many, how many times? How many times have you heard, "It is what it is"'?

'Notice what's happening here? Can you see what's happening here? Every time you hear the phrase, every time you use the phrase, every time you say, "it is what it is", you're saying. There's nothing, nothing, not a single thing I can do. I can do – nothing.'

'Let's see about that.' Applause, cheers, whistling. 'Any friends here who love the presence of God?' Phoebe called.

'Yes!' The worshippers' responsed, some stumbling, knees trembling, giving out.

'Any friends here? My friends are you here to experience an incredible God encounter?'

Keith Evans stood mesmerised, barely conscious, alert enough though to crush a bundle of notes into the bucket passed around. Keith felt himself come alive at these services.

'Yes,' he shouted, 'I am here to experience.'

A poor, single mum wasn't enough family for Keith, a computer science degree - not enough for Keith, having to save, or worse, do without, because you couldn't get credit – not enough. Enough too, of no friends.

A former colleague had taken the lonely Keith along one evening to a Phoebe Lang service. He was evangelised within a week, seduced by the inspiration that the quality of one's spiritual life is measured by one's temporal life; wealth, or at least looking the part, evidence of God's love. Goodbye not enough. Asher Ministries, like the first drink for an alcoholic, Keith wondered how he'd lived without it, his answer of course was obvious to him now, he hadn't been alive before, not really.

'My friends,' Phoebe lowered her voice taking them into her confidence, 'here's the thing, when you resign yourselves to believing there's nothing you can do, you're not encountering God. You are walking away from the presence of God, you're taking the other path, you're asking God to leave us as we are, to leave us resigned, to leave us without hope. AND HE WON'T DO THAT!'

Phoebe disappeared. Strobe lights replaced spotlights, solo drum introduction, strong bass, lead guitar over the top to playful lyrics, or would have been if they were heard. Flirtatious backing singers: Keith Evans writhed, amazed at his lack of control, although drug-free.

Phoebe, her stage manager, and her choreographer judged it was time for calm, an Asher audience too exhausted for tithing was just a crowd. The music dropped, the singers vanished, strobe lights off, stage dimmed. Phoebe reappeared, just walking along the stage, picking her way across power cords, leads, instrument cases; just a woman walking, no need to clap or cheer.

Her path took her to a microphone stand where she stopped and said, 'let me talk to you about parcel tracking,' some in her audience looked at each other, back to Phoebe. 'I've had some blogs, emails, voicemail about prayer. About your prayers not being answered. "Is Jesus out?" You asked me, "not at home? I prayed and he didn't answer."'

Phoebe had stepped up the pace and the volume, teasing her followers. Now, she slowed, dropped her voice.

'Let me tell you something about Jesus,' she said, and the lights dimmed except for the cross which shone brighter, 'he revealed something about prayer to me. Can I share it with you?' She raised her voice, 'well, can I share Jesus' message with you?'

'YES!'

'Well,' she began, 'let's say you want to send a friend a parcel, might be one of my books, hope it'd be one of my books. So, you buy it from the store outside, only fifteen bucks, take it home, bubble wrap it. Now, courier or post? You choose. Either way, you get a tracking number, so you know when my book reaches your friend. Because you know, you know, you don't just post a book and have faith it'll reach your friend. No, you want a tracking number.'

Her audience remained silent, but felt a bit agitated; no music, dimmed lights, no spectacle.

Phoebe pounced, 'you know I think some of you believe Jesus is Australia Post, can't be trusted. Here's the thing,' louder now, 'you pray to Jesus and it's like you want a tracking number on that prayer! You pray for something, in two days your something is not there! Look up the tracking number! Call Phoebe, she'll know where your prayer is at! Where did you get the idea that you don't have faith in Jesus?' Cue industrial level music, feverish lights, and Phoebe screaming now, 'NOT HERE.'

Twenty minutes later, final entreaties to give joyfully, promise of receiving more from God, reminder about her book, and she was finished. She left an arena of thousands of screaming worshipers, eyes glazed, bodies moving, hands waving, an early Beatles concert audience, with perfect teeth, torn jeans, and tattoos.

In her dressing room Hudson dismissed the beautician removing Phoebe's makeup.

'The blogs, media going over those lies, we are still under spiritual attack.'

'Or, this is just a test of Jesus' plan,' said Phoebe scrubbing her face, 'of our love for those who most need our generosity, our breakthrough to our wise elders whom we have welcomed into our Asher House ministry. Jesus doesn't talk about the social issues of ageing; he talks about the heart of a person. It's not our job Hudson, it was not Jesus' job, to preach ageing.'

'We'll have our lawyers help us with this. Let's take their advice. Maybe you could get on to the Attorney-General to do a bit more too?'

'OK Hudson, I'm seeing her tomorrow, she wants to get to the Parliamentary Choir practice a little earlier than the others. Do you have the time now to go over the schedule for me becoming a senator?'

'Sure, I'd love to help. Such a huge step.'

'It's a temporal step honey; not a spiritual one; but think of the leverage in Asia?'

'How does the schedule go again?'

'Senator Karsen resigns. NSW Parliament will nominate me to fill the vacancy. Media conference. Short video on our social media sites and our YouTube channels. There'll be a bit of a fuss about same-party nomination, but I'm told there are vacancies to be filled on some government company Boards, so the fuss will be for show only.'

'Those government Boards,' said Hudson, 'what are they? Can we get onto any of those? Do they pay? Can we use them?'

'After my appointment is confirmed by Parliament,' said Phoebe, 'copies of my Mary Magdalene Gospel will be promoted, sold as an eBook, audio book, and serialised in the Daily Telegraph. Signed up and sworn to secrecy until it all comes off. Our lawyers are all over it.'

'And the trigger?'

'Karsen's resignation should be on the news this week. He's told them he's going to resign.'

'OK,' said Hudson, 'now, what do you need from me?'

'I need you not to go on about government Boards,' said Phoebe. 'we don't need the attention. We've got a lot on. The money's coming in and everything's been quiet, now; the Senate, this media shit, what if we can't keep a lid on the complaints? Can't have you tied up on some government Board.'

'What do you suggest? Are you suggesting we do anything, or just laying out where we are?'

'In the next few days,' said Phoebe, 'we need to sit down with everyone who knows a piece of what's ours and remind them we're still here. Have Jackson pick them up and drive them here, another reminder.'

By the numbers.

Twenty-seven friends of Asher House Woden; hands and faces freshly washed, for some the wash shouldn't have ended there, making their way to their seats. Walkers, wheelchairs, canes, and sticks; clattering, out of sync with the pulse and empty lyrics of Asher Ministries' latest playlist. Some talking, meaning almost in the noise. Jeans, skirts, shirts and blouses, housing flesh, loosely packed. Traces of soap, detergent, vinegar, soup, farts; the dining room simply smelt of itself. Neglect.

The door opened admitting fresh air, it was enough for all twenty-seven to turn around, noses wrinkled. The kitchen staff thought one of them had escaped so one went to check.

'The guy at the door said everyone would be in here,' said the younger of the two women.

'You're not supposed to be in here,' challenged the kitchen hand, 'they get all worked up when the routine changes.'

The two visitors stood still. The visitor who hadn't spoken opened her satchel and took out an envelope, held it to her side.

The kitchen hand frowned. 'Look I suppose it's all right. Security let you get this far. Just don't disturb them though, they're about to eat and we'll be busy cleaning up after them. So, don't disturb us either eh.'

'I'm glad we got that sorted,' said the younger visitor, 'makes our report so much easier. Don't suppose you knew we were coming did you? Only we find most bosses do that. Don't let you know. A spot check, as long as it's not on them.'

'Yeah. No, you're right. We didn't know you were coming. Can you give us twenty minutes to feed them and clean up, at least the messiest? Then we can talk.'

'Sure,' she said, 'we'll take a quick look around and meet you back here,' looking at her watch, 'in twenty-five minutes? You know what, make it half an hour? Grab a coffee if you have to wait for us.'

The two women left the dining room.

They checked rooms; bare, no personal belongings, no photos, each room the same as the next. Lockers, few clothes, maybe one or two pair of shoes, again standard issue.

'See anything?'

'No, dust. Just dust. A little triangle in every corner.'

'Yeah, me too, maybe they keep it as pets?'

'Seen any double beds yet?'

'No, so sex is out then?'

'Don't think even I could manage it on these narrow cots!'

'Nothing like a challenge!'

Cupboards next. Again, contents all squared away. They took out the spray bottles, sprayed and sniffed.

'Vinegar?'

'Correct. Asher House vinegar could be your special subject.'

'Medicines, medication, hand sanitizer, denture cleaner, pills, tablets, eyedrops, creams, gauze, cotton wool, toothpaste, disinfectant, band aids?'

'Not an aspirin to be found. Let's go and talk to them.'

The two investigators returned to the dining room. The meal was ending, tables were being cleared, cleaned, friends also. One of the kitchen hands moved walkers and wheelchairs over to the tables, those needing canes, sticks fended for themselves. Twenty-seven older people made their return journey to the rec room. The staff made sure none of them could engage with the two visitors.

One of the staff stayed with the group, organising seats, cushions, a footstool for one, adjusted throwovers, leaving two to answer the investigators' questions.

'So, who do we talk to about medical records, falls reports, number of consumers...' she stopped, smiled, 'sorry, these people are friends, right? You don't call them consumers? So much more personal. So, how many friends were restrained in the last week? Where do I find those records? And pressure areas? Who can show me the records showing how pressure injuries are treated? It's a lot of questions I know, still, it is a spot check.'

'No use asking us,' said one of the kitchen hands, 'spot check or not. We don't know what you're on about. The records are all at the medical centre, where they're supposed to be. Their medication is locked away, we don't have a key. Hey! What are you doing?'

One of the investigators was taking a sample of the soup, ladling spoonfuls into what looked like a specimen jar. 'There, 60 ml or so, should be enough. Don't mind me,' she said screwing the plastic cap on, 'I'll take a few photos of what's in these cupboards, the fridges. Cool room? Pantry? There's not much space here.'

'I'll just take you, it'll be easier,' said the other kitchen hand, 'through here.'

'We've never had this kind of spot check,' said the woman, growing uneasy as she realised how little she knew.

'Oh,' said Darby's investigator, 'what are you used to?'

'Lots of last-minute changes, new staff with no training...look, it's worth my job this.'

'Talking to me? Thought we were just having a chat, bosses the same all over, aren't they? Mine likes to play music in the office too, says it helps him think,' she smiled. Thinking Darby would be as likely to have music in the office as no beer in the fridge.

'Oh shit, excuse my Strayun, it's on all the bloody time. Course they,' flinging her hand at the rec centre, 'don't care, can't hear it most of them anyway.'

'Yeah, you know I kind of expected to see more hearing aids, and then I thought maybe they use the really tiny ones?'

'Yeah. No, the specialist that comes here reckons they're better off without them, less noise is good for them. What with the cleaning robots buzzing around and the music? Anyway, we only let them have them in when they get visitors.'

'OK. Sounds sensible. Sometimes I wish I didn't hear stuff!'

'Yeah, me too. Get everything you need from the pantry, cold room love?'

The investigator and her pantry guide had joined them.

'Thanks so much,' she said, 'you've all been very helpful.'

'For our records, who do we say was here?'

'Oh, for your bosses you mean? I wouldn't worry about them, our boss will be on the phone tonight, we'll put in a good word for you. Thanks again. We can find our way back.'

They found their way back to the front desk where Alex Briggs waited for them, in deep conversation with the security guard who had bought his story about a spot check from ACT Health.

Safely in the car, one of the investigators said 'Alex, you wouldn't believe it.'

'No,' said Alex looking at her in the rear vision mirror, 'not here, and not before you've written up your report.' He looked to the road, 'you'll both brief Mick.'

Mick and Alex.

Alex Briggs held the door open for Mick, went around the front of the noiseless car, and drove off, startled.

'Not quite used to this hybrid, Alex, are you?'

'Never realised how much information you get from noise, Mick.'

'And that sums up the meeting I've just been through! I know it's early days mate, but that timeline? Are you on it?'

'Yeah, we've mapping how it is now. Then the team will build backwards. One of them, for example, is working people backwards; like what did the Aged Care Commissioner do before she got that job, are there photos of her at Asher Ministries? When did she meet them?'

'Good,' said Mick, 'the timing, it's going to be crucial, this circle of virtue didn't just magically appear.'

'Maybe it was revealed?'

'Not you too?' laughed Mick, 'You know, I went along on Saturday to see what they do with their preaching. Different take on faith and wealth. It's all about what you can get now, money a proxy for faith. Religions I've been used to stressed the afterlife. For these guys though, there is no future outside the present.'

'Bit deep, Mick.'

'Yeah, I was drowning in there. I'm having a drink with Molly Lavandar later this week – could you make sure our file on her is up to date please? Include her vetting for the Chief of Staff job she has now.'

'Sure,' said Alex.

Mick sat back in the front seat, mind wandering as Alex talked about the Raider's chances this Friday night. Alex's favourite conversation, soliloquy really, and it suited them both. Mick made an obligatory mumble now and then just to show he was listening. Alex would lay a trap or two in the conversation, interested in whether Mick was paying attention.

'Do you think I've lost it Briggsie? Ricky is the coach not the half.'

'My bad, Boss.'

'You've had your boys again this week, haven't you? Some good came out of your marriage mate. They're a bad influence on your language skills though, such as they are.'

'Mick,' said Alex, 'speaking of bad influences.'

'Something tells me I should be listening,' said Darby, half turning in his seat to face Alex.

'We got into Asher House Woden. ACT Health were really helpful, they'll be good allies in this. There is one thing though, I didn't use one of Harriet's operators, thought we'd best keep this to ourselves. There's too much chatter over there, and it's about an Asher nutcase; Evans, Keith Evans.'

'Too risky?'

'Yeah. Some of them, Harriet's mob, they moan about him a lot. Be just our luck to have one of them let him know that his precious Asher House is crap. So we went in alone.'

'What did they find?'

'Mate, the fucking RSPCA'd shut it down. I'd like to get a look at a few more Asher Houses. This can't be a one-off.'

'Look', said Mick, 'if you can find a way to confirm what you have now, without going in, then do it. Thing is, if we're seen to have enough to shut it down, shut them all down, then we'd have to. It's too early, I want them for everything they're caught up in, not just what they do to old people. Everything. But, not stuff they can get out of easily, I want them on what they can do with the robotics; cybersecurity, unlawful surveillance, surveillance of government ministers.'

• • • •

My bad boss indeed, mused Alex as he checked Molly Lavandar's files. Alex was employed by Parliamentary Security, permanently seconded to Mick Darby who regarded him as his offsider.

Alex knew his boss would put Research to review the Lavandar file and provide him notes to review before drinks. He also knew his boss relied on Alex to read between lines, to hear what wasn't said. The researchers covered a rational approach, logical, fact finding; would be all over the files; in-depth reports, interviews, any video recordings and wiretaps, assessments. Alex relied on his gut feelings. Mick would have the benefit of his researchers' logic and Alex's intuition.

Alex closed the file summaries, locked his laptop and his notes in the office safe, left the building. He walked the grounds of the War Memorial and mulled over Molly's disinfected story.

'Once upon a time', he began, 'there was a young woman called Molly Lavandar who came to Canberra thirty years ago. She's now Chief of Staff to the Attorney-General.'

He didn't trouble with her well-charted rise through the public service; however, he did think her network was interesting.

'Molly, and her closest friends from ANU days were or had been, senior public servants. Chief Scientists, Secretaries, Chiefs of Staff, Deputy Secretaries, Commissioner, medals, rank, and privilege. They stayed in touch. She lived happily ever after 1995. The end.'

Late the next day Alex told Mick his thoughts. Mick had her file and the briefing notes open.

'Well?' Mick asked, 'what can you add to this?' He paraphrased as he read, 'the career you'd expect from a smart country kid; dux of her school, school captain, university medal, honours degree in Politics and a MBA. Started in Canberra as a graduate, steady promotions, then rapid move through SES, overseas with DFAT,

Competition Council, ATO, on secondment from the Public Service Commission to Chief of Staff, Attorney-General.'

'It all checks out,' said Alex. 'Typical for a senior Canberra bureaucrat; lives in a three-storey penthouse in lakeside Kingston owned by a trust fund, owned by a trust in Vanuatu, she's the sole beneficiary. She was interviewed once after receiving the Public Service Medal and mentioned an uncle who had gone to New Caledonia in the 60s, details are all there. No career setbacks, no scandals, highly regarded by both sides. No fan of Asher Ministries. She even has a hobby, collecting antique ceramics. Has a well-known collection.'

Mick had a few questions, 'Vanuatu? Tax haven? Nothing there?

'I checked a few files of people with Vanuatu connections, all those files are a bit vague about Vanuatu. Not Molly's, every day she spent there accounted for.'

'And that's unusual?' Mick said, 'not only is she clean, she's also cleaner than clean. That fits, doesn't it?'

'There's a problem.'

'How come?'

'There's no story Mick; that's the story, and it's the story of a problem. I mean, cleaner than clean, when's that not been a problem?'

'Seriously?'

'Prepared for publication, it's just like Canberra – planned to within an inch of its life. Life is organic, messy, a file should reflect that. This city is planned and imperfect, Lavandar's files are planned, and, perfect.'

'Mate – interesting,' said Darby rubbing the side of his face. 'Molly, a real Canberra product. Habits? Interests? The Canberra trifecta; theatre, music, art? I don't need any more for the meeting with her; she is worth a closer look though. Who did the security check for the Chief of Staff job?'

'Alan Bates – you were at his retirement last month and he's in England now.'

'Batesy – he never filled me with confidence, so another thing to review. Mate I need detail – the Master would have relied on other people doing the work; so, find out - who asked the questions, who took the notes, find out who filled out the forms, go back to other documentation and find out what data was gathered from paperwork, find out who did the original paperwork, it'll come down to people leaving stuff out or leaving stuff in, always.'

'Chief Scientist? You mentioned a scientist among her colleagues?'

'Yeah, Sturgess, Aged Care.'

'Sturgess? Name came up earlier this week, he's the bloke in charge of some serious research on robots in nursing homes, not that there aren't enough there already. Asher Houses. Only they have the exclusive on this trial. Let's look at him too.'

'We knew that,' said Alex, staggered at the robot reference, 'I thought we'd agreed he was harmless?'

'Well,' said Mick, 'the stuff he's running now; sensors and bracelets, that detect and alert project. Don't see any harm in that, seems to be useful and it's going into all aged care. But, the robots, these robots; you can talk to them, they talk back, use them to organise your day, schedule medication, use them in rehab, walk with them. Bluetooth, facial recognition; scary stuff the data collected. Now, add a drone into the mix, drone with facial recognition.'

'Why are you so bothered by it?'

'Well, I'm not bothered by that, not by the technology. I'm fucking bothered that a scientist can slip this stuff into nursing homes, unsecured; and we can't even use it! I mean, facial recognition? Must be signed off by a judge, that's after the request has gone through my boss.'

'Shit', said Alex, 'I didn't know it all had to be signed off by the Boss and a judge. With what we've got, they must be signing ten a day.'

'Well, I might be a little behind in my paperwork,' said Mick. 'And now, Asher House gets it without even a second look. What do you reckon that holy roller, Hudson Lang, will do with it? That bothers me.'

'Mick, how far behind are you in your paperwork?'

'Not as far behind as you with the robot intel.'

'Mick, the robotics. We're finding nothing. My take? There's nothing to be found.'

'Or,' said Mick, raising one finger, 'you've found nothing. Don't confuse the two.' Darby pulled a sheaf of paper from his satchel, rolled the papers up, poked Alex on the forearm, 'get your boy and girl geniuses to check this shit out, research. Israel,' he poked, 'Canada,' again with the roll, 'Italy. Robotics research, exactly as I've talked about. I bet that prick Sturgess is going to these places,' again poking, 'get onto it. Once I start looking for the pattern, I see it everywhere.'

'So,' said Alex, 'do I log this as evidence? What's the custody chain?'

'Just fucking read it.'

Community Worship.

H iba started her shift in a meeting. A young woman letting them know they were training for the next two days, a new shift was to relieve them straight after handover. Handover and the rounds, then to a minibus and another Asher House facility in a nearby suburb.

With barely an introduction the session started. They were to learn new dance routines. Group activities, physical activities the instructor explained. Simple steps with countless variations in sequence, pace, and music.

'Group activities?' Hiba asked. 'The physiotherapy we've been used to is for each person, fits with their pills and what they can do.'

'You have described the problem with what you used to be doing perfectly,' peering at the name tag, 'Hiba,' she said. 'We'll do more on the theory later. For now, the theology of physical movement and group dynamics in Asher House is based around community.'

'We're building people's faith into their lives; a cornerstone of the build is community worship. You know the reason we are Asher House, part of Asher Ministries? Asher is the gate to Jesus that leaves people feeling calm. You would have been concerned at the number of falls under the outdated physiotherapy.'

She was right thought Hiba, there were many falls. 'Old people fall,' her supervisor had said, 'just like wrinkles, it's part of getting old. And, we report it to the Benchmarking company, they do all the paperwork.'

'This program has a real prevention focus' said the instructor moving from one foot to the other, 'the one-on-one programs which took so long, and the paperwork; just severing the ties that bind them to each other and to Jesus. No more.'

'You'll see a double row of XX's in red tape on the floor, so please stand on one, and face me for the first demonstration.'

The instructor thumbed an iPhone; music started, a row of dancers stepped out and took four steps forward from the open door behind her, paired off and facing each other, executed a perfect Do-si-do.

The flatmates shrieked, clapped, and were won over. Paired up with the demonstrators they had not much opportunity to talk among themselves. If they'd had any time to themselves, it would have been spent letting each other know how much they were enjoying it.

And so, they spent two days on the revised physiotherapy program. The paperwork was so much simpler, community movement programs slotted into the care management programs and all approved by a qualified physiotherapist. They were told to have the friends remove their bracelets so the sensors wouldn't continuously shriek, shown how to include those wheelchair bound in the community exercises and reminded, 'Asher House is an inclusive, faith-based community.'

Back at their facility the carers took to the community worship and movement program enthusiastically. The number of falls among residents didn't change. Where the falls occurred did change. Fewer falls occurred in the common areas, more falls occurred in bathrooms and bedrooms. The physiotherapist on his monthly round with each facility assured staff that the revised program was working – fewer falls where the activity took place. Generalisation of enhanced mobility would take a little more time 'in line with best practice expectations.'

Phoebe Lang had seen the opportunity and replace professional physiotherapy with community movement and worship. In the previous months, she had done the rounds of some Asher House facilities, a little preaching, a little handholding, a little reassurance, and a lot of watching. Seizing an opportunity to direct more money their way, she cancelled individual sessions with physiotherapists.

Phoebe met with her chief choreographer. The result of that meeting was the training program Hiba and her colleagues had just completed.

Phoebe claimed the costs of the training, including wages and replacement wages against the Commonwealth's traineeship program. The community worship and movement program documented as individual physiotherapy, and rebates claimed from Medicare for each participant. The savings and the false claims swelled the bottom line.

Just tell me what to do.

Phoebe hit return and a few seconds later saw her text delivered. 'Read' had been disabled so she wasn't to know when the Prime Minister got to her text. Not that Phoebe minded, the PM entitled to some privacy.

Phoebe's text conflated weekly worship numbers, book sales, music sales as a demonstration of the influence Phoebe would bring to the Senate. It pressed the PM for news on Karsen and reminded her about choir practice.

She texted a picture of the Attorney-General at her Asher House visit juxtaposed with a photo of a prurient headline, asking 'why?'

The Attorney-General quickly messaged back, 'don't stress, we're onto it.'

Hudson and Phoebe worked their contact lists. Their messages and calls were mostly brusque, insistent, and successful. Hudson demanded an update from Ian Sturgess on the clinical trial. Texted the Aged Care Minister that he'd expected to hear some good news about the increased subsidies for aged care by now.

Jackson had his roster and his instructions for the next few days, he was sure he'd enjoy them. In short pants Jackson had learnt to eavesdrop to avoid harm, still, in long pants, he eavesdropped to learn. A worrier in a warrior's body. Just as he closed the door on Hudson and Phoebe, he heard her laugh, 'where did you find him,' she said, 'the circus?'

Stepping back inside the room Jackson said, 'this'll take more cash than usual.'

Jackson was a big man, heavily tattooed and ex-military. Hudson alone knew he'd served three years as an Army clerk where all he'd really pounded was a keyboard, something not well conveyed by the phrase 'ex-military'.

Hudson stood and guided Jackson out of the room, handed him a roll of notes, 'was waiting for you to ask.' He smiled.

. . . .

First pick-up was the head of the medical centre used by Asher Houses. A doctor turned entrepreneur; alerted by the receptionist he was waiting for Jackson in his office, door closed.

Jackson just walked in, 'bring your phone,' he said, 'you'll need to call someone to get a lift back here, that's if you're coming back.'

Hudson and Phoebe had the medical centre cash flow set out in front of them, the doctor saw, blinked, certain they were accurate.

Phoebe put her hands on the statements, said to the doctor, 'these are not why you're here.'

More confused now, he blinked again.

'Maybe you'd better have your eyes looked at,' said Hudson, 'all that blinking.'

'You are responsible for the centre,' said Phoebe, 'everything. From cleaning to staffing. That's why you're here. Our expectations, we're not sure you understand.'

'Make sure the medical records are faultless,' said Hudson. 'Those we care for in Asher Houses leave us one way or the other. Some to hospital, some to rehab, some...well, they leave. Now, patient transfer records are becoming stricter; we, you, need to make sure our records pass every test.'

'Oh, there's no need to worry about the records; we keep two sets of course,' said the doctor.

'Well,' said Hudson, 'we've one nosy carer who thinks a medical record is false. I've had the woman who left the records unattended sacked, so far, the carer has the message. Maybe the second set of records should be kept in the safe at the medical centre rather than the facilities? Think you can manage that?'

The doctor nodded.

'OK,' said Hudson, 'now there's one more thing.'

The doctor shivered, no matter how many times Hudson ended, or you thought he'd ended a conversation, it always came back to this.

'You might wanna get that tremor seen to,' said Hudson, 'I can recommend a useful doctor.'

'Was there something else, Hudson?'

'Now you mention it,' said Hudson,' there is, and thank you for the reminder. Do you realise that most of the money spent on an older person's health is spent in the final years of their life? It can be as high as ninety percent. So, you need to be charging Medicare and insurance companies for more medical attention, it's expected in aged care. I don't wanna get investigated for under-spending.'

· · · ·

Hudson met the complaints boss, as he called her, in the Ministries' café. 'Tell me what's changed,' he said.

She was the Commissioner for Complaints about aged care; newly appointed, devout Asher Ministries worshipper. 'As you suggested, I sent our assessment of grievances against Asher Houses to Ethics Australia asking them to review how we'd handled them. I got a call from Harriet Cooper who heads it, that we're all good, model grievance procedures, she told me. I expect the report in the next few days.'

'OK,' said Hudson, 'send me a copy when it's in. Now, nothing else is to go to Ethics from you, no need. You have their seal of approval, send anything else and it'll look like you're currying favour. Just send any complaints to me, so hard sometimes to get people to understand we're doing Jesus' work.'

'Oh, yes,' she said, needing to feel like a good person, 'you know I'm bringing along all my executive to hear you and Phoebe preach next week.'

'That's great,' said Hudson, reaching for her hand, 'remind them we need all the donations we can get to pursue this work. Now, that lease on your car is just about up. One of the directors of our centre,' he looked all around him, 'a real servant of this place, leases cars. I'm sure he'll have a replacement; I'll get him to come around.'

• • • •

Later the same night Hudson met with Jackson again. He wanted Jackson relaxed and confident, so they met at Jackson's gym. It was quiet, no-one else lifting weights. They spotted each other; Hudson completed fewer sets.

'I'm out Jerry,' said Hudson.

Jackson sniggered at the Seinfeld reference, 'you should be doing this more often.'

'That Harriet Cooper woman,' said Hudson.

'Her security is beefed up,' said Jackson, 'no way we can get near her. Those guys are good, reckon they could be stalking us.'

'C'mon, why would they? OK, leave her alone, no more. OK?' Phoebe had assured Hudson that Harriet Cooper would be finished once she was a senator, not long to wait and not worth the risk.

'Yeah, you got it,' said Jackson. 'Too hard anyway.'

'Mai and Keith Evans?'

'Yeah? I think she's done enough.'

'Not your call,' said Hudson, 'she needs to stay close to him, get closer, get him used to her being around, in his house. Belts and braces. Understand?'

'Belts and braces,' said Jackson, who didn't.

If it can be thought it can be done.

Harriet replied to a text. One of the two security officers outside her door opened it and Mick Darby filled the doorway.

'Harriet, please don't get up,' he grinned.

'Mick, always the gentleman.' She stood, stretching, which turned into a hug.

'Drink?'

'No, I'm good, thanks.'

'Really?'

'Really. There's a bit on. The stalking.'

• • • •

Six weeks earlier Harriet had given Mick a USB which she had found in her coat pocket. She hadn't opened it, it wasn't hers. But she thought she knew how it got there. Not looking where she was going as she stepped out of a deli Harriet bumped into a woman, who stumbled and clutched at Harriet's coat as she fell. The woman just glared as Harriet helped her up. Harriet's car was ten metres away and when she reached into her pocket for the keys, found the USB. The woman had vanished, there was no one else around.

Mick had become worried when he had it opened, saw the photos of Harriet's Canberra house in flames. Mick had taken the USB unofficially to the feds.

'Mick, you know there's no crime here.'

'Yeah, I know that, but what do you reckon? If I increase her security, can I rely on you for any support? If we get anything; you'd run a few plates, check out a few names, have a chat?'

'Yeah, that's fine. Any ideas on who's involved?'

'No mate, no leads. She's getting up the nose of Asher Ministries though.'

'Really? She'll get anything she wants from me then. I've had the Minister's office onto me about the journos outside the Lang's house over the weekend. Bastards.'

Darby wasn't sure whose parents were maligned here, the paper shufflers or the Langs, didn't wait to find out, 'thanks mate.'

There were two more incidents, both emails, both doctored photographs, Harriet's car in flames and the Gillard Building in flames. All three incidents occurred within ten days, there had been none since, and no reports of threats to any Ethics' staff. Since about half of all stalking incidents of public figures occurred in a two-week period, Mick and the feds put the risk of further incidents at medium.

Mick, though, maintained a higher level of security for Harriet, her home watched, had her discreetly shadowed. The first incident was unusual. If stalking escalated beyond threats, the sequence was from communication to approach. This case was odd, it had started with approach and continued with communication, the emails. Stalking incidents frequently lasted two weeks, then nothing; he hoped this would be the case here. Darby didn't like odd.

• • • •

'So, nothing to add on the stalking Harriet. No contact now for four weeks, no reports of anything out of the ordinary here, your office, or any of the staff. Nothing either on the CCTV.'

'Thank you,' said Harriet, 'so these guys,' she indicated her office door, 'they can go home now? What's the usual way to thank them? They have been...I've felt quite safe.'

'I want to keep the security. The evidence, the usual pattern says it's over. But let's maintain the setup until it's over?'

'Until it's over,' said Harriet, 'OK, until what's over?'

'Asher Ministries; I've got the go-ahead to run a joint op with you and your team if you're in. Well,' said Mick, 'what he gave me the go-ahead for was to ask if you think it's what we should do. My boss will OK it if we both agree and give him a joint plan.'

'He's polite, your boss,' said Harriet.

'Can be,' said Mick, 'are you in?'

'Yes, I'm in. Not that there was a choice, but I'm in.'

Mick and Harriet talked through Mick's team findings and where they got to on the weekend.

'After Monday's meeting with the A-G, I'm even more sure it's what we should do. Let me fill you in on that, there's more to the story.'

'Isn't there always?'

'Had a drink with Molly Lavandar last night...settle Harriet,' he grinned.

'She must have some explosive dope on the A-G,' Harriet said. 'She must have her in debt over something or someone.'

'A couple of things, first; there are some contradictions. Molly has too clean a slate. She also has no time for Asher Ministries and their hold over the PM; and her boss now, the A-G, is a happy clapper too.'

Harriet laughed, 'couldn't possibly comment,' she said.

'I figure Molly has worked out all the angles; if she gets you to assess whether there's a case for investigating Asher for corruption, she wins whatever happens. If you don't take it on,' he raised one finger, 'well what are you here for?'

Second finger, 'you do take it on and find nothing, your professional judgement is discredited, she wins again. You take it on and find there's a case to investigate,' third finger in the air, 'that'll be enough to ruin the partnership between politics and the Langs' brand of religion. That connection, it's over ten years old Harriet.'

'She told you all this over drinks?'

'Yeah sure,' he grinned, 'she did tell me if your resources are thin, and she knows they are because I'm sure she thinned them, she reckons she can find a few bodies to second to you.'

'Who would they report to I wonder,' said Harriet. 'No. No, she was letting you know she already has someone here feeding her what's going on! Or, more likely, she's messing with your head. She'd know we'd talk about it.'

'Yes to all of the above, but my money's on she's playing games. So, the Attorney-General is pissed at the leaks about the Asher Ministries complaints. She wants the leaking investigated.'

'Of course,' said Harriet, 'to do that we'd have to open the matters that were leaked, the ones she just sent on to Asher. I can see what's in it for Molly.'

'Thing is for us, investigating the leaks is our Trojan Horse,' said Darby. 'There may be more to it than that too. State capture? What do you know of that?'

'A lot,' said Harriet, 'state capture, so, you're talking subverting public interest to benefit private interests. At The Hague, most of my time was on that. Where are you going with this? State capture? Here?'

"I know,' said Mick, 'what if the focus wasn't the country, just one arm of government? Aged care, for example?'

'Fuck!' Harriet sat back, exhaled deeply.

'What my boss said.'

'If he's up for a joint op, he sees a strong enough case to take a closer look? This is a lot to take in. Oh, Karsen; remember him, six weeks away?'

'I'm across that; Karsen's told them he's resigning from the Senate in six weeks and has not resigned yet. Yeah, I know Phoebe Lang has been tipped to replace him, and if she gets in, they'll have the numbers to cut your powers, water down the lobbying and electoral spending laws. The thing is so far, it's verbal, Karsen's not resigned, and Lang hasn't been nominated. Only you and I know this, Karsen won't resign until he's told.'

'Your part in this Mick; Karsen, what's he to you?'

'Karsen? Not so much Karsen, if not him it'll be someone else. Nah, Harriet, having Phoebe Lang in the Senate, with her influence, power from that one vote, it'd be a fucking disaster.'

Harriet listened.

'I think the Langs have ring fenced aged care, are ripping it off in the name of Asher Ministries.'

'Not sure you have enough though,' said Harriet. 'What more did you have for your boss?'

'Now I remember why I like working with you,' said Mick, and he told her of his concerns about the social robotics research in aged care.

Always hiding something aren't you Mick, thought Harriet, sleeves full of tricks.

'So, you like Asher Ministries, Hudson and Phoebe, for a national security threat?'

'Sounds ridiculous. I know. Well, everything they touch turns to gold. They are protected by the PM, Attorney-General, other pollies, bureaucrats. I've had a team doing a little bit of work on them, I reckon they're dirty. But are they that organised? Organised enough to do more than run a scam, to be a threat?'

Mick was looking a little less like Mick, thought Harriet. Playing with his cufflinks, voice flat.

'What's on your mind?'

'Everything I get on the Hudsons. The layers of bullshit over their money, even how they pay for petrol is hidden! Everything points back to them, Hudson, and Phoebe. There's a Board of Asher Ministries, Canberra's finest, we'll take a look at them too. It's just...I don't get it. I do get that you don't get between the Langs and a dollar.'

'Yeah, we're getting across that too. Lawyers, threats, more than a soupçon of violence, nothing concrete though,' said Harriet.

'So, the move into social robots,' said Mick, 'and everything that goes with that, tracking, facial recognition, video recording. Surveillance, we call it. It's seems too big a step up from theft; and yet, but they're all over it. The other thing is that if we just get them on fraud, poor quality care, even laundering money, we freeze their assets. But,' he paused stood, paced, 'their lawyers and political connections'd get the freeze delayed. Any prosecution would get postponed with every delaying trick. I think we have one shot at them and it has to work, cost them everything. '

'State capture,' said Harriet, 'bit beyond them too?'

'Like the rest of it,' said Mick, 'there's yes and no. I favour the yes.'

'The robots, socially assistive robots Mick, tell me more.'

Mick stood, paced the room, running words together, 'surveillance, trusted confidantes, whispering euthanasia, change your medication love, change your will, Hudson and Phoebe've been good to you, bequeathe them your house, your shares, your art, especially your art, don't ket your daughter in. The fucking moon-faced robots, like Russian dolls, layers of audio and viseo all fed back to Hudson.'

'Mick, is any of this possible?'

'All of it,' said Mick and slumped into his chair, 'I've had Alex and his team working on this day and night, they're so close.'

'It's just that I didn't see this in the paperwork for our working together. So, let's keep it separate. I know you think that the joint op means the Oversight Committee can't investigate this piece, but that depends on your boss releasing his paperwork to the Committee. If he doesn't I can't release it, and so they can examine every detail. I'd not want them getting hold of the robot allegations.'

'Allegations, they're not allegations Harriet.' Mick on his feet again, 'I tell you Harriet, I know it.'

'Come back with a robot then.'

Mick laughed, reached for his chair and sat, 'I've missed this you know. This to and fro,' he leaned towards Harriet.

'I can't say I have,' said Harriet, 'it's wearing.'

Mick sat straight, lectured, 'the good thing is we have a great chance now. The A-G and the Langs are so angry at the Kiernan stories, the fact the stuff was leaked to her, so pissed that they've invited us in. They've not thought this through. The A-G's got Asher Ministries' full cooperation to assist the investigation, so you're in! You've got secrecy provisions, your people interview an Asher employee as part of an Ethics' inquiry, they can't disclose it, if they do, prosecute.'

Mick made them a drink.

'Cheers,' said Mick clinking Harriet's glass, 'this is starting to fall into place.'

They both sat, still, excited, tense.

'Why don't we call it a day?'

'OK,' said Mick, 'we have to get a briefing from the two officers who went through an Asher House, forget which one."

They found times in their diaries. Mick texted Alex, arranged the briefing.

'There's one thing you have to have sorted right away,' said Mick.

'Oh?'

'The infighting among your staff. Don't look so surprised, it's all over my office. They need to get their shit together, whingeing about each other, it's contagious. I can't put my investigators with yours until there's a way ahead.'

'OK, I'll sack him, Keith Evans, he's ...'

'Harriet,' Mick interrupted, 'it's never about one person. OK, Evans, he might be a problem. But the bigger problem, the bigger problems are in the way the people around him let him get away with it, whining about him while they look on. His peers, his boss and even you. Now, I know a guy who's a specialist in this stuff.'

'Keith Evans, he is very good at his job, it's just the way he is.'

'Bullshit,' said Mick, 'it's the way you've let him be. I wanted one of your people with one of mine to inspect that Asher House, Alex wouldn't be in it. Wasn't prepared to trust any of your investigators not to whinge, give away their cover. They went in as ACT Health. Serious Harriet.'

Harriet sat, very still.

'The bloke you want for this is Thomas Bain,' said Mick. 'He's the best. None of us can do it, we're not independent. Has to be an expert outsider, he's it. He just gets people to talk.'

'They're public servants. They investigate, they interview; their expertise is getting people to talk, not divulging what they think.'

'Bullshit again,' said Mick, 'they're on the phone and in little huddles divulging what's on their mind to each other and to my people. They're fucking talking all right, that's a bigger problem now than Evans. It's the way they deal with friction, which won't stop when Evans is out.'

'So, is this a show-stopper?'

Mick nodded.

'Give me his number.'

Molly Lavandar.

Molly had been meeting with Ian more regularly since the approval of the ElderTech clinical trial. She was monitoring its implementation, reviewing progress. She monitored Ian.

The meeting of the clinical trial oversight group had been scheduled for an early Friday morning at the Aged Care Research Centre. The Centre was to the southern end of the Australian National University campus. Equipped with state-of-the-art conference rooms and laboratories, by comparison the offices were cramped; poorly set out, cheaply furnished, embarrassing for Sturgess. He couldn't even get laptops for his staff on time.

Late the evening before, Ian Sturgess rescheduled the meeting, after carefully checking diaries, to make sure few could make the amended time. The meeting went ahead with apologies outnumbering those present. The meeting approved his proposal for phase two of the remote monitoring of seniors in aged care, literature review, extensive study tour.

Flushed with success after the meeting Ian had rung the Aged Care Minister's news and communications team head.

'I'm calling to make your day, got a pen?'

'Ian, I do – I'm getting my nails done Tuesday though any other day is fine, except Wednesday – hair appointment,' she teased.'

She had a few questions about the research, background 'just in case he asks.'

Ian blustered, 'Really, do you think the research oversight group would let just anything get through?'

He named some of the more senior members, none of whom were at the approval meeting.

Head of Comms drafted the release, checked it with Ian for technical accuracy, and took it to the minister's Chief of Staff, briefing her on her reservations. The Chief of Staff was keen to make no errors. 'Two heads are better than one' her father, a Canberra veteran had told her. She called her mentor, Molly Lavandar. On hearing it wasn't urgent, the project had just been approved, Molly promised to get back the next day.

• • • •

I an agreed to meet up for a drink with Molly, the 'Tipsy Bull' she suggested. She thought it appropriate. He had no idea.

Molly sat up straight, hands on the table, right hand over the left, resting. Shiraz gin with Strangelove Bitter Lemon was delivered by the waiter. She continued to ignore the looks that had followed her all the way to the table reserved at the back of the bar. Ian rather enjoyed the envy generated as he kissed Molly hello and sat opposite, a few minutes later.

Molly, who had barely moved, opened her right hand, and said, palm up, 'so, tell me, what happened.'

'Let me get a drink, you?'

'I'm good thanks.'

'Scotch, house,' he said to the passing waiter, 'double, no water, just ice, on the side.'

And he talked. Nigel Blakeley, ElderTech, the clinical trial, the oversight group meeting, the post-graduate student who had finessed the research proposal, the Dalmeny bathroom finished, work on the kitchen started, a lease on an apartment in Reid.

'So, to fix this, now...' said Molly,

'I need your help. Everything's coming together for me,' he grinned, 'I've a girlfriend too.'

'There'll be no media release, I'll sort that. You swamp communications with research data she's no hope of understanding, offer to explain it over lunch, and then withdraw the idea of media. Wait until the minister can do a site visit, near a winery in spring, photos with happy stay-at-home seniors, and a day or two of cellar doors, a compliant junior staffer perhaps. That should be it.'

'But' said Ian, 'I've had a journalist, Marcia Kiernan, on the phone asking questions about the research program. I fobbed her off and told her the research was approved by the Ethics Committee. All approved, out of my hands.'

'Ian, your department has a media liaison army, use them, call comms, it's her job to handle this. Tell me where you're up to with detect and alert.'

Molly listened as Ian summarised; she figured Ian must have two separate brains. One, lucid, intelligent, rational. The other, all over the place like a baby's breakfast. Lucid Ian was finished and before he shuffled away, she spoke.

'Here's what has to happen. The trial is finished, get it written up and present the findings, let the committee evaluate them. Your recommendation is the detect and alert technology is now available for implementation. You want detect and alert in every nursing home don't you?'

'Absolutely,' said Sturgess, 'it's a winner; saves money, safety, security, builds confidence.'

'OK. So let's not have any distractions. No-one will notice minutes of a meeting they did not attend. You step away now.'

'Now? Walk out now, I can't,' said Ian, leaning forward, spilling ice, 'now is the best part, big reputation boost.'

'What? Where's the kudos in detect and alert? You've built your career around science and research, and you'll only face scrutiny if you continue with this and extend it beyond its use by date. Your unit does not do implementation. Get involved in some of the other trials your teams are working on – I'm sure they'll welcome your interest given you've been absorbed in this for so long.'

'This is what it takes? But my reputation?'

'Ian,' said Molly, 'you bought and sold your reputation years ago.'

'That's unfair,' said Ian, but his heart wasn't in it.

'Bullshit. I got you out of that didn't I? Think I'd forgotten?'

'So, so, this is all about payback?'

'No, this is about me getting you out of the shit again. And, you know it. The second phase, assistive robots? You've got approval for a literature review, right?'

'Yep,' said Ian, 'and for more than that, got the go ahead for a study tour,' he added, 'for two of us.'

Ian drained his glass, looked for the waiter.

'Ian,' coaxed Molly, 'you don't need a drink to listen.'

'You're right. And I'm going out tonight. OK. What's next?'

'Let Nigel know the clinical trial is finalised. He'll be fine as the Commonwealth will purchase whatever inventory is available, a stockpile, for distribution to aged care in all states. Polonius can handle that order; authorise an advance under those small Australian business rules, it should be around forty-five million dollars. Monitor this one personally, Ian. Let me know, and I'll make sure the trip's approved.'

'I told you,' said Ian, 'the trip's approved.'

'It's been passed by your dodgy committee, it still needs funds authorised.'

'But, there's money in the budget. Chief Scientist,' Ian brushed his hair back with both hands, 'look, I can move money between budget line items.'

Molly shook her head, 'means nothing. Overseas study tour, assistive robots, artificial intelligence; needs my minister's signoff.'

Ian shifted, which Ian have I got now wondered Molly. She thought she'd hooked him with the sale of the orders to be placed with Polonius, sure he was calculating his cut.

Lucid Ian said, 'Makes sense, I'm to meet Nigel next week and we were going to discuss the rollout, so that all ties in, he'll be interested in the stockpile.'

Bullshit thought Molly, really, meeting with Nigel, diarised? Molly let it slide for now.

'Thanks mate', she said as she leaned to peck his cheek, 'your shout, let me know how it goes with Nigel. The order in the morning? Let me know. I really have to get home tonight'.

· · · ·

Molly collected antique ceramic bowls; she had an arrangement with specialist galleries to rotate her collection. She'd have pieces in her home, buy other works, have some taken away and stored to make room. Right now, she was collecting Clarice Cliff so when one of the galleries called to say they had one of her Bizarre Ware pieces, she asked them to bring it.

Later that night the uniformed driver of the gallery van carefully carried in a bubble wrapped box, smiled at the concierge, who asked him if it was for Ms Lavandar, and pointed him to the lift.

'Not the usual bloke,' said the concierge.

'Did his back,' said Johnny Koh, 'compo for a week they reckon.'

Molly opened her door, stood aside, and poured Koh a Tasmanian whisky.

'You collect no works by Australian Asian artists?' Johnny asked.

Molly laughed, 'what? You want Ahn Do to invite me to share my moment of truth on the ABC?'

She told of her conversation with Ian, shared their concerns and agreed to leave him for now. Polonius would get a Purchase Order and pre-payment from Sturgess.

'Sturgess? No, he's not a problem,' said Molly, 'he's distracted by stage two, the robots. The robots, brilliant distraction. He's way over the extension, the rollout, the forty-five million. He'll just sign it.'

'Once you have the PO, get the money into the account. That's it, we walk away now.' Molly handed Koh a four-page gallery brochure, 'the serial number of the Cliff teapot is the start of the account number for the forty-five million, just add these numbers,' Molly wrote on the back of the brochure.

The Cliff piece replaced an art deco bowl which Koh wrapped and drove it back to the gallery.

Yes Boss. No Boss.

'Let me go over what's at stake here, Mick.' Darby's boss held up one hand, rough blunt fingers. Tapped the little finger of his left hand and leaned back in his chair.

'Look,' Darby shrugged, 'I know my job, what I've been put here to do.'

'Maybe,' the hands didn't move, 'but, you don't know what's at stake, so I'm going to tell you. One.' Tapped the pinkie again, 'Asher Ministries, there've been complaints...'

'Complaints? Hudson Lang? Complaints - not about him, from him? That's what this is about? What if Asher Ministries ran a mosque? What if Hudson didn't tout himself as a pastor but as an Imam? You'd see crimes which are not there. There'd be no trouble getting the go-ahead to shut it down.' Darby stood, slammed both hands on the desk bouncing his tablet, 'just because Asher is a happy clappy tent, you refuse to see what's obvious.'

'And you Mick, what do you see? Our job is mistrust, suspicion, disbelief. But, I'm saying I need more than suspicion. Suspicion works both ways. If we can't get something solid on the Langs, and remember how well protected they are, we're not even going to try. If it's suspected that you're after them, it'll be all over red rover. It'll be over for you and our Committee. So, either we do nothing or we catch them good and proper and follow up with a fair trial. Now sit down, bring me up to speed.'

'You're right, 'said Darby, sitting down hard, 'I am seeing things, things are there to be seen. But I'm not seeing enough.'

'You know Mick, most mornings I read the paper, have a coffee at a place near me. It's a bit quiet so this morning I'm chatting with the barista. The bloke at the next table asked for his coffee extra hot.'

'Baristas hate that,' said Mick also eager to ease the conversation, 'something about the perfect temperature for coffee, any hotter and the milk caramelises, destroys the taste.'

'So, you know what they do? He told me their secret. The good baristas? They run the cup handle under boiling water, hand over the coffee. The bloke getting his coffee picks it up, says, "shit this is hot, really hot, not everyone'll do that, thanks". Everybody happy.'

'Deception Mick, currency in this town,' said his boss. 'Even a cup of fucking coffee, cappuccino, ya can't even trust that. Some people, they read coffee grounds, "could see this, might see that," very even-handed your coffee grounds' reader. Not us Mick, our coffee grounds must not be open to interpretation, one version only. So, Lang, what do you have?'

'You want to know what I've got or what I make of it?'

'Mick, fact you've got to ask bothers me. Give me what you have, I'll draw my own conclusions. Time for sharing, mate. You've got a degree, you did sharing at uni?'

Darby listed what he had, occasionally turning his tablet to show a graph, a table, a timeline. Darby started with the most serious findings, rated progress on each one towards securing evidence on a scale of one to five. Categorised each allegation on ease of blaming someone other than the Langs; poor record keeping, confusing regulations. Few items would lead to prosecution of the Langs. None would lead to prosecution of government ministers, a few bureaucrats maybe.

'Ok,' said Darby's boss, 'where do you think the threats to us'll come from?'

'Lang lawyers, Prime Minister through the Attorney-General when Phoebe claims her senate seat gutting Ethics Australia, Minister for Aged Care, backgrounding journos about the need for greater accountability of security and intelligence agencies, stop them interfering with health,' he scowled, shifted in his seat.

'What's on your mind? Other threats?'

'Our own side,' said Darby, 'Intelligence Committee, some of the other security agencies. If we launch a false start, some of those bastards have never been known to join a losing side. They could do me discretely, withdraw funding, shut access to resources. Then they'd bargain for more powers for a watch dog to which they'd get one of their own appointed. This whole thing,' Darby swept the tablet aside, 'it'd be as effective as dropping a stone into a bucket of water, one ripple, then nothing.'

'I want us to go through this all again,' said his boss. 'Here's our we do it, you'll drive that tablet. I want a spreadsheet, list every alleged offence, you keeping up Mick?'

'Let me draw it first and then I'll use the tablet.'

'Old school? A good way to start. Then columns, and you'll have a better idea of the order in which you put them. Give each offence a score out of ten; ease of securing a conviction, strength of our case to the federal prosecutor, impact on the Langs, impact on the relevant minister, impact on the government, then list the agencies we'd rely on for resources, estimate the cost of pushing ahead.'

'That it?' said Mick.

'No doubt you'll think of some more. OK, once you've set that up in there,' pointing to the tablet, 'we'll fill in those columns, use the numbers, we'll see how they weigh in. Know where we start, what to give someone else, Medicare, the Feds, ATO...whoever. Give em a secure conviction, they'll love us for life, or long enough to work out what's next. I'll bring you back a coffee, and don't make me ask for extra hot.'

It took them two hours, some more coffee.

'The spreadsheet, the numbers tell us where to start, gives us the priority. What's your gut tell you Mick?'

'I need just enough to freeze his assets, and Asher Ministries. Then I think the empire will cave, he's a late payer. It's not that he doesn't have the money, or can't get hold of it, he's just severely allergic.'

'Anaphylactic shock,' said Darby's boss, 'explains his writhing and thrashing around on stage.'

'Pushes all his invoices out to one twenty days, more sometimes. Often, he pays half, and gets another one twenty days to settle. Thing is he's into them for so much his suppliers have to wear it. Not as bad for staff wages, but he underpays, gets caught out and makes up the difference in instalments, way behind in super too. So, if we freeze it all, his creditors are already months behind, and I think a few will turn, expose him when they see how much they stand to lose. Their aged care will fold in a day, so we'd have to close those facilities, relocate the wrinklies.'

'OK,' said Darby's boss, 'you get his money. Good start. It'll take months, years maybe with delays to get through the courts after fights over jurisdiction, he'll win an appeal to unfreeze his money. Aged care? No, we need to get him on the lot, the wrinklies will just have to wear it a bit longer. What about his clout? How do you isolate him from that crowd at that soiree? They'd risk the clap to stay close to him. Being loose with other people's money is part of the entrance fee to that pack. Mate, we can't wait til Sunday to find out Saturday's race result, we need to know it on Friday. If there's to be a day of retribution, it's got to be complete, instant, not a false reckoning.'

'Robots,' said Mick.

'Robots? You're fucking crazy. Hit him with a drone! Has some merit I suppose.' Both men laughed.

'Thing is,' said Mick, 'to make certain of cabinet support he's promised to give a prototype remote processor to each Cabinet member. Imagine, in every senior minister's office a device with remote audio, video recording, GPS tracking. Thing's about as big as a mobile phone, some of them will take it home, wherever, with them. We get him on that, espionage, cybersecurity offences. He'll be dropped, like that,' he slammed both hands to the desk, just missing the tablet. 'They'll be begging us to lock him up.'

'You had me at drone. There's a bit of a wait and see for the robots isn't there? He hasn't got them yet.'

'I suspect the robots are closer than we think, but you're right. Not here yet. The bracelets are all so far, they're doing a trial run with GPS fitted too, for dementia patients. We suspect the bracelets are a bit of a scam, clever, and not all bullshit. I think the scam just goes to providing them to older people who don't need them. Over supply of medical equipment? Half the doctors'd be on a charge. He's probably charging for them as well, we have some suggestions about that, none of it would worry his lawyers for half an hour.'

'What about the next phase of the bracelets, detect and alert? Close to a hundred million to provide them to everyone in aged care, public, private, home care.'

'Yeah,' said Mick, 'that's just the bracelets. The logistics of monitoring alerts, organising responses to breeches, that'll be outsourced separately. Nothing to do with Asher Ministries. I'd want to leave the bracelets alone, wait for the robot technology.'

Darby's boss thumbed his phone, 'OK with leaving the bracelets, we won't stop the money. Can you keep going with other ones on this list,' he pointed to the tablet, 'keep it quiet?'

'Some of it I can move along, especially now we're working with Ethics.'

'How is Harriet?'

'It's working well, the joint team, she's totally on board, corruption, state capture, she's onto it.'

'Well, keep her that way, get onto it, Mick. No church is too big to fail, no matter how many Commonwealth Ministers they have in their pocket.' He stood and came around his desk, put his hand on his Mick's shoulder, 'we're under starters orders old mate.'

Thomas Bain.

'Thomas Bain? I'm Zoe Saunders, CEO Ethics Australia, we'd like to talk to you about some problems, people problems, to see if it's something you could help us with.'

'Zoe I'll be in the office in about twenty minutes.'

He got her office number. A Canberra number. Googled Zoe Saunders. Checked her out on LinkedIn.

Zoe answered on the first ring, put him on speaker. He provided a little background. They talked a little about some counterproductive behaviours and some interpersonal conflicts. Thomas and Zoe agreed to a meeting in Canberra in two days.

Bain was intrigued by the phone call.

It had taken years for the Australian government to create Ethics Australia, the federal government's version of state anti-corruption authorities. Successive governments had raised 'doing nothing well' about federal corruption to an art form. Former prime ministers had channelled a parent's condescending language, calling a federal anti-corruption commission a 'very, very, very bad idea'.

The first iteration of the commission was welcomed by the kinds of organisations used to fronting the state-based bodies. Political party hacks, police associations, developers, backbenchers, government ministers, union leaders, industry association executives, shock jocks, public servants, lobbyists, and university professors delivered a firehose of posts, tweets, opinion pieces and media interviews favouring secrecy over transparency.

They embraced holding corruption enquiries in private, voting 'no' to public hearings, and 'no' to taking public complaints. They were seen off by leaders of the state corruption bodies, judges, whistle-blowers, some media, and some great PR. Lines like; 'the idea of exposing corruption behind closed doors is oxymoronic', helped cut through the bullshit peddled by all government ministers about the 'sharp teeth' of the new body.

Ethics Australia - the final version - defined corruption broadly, conducted public hearings, and investigated complaints about the public service, ministers, members of Parliament or their staff. Ethics decided how to investigate what was reported to them, but for matters referred to it by Parliament or a government agency. The oversight committee could review its operations. It was also poorly funded, constantly criticised and a stressful place in which to work. Ethics Australia had won the battle over being created and was losing the war of attrition.

Bain emailed Zoe an agenda for the meeting. Drafted a form of words to let the staff know what would happen once he started and printed the paperwork for Zoe to sign. He wanted to walk out of the meeting with all the administration out of the way, staff names and contact details, next steps agreed.

Buyer's remorse tormented those hiring consultants. He'd found the best way to handle it was to agree an action plan at the start so everyone focused on what would happen next rather than if anything would happen. There'd always be some ambivalence after they had decided to deal with their problem. Their decisions would be second guessed, and blame-free workplaces were still a dream.

Asher Ministries.

I t's vital to keep Board members enthusiastic about their role, to maintain and yet gently restrain their self-importance, and above all, continue to have them set the lead in tithes and special-cause donations. Of course, they reclaim all their donations and tithes as directors' expenses, no fees are paid to directors in keeping with the brand.

A Board must look the part so that when the reader casts an enquiring eye down the list of directors she is immediately impressed with their company experience, business savvy measured by wealth, and their altruism. It's a tricky balance as you want everything bar the altruism left at the Boardroom door, all you want inside those four walls of artwork is the blazing heart of emotionalism. In short, the Asher Ministries' board needed to impress the uninitiated as experienced enough to be strategic, yet with enough heart to live compassion for the cause – guardians of the heart and soul of their church.

Most important of all though to Hudson, the Board had to be biddable. Hudson was surprised at how easy this turned out to be. Directors. Successful businesspeople. Their lawyer talk, their strategy talk, their finance talk, their business speak; all simple costumes. Like the robes of the ministers of the dinosaur churches, their language was cloth to enhance their status and to mask their insecurities. Cloth he could render, status he could build, and insecurities he could exploit.

Hudson made sure that every Board meeting began by giving praise for the blessings received since the last Board meeting, for all that God had done for them. He enhanced this with a slide show of artful photos of Board members at worship, with celebrities, visiting preachers, handing over cheques. He still rode with the members of his old gang who had prospered. Some of them had grown rich beyond their wildest dreams from family connections in Griffith, and now ran successful gyms, car yards, and even a string of florists. Some of their sons and daughters ran legitimate businesses, others became lawyers and accountants devoted to exploiting loopholes.

Hudson was attracted to those who most resembled him as a youth. Those who considered following the law, an option, compliance a weakness. Among these he found computer hackers, buyers and sellers of information, muscle, and accountants and lawyers known as enablers. Jackson, the muscle, bothered him, Hudson was attracted and a little repulsed by his misogyny and violence. Jackson, along with some others, were invaluable in making sure Hudson's buildings were completed on time, complaints didn't progress, and threats were believable. Jackson had only had to sit beside a journalist intent on finding fault with Asher Ministries' services to deter. Invaluable and expensive, like his belligerent lawyers.

It was to hackers he turned for help to exploit Board member's insecurities, frailties, and uncertainties. The respected financial wizard on the Asher Ministries' Board with the secret collection of Asian pornography was always featured on Hudson's slide shows surrounded by young Asian worshippers. Those photos at Board meetings made him uneasy; not enough to call Hudson out, but more than enough to make him wonder, certainly enough for him to not question. Hudson's carefully designed slide shows for every Board meeting contained a message for each Board member, along with the implicit promise the message would stay hidden for as long as...

Today's Board meeting was no different. A short video highlighting each director's contribution to the church since their last meeting, cameos of them arriving at functions in their late model cars to remind them of the wealth they were acquiring thanks to Hudson and Phoebe, shaking hands with politicians - again a reminder of their status and their debt. And reminders of their vulnerability - should their secrets be outed – reminding them of the value of compliance.

'Asher House,' said Hudson, 'we are facing a spiritual attack here on our good work with older Australians. It's disappointing and stressful, let me provide some background, and outline an action plan.'

'We had the Complaints Commission seek detail of our complaint handling process, based on our compassionate response to the grief-stricken son of one of our elders who passed while with us. There was a slip up with the records, which could happen to anyone with so many records to keep, all of them imposed on us by government which sought a record of our records!'

Hudson continued, only to be interrupted.

'Hudson,' said one of his directors with a mother in a nursing home only an hour from where she lived, whom she visited annually, 'there's also some concern at the number of older people passing at our facilities. How are we monitoring the level of care?'

'Certainly, more thorough than the audit we are required to conduct...quarterly, independent,' said Hudson, relishing the guilt-stricken look on his director, 'we use an international benchmarking company. They visit each place every quarter, like, they'd see your mum four times a year. You would have seen their invoices in the accounts.'

'I'm sure we're...'

Anxious to close the conversation now aren't we thought Hudson.

'No, it's important enough to ask at our Board meeting, after all that's why we are here, oversight. Our aged care programs reach out to the most vulnerable of older Australians. Those who need assistance to live longer in their own homes, and at the next stage who need residential care, we're extending the lives of the most vulnerable Australians. Guided by Jesus's grace and wisdom we offer care to those elders whose life expectancy is lower than that enjoyed by the rest of the population.'

Directors sat silently, still; aware Hudson would focus on any gesture.

'The data show,' said Hudson, 'as you've raised, that we offer our care to the most vulnerable. If the median age of death of those with us was higher than for most Australians, what would it mean?'

'It would mean we are ignoring the most vulnerable – not what Jesus wants from us.'

'Hudson,' she continued, 'it sounds circular, your reasoning.'

'Maybe we need to renew our scripture study,' bristled Hudson the preacher. 'Remember Jesus sits above the circle of the earth, enthroned, there are no circles in nature the scripture reminds us, the Hebrew word recorded as circle, actually translates as compass, the way to Jesus. Jesus, of his own will, brings us to the circle of truth. In my own humble way, I'm guided to the circle of truth about our elders – yes, they pass on earlier why, because they are more vulnerable, that's why we reach out to them.'

'Yet again Hudson,' said the chair, 'we are reminded of your command of the scripture; to live your life in the presence of the Lord, I think we can move on, don't you? Are we agreed, Hudson? I'm confident, as I'm sure the Board is, you'll have a well thought out plan to dismiss these minor obstacles to our good works? Now, your invoices? I expect the approval is unanimous?'

Directors concurred. Hudson invoiced Asher Ministries for the sermons he and Phoebe preached. The invoices were paid monthly, the Board approved them each quarter. Transparent, taxes paid, even a small contribution of GST.

Hudson nodded his thanks to his favourite director and the Board's chair. He loved this guy; he had known him for a long time from Sydney's inner west where Hudson knew he owned two restaurants and a popular café. He had been raised Catholic, Hudson's preferred recruiting ground next to those who came from no denomination, as he'd explained to Phoebe many times.

'Ex-Catholics suit us because they have absolutely no scriptural knowledge, there's nothing they have to unlearn, we just teach them how it is. Those who attended Protestant churches though, they want to argue the interpretation, I prefer to weed them out early.'

Hudson explained that the complaints had been reviewed, the files were closed. He'd been notified that the complaints were dismissed as vexatious. Hudson had the lawyers write to the complainants and a particularly tenacious journalist, aggressively warning them off. Still some blogs continued the harassment, and these were picked up and repeated by mainstream media. He circulated a press clipping; the Board was impressed at the alliance of labour and faith.

Hudson read the part from the clip he most liked; 'Health Workers' spokesperson Ajay Sirenti noted that investigations of all complaints lodged about Asher House facilities had been concluded and had been found to be unsubstantiated. The complaints were found to be vexatious. The process of being investigated had a deep effect on our members, yet they had no come back against those found to have made frivolous complaints nor against those continuing to harass by raking over these closed investigations...'

He assured the Board any leaking of the details of the investigations would soon be over as the Attorney-General had assured him and Phoebe. Hudson knew that the mess had been referred to Ethics Australia. He thought that Harriet Cooper would likely fail to find the source. Or do nothing his lawyers couldn't do, providing more reason to sack her, and leash Ethics Australia. No downside.

Keith Evans.

Keith Evans had been victim of prolonged bullying at Defence, and was now the butt of many jokes in the Ethics Australia office. He was safe inside his Woden apartment, surrounded by the boy's toys he would play with when he was accepted in the Pastor Leadership program. His mountain bike, electric commuter bike and surfboard hung on the walls. A white-water kayak, still water kayak and a surf ski, along with the paddles for them, suspended from his single car garage ceiling.. He did use the gym gear though, and he ran. he found the phrase 'financial blessing and good health – the will of God', so inspirational, he'd painted the line as a word cloud on his garage walls.

Not that Keith knew it but, he'd been approached by Hudson after the Harriet Cooper briefing on what to advise the Aged Care Complaints Commission about strengthening their grievance investigation methodology. Keith was appointed Program Manager for a cross-agency team to collate data on age of death rates of seniors receiving any level of aged care assistance.

At his bus stop the day after his appointment Keith sat with an attractive woman wearing a 'Magdalene Saves' T shirt. They starting talking, went for coffee, dinner, saw each other daily for a week or more. Nothing more than that. She'd said, 'I'm loving this conversation Keith it's our loving conversation and the context is not just right for us yet.' Keith had no idea what Mai meant, other than he wasn't getting laid, but he felt grace.

He was soon mixing with a small group of wealthy, powerful, thirty somethings. Keith was the life of their party. One of the guys he met was awfully close to the Health Minister – it seemed every time they were out, he'd excuse himself to take a call. After one of these calls the guy took him aside and asked Keith if he thought he was able to do something for the minister. A good word from the minister would not just clean his slate from Defence but gild it, Clinton guaranteed it.

Mai had introduced Clinton to Keith.

'Keith, yeah,' said Clinton, 'I've seen you here a few times, just recently. God, our perfect friend, right?'

'Exactly,' said Keith, unsure of what to say among the blessed.

'You're not sure, are you?'

'Well, I wouldn't say...'

'It's fine,' said Clinton, 'it's just like Phoebe says, talk to God about your day, keep a journal, I mean, you could write to God, sort of like a pen pal.'

'A pen pal? Talk, like pray?'

'Talk it over with Mai,' Clinton said, 'you know, someone like you, so much to offer our work; it'll be so easy for you. You'll be asked to earn revelation. So much is expected of those with so much to give, like you.'

Keith stumbled; Mai held him up.

'I'm fine,' said Keith, 'just, this is so much.'

'Doing something for Jesus,' Clinton in his ear, soothing, 'you can't just turn up at Asher and expect a revelation, you have to work at it. You're beginning to feel that, physically. You can feel a tap being turned on, can't you?' Clinton put his arm around Keith, 'Even I can feel it.'

Keith stumbled again, a knee giving way.

'God's power just knocks you over. How can you use your power to do something for Jesus? That's why you're here right? To work for Jesus. To defeat his enemies, before he defeats your enemies. You know what Jesus can do, but does he know what you can do?'

'What can I do?' Keith's voice broke, sounded pubescent.

Clinton explained about the mortality data and how Keith could keep Asher House safe from its enemies.

'It's risky,' said Keith, 'I wouldn't want to get into any trouble.'

'Mate,' Clinton said, arm around Keith, 'so, let's make sure you're not. Anyway, taking a risk for Jesus. I mean, it's not like he's done anything for you is it?'

'No,' said Keith, rushing to defend his new and invisible friend, 'he's done so much for me.'

'You're the Program Manager, right? Leading the mortality data team, the team would do what you want, that's what leading means eh?'

'Yes,' said Keith, 'they'll do what I need them to do.'

'Think of this as a charismatic moment,' said Clinton.

Keith relished the opportunity to gild his slate and impress his new friends.

Keith was to a spreadsheet what butter was to a hot BBQ plate; he slid all over it. He talked up an array of colourful, interactive, immersive dashboards and metrics. He didn't try this with the data analytics project team though. They would see through the manipulations. So, to make sure the different sources of data were not pooled in meetings, he cajoled, threatened, and belittled team members. He'd had to pull the data integrity card, and then trump them with the Chief Commissioner card 'Harriet wants this yesterday.' The analysis was now complete, the data packs with Noopur for the Chief Commissioner.

Not complete enough for Keith, he wanted to dive deeper, to make sure he knew what he was protecting. What was it and what might it be worth? With Asher Ministries playlists softly in the background Keith fed his fish, never tiring of watching his ecosystem, his creation. He opened his laptop. A personal one, he didn't want this activity tracked at work. He'd downloaded the data he wanted from Genelle's pc onto a flash drive. If it came out, she was downloading data – well, she deserved whatever happened to her. She'd not only not gone out with him, but she'd also laughed at him.

Armed with Excel and good enough knowledge of Power BI, Keith turned the cherry-picked data into information, worked out correlations and regressions. Four Red Bulls, thousands of lines of data and five hours later Keith was sweating.

In the sample he'd constructed, he manipulated averages and percentages, settled on reporting averages - average mortality rates for elder Australians were falling. This fall despite a rise in elder mortality rates among indigenous Australians, despite public assurances and statements from the Minister for Indigenous Health – now part of Australian Health – that 'progress was on track to achieve government targets jointly established with ...'

When he cut the sample data by aged care program, again he found that mortality rates were falling – home care, aged care homes - whatever care elder Australians were receiving, they were living longer.

He moved from the cherry-picked data to the population data – the parameters he'd spent hours on had delivered the sample he'd needed for Harriet. He'd been successful in reporting only aggregated sample data on elder mortality. Keith unified all data on age of death over seventy-five, used the median. Varying the age of death data point yielded different median values, so he knew he could get away with the data he'd cherry-picked – the variance could be explained. What worried him was age of death data in Asher House aged care facilities or where it provided home care, or residential care programs. The age of death for males and females was significantly earlier here compared to any other provider. So that was it, Keith warmed at his cleverness.

At his next meeting with his pastor, he let her know that being in Asher House didn't lead to a longer life. Two days later he was asked to meet with Hudson Lang, global co-pastor Asher Ministries. Keith was on a high, felt blessed he confided to Mai, who stayed over that night.

Hudson also was on a high. His lawyers had let him know the Ethics Australia report to the Aged Care Commission was complete and included no adverse findings, just a recommendation to strengthen some admin. They also advised him that the Attorney-General had referred his complaints about public leaking of investigation details to Ethics Australia. They would be hunting for corruption in government departments. While he welcomed both details, he also knew he had to find out more about Keith Evans who he thought was trying something on.

Hudson showed Keith his remarkable understanding of a bigger picture, a visionary's picture. Asher House programs and facilities extended the lives of the most vulnerable Australians. Asher House chose, guided by God's wisdom, to offer care to those elders whose life expectancy was lower than that enjoyed by the rest of the population.

'Just what your data shows,' said Hudson. 'Here, I got you a coffee. Your data analysis shows that we offer our care to the most vulnerable. If the median age of death of those with us was higher than for most Australians, what would it mean?'

Keith could barely hear Hudson. This guy brought me a coffee, too excited to drink it.

'It would mean we are ignoring the most vulnerable,' Hudson said, 'not what Jesus wants from us Keith. Those not with us, would not understand that. And we're not about to disrespect elder confidentiality and privacy by speculating how long these, the oldest children of God may have lived without our care...'

'The thing to remember Keith is that numbers and narratives go together, and you've been tasked with focusing on the numbers. Brilliant job too, it's exactly the kind of motivation we need – I'm sure you'll find yourself among the intake in our Summer semester advanced ministry diploma. Now the narrative here with these numbers is so important. Together, they complete the picture. The complete picture is more important than either the numbers or the narrative.'

'You get that?'

Keith couldn't nod fast enough and stammered his thanks. Sipped his coffee, now cold. He thought he might take his coffees cold from now on.

'Now Keith, this is important,' said Hudson. 'How many other people do you think should be brought to this understanding you and I have. Our appreciation of the numbers and the narrative, the complete picture. Who would you want to share this with?'

Keith thought that knowledge only he and Hudson shared would be cheapened if exposed, and said so, 'Pastor...'

'Hudson, please.'

'Pastor Hudson, no-one. I work with some pretty smart people; no-one knows anything about this. I mean, the people I work with, they don't worship, so wouldn't understand the vision you have, they wouldn't understand what I've done.'

'Good man. You must keep it that way. If you can't be trusted Keith, you can never run away from being untrustworthy. Can I rely on you?'

'Yes. Yes, you can, you can rely on me,' said Keith, speaking fast, voice raised, yet frail.

'Has anyone ever asked you before if you could be relied on, if you could be trusted?'

'No,' said Keith. 'Oh, maybe, I signed a security clearance.'

'Face to face? Man to man? Has anyone ever said to you, "Keith, can I trust you?"'

'No,' said Keith, loud again.

'Well now, I have, and I like your answer. I know I can rely on you,' said Hudson, patting Keith's shoulder as he stood. 'And Mai, how's Mai, how are you two getting along? I see her at the services, and she looks radiant just now, she must be happy.'

With that Hudson was gone, moving away, allowing for one long look at Keith who had his head down over his phone.

Keith texted Mai, 'H knows about us! Excited much.'

Finding the leaks.

Harriet Cooper had an early morning meeting with Mick Darby.

'I know you're worried about the timing, ' said Mick, 'let's remember I have a team available too, with the added resources there'll be more than enough time if we all move fast. You'll get the referral this morning. Ethics has to investigate the leaks because the Attorney-General referred it, but your Assessment Panel determines how to investigate.'

'The tricky part is,' said Harriet, 'that because the government referred the leaks, I could be, probably will be, called before the oversight committee on how we run this investigation. Mick, we'll need to be meticulous about how we go about this. Ministers and bureaucrats puffed with paperwork, pride, and lunch, they'll line up to see me grilled.'

'Meticulous? You got it,' said Mick.

'You don't seem concerned.'

'The joint operation is quarantined from your Oversight Committee,' said Mick.

'OK,' said Harriet, brushing hair from her face, 'we're trading words here. I don't want to provide the Committee with an excuse to trade words. So, meticulous, we quarantine the different pieces so I am only exposed to Oversight on the leaks.'

I will have to warn Noopur and Zoe about Mick, thought Harriet, wondered if he was beyond Alex's calm now.

• • • •

Harriet went straight into her next meeting with the AG. This meeting took a little longer as more people had to make their attendance felt. Philistines on brevity all. Harriet reported the

Parliament House meeting results to her senior staff. The minister's final point had been that leaking of government data was a fact of public life, a Canberra building block. Backgrounding, briefing, off the record, leaking, senior source comments – all cut from the same duplicitous cloth.

'That being said, Harriet,' the A-G had lectured, 'leaking details of internal investigations risks breaching the public's trust in government to manage the public interest – that seriously concerns me. Data breaches are also costly because of the negative perception the private provider now has of the compromised government departments.'

The A-G came around her desk, stood close to Harriet, 'now the provider in this case is Asher Ministries.' She handed Harriet an envelope, 'it won't surprise you that the Langs are seething about this, this fuckup. So much so they've written to me offering to open their offices, access to their staff to your investigation. I suggest you take them up on it.'

• • • •

H arriet called her staff together to let them know about the referral to investigate the public data leak.

'That's all I have for now,' she finished up. 'Noopur and Zoe will form teams, assign tasks, and I expect they'll be talking with you for most of the morning. They'll be with you in half an hour.'

Harriet, Noopur and Zoe made coffee and settled in Harriet's office. Zoe asked about the report on aged care complaints procedures.

'I signed it off the other night,' said Harriet picking up her copy, 'and I've briefed the Aged Care Complaints Commissioner. It's not part of this remit. Noopur, you still have the data though and the analyses, they might be useful.'

'Separate team.' Noopur said.

Harriet nodded, 'with what we've learned from this,' she waved the copy, 'and what we expect to get from the leaked complaints, we've enough to start our own investigation. Just collecting data for now. The real focus must be on the leaks. We can get called before an oversight committee, so our proactive work must be kept apart.'

'Now,' she said to Zoe, 'how did you get on with Thomas Bain?'

'Spoke with him yesterday, Harriet. He starts Monday. Do either of you want to speak to him, meet him?'

Harriet spoke for herself and Noopur. 'Maybe along the way, not at first though, thank you. We'll catch you up at lunch in here, you will join us?'

'I met Mick Darby yesterday,' said Harriet, 'he had some useful background to the referral, and can provide some intelligence services where we need them. You'll be interested to know Molly Lavandar has offered me some people too.'

They grinned and settled into discussing the broad strategies for the investigation. Zoe would continue the day-to-day managing of the teams, as well as the Bain piece.

'This won't be a simple investigation. The allegations that are now public, thanks mostly to Marcia Kiernan are based on the detail of the complaints. They include falsifying trainees' records of competence, failure to supervise trainees, medication errors, OH&S violations, and failure by the Asher Ministries' trustees to manage conflict of interest in related party transactions. Oh, and there is also the matter of failing to comply with previously issued directions from the regulator.'

'Has the Attorney-General put a deadline on us?'

'She's not that explicit,' said Harriet, 'she just reminded me there's an oversight meeting in four weeks, although there's no agenda set for it yet.'

'Four weeks?'

'Put it out of your mind. She'd want us to rush it, give the committee something to get quoted on. Just a bluff, and if it's not, we'll deal with it.'

'Oh, Harriet you're so calm,' said Noopur.

Harriet continued, feeling anything but, 'wait, there's more,' she laughed. 'The allegations are public, available on social media, amplified, feeding the conspiracy of a systemic whitewash. Those with whom we want to talk know we are coming, and if they haven't rehearsed their stories, they have time to do so, or destroy or fabricate any evidence they have not already destroyed.'

'Such an emotional twist too,' said Noopur, 'more bad news about older people. Whether it's us reporting neglect, or Asher denying it; it just means sorrow to some.'

Thanks for that, thought Harriet, visualising her mother. 'Or apathy,' said Harriet, 'many may just assume there's nothing to be done. So common is older abuse, it is no longer remarkable. She turned to Noopur,' 'make sure our people do not find this unremarkable.'

'Got it.'

'We need to be explicit, repeat this every day in every conversation, Harriet leaned forward and raised her voice slightly, 'who leaked the data and why is within the scope of this investigation and nothing else. Have an open out of scope file, and everything other than who leaked the data goes there. It'll help us assess to investigate further. I think the out of scope log will grow.

'Oh, it will!'

'What do you know?' said Harriet.

'So, as of six o'clock this morning a hundred and seventy-eight (including the fifteen in the referral) complaints have been lodged against Asher Ministries, I don't know if that's all there are. I've collated all the responses I have, here's a preliminary breakdown,' Noopur swiped her iPad. 'Some standout numbers, all the complaints were raised by members of the public, eighty percent were anonymous, almost every aspect of Asher business has been complained about – aged care (the most), childcare, overcharging, staff harassment, health and childcare professional standards, working conditions, financial irregularities, favouritism, property development, privacy violations, conducting clinical trials without permission.'

Harriet wondered if Darby already knew some of this.

'No complaint was found,' said Noopur, 'not one. All dismissed, found to be frivolous, settled during an investigation, withdrawn or referred to Asher Ministries for their action. Table three has the exact breakdown.'

Harriet saw her mother's face in the data, smelt the disinfectant in her room.

'Finally,' Noopur looked up, 'only fifteen have been reported in the media, no media coverage on a hundred and sixty-three complaints. What's with the fifteen that's not with those?'

'Keep it separate', said Harriet.

'Yes, this question may go to why and that will narrow who. So, it's outside the scope of the referral, and may lead us back into it.'

'That's a big question.' said Harriet, 'we all know what's next; source the data, verify, confirm, validate. Let's get Zoe back in, take her over these data. Then, your teams can be tasked.'

Detect and Alert trials end.

Nigel was insistent, Ian Sturgess was to meet him in Civic. Ian had signed off the completion of the clinical trials of domestic sensors and monitoring devices. Based on the success of the trial, and at Molly's beckoning, he also authorised the procurement of enough electronic sensors and bracelets for all aged care facilities.

It wasn't unusual in Aged Care, Health – it wasn't unusual throughout whole of government for the proponent of a clinical trial to be private, head of the trial a public servant, trial approved by a public servant, procurement of the technology private, conduct of the trial a different private sector company, trial evaluated by the public servant who approved the trial, the same public servant to authorise the Commonwealth paying the bills. Ian saw it as custom and practice. So was his personal use of the Special Purpose Fund he set up to separate clinical trial funds from his unit's operating budget. He opened the account and was sole signatory, he was Chief Scientist. No longer using incel sites he'd made a modest, by his new standards, donation to one, acknowledging their support for him over the years.

The abject figure Nigel had first met now sported a hundred-dollar haircut, a condescending attitude, boasted a string of one night stands, and a cavalier approach to public money. Nigel was confident Ian would get away with it, after all the health budget was in the tens of billions. Nigel wasn't averse to a cavalier approach to others' money, though he was risk averse. Ian had no acquisition plan, no installation plan, no documentation other than a purchase order, and no negotiations with aged care service providers had begun. He hadn't thought about where the material would be stored once it arrived at his office.

'Mate this is very impressive...' Nigel said. That's as far as he got before Ian interrupted,

'I'd expect that ElderTech would be closed now as its business is done, the trial is completed. The purchase order is for Polonius, and I'd expect a contribution from Polonius, based on a percentage of the purchase order amount, to the fund I've established for technology education.'

'If I could make a suggestion, Ian, it's your decision of course, absolutely. Why not consider letting Polonius know what you've decided and your strategy in advance of delivering the Purchase Order? I don't know the reporting structure there and I'm sure someone there would like the opportunity to prepare the ground. Aged care gets a lot of media attention, the national dailies still run aged care stories for free to non-subscribers – contract this size? Stockpile? Media scrutiny? Do you want that camped outside your office, waiting for you when you finish kayaking on the lake?'

Ian's hundred-dollar haircut let him down. 'Fuck no. No journalists! Maybe you could reach out, get a sense of where they would be with this, and circle back. Shit, where would I be without you?'

Queanbeyan, in ever decreasing circles, thought Nigel. 'Mate – be happy to try and take it up, I don't know anyone there though. I'll get back to you.' He simply couldn't find his way to say, 'circle back.'

'You'll let me know soon as. I'm going to Dalmeny and there are blackspots – so just keep trying.' Keen to get away, Ian was to pick up his latest Tinder find, plan their study tour, let Molly know in the morning.

'Right,' said Nigel, 'a detail may occur to the guys at Polonius.'

Ian shrugged, looked at his watch, 'a detail?'

'Yeah,' said Nigel, 'where do you want the gear delivered? Address?'

'Oh fuck!'

'Tell you what,' said Nigel, 'if you get that order to Polonius tonight, first thing in the morning at least, you can use my warehouse. It's nearly empty now, will be empty by the beginning of the week. I'll text you the address.'

'Tomorrow morning?'

'Mate, I can't keep it vacant forever. I've got guys want the space, keen to rent it.'

'Look,' said Ian, putting his arm on Blakeley's shoulder, 'PO by the end of the week, promise. Text me the rent with the address, I'll pay whatever you reckon. Best I can do, Friday? OK?'

'Righto mate, that's fair.'

• • • •

Two men in overcoats, scarves, collars turned up, one with a black hat, the other in a black watch cap. They seemed comfortable in the cold, sitting under the gas outdoor heater. Watching from the expresso machine as she made the two short blacks, adding a slice of lemon to their carafe of water, she wondered if they were European, or at least used to European winters. They were dressed for the weather and not bothered by it. Her regulars were huddled inside, if they had been outside, they'd be shuffling chairs away from the heat, then back to it – that dance with heaters Australians did when exposed to anything below 10C, even Canberra natives. She was Polish and this wasn't cold.

She knew they'd stop talking when she reached the table. Sure enough, the guy in the watch cap looked up, smiled and after she'd put the tray with their order down, he politely handed her $20.00, 'Thanks, he said. 'You're very kind,' she replied, as he saluted her with his coffee.

'She'll remember you,' said Blakeley.

'Yeah - a polite customer in this town.'

'Tell me about Udson with an H.'

'Udson with an H. I'd forgotten that old fart selling timber! Most of what Lang said about the music industry is accurate –

although he may have upped his role, the technology side is right, and he has made a production line out of it, a model student of Henry Ford.'

Johnny Koh sipped his coffee, Blakeley continued, 'Must be the most profitable not-for-profit since that other mob now gone to the US. There are seven different corporate entities registered with the Charities Commission. Rapid expansion, and clever.'

'Clever?' Koh put his coffee down, 'how's he clever?'

'Well,' said Blakeley, 'his first centre was in Petersham, now Hudson concentrates resources in a geographical area which gives easy access to land, big convention centres, population growth to feed the churches, childcare centres, co-located aged care centres, and to recruit juniors as low paid trainees. Once an area is dominated, he moves to another and repeats the model. Like Bunnings, squeezes out the competition and recruits well known locals to feature prominently in media. They get a callout in the preaching, they get photographed at events, with visiting celebrities.'

'I get that.' said Koh, 'You know what I don't get though is how much he seems to make by convincing people you can buy into a heaven. Maybe I should have gone to Sunday School more often as a kid? Seriously,' Koh continued, 'it does my head in. Mate I keep imagining a huge cosmic trading floor, angels on phones, flying around. When people die; all their money, properties, trust funds in different currencies, shares, bitcoin, tax haven billions, cars, paintings,' he held his hands out, shrugged his shoulders, shook his head, 'all that fortune. Options, margin loans, credit card debt, probate, all sorted. It's suddenly converted; 'converted? Shit, did I just say that?' So, there's a reckoning of all that wealth into some spiritual coin, buys you a place in heaven. People buy that?'

'Mate', said Blakeley, 'literally!'

The two men, serious men, cracked up, laughing: attracting the smiling attention of those inside the café.

'Ah, mate, seriously, maybe we should start a sect?' Johnny Koh leaned across the table, 'another coffee?' He stood and signalled to the woman who had served them earlier, drew a circle around their table with his finger, mouthing, 'same again?' She nodded, he mouthed 'thanks.'

'OK Nige, back to Hudson?'

'Greedy, he's more greedy than clever though. He charges people for the ElderTech devices and sensors – which he got free and installed free as part of the research piece. Also, he's discovered a state-based government technology fund – money specifically set aside to spend on seniors living at home; he plans to get a grant from that fund to cover the costs of the devices supplied by ElderTech free, paid for again by residents. He figures the feds will never check. If they do, I guess he'll blame underlings and excommunicate them.'

'Excommunicate?' Koh sat back, scratched his head.

'I don't know, voted off the island? Cross Hudson, you get your arse kicked, social media, lawyers.'

'He believes his own bullshit, so he has to protect it; is that it?'

'Mate,' said Blakeley, 'he's so far up himself. His missus is totally wrapped up in herself and her acts. He runs the money side, by himself, no oversight.'

'What about an accountant? Financial records? Even a church has to file reports.'

Blakeley scoffed, 'Yeah, tame accountant, a Board and they do what he tells them, locals mainly, a real estate guy, another guy who sells luxury cars; mercs, beemers, Porsche, Maserati.'

'Well, that's a proper gang right there,' said Koh.

They both laughed, 'with a dozen accounts in local banks, he's always got money. And aggressive lawyers. You know,' Blakeley finished, 'he's a risk we need to plan for. Sturgess may be a risk too.'

Blakely went over his conversation with Sturgess.

'This inquiry,' said Koh managing to look more relaxed than he felt, 'Aged Care complaints? Have anything to do with what Sturgess wants to do?'

'It's another thing we know, that's all it is now,' said Nigel. 'We know the clinical trial is over. There's to be a stockpile. We don't need ElderTech anymore.'

'None of these dots can be connected?'

'Mate – they can always connect dots; the secret is to not give them a reason to.'

'OK, the journalist who used the leaked investigations?'

'Scared off by Molly Lavandar,' said Blakeley, 'threatened her with the feds and barred her colleagues from ministerial briefings until she calmed down. She calmed down – peer pressure, a wondrous thing. The journo who shares her pod told me she was shit scared.'

Johnny double-checked that the dots couldn't connect. 'Sturgess. He has met you but has no trace of you?'

'Right,' said Blakely.

Koh said, 'Molly Lavandar?'

'Know about her. Never met her, never seen her,' said Blakeley, 'Sturgess may have mentioned me. Same risk as Sturgess I reckon.'

'That leaves Hudson,' said Koh, 'what are you thinking?'

'He had his lawyers jump all over that journo as the investigations were all into Asher. Even though they were cleared, he doesn't do criticism or even questions. My take is he is unlikely to talk. My worry,' Nigel continued, 'is that he overreacts, and his lawyers' aggression draws attention and can become the story. The exit strategy? Time for that now? Time to get out, I reckon,'

'That's it. Time to get out. There's nothing to find in Polonius, it's a shell. It all happens with email, banking transfers, a trust fund puts money into my account. All the orders through to an encrypted email account.' Johnny said.

'Well, if Polonius is out, 'said Blakeley, 'then that takes ElderTech out of the loop. Remember, never registered it, the ABN is bullshit, just used it to supply Hudson Lang from Polonius. You know, he's pressed me a few times on the cut it takes, hinted he'd like to invest in it. Reckon we see if he'll buy it before he knows about the stockpile?'

'Before he finds out Sturgess will order direct from Polonius, and stockpile the tech. He'd be sold a worthless company.' Johnny laughed. 'Serve the prick right. How much?'

'Go for a multiple of two times the value of the orders last financial year, and settle for one, that'd be seven million dollars, two now, and the rest over twelve months. Be a neat million each. We won't get the rest!'

'Any comeback?' asked Johnny.

'We could cross the guys from Sydney. His chairman, Riccini, he's connected. But I think Hudson can get his hands on two million. I think he'd jump at buying this himself. And then when it sours, he can only go to Riccini by fessing up to cutting him out. Can't see it. The real risk is the young guys into drugs, and fights they can win, mainly a clown called Jackson. Hudson uses him a bit. Figure we can handle him.'

Johnny intrigued, 'Let me get this straight. First generation into Leichhardt makes it with crime. Second generation gets out of that and run mostly legitimate businesses, and you tell me the third dips back into drugs and muscle?'

'Yeah, and some hacking. Mainly social media, ex-girlfriends, blokes they've fallen out with – nothing financial or legal.'

'Idiots must be costing a fortune in their parent's legal fees and paying cops! Wonder what the families think of that. So, you think Hudson will see fourteen and two, figure he's just saved twelve million?'

'Yep. For a couple of hours getting the books straight including next year's forecast, false ABN, ASIC registrations, so he can have them for 'due diligence', sitting down with Hudson again, insisting on a decision in twenty-four hours, it's worth it.'

'I'm in mate – very generous of you. You know, you could have gone to Hudson on your own.'

'Not if the books show a note from Polonius,' said Blakeley reading an email on his hand, "looking forward to our expansion in the next few weeks and inquiring about any investment opportunity to boost our warehouse capacity."'

'Exceptional mate. You'll have the note tonight.'

'OK, let's get out of this fucking cold. Get a drink.'

The Bain workshops begin.

N atasha met Thomas in the Gillard Building lobby. She took him over to the security guys, introduced him. They needed his photo and signature to complete his pass for the building. They even had a car space for him, so they asked for his car make and model, registration.

'Thought you'd be a Ford man', said the older of the two uniforms.

Bain laughed and said, 'what's next - Elvis or the Beatles?'

The guard's turn to laugh, 'I've seen Elvis here a few times late at night. Here's your pass. We've put it on a lanyard as you'll always need to display it. Thank you, sir.'

Bain and Natasha headed for the lifts, he used his pass for the first time and the guards also checked it worked.

The room where he could interview staff was out of the way. Perfect. Those he talked with wouldn't have to run a gauntlet of their colleagues trying to avoid eye contact as they trooped past. He plugged in his laptop, arranged a box of tissues, notebook, pen, and a copy of the email Zoe had sent to the staff. He had the list of staff and a schedule of interviews. He'd asked for forty-five minutes for each interview, and it looked like he'd be here for the week. Some would take more time, others less.

These first interviews, free narratives, – conversations he'd call them – looked unstructured. He was asking for each person's perspective on what was happening at work. He'd begin by making sure they had heard Zoe's explanation and seen her email. He'd set a copy in front of them. Then he'd ask if they knew why he was talking to them. The question was enough to get people talking.

His first interview. He greeted her, she introduced herself, and settled into the chair nearer the door, folded, then unfolded her arms, sat up straight.

'I wanted to go first and get this out of your way. Waste not your time nor mine, I can't see why you'd want to talk to me so this won't take long, and you can get to the people you really need to talk to', she said.

He pushed the copy of Zoe's email towards her and opened his palms, raised an eyebrow – he was all invitation.

'I'm not happy. I focus on the work; it suffers though because I get information late in the process and then must rush to accommodate the 'new', even though others may have had it much earlier. One time there were three of us over at the Commission talking to different people, we only realised when we saw each other in the lobby! Really?' 'We're Ethics Australia – we should work together. It'd be like Tax people not completing tax returns, Archives not managing data well – oops bad example!'

He only had a few more questions.

'When you walked in and sat down, I think you said something like...get this over with so I can talk to the people I should be talking to. Who would they be? Are they on this list?'

She glanced at the one-page list of staff.

'You're talking to everyone on that list?'

He nodded.

'Well – you won't miss them.'

In the next four hours six more people had talked about their experiences of the workplace. Bain was told there was a flat structure, the office was non-hierarchical, and everyone got along professionally. It was a team environment, regular meetings, and a valuable information flow. He was also told about the poor work environment, the low morale, some felt disenfranchised.

Bain finished day one, gathered his stuff, went by Zoe's office. She waved him in. He didn't want to interrupt, left her with Natasha finalising a slide deck. He told her that her people were all keen to talk, and he was looking forward to tomorrow.

By the second day's end another eleven staff had sat opposite him. He learnt of a few more sources and contributions to friction.

Everyone was positive about working in the Gillard Building, thought it was a fitting tribute and acknowledge of the former prime minister. The name, the architecture, the office layout, the position near the lake. They all rated the job a positive, just some of the people couldn't get along, the hostility contagious.

Bain left, taking his car this time. He changed into walking gear and headed for the Black Mountain track.

The Kiernan papers.

For the investigation of the leaked complaints, Noopur organised four teams.. One team each for the three areas of the complaints – aged care, traineeship, and financial entities, the fourth team on commonalities between the three areas. Each team included someone working on the broader search for corrupt behaviour by directors and employees of Asher Ministries and Asher House.

'We have to give this a name,' said Noopur, 'enquiry, investigation about Asher Ministries. It's too confusing, so let's call this one the "Kiernan Papers", so we know we're not talking about the Complaints Commission or the Attorney General's investigation.'

Within each team, members focused on either the people or the data. They soon realised that thousands of officers in a dozen different federal agencies had access to the information that was leaked. Noopur also stressed that the usual data forensics, cyber-attack protocols, were irrelevant.

'The key to the sources is personal relationships. This wasn't some actor in an airconditioned room full of teenagers stinking of energy drinks,' she said. 'This was people talking to each other in a cafe, pub, on their phones deciding to use the media. Somehow, an individual or a group found Marcia.'

The scope of the investigations threatened to overwhelm. The media reported confidential information of fifteen internal investigations – so fifteen leaks, fifteen documents? They were guessing. Fifteen leakers among thousands of candidates of authorised and non-authorised users.

Noopur was to interview the journalist, Marcia Kiernan. Megachurches were not among Marcia's usual interests, nor aged care, traineeships. Marcia's series of articles exposing climate change lobbyists in Australia and New Zealand had seen her nominated for media awards, vilified on social media, and promoted. So, what was she doing with these twelve cases?. Noopur would ask her.

Noopur met Marcia in a cramped, windowless office of her employer's building, National Media, three chairs and a table were pushed together to provide space for a credenza without legs and parts of what looked like two coffee machines. Noopur wondered, was the room a physical cue? Marcia wouldn't be open to talking?

Marcia's warm smile made her feel welcome. 'No one will interrupt us here,' said Marcia.

'Guessing you do know why we are talking?'

'Well, I'm not talking yet,' she smiled. 'But I do know why you're here.'

Noopur explained about the investigation and the Commission's obvious interest in Marcia.

'I've been threatened defamation over those stories and risked my colleagues' access to ministers. I need to know where we stand before I talk to you. We're in our building, so our in-house counsel and my editor are able to join us easily if they need to.' Marcia said.

'I'll let you have my questions, and you can decide if you want them to join us?' Noopur flipped open her iPad.

'Really? These questions, why?' Marcia sounded surprised.

' Your complaint stories are way outside the material and the people you write about, so I'm interested in why they became important enough to you to take the personal risk and potentially expose your colleagues. And of course, I'd like to know how you got the data – we all would!'

'Fancy a coffee?'

Noopur, glanced at the coffee machine bits. 'Not sure these will give us one.'

'Let's go downstairs. I'll let them know they won't be needed,' as she texted.

They settled into a sunny corner of the café and ordered. 'So, what's interesting is that no-one has asked me your questions. I had one meeting over the inquiry and was advised by whoever did the arranging to bring counsel. I did, and we walked in, and the Commonwealth lawyers listed my two stories, summarised their content in their archaic language, then simply threatened defamation if we continued to publish.'

'The third person on their side of the table – it was all very formal; she threatened our access to ministers. It was all cease and desist.'

'So, can I ask why you wrote?'

'Sure, my mother died in one of the Asher House places. I was really upset because I had moved to Canberra to see more of her, we were each other's only living relatives. Selling up in Sydney, whatever, by the time I got here, she had died. I met a woman who had befriended Rose and we clicked. I met her family; she has a young boy who loved Rose. They had Rose over to lunch a few times – I was so, oh I don't know, it made me feel so happy for Rose and a little jealous of the family. I had lunch with them too, my mum, me and an uncle of theirs. Shit, I never got back to them.'

'Back to them?' said Noopur.

'Oh, it was nothing really. Mum wore a bracelet, like a monitoring bracelet, but she had nothing to monitor. So I asked about it at Asher House and they told me they were just getting some of the residents used to the bracelets, so they'd have no problem using them when they needed to. Sounded sensible, you know how many older people find change a little difficult. Sometimes. I said I'd get back to them about it, and I didn't.'

'So you talked to this family at the funeral?' Noopur reached out, softening the question.

'I told her I was a journalist and she opened up about some of her concerns I guess, not too strong a word, about where Rose was living. I went there, to the Asher House, saying I just wanted to get a little of the atmosphere where Rose had been. I mean there was no trace of her of course. I met a worker, Hiba, there, she remembered Rose very clearly, and they got along so well – I was jealous again.'

'A friend of mine worked at the Productivity Commission a while back on their aged care inquiry, and I had a bit of time off, so we got talking about aged care and I told him. He set me onto the Complaints Commission, and I emailed a few general inquiries. They saw through that and asked for specifics, so I emailed a little more specifically.'

They'd finished their coffees and ordered more.

'Talking with you now, if Rose were here to listen, she'd have loved this story,' said Marcia. 'She protested against the Springbok tour in 1971, I think, got arrested! She'd have been proud of me for earning a defamation threat.'

'What happened next?'

'I was emailed the complaints handling process used by the Complaints Commission. So, I got back straight away with a thanks but that wasn't the question I asked. Asked to meet with them.' I got nothing from them, no reply. The next day there was a package left for me at reception. It was a toy Viking, I left it on my desk. One of my colleagues walked by and picked it up. "Mate it's yours, I said." He laughed and accused me of being un-Canberran, said it was old Canberra Raiders' merchandise. He told me to open it, see what's on the thumb drive, probably porn, he'd winked.'

Marcia saw Noopur's flat face of professional interest shoved aside by dilated pupils, open mouth, harsh deep breath intake of surprise.

Slapping the table Marcia pounced, 'Well, would you open the Viking, plug it into the drive, see what's there?'

Noopur, surprised again, 'Open it? Fuck yes!' Her voice a little loud for those at nearby tables.

'You can have it,' said Marcia. 'A copy. My editor said if you gave me the courtesy of asking where I got the information you could have the USB. It identifies no source. Our counsel came around as long as you sign a couple of pages of indemnity and waivers.'

'That is great,' Noopur emphasised each word, also thinking that she had just given a journalist a contact in Ethics Australia. 'I'll call my boss just to see if she's fine with me and your paperwork. We'll want the Viking USB, not just a copy of the contents.'

Noopur signed the paperwork.

• • • •

B ack in the office one of the digital staff ran a virus and malware check on the flash drive. Safe, she copied the files and logged them.

Then she led Noopur into the Gillard conference room crowded by the investigation teams, where she opened the folder of files, now displayed on the widescreen.

'You are looking at the contents of a smoking flash drive,' opened Noopur. She'd made a brief introduction to the flash drive around three points; here is what we have, this is how I got it, this is what it may mean. She finished by saying, 'Marcia told me no-one else asked her about her source(s) for her stories or why she wrote. So, a big shout out to you two" as she pointed to a couple in the back row, 'for the questions!'

High fives all round and, buoyed by the breakthrough, there were no latecomers to team meetings to review the new information. Data about the flash drive were circulated to everyone. It held twelve pdf documents in one folder, called folder1, the date modified columns showed they were all copied to the drive within a minute of each other. The speculation was they were now looking for one person with access, authorised or not, to the systems where the reports of fifteen investigations were logged.

Bailey and the Asher Board.

A sher Ministries' directors strutted into the Boardroom at the back of the lifestyle Hub. Some had met earlier over coffee in the café at the front of the Hub, others found themselves in the carpark at much the same time and joined up in the walk, around the restaurant building site, through the Hub to the Boardroom. Service greeters welcomed them to the Boardroom, served their coffees; preferences memorised.

They could hear the replay of last week's service well before they entered the room. The catchy song lyrics, followed by Phoebe's emotional plea, 'Are you desperate for God to step into your finances? If you honour the Lord with your possessions, and with the fruits of your growth, your barns will be filled with plenty, your vats will overflow with new wine.' Finally, Hudson's cameo appearance, pumping his fist, to let the crowd know about credit card facilities, the app, and that cheques should be made out to Asher Ministries.

'Let's pass those buckets along!' said the Chair as he sat at the table surveying the room, surprised to see the finance guy with the real estate guy – a document in front of them.

A few minutes later Hudson Lang took his seat beside the Chair, after going around the table greeting everyone in the room, high fives, hugs, clasping hands, thanking them all for their efforts in pursuing Jesus' work.

'Let's start this meeting', said the Chair, 'we all have the agenda, so I draw your attention to item one.'

'Can I interrupt you there please? We don't often do this, so it makes my request more important, I have an item I want added to the agenda please, super urgent, and as it speaks to many of the items on our agenda, can I suggest we deal with it first?'

Bailey, who ran one of the biggest real estate businesses in and around Canberra, sat back, unsure what reaction he'd provoked. He wasn't disappointed.

Hudson interrupted, 'One of the reasons we don't change the schedule often is we don't need to, so much of our time goes into doing God's work we wanna get through the compliance stuff fast. Give Caesar what we need to and no more. This is a well thought out agenda covering what we must review, not what we might like to talk about.'

Bailey hit back, 'this is a chance to be an independent Board of Directors. Question is do we want to take the chance?'

Hudson, pointing to his lawyer, and Board member, said. 'If this is defamation, I'll sue.'

'Suit yourself,' said Bailey, 'pun intended, I'm just trying to help you out for when the Feds knock on your doors.' He had their attention now. 'Listen, I've had Tax Australia for the last two days. Can you believe I had to get their approval to come along here this afternoon?'

He lifted his hands to a chorus of voices, Hudson now watching intently.

'Hang on, hear me out. The letter I had given to me said I was the subject of a random audit of real estate firms which had handled deals with overseas buyers. Of course, we do I tried to explain, this is Canberra, huge population of non-residents. Anyhow, they're still there going over the books, interviewing staff, checking files and tomorrow they're meeting with my directors. They're checking whether we undervalue or overvalue properties, what conveyances we use, what banks we have deals with, our rental agreements. Here's the thing, my directors will be fine, they've all done the company directors course, we have the right committees, audit, investment, people, compliance. But here, Hudson, we have none of that.'

'And your point would be?' Hudson said quietly.

'My point is that right now as directors we're exposed because we don't have the information we'd need as directors if we were to be interviewed by any of the regulators. No governance oversight, no committees.'

'You do have all the information you need,' said Hudson, 'you get it from me in my reports, in your visits to the centres, to the Hub, participation in our services – you get to observe our ministry firsthand rather than rely on paperwork. Do you not feel that personal witness of the miracles we perform every day, do you not accept it's God's will, not governance policies, that we prosper? Bailey, you introduced this trip through your company problems – yours and not ours, by saying 'I'm just trying to help you out for when the Feds knock on your doors'. So, why do you think the Feds will knock?'

'Hudson, sorry, I don't think they will come here, there's nothing for them here. I was trying to get your attention. My directors could answer lots of questions about my company, but as a director I don't know how I would answer similar questions about Asher Ministries.'

Hudson, texting, looked up, 'Bailey – we've been evaluated by the Charities' regulator against international governance standards. We're fine. You're facing a loyalty test, a test you can't study for. Feel for your answer. Where is your loyalty? Maybe sit out this gathering today, I'm sure the chair will note your apology.'

Hudson had required the accountant complete the regulator's self-evaluation, Hudson coaching her on how to respond correctly.

Bailey, dismissed, gathered his papers, and left. As he opened the door Jackson met him, took his papers, handed them to Hudson and escorted Bailey to the carpark.

Hudson, 'Let's get on with our meeting.'

The meeting continued; members subdued. For the Chair it was a perfect meeting, no questions, lots of praise for the worship attendance numbers, podcast subscriptions, downloads, playlists, bible study apps. Hudson brooded, planned a closing few words, made a list of the directors to call that evening and a few notes on what to remind each one about.

With a few reminders about the week's coming events, the Chair closed the meeting, as the end-of-meeting paper shuffle began.

Hudson, Columbo like, 'Oh, there's one more thing. We do respect the processes of being a director, a company director in Australia. Our higher call is the gospel. Christ's death overcame the curse of the fall from grace, and it also conquered the consequences of the fall – sickness and poverty. Especially poverty, for all the other consequences of the fall seem to follow poverty. Let's pray for our colleague.'

Frank Riccini was Hudson's idea of a perfect director to chair his board. He rarely questioned Hudson, when he did it was almost apologetic, a gentle course correction. To the men whose business interests Frank represented, he was also the perfect Chair. Awash with cash, Hudson had approached Frank some years ago, who had arranged for Hudson to put millions of dollars in companies whose owners were known to him. Their arrangement was simple. Over the years the businesses issued Hudson false invoices, with severe late penalties. Hudson paid the statements and the penalties in cash. To get to his money Hudson and Frank had an endless variety of schemes hatched over Italian dinners. Frank issued Hudson with gift certificates redeemable for clothes, shoes, furnishings, restaurants, luxury getaways, anything really. Sometimes they used Woolworth's vouchers, or Frank paid Hudson and Phoebe consultant fees for corporate retreats for Frank's staff, for the staff of Frank's business associates. For bigger amounts; land, buildings, Hudson would buy artworks from unknown Australian or Asian artist and sell it to Frank for a hundred times what Hudson paid for it. Frank gave the pieces away, his grandchildren's schools, wedding gifts, housewarming presents

. . . .

Frank was trusted to oversee Asher Ministries for these interested parties. The group met weekly for personal, family and business reasons. Frank told them what Asher Ministries was up to, detailed Hudson's performance and listened attentively. Frank also talked with each Asher director between Board meetings, again, not saying much but listening, getting their feel for things. He also managed to 'bump into' Hudson's senior staff, and again, listened. Sometimes he'd mention to Hudson something that may have come up in these conversations, usually not. Over the next few days, he listened to the Asher directors talk through their misgivings. Every one of them was doing well out of their connection to Hudson, but, as a couple of them reminded him, director's responsibilities and liabilities were not less onerous just because you were a director of a charity.

Frank's assessment was that Hudson equated talking out of both sides of his mouth with talking in tongues. It confused his followers, and convinced them that he was a spiritualist.

One of the reasons his associates trusted Frank was that he never shirked passing on bad news. He sat with them in a Leichhardt trattoria and after the meal was finished, more wine was poured.

'Let me make some observations about Hudson Lang, and then I'd welcome your thoughts, and well – then we take it from there.'

The men listened until Frank stopped talking, having detailed his observations on Hudson's state of mind, items discussed by the Board, and the matters they would all expect a Board to discuss, and which were not. He gave them the perceptions of the other directors, and Asher's senior staff. Open for discussion now, there were a few questions clarifying detail of Frank. He invited others to add information. Some did and that was mainly about Hudson's increasing reliance on aggressive legal tactics, on persuading people to drop complaints or change statements.

'Is it true he calls them his Leichhardt army?' asked one.

Some were concerned at Hudson's political activities, 'What do you know about his missus running for politics?'

As their excitement mounted and attention wandered, Frank gently guided them to talk through the information. 'Let's get the story straight before we try to figure out what it means.'

Over coffee and pastries, the mood lightened. 'Frank, I've been meaning to thank you for being part of this Asher Ministries, what do they call it a megachurch?' Among this group a compliment usually signalled the speaker was about to take the piss.

Said Frank, 'I know I'm taking one for the team here,' he offered, 'you take my place.'

'Sure, mate, and me a good Mason. I heard Hudson interviewed saying financial success was proof of God's love, wondered what you thought?'

Frank fed the laughter, 'Looking at you, around this room, I would say it's proof of dumb luck.'

Over the next hour they figured out what the collected information meant. The Langs were overexposed, overextended, moving too fast.

One of them noted, 'They're out of control,'

They agreed that they needed to safeguard themselves.

A sher Ministries' Lifestyle Hub was now free of builder's rubbish, temporary fences removed from the carpark, and the gardens restored. The result of months of interruption was an impressive fine dining restaurant. Hudson had appointed a chef to design and configure the kitchen, and a design team to coordinate the dining décor with the Asher Ministries' lifestyle image. To attract the wealthy, young, mostly single public servants – significant contributors to Asher Ministries - his restaurant was to be nerve-soothing. A welcoming ambience, booths to allow young professionals to relax privately. A variety of dishes prepared at the table, a feature guaranteed to make guests feel special, the right level of indulgence. And of course, five percent of every bill donated to a charity supported by Asher, he'd encourage cash for this.

Chef wanted daily deliveries of local food, grain-fed meat aged and local, to cater for Canberra's locavore devotees. Vegetarians weren't ignored either.

The Hub café prepared light meals with premium fruit and vegetables, speciality grocery products. Specially blended, locally roasted coffee and artisan bread. Hudson had the invoices for the premium food made out to Asher House. His driver collected the goods and delivered them to the Asher café, meanwhile much lower quality food ordered by the café was delivered to Asher House facilities. The inflated food costs of aged care were covered by government money, so the café's books looked remarkably profitable. He'd do the same with the restaurant.

Chef saw Hudson drive in, park, reach around the back seat for a leather folder and his coat. He watched him as he took little steps from the car to the café, checking himself in the car window, café windows, the café door, probably the polished fridge doors too. Hudson was expensively dressed, black denim jeans, baby alpaca silver polo neck jumper, with a scarf – the light blue cashmere, and double breasted, three quarter length coat in charcoal. A little too well.

'Chef!' called Hudson, 'I would have thought by now that your menu was drafted for me to approve?'

'Hudson,' he began, 'your choreographer wouldn't have the dancers perform live without rehearsing until she was satisfied. Let's apply that to the menu, You, Phoebe, and a table of people you want to share this with, judge each plate. I'll sit down and guide the talk through each plate, presentation, flavours, ingredients, pairing. The experiences we use to finalise the draft menu for you to approve.'

Hudson was comfortable with that, 'and the costs will be low because we're not serving big amounts, eight people, right?'

'Samples,' agreed Chef.

'OK great, email me the details.'

. . . .

Queanbeyan Golf Club bistro is quiet during the week. Two well-dressed businessmen took a window table for lunch, ordered straight away. Pleasantries exchanged over sparkling water, chit chat over lunch – fish and salad both, they were down to business in twenty-five minutes.

A few days earlier Nigel Blakeley had a lawyer draw up the legal documents necessary to sell a business. The same lawyer prepared a business valuation, signed them as business broker, and had the paperwork witnessed. He also had an official-looking document addressed to the Chief Scientist Aged Care Australian Health, accepting the results of clinical trials of remote monitoring of seniors in home-based aged care. The document went on to state that the technology was now to be supplied to the aged care sector and that a rollout schedule was now awaiting sign-off.

'Hudson,' Nigel began, 'mate I need your help. Business help. As you know ElderTech supplied the technology for the clinical trial of remote monitoring. Thanks to you and your staff, the federal trial team, and the government scientists the trials have been more successful than imagined, especially the money saved. The politicians are over the moon – I guess they know a good news story when they see one.'

'Well, the thing is they want to roll out the monitoring program. Yesterday. Make the technology available to aged care facilities nationally. Government subsided ones initially, followed by the private sector. Their procurement people emailed me that the Purchase Order is coming – even gave me the reference number. They want as much technology as I can get straight away so the distribution is smooth. They want to pay half the estimated amount up front and follow that with a schedule of fixed price payments, adjusted for cpi, plus pay for the storage costs as they know their rollouts are never trouble free. Pretty big huh?'

Hudson congratulated him. 'I have some initial thoughts, but I'd like to know what you think I could do for you?'

Use the bait this fish likes thought Nigel. 'I'm not sure where to start Hudson. We've had a great year, highly profitable and I invested that in trials of some visionary AI for aged care. I'm talking wearable devices that learn a person's gait and warn if they are about to fall, three-dimensional motion analysis. All the profits went into that. The prototype devices do not work, funds done, project over, I pulled out and the teams disbanded. We never even got to trials, looks like the idea is impossible just now.'

Hudson looked sceptical.

'Look, R&D funds I know,' said Nigel, sheepish. 'I have our auditor's report here, we need it to claim an offset.'

'OK,' said Hudson, 'let's clear that up first,' holding his hand out for the paperwork. He flicked through the pages, saw it was signed, hesitated over some acronyms, 'what's this mean?'

'RSP? Another language tax, isn't it?' Not that you'd know thought Nigel.

'To offset research expenses, you have to work with a Research Service Provider, that's the RSP, registered with the Innovation Council, so the auditor is verifying we're kosher.'

Nigel had the paperwork ready to show Hudson, the research expenses he thought would prompt questions from Hudson and the verification story would only enhance the credibility of the figures in the document. Hudson barely glanced at the balance sheet, was entranced by the P&L. What he saw there was ElderTech imported monitoring and sensor devices for a low cost and sold them at an exorbitant mark-up to Polonius. Operating costs were minimal, zero debt, R&D expenditure which would never happen again.

'You expect to import, what double, five, ten times the number of devices?'

'Shit no, more than that. We sold 1000 for $7000 each. They want 30,000 at $1500 each. It's a different cost because the order is bulk. They want to pay half upfront, and there are no research costs. We'll get them cheaper too because it's such a long production run.

And, we have the single source paperwork from the department. The thing is – I don't even have a storage site, a warehouse. Polonius have offered to fund a warehouse for equity, but then I'm locked into them for everything.'

'They give you a number?'

'Fifty percent.'

'For a warehouse?'

'They have it – warehouse space here, Victoria and NSW are rare, everyone stockpiles these days.'

'How much does a warehouse cost.'

'For our needs, two million dollars, state of the art temperature control, sensor protection, remote controlled pick and pack, electronic security. We're going back and forth a bit, professionally not personally, that investment is not fifty percent equity, more like somewhere between twenty and twenty five percent.'

'So, what do you really think you're worth?'

'Turnover of seven million in one year, no debt. Purchase order to the value of forty-five million, half up front, I can't wait until I've got the PO because I'll need the space within a week of placing the order – I'm taking all the manufacturer has to start with, it's on the wharf now.'

'Before the PO is signed?'

'My lawyer's advice, based on the order's reference number, the paperwork from the department, is that we should go ahead. The company's valued at fourteen million – multiple of two, based on the forecast.'

'Well, you're lucky you came to me for advice, Nigel, The company's worth seven million not fourteen. Multiples don't enter the equation in such a short trading time. The order is fantastic, and you're right, difficult to factor into the equation until the upfront fee is secured. The single source status too is important. But do you have the manufacturer locked in with you as the sole purchaser of the technology? You have a legal agreement stating they can't supply anyone else right?'

'Shit,' said Nigel.

'Hudson came around the table, moved his chair beside Nigel, took his hand, 'I'll give you seven million. My Board would not approve more. If I could, if was just up to me...'

Nigel suggested they go for a walk; he got their coats while Hudson paid. Outside he said, 'Can we just walk for a bit while I digest this?' He soon began to talk, 'Putting a value on technology, I'm good at that, I thought valuing a business would have a few rules of thumb, I'm not sure, I tried a few experts, a few different worksheets, I'm not sure any of them are useful.'

'Your choices are tough,' Hudson said. 'You have a phenomenally successful company. You are used to doing things your way, answerable to your one shareholder – you. Taking an equity partner, you now have other shareholders, what if their expectations are different from yours? And fifty percent - you'd have to agree on everything, you can see they are hagglers, cheats really, trying to take three million dollars away from you. That haggling won't stop after you have signed away half of what you have built. I'm guessing they'll want fifty one percent, and then, to use language unbecoming of a pastor – Nigel you'd be fucked.'

'You're right, I hadn't thought it through. The idea of partners – man, I don't play well with others. I'm kind of all or nothing.'

'With them you'd go from all to nothing, believe me. What I can do is this – if you're agreeable, is pay some of the buyout up front and the rest over a year, because I'll be able to pay from the money generated, thanks to your work this year. So, some cash and the rest on a schedule, get our lawyers to agree the schedule so it's not just my word.'

'I can't get over how they planned to take three million from me. So glad you pointed that out, I learned a good lesson there.'

Hudson, low key; 'let's make it two million cash up front, tomorrow, come to Asher Hub, and the remaining five we schedule over the year in ten equal instalments, starting the first of next month. I can do that if you have the company paperwork, ASIC registration, that manufacturer locked in, legal documentation ready for me then. If you can move as fast as I'm prepared to, two million in your hand before lunch tomorrow.'

Nigel stopped walking, turned to face Hudson, studied his face, 'you're serious?'

'You text me,' said Hudson. 'I'll leave you to weigh my offer up against the risk of not being able to be your own man. Not now mate – don't say anything, let the Lord into your heart.'

Bain talks to Keith.

Bain had sent a quick email to Zoe with the points he wanted to go over with her.

'So far, I've talked to twenty-five people and there are about eighteen different topics coming up in those conversations. I have three I'm yet to talk to.'

'I thought some of our people might be disgruntled about that and bitching about it in the office. I just thought there'd be a few people who would go on and on talking to you - but everyone?'

'It's common to talk about a few bad apples,' said Bain. 'But our relationships at work are much more complicated. Let me catch up with those I've yet to talk to, then I'll know what's needed to be talked about in the workshop.'

'So, where are the complications?'

'The role of the Program Manager is unclear – how the distinction between program matters and people matters, how does that works. The vague boundary is a problem for them. Another problem is the guy who is the Program Manager, Keith.'

'Well,' said Zoe, 'something where we're agreed. Keith Evans.'

'Your teams are getting through their work; and they produce results while dealing poorly with friction, and with each other, which suggests to me they won't maintain high performance, without addressing how they feel about each other. Can we schedule the workshop for the end of this week – Thursday or Friday?'

• • • •

Bain finished some short notes, left Zoe's office to find Keith Evans for his second interview and while he walked, he mused over the issues he needed to discuss. Keith was the Program Manager; in his first interview Keith had talked at length about the role, how it was new, how much he enjoyed it and how well he was performing. The last claim was at odds with his colleagues' view. He had a few things to review with Keith and he wanted him to take the lead on introducing the discussion about the Program Manager role at the workshop.

The main concern was with the data analytics project which was not an in-house Ethics Australia team, it comprised experts from Ethics and others drawn from the government agency with expertise in the field of enquiry. So, in aged care – data analysts drawn from Centrelink, Health, Veterans, Tax.

The role was an experiment. It cut across line managers who were responsible for people, and project leaders who were responsible for teams pulled together for projects. Internal liaison and external too – responsibility for making sure information was shared, trust between team members was credible.

The message Keith would be getting from his colleagues would indicate little trust, poor communication, and little sharing of information between the team and him.

He figured Keith was shy of accountability, 'I'm from Defence originally and this (Ethics Australia) takes some adjusting – consulting over directing, soft management compared to the hard nose defence way I'm used to...' He used this bullshit a couple of times, 'it just makes the coordinating, liaison role problematic.'

Problems Keith had with his colleagues' work included missed deadlines – material to be delivered to partner agencies may be late, incomplete, or contain factual errors. Partner agencies never missed deadlines, again not a claim made by his colleagues. None of these experiences with information sharing had been raised by Keith with his colleagues and he stewed over it.

Bain was also bothered by some of the language Keith used.

In talking about his colleagues' work Bain had probed, repeating a line of Keith's, 'bothered by your colleagues...?'

To the contrary Keith had asserted, lecturing Bain; 'what many do not seem to understand sometimes is the distinction between who people are and the work they produce. I love my co-workers as people. Sometimes they let themselves down with inferior work, denying themselves opportunities for holistic empowerment. So, no, they don't bother me, their work does at times.'

Bain had no fucking idea what was meant by holistic empowerment and saw no reason to ask.

· · · ·

Keith saw him over the partitions, moved to greet him, and they walked to Bain's office, getting any small talk out of the way.

Just before they got there, Bain opened a notebook, glanced at the page and, casually, 'since we last talked, most have had the chance to speak to me about what's happening here. I just need to go over a few things with you.'

'Let's start with you taking me through what happened when you held the meeting about some specific data, mortality rates in aged care, two weeks ago.'

Keith launched, 'What you have to understand as someone unfamiliar with the way we work is...'

Bain didn't think he did have to understand and noted Keith's defensiveness – it would likely come out in the workshop too.

'So, Keith, the meeting, tell me what happened at the meeting, mortality rates...?'

'...I may have been a little abrupt, a little animated, some of the print outs slipped off the table. Sometimes we need to be forceful to get our point across to help staff see what's important...This aged care inquiry, the background data.' Keith sighed, 'I just wanted them to be really clear that the data required did not need to be broken down by aged care provider. I wanted a helicopter view, the helicopter airborne, not on the ground.'

Bain interrupted. 'Keith, that's just an excuse - we're having a conversation about stuff we find difficult to talk over. Let's go back to the meeting and take me through what happened.'

Keith's response to the idea he was behaving defensively was to get angry.

Bain wondered if he would work his way through all the major defensive strategies, denial would be interesting. He hadn't expected martyrdom.

'Look Thomas, if it helps the team move forward, it's an encounter I'm not unwilling to face, I respect your process. OK, so the way I managed that meeting, well not everyone was happy about it.'

It was enough for Bain to begin work with, and with some tears, and an hour later, Keith was getting his emotions around the idea that some of the things he said and the way he said them, made co-workers uncomfortable.

'What about friends at work Keith? Hanging out with anyone in particular?'

'No, not at work.'

'Get on better with some though, more than others?'

'Not really. Genelle's OK.'

'Is there anyone else you think I need to talk to?'

The question seemed to panic Keith, 'What do you mean by that?'

'If there's anyone else, maybe not on this list,' he slid Natasha's list to face Keith, 'anyone else you think I should talk to?'

Keith, 'No, we're all there.'

'Outside work, maybe?'

Keith was defiant. 'Outside work is outside work.'

'Nothing to be concerned about there, I hope I didn't...'

'None of anyone's fucking business, is it!'

'Absolutely.'

They decided to meet again, go over the feedback again, and continue rehearsing Keith's part in the workshop. As they went to Keith's desk, Bain asked him about meeting tomorrow afternoon. Keith checked his diary, they agreed 1600 hours.

Bain was exhausted. Talking to Keith was like taking his puppy for a walk. Answers to some of his questions were supposed to be as straight forward as the 200-metre path from his house to the local park. With the puppy he called it the walk of distraction, for the puppy, anything along the way – an ant, a leaf, a piece of bark meant a five-minute delay. Keith was the same, his distractions were defensive tactics, about as productive as a piece of bark and more time consuming.

• • • •

Keith Evans texted Mai and arranged to meet at the Hub. He hoped his Pastor would be there too, although she hadn't replied to his text. He didn't like Thomas Bain, didn't like his trick questions, really didn't like the way he couldn't tell what Bain was thinking. With his headphones on and a blank face, Keith looked like any anonymous Canberra commuter. He had his backpack beside him, seat signalling. He ignored a woman standing; yes, he needed two seats.

Keith suspected that Bain was in their offices talking to people about him. Conversations ended when he came into the tea-room this morning. He'd heard people laughing and it stopped when he walked in. And that old guy, Vic, patted him on the shoulder and said, 'thanks for your help today Keith, good of you.'

He got off the bus and found Mai in the café at the Hub, went up to her.

'You wouldn't believe my day, Mai!'

'May day, may day, may day' Mai danced around him, said, 'oh, hi Mai, how are you?'

'You know Vic? I've told you about him before. Well, yesterday he asked how to, look it doesn't matter what he asked me to do yesterday. Thing is, he asked me the exact same question again today. Today, not even twenty fours later. I mean, unbelievable.'

Mai stopped dancing, I hope Jackson doesn't go out tonight, she thought, or, if he does, takes me with him.

'Keith, honey, what did you do with this dick?'

'No. Vic,' said Keith, 'oh yeah see what you mean,' Keith forced a laugh.

'I said that I'd told him yesterday. He reckoned it was new to him and he needed to hear it again, so I said I can't be repeating myself every twenty-four hours.'

'Oh Keith, bet that showed him,' said Mai, giving him a light kiss.

'But,' said Keith, 'that consultant guy Bain. Even tried to suck up to me today, talking about running. Asking me all his questions about my work, who I see outside of work, that project that Clinton has me doing for Hudson. I don't think I'll talk to him again, I don't have to, I'm pretty sure it's voluntary.'

'Maybe... if you talked to me about it,' said Mai taking Keith's hand, 'hot chocolate?'

Keith talked and Mai listened, as long as that's all I have to do tonight Mai thought, it'll be a good night. Keith headed for his bus with the promise of calling her tomorrow. Mai texted Jackson.

Hudson and Phoebe spend.

Hudson and Phoebe left their house early. Both wanted a run outside without a crowd. After running most of the trail through the Jerrabomberra Wetlands, they strolled back to their car, parked off Dairy Road, the dairy long gone.

They used the time together to catch up. Phoebe asked, 'What do you know about this Senator Karsen who has said he'll resign and hasn't yet done that, hasn't put it in writing?'

'I don't know him at all, 'said Hudson, 'What do you want to know about him?'

'I don't know,' she said. 'I've got the office pulling his profile off websites. He's asked to meet me this morning and he's coming over for a coffee, at the Hub, nothing formal from the way he spoke.'

'How about we talk about him over lunch, somewhere nice, Topkapi? We will own a new company by then!'

'Hud, really?' Phoebe shrieked, grabbed his forearm. 'What are we doing?'

Hudson told her about his conversation yesterday with Nigel Blakeley, explained the deal, how he'd landed Blakeley on the cash – two million.

'Two million now, maybe the five later, much later, I'm sure our lawyers will be able to stretch the schedule, and the contract for the technology is for forty-five million and half upfront. Hud – that's a great deal!'

'He texted me already, the paperwork is ready for me to have, ownership deed, ASIC register change, passwords – everything, he sure is an organised guy. Two mil, I have most of that in cash already and need to make a few withdrawals, you know the ghost employee accounts we use to get the money we invest with Frank and the guys I went to school with?'

'You're not telling Frank about this. He'll want it.'

'No, not at all, you're right. No-one, I've told no one except you. This is ours. You know I've got so much going on, this, the restaurant, you a senator soon, all the effort with the bureaucrats who persist with their unreasonable attacks. I'll feel so much better with something you and I have that is separate from our ministries – unrelated. Everything else is legally isolated but it still involves others, our members.'

'You'll have this done by lunch?'

'Yep, enough of it anyway. All I want are the deeds, transfer of ownership certificate, single supplier certificate, and give him the money. The rest of it we'll do our way when the Purchase Order comes in later today or tomorrow. Thing is the department has issued the PO and doesn't have a contract prepared yet, because it won't go to tender. I'll need the name of the procurement guy just in case I need to chase him up. So, our lawyers will draw up a contract for them to sign, they'll go back and forth, and the result will be a better deal for us, stuff like storage at the Commonwealth's expense. I've got a few ideas!'

'Got any ideas about this Karsen then? I want it over with him before we have lunch, it's getting close to my nomination.' Phoebe's phone chirruped, she showed him a text from her office, 'what do you make of this?'

'Karsen,' said Hudson, 'all these photos with young women? Think I'll run for the Senate.'

'Jealous? I think I'm getting the message about our Senator Karsen.'

· · · ·

Nigel texted Hudson again, he thought they could meet at the National Library, leave their material in the lockers provided, swap keys as they left. Nigel would have brought the paperwork, Hudson the downpayment.

Hudson wanted to see the paperwork first though. What would be more natural than paper in a library? Two million, not so much. They were to meet at the lockers, Hudson to put the money in one, pass the key to Nigel when he'd read the material.

Both men then made their way to the music collection. Hudson wore headphones while he went through the papers Nigel handed him. He nodded, smiled, and passed his locker key to Nigel. As they left the collection a guy in a hurry bumped Nigel, who passed Johnny Koh that locker key. Hudson was impatient, keen to meet Phoebe as Nigel distracted him with whispered comments about the moat around the building.

Hudson, stopped him, smiling, 'Nigel, I don't know if you're making this up or its true, but I don't have time to find out now! I'm to meet Phoebe for lunch and don't want to keep her waiting. So, can we get going?'

'Mate – you go ahead,' said Nigel as he passed Johnny Koh holding an issue of Spectator, 'I do love this building and I'll have a bit of a look around. I've got the key,' patting his pocket, 'I trust you.'

Johnny Koh texted Nigel that Hudson was gone, having watched his car turn into Flynn Drive to cross over Commonwealth Avenue, safely out of the way, he wouldn't see them together.

Nigel now wearing a knee length red puffy jacket and a matching cap walked out of the library, caught up with Johnny carrying a backpack holding Hudson's bulky package.

'Love the red,' said Johnny.

'Mate, you couldn't afford it.'

'Yeah? Check out that bag there.' They found this exchange very funny.

• • • •

Phoebe's meeting with Senator Karsen started off less enlightening than Hudson's with Nigel. Karsen had no stories of moats or robots. He was not who she expected, and just as expensive.

Karsen was all over the place, Phoebe assumed nerves. Karsen was nervous, after a threat from a guy whose name he hadn't given, about when he'd resign from the Senate. If it's that important he'd thought, there might be some money to be made from Phoebe's interest in the nomination. And then Mick Darby. Darby had beaten him to Phoebe's money, suggesting she was open to being bribed. Karsen could keep the money, if he could prove, just to Darby, that Phoebe paid him for his seat. Now, here he was, and could not get the ask out. He couldn't say he'd been threatened as no-one could know of the move to Malaysia, he had no leverage with nominations, had no insight into how the Senate worked because he didn't know. He did know lust well and thought it pretty close to greed.

With some flirting from Phoebe to calm him down, she asked him to be frank. Karsen posed the question he'd struggled to form.

'Phoebe, the wall of photos with the rich and powerful shows you to be extraordinarily successful. Can I ask what value you put on being a Senator?'

Phoebe who rarely blinked (Botox) and then never first, 'it's another step isn't it, albeit a temporal one. The spiritual step is so much more precious don't you agree? What value do you think you're relinquishing?'

'Value,' said Karsen, 'you never surrender value, do you? Value is exchanged. What you value today, well, tomorrow, you might find something more valuable. Phoebe, let me ask you this, you become a senator, tell me what new photo goes up on your crowded wall? And what photo is taken down?'

Phoebe smiled, 'maybe I'd build a bigger wall?'

'So, politics for you,' said Karsen, 'is about building walls?'

'More about silos,' said Phoebe.

'Silos,' said Karsen. 'Silos are misunderstood. People use silos to talk about keeping things apart. The thing about silos is they stand on common ground and open to a common sky.'

'Common ground?' asked Phoebe, 'an agreed way ahead? So, the ground, the air, the planet, Jesus will take care of it all. You know, Jesus designed us to sit just lower than the angels, dominion over everything else because it's below us.'

'To be crowned with honour and glory, I hope.'

'Shame you're leaving the Senate,' said Phoebe, 'they'll miss your talents. Now, each according to his deeds is how the reckoning goes. Let me start with,' she paused and wrote down a figure on paper, 'unless you'd rather?'

'This is your office,' said Karsen with a broad sweep of his hand.

• • • •

Topkapi counted Hudson and Phoebe among their favoured customers, welcomed them both, guided them to their secluded table, and indulged them with some of chef's more intricate dishes, although Phoebe resisted dessert. Topkapi even waived the bill, which Hudson on the way home said was handy, as between them, they'd spent enough for one day.

The cyclist.

The next morning was clear and cold. Thomas Bain left his key with reception, declined the offer of a map, stuffed his licence in his shorts.

He walked briskly and soon warmed up, except for his hands. Set off running from the rose garden outside the old Parliament building and joined the track around the lake just off the Patrick White terrace. Enjoying himself, he found a rhythm right away, darkness receding.

He woke up in hospital.

ICU, he recognised the murmur of machines, the constant beeping of monitors, the shallow light, the unhurried voices.

'You're awake love; I'll do your obs.'

He opened his mouth to talk, and she slipped him a thermometer, noted the oximeter readings in her chart and folded her arms.

'You took on a cyclist, nearly took a dive into the lake – wouldn't advise that love. Lucky for you a running club group found you, one of them called the ambos, stayed with you until it came. Down behind the High Court building full of lawyers, which'd be funny if you decided to sue.' Wasted on him, she thought. He'd drifted off.

He was discharged the next afternoon. He'd been out of it all day and they wanted to keep him for observation. No stitches, a head knock and bruised back. They gave him codeine, advised Panadol if he needed anything else. As he collected his glasses, his licence, he almost said the small card envelope was not his. He stopped himself and put it in his pocket. He'd showered and put his running gear back on, realised it wouldn't be the most useful now.

Looking around for a phone near reception on his hospital floor, he recognised one of the security guards from the Gillard Building. The 'Ford or Holden' man.

'Mr Bain, I've brought you a change of clothes, it's a bit nippy outside and you'll need these'. He held them up and led Bain to a bed, closed the curtain. 'Be back in five', he said.

Thomas dressed, couldn't quite figure out the clothes, the guard.

'If you'll follow me sir. 'My name is Alex Briggs. Mick Darby arranged for me to collect you.'

He took him outside, opened the passenger rear door of the BMW with a discreet Uber sticker on the back window.

Bain threw his running bag on the back seat and turned to the front passenger door. 'Not sitting in the back, mate.'

Alex relented, shut the rear door, opened the passenger door, and closed it after him. A small victory thought Bain. He felt he was in control of something at last – even as small as where to sit.

The drive was quick, not to Barton where his hotel was, not to Parkes to the Gillard Building either. His driver said nothing. He turned off to the lake and parked near the Kings' Park. Park, handbrake, aircon running.

'You'll have a few questions, Mr Bain.

'Don't call me 'Mr', said Bain. 'It makes me feel old. It's Thomas. You're the bloke with the coin; Ford, Holden?' They shook hands.

'Now Alex – what the fuck is going on? A BMW Uber driver from Mick Darby?'

Alex shifted in his seat, slipped it back so he could face Thomas comfortably.

'You will have been given a card envelope at discharge. I'm told it holds a photo. Mick says it was planted; he'd like your thoughts on what it means.'

'Mick would, would he? So, the cyclist, two days in hospital was all about a fucking photo!' Bain pissed, sat back into the seat.

Alex didn't change, but he did suddenly seem a lot bigger and more powerful to Bain.

Thomas softened his voice, 'And what's Mick up to these days?' he asked.

'If you asked, he said to let you know he was with a think tank, the Helping Hand, sir.' Alex said it as though he were announcing a guest at Yarralumla.

Bain was impressed with Alex's delivery and the bullshit. They both laughed, any tension gone.

'With all the fuss,' Alex said, 'I'm now on the floor with Ethics. The additional security risk that goes with the general uproar. The hotel has upgraded you to a suite at the end of the corridor on Level Two. They are anxious to repair your experience of Canberra; your stuff has been moved. I have a couple in the room opposite yours, and in the room beside yours. No more cyclists.'

So, back to Barton. The hospital staff thought he'd called an Uber to pick him up, the hotel that he'd been lucky the night before and Zoe and her staff were told it was an unfortunate and all too common accident.

'Thanks Alex, catch you Monday morning. If you see Mick or message him – tell him thanks too, please.'

Bain reached over the seat for his bag and was reminded he'd bruised his back. Alex was out, bag in hand, grinned. 'Might take a while,' he said.

In his room with Panadol washed down with a glass of red, he opened the envelope. It was a photo of a car taken side-on. His car, ageing VW convertible. Photoshopped with the front, rear, and side smashed, roof shredded.

Investigating the leaks.

Noopur and one of her colleagues walked from their office to Barton to interview the two officers who conducted the A-G's inquiry into the data breaches. They were older than their colleagues in their open office, both grey haired, grey suited, and their faces, pale. They were very much at ease, sharp eyed and a little overweight.

In a private meeting room, they seemed to hold nothing back, provided full answers, did not come across as embarrassed that their inquiry was being raked over by Ethics Australia.

'How come you guys got this inquiry?' Noopur asked them.

'We wanted it,' said one, Sandy.

'Yeah,' said John, 'volunteered. Now, before you ask, let me tell you why,' he grinned and leaned forward. 'The brief was to identity whether any public service employee(s) had violated the APS code of conduct, unlawful disclosure of government information.'

'The brief was displayed on an electronic whiteboard, and one of the senior execs talked through it. John and I texted each other during the presentation, initially to stay awake, and then we got interested.'

'Very interested,' said John, 'the scope didn't extend to Marcia Kiernan, the journalist or her editor; not public servants. Code of conduct breach? They could have gone harder and included identifying improper or criminal conduct. The Charities Commission has a secrecy provision, breaking that is not only a code of conduct violation.'

'We finish each other's sentences, I know,' said Sandy, 'The other thing is that the suit presenting suggested where we'd find the source of the leaks. Nothing overt, no nudge, nudge...but the music to us was very loud. The source would be non-believers, hostiles to Asher Ministries. Now, both of us think you can't get too many non-believers of these charlatans.'

. . . .

'Now, let me go back to the presenter. We thought he was trying too hard to say that an employee or employees with the access, who stood out due their feelings about Asher Ministries would be obvious candidates for leaking, therefore it would be difficult to not overlook them.'

'Now, that's not poor advice.'

'Yeah,' chorused Sandy and John, 'our question was, out of all the advice he could have passed on, unnecessarily to a room of seasoned investigators, why pick that?'

'Everyone else in the room saw the politics and stepped away. We volunteered, got the gig, and started the next day. We didn't see the motivation as only political. We wondered why we were being directed? '

'We focused on the Charities Commission breach. Aged Care and vocational training, they each have a library of reports of inquiries, investigations into them, many pages of behaviour and conditions far worse than the complaints investigated here, and all in the public domain, so we went for the money complaints.'

Noopur nodded, 'Makes sense, what were your thoughts on the motivation for complaining that they should be paying taxes?'

Sandy sat back, hands on the table, 'Well that question takes us to a conspiracy,' he grinned.

'And conspiracies cost coffee, right John?'

'Right,' said John.

John explained that their investigation concluded there was serious misconduct, criminal charges could have been laid against those leaking the Charities Commission report.

'We just played what we saw. But no joy in finding the source of the leak. The report we wrote included some of our hypotheses if you like, and our findings, why we rejected our hypotheses about the motivation of the source. We figured the dead ends would help anyone who would have to pick it up. The political pressure to find the source from the A-G's office has only increased. Bosses all shouting about 'upstairs'. The final report doesn't include our thinking, leaves out our conclusion about criminal charges, just has the nil finding, list of people interviewed, and recommendations to address some pretty ordinary information management and security practices across all three agencies.'

'So, I asked why our unsuccessful attempts, our dead ends if you like, were excluded from the report, and Sandy was pulled aside and told I was an embarrassment, and not to work with a fuck up!'

'The conspiracy,' prompted Noopur.

'The source is not meant to be found. The journo wasn't asked for her source – just told she was a very naughty girl. Now the next question is why, and we reckon we know.'

'Our thinking is there is nothing mysterious here, for us the simplest explanation is the one. Marcia Kiernan, the journo, was just threatened about her stories. She wasn't asked to reveal her source because she's got the journalist shield of protection, doesn't have to reveal sources. So, we close our investigation and it gets referred to you, Ethics Australia, because you guys can compel a journalist to reveal sources.'

Sandy picked the theme up, 'we think there's more to this though. Our boss came and saw us late yesterday afternoon and we went for a drink. He told us we'd done as much as we could do. Not to worry about the bullshit from upstairs. He reckons the A-G wants to wind back the journalists' shield and change the privacy laws to remove their protection. She'll claim the powers of the Attorney-General as chief law officer are too restrictive, even her office can't do a proper investigation.'

'So,' said Noopur, 'you reckon this is a step in some long-term strategy by the Attorney-General.'

'Yep, the long game.'

Sandy gave Noopur a flash drive of their draft report, some other investigation notes, the dead ends they stumbled into, and an invitation to call them if she had other questions.

· · · ·

Noopur texted Harriet and arranged to meet her, brief her on the interview when she got back to her office.

'That's what they think, and that's got some traction in the A-G's department,' Noopur shrugged and closed her tablet.

'Any thoughts?' said Harriet.

'I think some of her bureaucrats are embarrassed they have a nil result, and they're just covering arse. If the A-G wants to change the privacy act, she can put up a draft any time she wants. Doesn't have to use us. Just a fuck-up, not a conspiracy. It's John and Sandy drinking with their old mate of a boss, breathing some interest into their boring lives. Waste of space.'

'I agree,' said Harriet, 'so, what's next?' Noopur's phone moved on the desk, 'take it,' said Harriet.

Noopur read a text, said, 'Harriet, the next interview's starting now. I just wanted to let you know about what we got from the A-G's investigators.'

· · · ·

This interview was with Naomi who had accessed the room from where the investigation into complaints about Asher Ministries to the Charities Commission had worked.

After twenty minutes of Naomi's transparent dissembling the interviewers changed their approach.

One of the investigators turned over a piece of paper on the desk, it was a sketch of the floor Naomi worked on. 'Could you show me where your office is? Communications right?'

Naomi pointed, marked an N.

'Ta, and the compliance team?'

'Oh, they are not on my floor.'

'That's very helpful, thanks.'

'Why? It's just an office.'

'Well, it shows us something of the quality of your relationships. You say the compliance team often ask for your help with drafting reports? The compliance team must get to a different floor, swipe in, and swipe out to see you and ask about verbs and nouns, sentences. Can you show me on the sketch the room where Nikki worked on the leak investigation?'

Naomi put her bag down. 'I'm not sure where that is. It's got separate access. She's on my floor though.'

'You don't know where she is or, you're not sure?'

'I know who you mean. I know Nikki, but I've not been to where she and her colleague worked that particular investigation.'

'So, just to be clear, so we've got this accurate. You've not been to where Nikki worked on the investigation?'

'What I said.'

'What if I were to say to you now that Nikki has a file note of when you came into that room, using your swipe card and asked about the progress of her investigation, specifically asking about whether the complainants had been identified.'

'Bullshit! That's what I'd say, I mean, how would I have access?'

'Let's come to that question, after you can explain why this access log,' showing Naomi the printout with the entry highlighted, 'shows you did access that room at the time of Nikki's file note.'

The investigator said as she fumbled with her iPad, 'I think Nikki has a photo of you there, for her records, because it was security breach.'

'Maybe someone took my card.'

'Tell me more about why someone would take your card, use it to access a secure area which your card doesn't do, does it? So, Naomi, we want to know a few things: who changed the access on your card and why were you asking Nikki the question?'

There were tears and a few questions about the end of her career, and what will happen to her.

The investigators walked away with the names, contact details, details of the approaches to Naomi of the consultant who wanted to know the complainants' details, and the technology contractor who upgraded her access card, and restored it later that day. They recorded it with Naomi's permission, and took detailed notes, then phoned for the next steps.

'Thanks Naomi, one of our team will be with you in a few minutes, and take you through what happens next. You've been very upfront with us, and that's all we ask.'

Natasha and an analyst came in to talk to Naomi.

The investigators left, out of earshot, one laughed, 'Photo?'

. . . .

Molly Lavandar sent her text and settled with a small glass of white in an empty bar.

John had his phone on speaker when he rang her so that Sandy could be in the conversation too. 'Take it off speaker,' said Molly.

'Molly,' said John, 'we were both there.'

'Well you'll have to take it in turns then. What do they have?'

'Nothing,' said John, Sandy echoing.

Molly shook her head, 'tell me.'

'So, that was it,' concluded Sandy, 'nothing right? Like we said.'

'Who were they going to talk to next?' asked Molly.

'We don't know, they didn't tell us. Look, they know shit.'

John winced as he heard Sandy, drew a finger across his throat. Molly said nothing. Sandy shrugged, shook his head, handed the phone to John.

'Molly? John. They are no closer to finding out about the leaks than we were. Two smart people, but nothing.'

'What did you leave them with?'

'Conspiracy theory as agreed. And the USB with our draft report, also as agreed,' said John

'Got it.'

Getting comfortable.

At an outdoor coffee shop Alex warmed his hand on an espresso, rolled his Ford/Holden coin across the knuckles of his other hand. To his west, threatening clouds over Black Mountain were skewered by the tower.

Alex sat back in his chair, head almost up against the brick wall. A few empty tables away and to Alex's left a small boy was watching him, steady gaze, attention unwavering. The boy's mother put a gelato in his hands, still the boy examined Alex. Alex tipped his head back further to the wall so the hard brim at the back of his hat just touched it. He then put his thumb in his mouth and puffed his cheeks, blowing through his thumb, tilting his head back. As his cheeks puffed his hat lifted at the front.

The little boy screamed, threw his hands to his mouth, dropped his gelato. The boy's mother reached down ruffled the boy's hair, cleaned his mouth and lap, and gave him her gelato.

In the line of sight revealed by the woman's bending down, Alex saw Mick Darby behind the wheel of a car parked across the street. His phone shivered on the tiled table. Alex put his coffee down and turned the phone over. 'Mick,' he read. He let the phone shiver, until exhausted it stopped, then restarted.

Alex wondered if Mick's appearance was connected to the two blokes who'd followed him all morning, decided to find out. He stood, adjusted his hat, poked his tongue out at the boy, and after staring down the traffic with the arrogance typical of Canberra pedestrians, eased into Darby's passenger seat.

'Not taking my calls,' said Mick, looking straight ahead.

'What,' said Alex, 'you can't see me.' Waving towards his followers in the panel van a few cars down, 'your puppies not telling you where I am.'

'So, what are you doing here?'

'Getting comfortable,' said Alex. He reached between his legs to release the seat back as far as it would go, rested his elbows on the armrests, wriggled into the soft leather, not taking his eyes off Mick Darby.

'You looked pretty comfortable the other night,' said Darby, looking straight ahead, fingers curled around the steering wheel.

'You'll have to be more specific,' said Alex who'd resumed rolling the disc.

• • • •

Mick had seen Alex leaving Harriet's house. Darby knew that Harriet's husband was on a regional tour, away for a few weeks. He'd sat in his car a few doors down from her place, squirming with indecision. He took the bottle of red, her favourite vineyard, out of its paper bag, replaced it, removed it, replaced it. The bag was tearing now. Not uncomfortable enough to either leave or to knock on her door. Trapped in his imagination. Working so closely together again. What if she didn't want him there. Could he risk that? Now or never. Darby shook his head, straightened his coat collar and as he reached to open his door, saw Harriet's porch light shine, her door open to spill more light from inside, and Alex Briggs walk out. Darby had called another squad as he drove away, and had had Alex followed, phone tapped.

Darby waved away the two men from the van, they scuttled back to it.

'Toss your coin,' said Mick.

Alex tossed, caught it, and trapped it on the back of his left hand, 'Ford or Holden?'

'Ford.'

'You going to turn it over?'

'What, a Ford or a Holden, be big enough to drag the right words out of your mouth Mick?'

'You've something stronger?' asked Mick, facing Alex

Alex saw the parking warden walk in front of the car, take out his mobile phone; only to be interrupted by the men from the van. Mick turned to the front, 'what the fuck.'

Alex knocked on his window, 'bus stop,' he said.

'I know it's a fucking bus stop,' said Mick, and punched the dashboard, 'only place I could park because of you.' He drove around the corner and parked, carefully.

'Because of me,' said Alex.

But Mick cut him off. 'Tell me what you were doing at Harriet's place.'

Unlikely, they'd talked about Mick, his robot obsession, agreed it a dead-end. Agreed also to not humour Mick anymore about robots. And, how did Mick know he'd been at Harriet's?

'I needed a second opinion,' said Alex.

'That's what I'm here for.'

'You don't have second opinions Mick. Not anymore.'

'Well, try me out.'

'I don't need to,' said Alex, 'got my answer. Call these fools off.'

'My question. You haven't answered.'

'My question,' said Alex, 'my question. My kingdom for a question.'

'Climb down,' said Mick, 'what do you want to know?'

'Harriet's place. Why were you there?'

I'm imprisoned in the past with too many memories.

'OK, they're gone, satisfied?' said Mick, as the van with the two followers drove by. 'Now you can concentrate, what do you have for me on the robots, read those papers?'

'Nothing more than last time we talked. Read the papers, case studies, as close to evidence as a taxi driver's chat. We called the researchers and asked for other studies, details of their other unpublished work in robotics, got nothing.'

'So what are you saying?'

'We're doing nothing more on it. If we get to interview Sturgess and Lang, we'll ask them about it.'

'That's it.'

'Yep.'

Mick fastened his seatbelt, started the car, 'you can get yourself home from here OK?'

Social network analysis.

Harriet, Noopur and Zoe met at the end of the day, settled into chairs around the table, shutting down phones and opening iPads. A knock at the door and Mick Darby was shown in.

'We're just about to go over what we have with the leaks of the Asher House complaint investigations, the Kiernan Papers,' said Harriet. 'Since you were with the AG when she decided to refer the leaks to us, you may have some observations, Mick?'

'Sure,' said Mick, 'can you give me a few minutes with Harriet first though?'

'Noopur, Zoe.' Harriet stood and opened the door for them, 'thank you,' she said, 'let's make it ten?'

'I've had a chat with Karsen, two actually. He saw me again the same day he'd met with Phoebe,' said Mick, 'and what do you know? He'll not resign until they drop Phoebe Lang.'

'Interesting.'

'Interesting? Interesting?' Darby stood, raising his voice, 'Stimulating? Exciting? Remarkable even? Worthy of comment? Oh, come on Harriet, it's the breakthrough we needed!'

'How so?'

'He found out about her views on climate change, actually denying climate change. And it's one of his few interests, outside women. He's really pissed off.'

'Remind me. That's a breakthrough for us? How?'

'She tried to bribe him.' Darby grinning, hands in front of his body, fists clenched, pumping them as he said each word. 'She. Bribed. Him.' He felt in his jacket pocket, 'got it recorded,' he said, a USB in his hand.

'"No helping hand," you said, "not even lifting a finger," you said.'

'I know,' said Mick, 'I don't need a lecture.'

'You know what, I think you do. Not now though, I won't keep them waiting any longer. Now, stay, and be nice.'

Harriet opened the door, spoke to Zoe and Noopur, looked around for Natasha. Zoe saw this. 'Coffee, Harriet?'

'Please,' she said, and led the way back into her office.

Noopur began, 'we've all seen the data from the interviews and the analyses, and the analysts' conclusions. So let me tell you what I think we should do next. My sense is we should stop the investigation into the leaks, deploy the staff to the covert investigation, report to the AG that we can't identify the sources of the leaks and recommend that the agencies involved tighten their data security. We have nothing to suggest corrupt behaviour.'

Noopur's recommendations created a flurry of talking, back and forth, some repetition, some resignation. Mick noticed Zoe had not been in the talking for some time. He caught Harriet's eye, tilted his head towards Zoe, and asked. 'Zoe?'

'I'm with Noopur on this. Maybe there's something else. What if the leak is not the main game? Harriet, your first briefing on this, you said the Viking USB was both key and a distraction. What if the key to the USB is that it is the distraction. Source can't be found, game over. Except what if it's not the game?'

Mick noticed a tiny flush of red on Zoe's cheeks, voice faster, not raised, just the pitch a little higher. The naval intelligence officer, he thought. The hunt is on.

'You do have our attention, Zoe,' said Harriet, 'What are you thinking?'

Zoe relaxed her breathing, 'Let's look closer at the fifteen complaints. These complaints have two common factors, they are about Asher, House, or Ministries, and leaked by an unknown source. Let's assume one source, it's all on the one Viking USB.'

'We also know the AG's concern was to shut down the media by the threats to Marcia and the aggressive threats from Asher

Ministries' lawyers. Her own investigators into the source of the leaks figure the source was not meant to be found, that no one expected them to identify the source. Their investigation was a sham. Just meant to close the story.'

'If closing the story is the goal, and not finding who leaked the story,' Noopur spoke softly, 'then do they already know where the leak came from, who leaked?'

'What if everything to do with the source of the leak is a red herring,' said Zoe. 'If we can get the data on the fifteen complaints, we may find some other common factor. We already have suspicions about Asher and complaints, and as Noopur found out, nearly 200 complaints and not one substantiated, not even Teflon's as good as that.'

Zoe continued, 'and we have the software to analyse the data overnight – if we can get the data?'

Mick, 'what data?'

Zoe counted on her fingers, 'complainant telephone numbers, email addresses, and access to their digital data including internet going back to the dates of the problems referred to in their complaints. If we could have data going back a month before the dates of the problem referrals, they will give us a baseline of regular communications?'

Mick said, 'I can get that to you tonight. Copy it, log it, establish the custody chain.'

'Let's assume it can be done,' said Harriet. 'Let's step back a little. You've told me how the communications data gets analysed. The conversation we're yet to have is why should we analyse these data. Just because we can do it, does that mean we should do it, or need to do it? What do you think we'll gain?'

Harriet led the discussion about why the fifteen complaints should be rigorously examined and all four agreed that the level of suspicion around leaking details of fifteen cases out of a hundred and seventy-eight was sufficient to warrant further investigation of those cases. They had one eye on the oversight committee. Their attention shifted to Zoe's investigation procedure.

'The assumption we're making is there is some factor common to the fifteen complaints,' said Zoe.

'So,' said Darby, 'how would you test that?'

'We test it by treating the complainants' digital data as a series of social networks,' said Zoe. 'We have the software to do this. The software takes the data you said you could get us, and displays links between individuals involved in the fifteen complaints. The analysis will tell us if there are any relationships between these people. If there are relationships or connections, it will show how strong they are, who else they are connected to.'

'Zoe,' said Mick, 'this software, Social Network Analysis? Ethics has this?'

'Yes', said Noopur. 'We have it, no one knows how to use it. The two analysts who were trained left us months ago, I haven't even thought about it since.'

Harriet, 'Zoe? You can drive this?'

'I used it in the Navy, and again a few months before I started here, when I consulted to the Inspector-General. I can use the package we have.'

'I'd train two of Noopur's people, it'll take two hours,' Zoe said. 'To use the software enough to test our assumption. We use the complaints about quality of aged care. If the analysis shows complainants talking to each other, we may decide to find out what they are communicating about, and who with. The software will have done its job.'

Harriet approved. Noopur wrote it up as a minute, logged it. Mick organised the data transfer. Harriet signed for it. Noopur chose Vic and Genelle, she figured investigators would be more useful quickly; she would deploy analysts if more detailed analysis was needed later.

By nine o'clock the next morning Zoe, Vic and Genelle had finished the training session. The first outputs from the software were available. They printed the graphical displays. The displays resembled a murmuration of starlings. Zoe left Vic and Genelle to make sense of the displays. They were thorough, not rushing, first agreeing on the findings, next discussing their evaluations, finally the decisions they would recommend to Harriet, Noopur and Zoe.

• • • •

Vic and Genelle stood ready to present. The displays were projected onto the wall and their presentation started with a short explanation of some of the legends. Thirty days before the date's complaints were first lodged was designated Day One, standardised for each complaint. Five complaints across four different Asher House facilities.

The first display showed Day One, five separate networks, nothing in common but for one exception. Some mobile numbers in two networks communicated with one landline, identified as the number of the Asher House facility where the family members of the two networks lived. The same pattern held for most of the days one to thirty. Network members communicated among themselves, with the Asher House facility and with the person in care.

In all networks the frequency and duration of calls to the facility increased immediately prior to the dates complaints were lodged. Members of the two networks where the residents lived in the same facility began communicating between their networks a few days before complaint lodgement day. The other change was members of each network communicating with the Aged Care Complaints Commission, and a burst of communications between numbers identified as owned by Aged Care Complaints Commission, Asher House facilities and Asher Ministries lifestyle Hub.

The first display acquainted Harriet and Noopur with social network analysis. Mick was on top of it and Zoe all over it. Zoe thought it a useful place to start, everyone now shared a currency of language. She had sequenced the displays with Vic and Genelle and signalled them to move to the next.

'Just before you move us on,' said Harriet, 'how do you know these numbers are owned by Aged Care Complaints, and Asher?' She turned to Mick, 'I didn't sign for records of their numbers, they would not be part of the evidence chain.'

'We have the phone records of the complainants and when we identified that members of the complainant networks communicated with all three numbers, I used Signal to ring last night, their voicemail identified them.'

'Thank you,' grinned Harriet, 'am I the only one who didn't get that?'

The final display featured eleven networks, the five complaint networks, Aged Care Complaints Commission, Asher Ministries and four Asher House facilities. The display standardised communications in the five days prior to complaints being finalised, either withdrawn, or found to be unsubstantiated. Intense traffic between the Aged Care Complaints Commission, Asher Ministries, and Asher House with members of each complainant network. Complainant network members also communicated frequently within their network and with other networks.

Noopur brought the discussions about the social networks to a head, 'If we go back to the start of yesterday's meeting, I think my recommendations stand, except for suspicion of corrupt behaviour. Close the leaks investigation, report to the AG.

'Thanks to Zoe, Vic and Genelle, we now have reason to investigate whether Asher Ministries influenced staff at the Aged

Care Complaints Commission about how the complaints were addressed, because that could be corrupt. Secondly, there is potentially criminal behaviour, in the substance of the conversations between Asher Ministries and complainants if they were pressured to drop the complaints.'

They decided to investigate pressure on complainants first and use any findings there to explore connections between Asher Ministries and the Complaints Commission.

'Next,' said Harriet, 'paperwork. I'll draft a report for the Attorney-General. Now, quite apart from that, I need phone record requests and seize orders for the complainants' mobile phones, tablets. Noopur, I'll sign them as soon as I have them.'

Noopur made a note.

'Mick,' Harriet continued, 'with their phones, tablets and call records, what can your team do?'

'Digital forensic experts,' said Mick, 'they can retrieve emails, text messages, browsing history, and even the GPS location of their devices, including what the users think they deleted. They just need phones, tablets. I'll know how much time they need when they have the devices. Who's collecting the devices?'

'Noopur,' said Harriet, 'it's your guys, I'm not authorised to get warrants to your people Mick. It's not covered by the paperwork for the joint op approved by your boss.'

Harriet took Zoe aside, motioned Noopur and Mick to stay too.

'That was a breakthrough Zoe, alerting us to what may lie behind the fifteen complaints. More impressive was you opting to train Vic and Genelle rather than do the analysis yourself.' She gave her a hug.

'I'm next in line,' said Mick.

'You certainly are,' said Harriet.

Harriet and Mick, now alone in her office.

'My lecture,' said Mick.

'The evidence log and the chain of custody,' said Harriet, 'these are crucial to our investigation.'

'Seriously,' said Mick, you're telling me that?'

'Where are you with the assistive robots piece?'

'Alex's best people are onto it.'

'What's changed since last time we talked, because then, Alex's best people were onto it.'

'These things take time, if it was easy the feds could find them.' said Mick.

'So, no evidence? Nothing for the log? Custody of nil information about the assistive robots.'

'Harriet, my instinct screams I'm right about this.'

'I cannot log your instinct Mick. You need to table evidence Hudson Lang is using robots to corrupt public officials.'

'I, I need to bring it. I thought this was a joint operation.'

'Well, you've just seen how our hands are full with information, some evidence, all to be sifted for intelligence about corruption in Aged Care Complaints and involving Asher Ministeries. So, when you bring evidence to the table about assistive robots and corruption, when you document it, log it, have it confirmed, have it independently corrobated; well, then we consider it.'

Mick stood up, leaned over Harriet, who looked him up and down, Darby sat, 'you don't believe me either do you?'

'You want me to log beliefs now, as well as instincts? hunches, suppositions, biases, prejudices, guesses. You know you need data to back your talk up, find it or stop talking about it.'

Bain is back at work.

A t 0400 hours Bain gave up the idea of anything other than a fitful sleep. He'd fall asleep on his side, roll over, wake up, fall asleep on his side...relieved he'd had the weekend to recover.

The gym was open, so he walked the treadmill – his routine was out of the question for now, and he wasn't going for a run.

He walked to the office, taking his time.

'How are you?' Zoe asked, 'It's dreadful....'

'It's nothing really, a few bruises, minor.'

• • • •

N atasha handed him a file with a revised schedule. By the end of the day, he had talked to everyone available. He had heard about low morale, unhappiness, and difficulty on focusing on the task at hand. Now to make some initial sense of it. He hunted through his notes.

He had two more days of preparation ahead, then the workshop, and he was keen to get away by 1900 hours. Packed his satchel and headed for the lifts. Walked back at the hotel, and headed to the bar for a restorative Guinness. Followed by another one and the lamb shanks. Executive comfort food.

• • • •

B ain had kept the morning free to prepare the workshop. He was scheduled to meet with each of the team leaders individually again at two o'clock to continue their preparation, and to rehearse their part in the workshop. It was not about learning a script for a role in a play, rather it was to make sure they weren't ambushed by the feedback on the day of the workshop.

And then there was Keith. Unsure how long it would take with Keith. He scheduled him for the end of the day, so their time together would not be rushed. Keith had so far shown a remarkable lack of insight into the effect of some of his behaviour on others, and even in the capital of government his defensive skills: to rationalise, to minimise, to trivialise, to dissemble, to deny, were of Olympic standard.

He read the files, background to the conflict in the office. He read about the Program Manager role and what he learned was quite different to how the role had been portrayed to him. He read that eighteen months ago Keith Evans had been on a six-month Performance Improvement Plan while with Defence. However, the plan milestones had not been monitored. It had not been signed off by Defence, had been discontinued at Ethics. It had simply lapsed.

And so, Keith, now in Ethics Australia, had been allowed to wriggle away from the uncompleted performance plan having learnt not much. On paper, the Program Manager role was strategic and not about people.

The complaints file on Keith was thick, some anonymous, none requested any action be taken. The complaints that could be followed up were and the complainants interviewed confidentially. All those interviewed wanted their concerns noted, asked nothing of management, and management, as usual, was eager to comply.

The complaints were about a threatening tone, and a harsh, abrupt manner. A couple also referred to Keith's attempts to evangelise at work, likened to door-to-door sales; repeated invitations to accompany him to worship, join a choir, attend a bible discussion. He was reported as not taking 'no' for an answer. One anonymous described an interaction with Keith as a 'faith trap'.

Bain checked his notes of the conversations – none of the proselytizing had been mentioned to him. He made a note to raise this with Keith. Superficially the notes suggested that without Keith, the office would probably right itself. If they moved Keith out, held a priority setting workshop for the staff...The problem was maybe not Keith though, the problem was his bosses' and his colleagues' inability to deal with him, and the friction they created by not addressing Keith, infected how they got with each other.

Keith and Bain got off to a good start. Keith wanted to know how much Thomas would dominate the conflict workshop. The question gifted Bain the chance to explain the process again, to let Keith know Bain's role was to make sure the steps in the process were followed, that Keith and his colleagues would do the talking.

Asked to go over how anything he may have said or done in the morbidity/mortality meeting contributed to the conflict, Keith started to talk about how everyone on the team had done the wrong thing, everyone makes errors. He may have too, they all needed to calm down he said. A beautifully played three-step washing away of any accountability thought Thomas. He'd made it sound like a syllogism.

'Keith, let me ask you again about how you may have contributed to the situation getting worse by how you acted in that meeting. Now, this time, I'm going to help you out.'

'I don't need any help from you.'

'How about I stop you when you mention what anyone else did, if you start to talk about the contribution others may have made, I'm going to stop you, and ask you to start again. If you start to talk about anything other than your contribution, I'll stop you and we start again.'

Keith shrugged, 'the ground rules for that meeting were clear, aggregated data only, just a pooling of what we had. There was to be no detailed talking through of any specific aged care organisation...there were no decisions to be made, and it was not about generating ideas. So, when Gail started to talk about the results of a deep dive into the data, she was clearly not...' Bain interrupted him.

'Keith, you are now talking about what someone else said, just take me back to what you said.'

'It's a team meeting, of course there are other people there...'

Bain again. 'It's not easy some of this, Keith, let's just go back to what you said eh?'

This sequence continued, Keith stood up over Bain few times, raised his voice, said he'd refuse to go along with this 'process', threatened to report him to the Public Service Commission. Bain ignored it all, and when Keith stopped talking, asked him if it was possible that people might have found what he said at the meeting difficult.

'How would I know what people find difficult? No-one has said anything, this is just like what happened at Defence. My pastor warned me this could happen again.'

'Pastor?'

'I suggested we start our meetings with a prayer, this wasn't the same meeting, it was the first meeting of this data team – six weeks ago. One at the meeting stood up and said he'd be outside and to let him know when the séance was over, everyone else stood up too. I said it's just the same as a value share – the way we start our meetings at Ethics. I talked to my pastor at Asher Ministries, and she advised me that sometimes people weren't ready to receive God into their hearts, to invite my colleagues individually to a bible meeting or prayer group rather than introduce prayers to a group.'

'So, what happened after you suggested the opening prayer?'

'Nothing. We didn't say any prayers, didn't do the value share. I just talked through the group's purpose, gave the highlights of my experience so they would understand where I'm coming from.

Then I went through my PowerPoint presentation, no-one had any questions and I set the date for the next meeting.'

'Thanks, you are being very frank. Let's move now to the mortality data meeting, and then I'd like to revisit how it's going talking about Asher Ministries in the office, that'll work?'

'My religion? What's that got to do with anything?'

'I'm interested,' said Bain, 'in what it's got to do with you, if it's OK with you for me to ask?'

'No. It's not.' Keith stood, 'discrimination, privacy, you're breaking all the rules,' smiling now, 'Mai said you would.'

Bain waited. Keith sat.

'I know what you're doing,' said Keith.

At least one of us does thought Bain.

'Mai is my girlfriend,' said Keith, 'Pastor Judee is not a data analyst; she's studied the theology of project team formation and leadership. So, she understands what I'm trying to get done, she's been a great help, and agrees that the greater the data aggregation, the greater the data integrity. The deeper you drill down the more you stretch the level of confidence in any interpretation. The error particular to small sample size. Still with me ? This is not a soft social science.'

'I think I'm following along OK, thanks,' said Bain.

'Based on the data, I recommended no action needs to be taken. Other people are looking at other elements of the complaint. I don't know where they are up to. One of the problems with Ethics though is that anyone can complain about corruption and all these resources get deployed and there's nothing there. 'I hope this is all useful', said Keith.

'Mate, you've got no idea,' said Bain, 'do you mind if I ask whether you take this stuff home with you?'

'What do you mean by that?' Keith, standing again, voice raised.

'Talk to Mai about it at home?'

'We don't live together,' said Keith, sitting.

'Talk about work? Her day, your day?'

'Just because we don't live together yet, doesn't mean we're not close.'

'What does she say about how it's going at work?'

'Oh work? We don't talk much about that.'

For another day, or maybe not, thought Bain.

'Keith, thanks, you've got a bit going on. The things you said and the way you interacted with others - that's something we're going to talk through at the workshop. Let's just go over that again.'

Keith talked through how he'd thrown the spreadsheet at an officer had started to distribute back at her; told the group he thought they were incompetent and couldn't follow even basic instructions, that he'd consider filing a formal complaint to Zoe, and other managers. He also said he'd threatened a religious discrimination complaint. He'd followed through with none of that. His pastor had been a great help and had shown greater interest in the aged care project than even his own boss Zoe.

An hour later, Keith and Bain were finished. Keith listened without any of the earlier histrionics, asked a few questions and thanked Bain for his time. Bain saw huge question marks over Keith. He had said some of the right things, had dropped the defensive behaviour, was prepared to hear the feedback and was able to talk through how he might respond to hearing how others had found what he'd done very difficult. There was so much inconsistency.

He'd also said that the prayer he sang regularly with his pastor was 'I haven't failed yet and I won't fail now'. Bain was confident the group would deal with Keith. He was also confident Keith would need some additional support to become a valuable contributor to Ethics Australia, whether the additional effort would be warranted was their call.

Thomas meets Harriet.

Walking back to his hotel, Bain was exhausted. Listening to Keith, paying attention, and trying to make sense, hard work. He thought his elbows would bleed. And the level of confidence Keith held in himself, inversely proportional to his colleagues' assessment. His relationship to his pastor would not be addressed in the conflict workshop. The betrayal of security with Pastor Judee, that would have to be dealt with before then.

Alex texted he was ten minutes away, and to meet him outside his hotel. Bain packed his notes, laptop in his satchel, put his coat on and took the stairs to the lobby. Alex had the front door open for him and put his satchel in the boot. He and Bain were happy to talk Canberra Raiders' chances until they pulled up at Manuka. Alex drove into the driveway of the two-storey house, garage door opened remotely, when it closed the lights came on to show a bare space.

Your place, Alex?'

'Thanks for thinking I could afford it – it's an address we use where privacy is more important than usual. Your satchel stays in the boot. This way.'

It was all he was going to get. He followed Alex through a door into a big, square room with dark wooden floors, boxy leather lounges, coffee tables and a kitchen along one wall of the square. Curtains ran along the side opposite the door he'd just come through, the other two walls bare. Alex motioned him to stay in the room, opened a door Bain had assumed to be of the pantry, and emerged a few seconds later with Harriet Cooper,

'Thomas, I'm Harriet Cooper, Chief Commissioner Ethics Australia. Call me Harriet please. Not all my meetings are like this, let me explain. I'd like to have your observations on Ethics Australia, and you may find we have more to discuss.'

'That's not a pantry you came out of there is it?'

'No,' she laughed, 'Mick Darby you know.' Bain hadn't seen Mick. Where did he come from, he wondered. They shook hands, sat.

Harriet referred Bain to the provisions of his security clearance, then gave what she called an executive summary of the challenges facing her and Ethics Australia.

'The reason for meeting here, having Alex pick you up and the security precautions is I am being stalked. We don't know by whom yet, individual or group? We do not know if it is personal or a threat to my office, or part of a wider threat to Ethics Australia. We are assuming the stalking – either by individual or group – comprises extensive monitoring of my whereabouts, including those with whom I meet. We'd rather them not learn anything.'

'Your collision with the cyclist. There is no video footage of the incident. The cyclist did not stop, just seemed to disappear. The onlookers didn't get a look at the person either. We have no leads, we're just suspicious that this happened to you. Forensics on the photo found on you and ones sent to me show the same digital footprint. So, we don't think the collision was an accident.'

'So, here we can sit,' she moved to the boxy lounges, 'Coffee, or join me in something stronger? We'll bring you up to date from our end, and then let's talk through what's happening with my staff. No one can hear us, that right, Mick?'

'Harriet?'

'Mick?'

'Yes, no recording.'

'He can't help himself.'

Thomas thought this exchange was for his benefit, these two were a team, formidable.

Harriet and Mick finished with the status of the reviews.

Mick began, 'maybe you could give some brief background to the approach you're taking with the relationship conflicts in the office. It'll give some context to any findings you may have for us now.'

Thomas summarised for them, 'Some of your team members are not getting along with each other. That friction is infecting those around them. My approach does not compel them to take a self-improvement path set by me. Rather it assumes they can figure it out for themselves, with some help. After talking to each team member, I am bringing them together tomorrow, to deal with their struggles and plan to decide how to make things better.

Thomas went through the key elements of the approach: heavy reliance on open questions, follow up questions, probing a little to get the stories out. Not arguing with the staff or defending the process.

'I have a couple of observations about two of the team. Keith Evans has shared some of the data he's working on with his pastor from Asher Ministries. She may be encouraging him to distort some of the findings. Zoe's just finished, two weeks ago, a group mentor program, some of the advice about team communication, the advice she's getting is poor, or she has poor understanding of the advice. It's unusual, each mentee has a group of mentors, they all meet at the same time, offering different perspectives to the issue the mentee brings to the table. One of her mentors is Molly Lavandar from Attorney-General's, one from the ATO, one from Human Services. She only spoke about Molly, I don't know her. I don't know the others,' said Bain.

'Let's take Evans first, this would be a reportable data breach?' asked Mick. 'Do you reckon we can turn Keith?'

Harriet replied. 'There are a couple of scenarios. We need to find out a few things about Keith. Right now, all we know is that he breached security by taking his pastor through our data.'

'Is he wrapped up so much in Asher Ministries that the motivation was about being part of that group, or was he induced into corrupting the data? If he's mainly about corrupting data then he may do more of that, without the regular contact with Asher Ministries.'

'Harriet – let's start a watch on Keith in the morning? Zoe?'

'I'll ask Noopur to talk with her, find out a little more. She can do that after the workshop – just asking how it went.'

Mick took care of another drink each, and sat.

'I'm a bit confused here,' said Thomas, 'I don't see how the watch on Keith follows on from what I've said. And I don't get the concern about Zoe. Mentoring is just part of the public service now.'

Harriet and Mick looked at each other. Mick sat back, opened his hands, 'this is your call Harriet.'

Harriet turned to Bain, 'there is a lot more to this than the group conflict in Zoe's team. After hearing from you just now it's clear to me, and I think to Mick, that you need to know more. From what you've said and from what others in Zoe's team have talked to you about we know that part of the group's conflict concerns the conduct of our investigations, goes to the integrity of our investigations.'

'And Zoe? You think, suspect she's compromised your investigations?'

'We don't know,' said Mick. 'We will have to assume Molly Lavandar's pumped her for everything she knows about the investigations. Another unknown is, what does Lavandar do with the information'

'Here's where I am now,' said Harriet.

At times walking the room, sometimes sitting, Harriet took them through the review of how the Aged Care Commission handled complaints about Asher House facilities. The review of the Attorney-General's office investigation into leaked details of investigations of fifteen complaints made against Asher House and

Asher Ministries, took a little longer. She gave the facts of other interviews and desk audits of the last few days.

'Our proactive investigation. Thomas, you may not be aware Ethics Australia has the authority to initiate inquiries. I can tell you that in addition to the two reviews we've just been talking about, we are examining allegations of corrupt behaviour by directors and employees of Asher Ministries and Asher House.'

'We're investigating dishonest financial benefits from Aged Care Research in Australian Health, and in fraudulent tax-free status claims as a registered charity and not-for-profit. A related investigation is whether any staff of Aged Care Research were involved in bribery or fraud. Persons of interest?', Harriet sat, took a drink, 'multiple. Now we include Molly Lavandar who maybe following our investigations, she's connected to Ian Sturgess who runs the research program.'

Darby added more water to his drink. Bain sat, taking in the information, reliving some of the interviews for a hint of what Harriet was talking about, a bit chuffed that he was connected to this.

'Taken on their own, no one single event or incident or report is evidence of corrupt conduct. Taken together, the matters raised in our reviews, together with the matters arising from some original complaints are serious enough to put to our Assessment Panel – do we launch an operation? We're meeting in the morning, without Zoe.'

Mick Darby's workshop.

Mick Darby brought together Alex and his senior officers, along with Noopur and her key investigators. His email gave the schedule, first a presentation then some skills practice, finishing up with a broad investigation plan.

Harriet joined them at the start, told them what she had decided. 'The review we ran for the Attorney General is complete. I'm signing off on her report tonight.' Harriet took a step towards the officers.

'That's over,' she said, throwing one hand over her shoulder. 'So, now we run our own operation. For now, so we all know what we're referring to, I'm calling it Operation Rose. I'll give you my reasons later. It's late, and you've a bit more to do tonight,' she gestured towards Mick.

'Proactive and beyond reach of the oversight committee, we'll do it by the book, and, we won't be second guessed on this one. Remember, investigations we initiate are not subject to review by government. You'll see me again Monday morning for the all staff briefing. Until then, this is just between us.'

The officers and investigators looked around the room at each other, grinned, a few nods.

For now it was enough to know they were investigating corrupt conduct of public officials and Asher Ministries for encouraging others to engage in corrupt conduct. Harriet briefed them on some of the challenges facing them; uncooperative witnesses, finding evidence where information was chaotically stored, incomplete or non-existent, the difficulty of acquiring whistle-blowers as many complainants had come forward in the past and were wary of speaking up again.

Additionally, many of the witnesses, among them; Asher House employees, Asher Ministries directors, public servants were once complicit in the activities they're now reporting so their credibility was doubtful. Aggressive lawyers would argue every step of the investigation, contesting the need for interviews, the jurisdiction, threatening complainants, and witnesses.

There were no questions for Harriet, so she thanked them, handed over to Mick and left.

'So,' began Mick, 'The Commissioner outlined some of what we have in this investigation. Let me give some examples of what we do not have - no scene of crime, no fingerprints, no DNA, probably no eyewitnesses, not who will talk to us anyway. The work we do together will only be successful if we sharpen our expertise in making it easier for people to decide to cooperate, to tell us what has been happening; forget the truth. All I want is evidence. This is expertise our guest today has. Let me introduce Marcia Kiernan.'

She was led in through a secure door at the back of the room as she was not to hear any of Harriet's briefing.

Marcia immediately captured her audience, 'me, an investigative journalist, threatened with arrest by colleagues of yours, attacked by lawyers you probably went to uni with; accepting an invitation to come into this lion's den. I think it's Mick Darby who has the expertise in making it easier for people to decide to cooperate. Let's see if I can help out,' she said, the merest of glances at Mick.

'You'll have aggressive, dominant, arrogant people in your interview room. They'll invite you to respond in kind. You'll end up matching wits, which both of you will enjoy. And then you'll realise they are getting more out of it than you. Why? Because your interview is a dud, you're not getting anything. Then you'll be pissed off, and then you know you've lost.'

Some in the room shifted, a little uncomfortable, exactly their experience.

'So, is there a middle way?' Marcia continued. 'Somewhere between accepting the invitation to be compliant before them, because that's what they usually get, compliance. So, somewhere between compliance and joining battle? Let's find out.'

Her audience was sold.

• • • •

Harriet, alone in her office except for the security posted outside her door, reviewed the report on the investigation referred by the Attorney-General. Her team had verified serious misconduct, not by whom, and had not identified the source of the leak. The report was silent on the Viking flash drive. She didn't want their investigation bothered by renewed calls for the origin of that. Also omitted from the report was the statement signed by Nikki, her allegations were to be pursued covertly as part of Operation Rose. There were many references in the report to poor data integrity practices in all agencies, including the Attorney-General's.

Major weaknesses related to poor controls of access to confidential information, and vague accountability for monitoring and reviewing user access to confidential information. Harriet noted some recommendations about agency use of plain English, rather their lack of use. Much of the information written for complainants was indigestible, resulting in numerous emails requesting clarification, each unnecessary contact putting complainant identity further at risk.

The report included as an appendix the full recommendations to improve data security provided by the Attorney-General's office to the agencies involved in original investigations of the complaints. The introduction to the appendix read in part: 'included in this report...as the desk audit findings reveal, while the recommendations were accepted in full by the heads of the agencies concerned, no actions have been taken to execute them...'

Heads of agencies may not have breached data integrity, however their continued failure to take it seriously enabled it. Breaches caused not so much by bad people but by security loopholes.

Maybe Mick is right after all she thought, a helping hand? Words, words, words, she shrugged; signed the report, and the covering letter.

Thomas Bain's workshop.

Bain sat up straight, checked the notes in his folder, a mud map of the day.

'Good morning. As agreed, we've come together to hear what has happened and find out how everyone has been affected. Then we are going to look at what might be done to make things better. Let's begin with...'

'We start our meetings with a value check.'

'Well, some of us want a prayer...'

Bain let silence build pressure.

'We're here together to hear what has happened,' Bain repeated, 'and find out how everyone has been affected. Then we are going to look at what might be done to make things better.'

It began; the first part of the conflict workshop where Zoe and the team leaders spoke to management style. Bain guided the conversation around the room, gesturing for each to speak, ignoring most interruptions.

There were frowns, lots of tears, and 'I didn't realise,' feet shuffled, legs crossed, uncrossed, apologies.

After an hour and a half, Bain suggested a break, the coffee was outside, and he wheeled it in, and took Keith aside. Keith assured him he was fine, ready to go next.

Keith had gone over the workshop with his pastor late yesterday afternoon.

'Jesus was merciful', she had reminded him, 'be guided by that. He was even kind to those who accused him. And Mary Magdalene, reached out to those who abused her, forgave them.'

Later, at home, he had talked it over with Mai, repeated what his pastor had suggested.

'When she said that it felt right,' said Keith, 'but now, it doesn't feel that useful. Like a Chinese takeaway - it filled me up at the time and a few hours later, now, I'm hungry again.'

Mai thought the observation insensitive, 'If you're hungry eat. Look, I'm not going to tell you what to say, Mary Magdalene didn't tell people what to say and she's good enough for me. You're doing an important job there for us, it's part of your calling. Non-believers want to use numbers against us, and you have proven them wrong with your insights into how data works. Remember the devotional last Wednesday "a setback is the start of greater prosperity"? So, you ruffled a few feathers – remind them it's for their own good, we're all on a spiritual journey whether we believe it or not. They may choose not to see Jesus, but they are always in his sights.'

Despite his glib assurances to Bain, Keith was not so confident. He hadn't fully confided in Mai and wondered if she'd have said anything different had she known more about how he'd treated his colleagues.

• • • •

As they took their seats around the room Bain studied faces and postures. He saw a technologist lean into Keith, didn't hear her whisper, 'you know what, earlier, my crack about prayer, meant it.'

Keith looked stunned, mouth open, just sat there, hearing Bain's voice, and not his words, from a long way away.

Bain again, 'Keith, would you just take us through...? Keith, as Program Manager you ran the mortality meetings, the Asher House data, what happened in the most recent meeting?'

'None of this is worth my time, the attacks on my faith.'

'Mate,' in the peculiar tone Australians use to indicate not a mate, 'a religion has to be more than about twenty-five years old, otherwise "Frontline" would be a religion; not a bad idea.'

'Just what I said', said Keith, looking at Bain, 'what are you going to do about this?'

Leave it alone, thought Bain. He glanced at the faces around the room.

'I don't understand this,' said one of the group, 'Keith, tell me more.'

The room silent, shoes and toes arresting everyone's attention.

Keith now, nearly inaudible, 'I'm just doing my best you know; you may not like it, I see it as doing God's work, we all are...'

Zoe, like many others, leaning towards Keith, 'Keith – could you speak up a little please, I can't hear you.'

'You hear me,' said Keith, louder, 'you just don't understand me!'

Bain held out until the discomfort threatened. 'Keith, the meeting, how did that start?'

• • • •

The weekend before Bain had let Mick Darby and Harriet Cooper know about Keith and his leaking of information to his Asher Ministries' pastor. Since many of the complaints under analysis were about the level of care in Asher Ministries aged care facilities, the nature of some of their activity programs, this was a security breach.

Mick had urged Harriet to take no action for now. If we do, he'd argued, Asher Ministries will find another way into your Commission. They decided to ignore for now the mandatory disclosure of the data breach.

• • • •

Keith's behaviour worried Bain. He had one person in his workgroup whom he said had been consistently friendly to him. Genelle had thought nothing of it, treated him much the same as anyone and was happy to sit beside him at the workshop. When

Keith talked about anyone else it was a mixture of wanting to be accepted by others, together with a lack of insight into how his behaviour towards them might distance those same people.

Bain was also concerned at how strongly Keith was attracted to Asher Ministries. Joining this group was a major change to his previous religious beliefs, he had professed to having none. None of anything really, no friends, no family, no gym buddies, a recent girlfriend. While it was an about-face worthy of Canberra, he didn't trust it. Poor record at Defence, security breach at Ethics, when it comes out his career is over. Bain wondered what else Keith would be prepared to do for Asher Ministries, or its members?

· · · ·

Keith started again, raised his voice, 'Let's just say I may have acted out, not my usual self. But you guys are not, are not easy to work with!'

Bain insisting, 'Keith, the meeting, just take us through, how did the meeting start?'

'We don't get on you and me Keith,' said Vic, 'I reckon I can work with you though. But it's a struggle this, why was that meeting so important?'

Keith rushed his exit. 'You weren't at that meeting, so I don't know why anyone not there has to hear about this, I mean the clearances about the data for one thing.... Maybe Thomas, we continue with those at the meeting, another day?'

They were all stunned thought Keith, pumped his fist to himself!

'That's one suggestion', said Bain. 'Let's hear of any other suggestions about how we talk together about that meeting?'

Zoe, 'well the housekeeping details if you like, security, is not an issue, Keith your clearance is either the same as everyone else's here or lower, it's not remotely got anything to do with this.'

'I'm happy to talk about the meeting, Keith can chime in when he wants.'

'I was at that meeting – feel like I still am at that meeting, so I'm going to talk about it.'

'So, Keith?' Bain asked.

Keith, repeating an Asher song line to himself, talked about the meeting. He had their attention, a command performance – surely not the same guy who had sat, squirming for the last ten minutes.

Conflicted all right, thought Bain, as he scribbled a few notes.

'I had the meeting papers organised and the spreadsheets, visuals, and the dashboard on PowerPoint. It was clear, self-evident, the mortality rates were not climbing, no matter how you cut the data. The only exception was indigenous rates, and they were not part of the brief.'

'There were some other spreadsheets showing a different story, they were, are inaccurate, so I asked Gail not to distribute them. She argued, I took them off her and threw them back at her.'

'Others said we should check it anyway, you,' gesturing across the room, 'had put a lot of work into it and there was a lot at stake – age of death rates, they go to the core of aged care, I think someone said that.'

'I'll tell you what's core I said, what's core is this is wasting our time.'

There is something about the data going on here. Bain wrote, circled 'data'?

'Keith – what were you thinking about then?'

'I was furious' said Keith, now he thought he was on much safer ground.

'Zoe wanted our compiled analysis for the end of the week, this was Tuesday. It was done, and the aggregate data showed people were living longer. I could get the report to her tomorrow, I thought Health would like to know that as soon as possible, my name on the report as the Program Leader, and now if we opened it all up again, there was just no need, so I was frustrated.'

'Why would Health want to know?'

The casual question threw Keith, he muttered, 'It's their reputation, Aged Care is part of Health, or was last week!'

A wry smile from some around the room, a public sector in-joke at the merry-go-round of department changes – combine, split, relocate, rinse, repeat. Keith, confident, warming to his task now the lie was done. Not off the hook.

Bain asked, 'Who do you think has been affected by what you've told us Keith?'

'Well, it's obvious I have been upset by the way I've been treated, the lack of respect for the Program Manager for a start. Going behind my back with the deep dive into the data after I had prepared all the aggregates.'

A deep breath from one of the team, then, 'Let me clear that up a little, I've taken a look at some of the data, and while some data are like you reported, the median tells a different story, and you don't report the variance. Your report is, at best, incomplete.'

'How fucking dare you.' Keith stood up.

Bain put his hands in his lap, eyes not leaving Keith. One of the guys stood.

'Testosterone boys,' said Bain, casually.

Keith slumped, shaking.

'Pissed off are we, Keith? You know I didn't think I belonged here, that's how I felt, but you know what, maybe you don't belong here.'

Bain looked at the faces around the room, locking eyes with any who held his gaze, a slight nod of the head inviting talk.

'Keith,' said one of the team, 'what is it, what do you get out of working with us?'

'You too huh,' said Keith, 'happy to pile on in here. OK, well, I'm going nowhere. I belong here all right.'

'That's good,' said one, trying a soothing voice, 'I'm still interested in why your part of the report is, like, less than what we expect?'

'The data are in the report. Incomplete? Says who? Harriet accepted it.'

'Trumps,' said Vic, 'the Harriet trump card. Mate, you've worn it out.'

Bain kept his eyes on Keith. You have the floor Keith, he thought to himself, keep it.

'Missing data,' said Keith. 'Do you own the data then? Do you own working on it? No!' He sat back in his chair, stuck his feet out in front of him, arms folded.

The room was still. People looking at Keith. Some at Bain, shaking their heads slowly, foreheads creased, biting nails, eyes wide open.

Bain waited. Anytime now he thought, I'm busting for a piss.

'Didn't see any of you work like I did, stay here most of the night,' Keith's voice rising, more jarring with every few words, 'take the data home then, work on it there. That's how much I care.'

'How did you take the data home?'

'Figured,' said Keith, 'none of you cared as much as me. Asher House do look after old people, they're good nursing homes.'

'Asher House? So, you did drill down?'

'I used a USB of course,' muttered Keith, 'that's how.'

'Who's at home with you Keith?'

'The drill down,' said Keith, remembering fragments of his conversation with Hudson, 'shows Asher House look after the most vulnerable. Of course we can review other data too, we still have time.'

'It's not about the data Keith, this is about you, and you don't get it, shit – you don't even get that you don't get it,' pressing. 'It's like you have no insight, a whisper here, a whisper there, here's a fait accompli, oh – you're upset and the next day there are pastries in the kitchen. The smirk, like now, and then you're nowhere to be found for the rest of the day.'

And this remark was shot to Zoe, 'I'm not working with him again.'

'I heard about the meeting in the kitchen,' said one of the team. 'You two were there making coffees. Another guy walked in carrying cups, they introduced me to him. I remember asking how it was going and you said, 'It's not'. From what they told me it's not how we get things done here. Analysis is analysis, it's not averages. The people side. Keith? You're a weird cat, I can never tell what's going on with you, I don't think even you know.'

Keith, chin up, upper lip slightly raised on the left, 'Nice to feel wanted.'

Voice dead. 'Mate – I don't think you are.'

Bain gave it a few seconds, which felt like sixty, then continued canvassing feelings.

Keith heard how his colleagues had been affected by what happened, heard it dutifully, unconvincing in his sincerity. He stumbled through his mea culpa, welled up enough and even managed a sly look around. Realised they had bought none of it.

Bain suggested if Keith struggled to find the words, he'd ask the group for suggestions. Keith bristled. A few others smiled.

From someone, 'Keith, my suggestion is, just say, 'I resign, effective immediately'.'

Bain ignored it, scanned the faces. Even he felt the silence.

Then Zoe, 'That's not so helpful. Keith, we are all struggling with this, only you can help us out, what might you say to us to do that?'

'Hey Keith, before you make up whatever you think will get us out of here with you still having a job, I have a question. Maybe I missed it earlier – but we have caught you red-handed manipulating the data. Did you make the data in the report look like the residents in Asher House places live as long as anyone else, whereas the other analysis shows they don't?'

Keith, red faced, angry, voice constricted, to Bain, 'This has to stop, it's an assault on my faith.'

Bain looked around, flicked his eyes from the questioner to Keith.

'Answer the question Keith, then we'll know.'

The mortality data were discussed. Keith scrambled for some control, assured everyone he would review the report in the light of other's contributions.

This was unreasonable to the group, and after a lot of talk, Zoe took the lead, volunteered to chair the project team. 'You have too much invested, Keith, to reconvene the project. The thing is the report has gone along with the data as Keith reported it, so the report lacks integrity. Harriet needs to know, I'll let her know.'

· · · ·

The group were chatting among themselves, starting to pack up, Keith included.

Bain stood, 'just a few more minutes folks, thanks for your patience, and well done. You've found a way to let each other know some of what has been on your mind.' He took his seat.

'So,' said Bain, 'Keith; taking data home, isolating Asher House data, talking over your findings with some who do not work here.' Bain looked around the room, saw no-one was ready for this. He looked to Zoe, 'needs an action?'

'Keith,' Zoe said, 'these are serious breaches.'

'Fine,' said Keith, 'I'll go home.' He'd call Mai on the way, ask her to stay.

'And the action, for the plan? What do I write?' Bain asked.

'Write this,' said Zoe, 'recommend to the Commissioner that Keith be suspended while his conduct is investigated.'

'Whatever,' said Keith. 'Let me ask this question,' he snarled at Bain, 'is that fair, reasonable?'

'Absolutely,' said one.

Bain saw heads nodding all around the room, wrote the item for the action plan.

Bain read back everything they had agreed. There was no discussion, they were relieved, vulnerable, pissed off, and tired, up for a drink. He asked for a few minutes to write up the agreement legibly for them all to sign. Finished, they all signed. Bain said he would email it to Zoe to distribute.

Bain took Zoe aside, 'Keith? What do you want to do?'

'I've done it; texted Harriet. He's suspended on full pay, effective now. We'll interview him on Monday morning.'

'Could I make a suggestion?'

'Sure.'

'How about also advising him not to discuss anything to do with Ethics Australia with anybody, not colleagues, not friends and not his pastor. I'll keep him here for a few minutes while you draft an email to him, tell him about the suspension, and send him the email, asking him to acknowledge it by return email. He's got his phone here, if he refuses – which he has a right to, email him straight away saying even though he refused to acknowledge the suspension, it still stands.'

'Got it,' said Zoe opening her phone.

'And Keith now?' Bain asked her.

'I'll ask him if he wants a drink. How about you? You've earned it, you too?'

Bain declined, packed up.

. . . .

Outside the building Alex was waiting for him. 'Toss us your keys, Thomas, Mick needs to talk to you, Ahmed'll take yours to your hotel, he'll be gentle, leave the keys at reception for you.'

Bain handed over the keys to a slightly built young guy with a ponytail, jeans, and a denim jacket. He had to laugh though, his aging VW convertible, a source of constant amusement to Alex and his team.

The Long Room.

Alex drove, Thomas nodded off, knackered after the workshop. The long room was exactly that. The door opened into an area the short width of the room, a table, and a few chairs, then straight ahead. Barely room to walk down the middle of the room without banging the backs of those hunched over a continuous metal shelf holding monitors, mobile phones in chargers, iPads, keyboards, and gaming consoles. Overhead, a dozen big screen monitors able to display what was on any one of the twenty or so smaller monitors. Down past the stations the room widened slightly, furnished with lockers, coat hooks of helmets, jackets, and an unstrung tennis racquet. Motorcycle boots on the floor.

The men and women in the 'long room' monitored the devices installed by another of Mick Darby's teams. Journalists, lawyers, coppers, politicians, union officials, criminals, judges, academics, bankers, prostitutes, zealots, teachers, public servants, irrigation consultants, lobbyists, advisors, nurses, councillors, priests, anyone Mick was interested in, and, as of this morning - Keith Evans' house was bugged.

The tennis racquet was a reminder to be careful. Years ago, the long room team also installed devices as well as running surveillance. Mick split the team in two when he was taught a violent lesson, two utterly different skills sets are required. One of the team was killed breaking out of a house where he thought no-one was home. The racquet was his, he'd kept in the long room just in case he could get a game in. He was shot after successfully fixing devices, so the long room heard it all. Mick was in the long room that night and crying with rage broke the racquet over a locker as his operative was shot. All caught on an unauthorised device, evidence inadmissible. Leaving Mick with only one sure way to convict the killer. The tennis racquet? 'Be careful', it said. The killer? Shot by his own blokes when they found out he was a police informer.

Mick gestured for Thomas to sit. Alex fitted headphones.

Mick explained the room and the details of some of the surveillance, observed that concentration and boredom continued a centuries old battle for the hearts and minds of watchers.

Thomas talked over the workshop with Mick. 'The key result is that Keith Evans compromised the data on mortality rates in Asher House facilities. They all know that in the workshop. Zoe will brief Harriet and Noopur, probably doing that now.'

'Undeniably nice work mate.'

Mick was excited, reached over and slapped Bain's bruised back, 'Oh shit, sorry mate.' Not sorry at all.

Then an interruption.

In Alex's earpiece, 'I've got your party at home now, 2017 hours.'

'You haven't. He's just caught the bus from the office, Ahmed right behind him, Danny behind him.'

'Wait one. I've got Asher Ministries' music, male voice, wait one-two male voices. They're turning the place over.'

Alex to Ahmed 'Stay with him, he's got houseguests, unexpected.'

'Alex, right behind the bus.'

Alex to Ahmed and Danny, 'Danny, pull up in next door's drive, siren and blue lights. Figure these guys will panic, leave and Ahmed will follow them. We don't want them thinking Keith's being followed. Got that Ahmed? Our bloke will be OK because they want something from him – otherwise they wouldn't be there now.'

• • • •

Keith walked up his drive, keys out of his pocket. Door open, Mia must be here. Smiling he heard 'what a beautiful name' playing loudly, too loud for Keith. As he opened the sonos app on his phone he was flung against the door. He took a step forward and fell on his face, heard a siren, and took brutal kicks to the top of his head.

Ahmed followed a dark blue Lexus to a Garran address. The car registration checked out, it and the house owned by a trust, of which the sole beneficiary was Hudson Lang.

'Mick, what do you want to do about the Lexus?'

'Let the locals take care of that, an anonymous witness will report two blokes in a dark blue Lexus, registration accurate, speeding away from this street. It's still at Lang's place, we'll see how that plays out for him. Let's see who comes to his rescue if anyone does come. And speaking of rescue roster a twenty-four-hour security on Evans.'

As he knew where to find the men who broke into Keith's place, and they'd not been there long, Mick didn't call forensics. With Ahmed at Garran and Danny following the ambulance, Mick had some housekeeping done at Keith's.

'Mick? We have the girlfriend, Mai, in Evans' house. She's asked us to leave. We were just about done here.'

'Good man. Alex will come over and let her know about Keith. You guys just leave the place please, but wait in the car, just in case. We'll watch what she does from here!'

Mai searched the apartment systematically, either she'd done it before, or she was following a checklist. She photographed everything and compared how she replaced each object to the photo, satisfied, she moved to the next. They let her finish the house before Alex appeared. She'd found nothing.

Alex sat her down, gave the news about Keith. 'She didn't tell me that,' she said, sobbing. Alex let her sob. Calmer now Mai told him of a phone call from Judee, Keith's pastor, who asked her to find a flash drive in his place. He wasn't expected home, so she had plenty of time, and he wasn't to know she'd been there.

Alex explained Keith's injuries. Mai lost her shit. Mick called housekeepers, and Mai was in protective custody. Anyone in the long room keeping watch would have observed Alex walk slowly through each room, touching nothing. Three times they would have seen him do that.

Mick called Alex on his way to Keith's house.

'Having a good look around, mate? He's hiding a flash drive there, or something like that. See if you can find it. I agree with the girlfriend, ex now I think, it will be there. We need it. He'd told Thomas Bain enough for us to believe the data he reported is incomplete. It sounds like he used it for his own benefit with Hudson Lang. We don't have enough yet to get Lang in, far less charge him. We get that material though...'

Alex asked Mick if he could return to the long room. 'I need to learn what we know about Evans before continuing the hunt.'

Alex read every note on Keith, examined the stills of every room, and asked one of the team for her thoughts on his kitchen.

'No, I'm with you,' she said, 'the kitchen gear is not brand new, just rarely used. He eats frozen meals, prepared meals, drinks bottled water. Clothes? Laundry come dry cleaner, including a bag of t-shirts, socks, and jocks. He even cleans his trainers after a run, pristine. Bikes too.'

He thanked her and went looking for Mick, Alex said 'The flash drive is in a pebble on the bottom of his fish tank.'

'How the fuck do you know that?'

'Aside from Evans, and I'm not even sure of him, the fish are the only living things there. He checks them daily; they were all he asked about in the ambulance. Everything else he touches, he cleans; he's obsessive. Fish are a natural hobby for this guy, so easy to drop a pebble in the tank, and he can't clean them every time he puts it back. He hides that drive anywhere else in that place and he creates a cleaning job, not so good if he's in a hurry. He's so compulsive he'd always be in a hurry.'

'I'm just not sure which pebble.'

'You know, I wasn't sure I believed you until you said that. OK let's go back.'

Mick watched, and the investigator they'd brought with them videoed, as Alex explained Keith's fish tank set up, 'These filters and the small pump are not even attached, not setup, just decorative. I think he put them there to be found, hoping to fool anyone looking into assuming they'd found hiding places. They'd have to be broken to be taken apart and searched, so he probably figured they'd be removed, nothing found, and they'd leave the tank alone next time.'

Silently observed by a few tiger barbs that retreated even further into the plastic ruined castle on the tank bottom, and by Mick, who moved closer, Alex removed the tank's hood, took out a white pebble, one by one, each about as big as an adult's thumb. The ninth pebble opened to reveal a flash drive. Evidence bagged, find recorded, evidence trail secured they left the house to log it all at Ethics Australia.

Operation Rose.

M ondays usually got off to a slow start, like the old physio joke, start the regime with a rest day, for the work regime commences in earnest on Tuesday, Monday is given over to exaggerating the weekend exploits. Not this Monday. Ethics Australia employees didn't dwell on their weekend, their conversations were dominated by the workshop on Friday and the news of the assault on Keith Evans.

Harriet had them called together, pressing even these exciting topics aside. 'A covert investigation involving Asher Ministries commenced some months ago, in parallel with the reviews you worked on for the government. As a result of these three separate and related pieces concerning Asher Ministries, we are starting Operation Rose today, now. This is a joint operation with Mick Darby's team from the Intelligence Committee. Mick Darby met one of the older women caught up in this, her name was Rose.'

'We are investigating allegations of corrupt behaviour by directors and employees of Asher Ministries and Asher House, in dishonestly obtaining financial benefit from Aged Care Research in Australian Health, and in fraudulently claiming tax free status as a registered charity and not-for-profit. Operation Rose also goes to whether any staff of Aged Care Research were involved in bribery or fraud.'

'We expect to find criminal behaviour that is not corrupt. We know we'll find evidence of elder abuse and neglect. We will investigate whatever we find, even though it may not all be corrupt, investigations may lead us to evidence of corruption.'

Her staff received a stronger message that Operation Rose was not solely about following the money. It was an investigation about following the people, money was simply the footprint left behind. Harriet replaced the photos of aged care residents taken when admitted, with photos of them in their twenties and thirties, wedding photos, graduation photos, military photos.

'The driver of this investigation is that these lives may have been cut short because some people behaved corruptly and made money out of it. Corruption in this sector of health, aged care, remains a lucrative opportunity for as long as we allow older people to be disrespected. Let's not be deceived into thinking their ninetieth year or their ninety first year is somehow less precious than their twenty-first, or their thirtieth.'

Her staff: lawyers, investigators, technical experts, forensic experts in all fields, witness protection, extroverts, other employees who could not look you in the eye when you talked to them, stood, and applauded her. Most of them knew of the terabytes of reports, data, minutes of meetings on aged care, and the nil changes arising from them. They wondered if the work they were doing, the long hours of screwing around with the little things was going to lead anywhere. They still may not know where the hours would lead, but they would put them in.

'This is just the introduction. Briefings will continue all day. For now, let's introduce ourselves to some not so familiar faces.'

People stood, introduced themselves, mingled. A coffee cart and pastries appeared, briefly.

Twenty minutes with Harriet and Mick, an hour with Noopur, Zoe, and Alex, team assignments. The day passed with closing all other work and focusing on new system passwords, document management protocols, two-stage triage process, first to determine whether information should likely be regarded as evidence and warrant further investigation. Second, which agency should investigate if the matter was not about corrupt behaviour.

To the casual observer this Tuesday was no different to any other. But there were no casual observers. For this was Canberra where the only casual observers were tourists, few of them hardy enough to brave the lingering winter days. Resident observers would have noted the signs of a fresh operation. Those headed to the Gillard building had the posture of those with whom a secret was trusted, head erect, confident. Even their satchels and backpacks spoke of coded scraps secreted in false bottoms. Inside the building the effect was more pronounced, printers didn't jam, the air conditioning kept pace with the external temperature, the lifts were there when wanted.

Noopur assembled the teams in the early afternoon. A light lunch ensured no latecomers. Under Harriet's tutelage she had learnt to commence an operation with a pre-mortem. Another tool pirated from business literature the pre-mortem was exactly that – a post-mortem conducted before the start of an operation. In a pre-mortem, participants first imagine the operation a failure, 'just think of it as Murphy's law on steroids' was her line.

Noopur set a brisk pace during the workshop and by day's end they had a mutual understanding of the main threats to Operation Rose, and a detailed action plan to address the risks before they manifested. Progress against the plan was to be reported at operational meetings, the pre-mortem action plan designated as serious as any operational plan.

Mick kept his own counsel during the pre-mortem. He'd long ago learned its value. Today he would speak once, aside from the pleasantries, and when he spoke, he transferred a thousand dollar casino chip from one pocket to another. For talking in a pre-mortem, he allowed himself a thousand, sometimes he carried smaller denomination chips totalling the thousand, today though he put it all on one observation. Moving the chip meant he had spent the money and he allowed himself no credit facility, so he could no longer talk. He knew he needed a disciplined approach to shutting up. Plus, he found he listened better, stilled some voices.

'I'm bothered by a few things,' he said, 'let me list them and my interpretation. Not in order my thoughts, so Friday night acting on a tipoff, anonymous of course,' the group laughed quietly, 'Federal police went to an address in Garran looking for two young men who were reporting speeding. We know they had assaulted Keith Evans. Evans is in an induced coma. The officers were met at Garran by a normal looking front door to a suburban house, but the door was steel set in a steel door frame. A quick look around the front revealed high security windows, more cameras than a movie set. The house was a fortress. The house is owned by a trust, of which the sole beneficiary is Hudson Lang.'

No-one moved.

'They could raise no-one at the house, so they turned back to their car. Silently and very quickly they found themselves surrounded by four heavily built men, some between them and their vehicle. The group dispersed as one guy politely let the officers know not to return.'

There were a few smiles at "politely".

'They didn't return. A specialist response team did, with a warrant. The place proved to be empty, wired for audio and video. I've had some work done through the weekend looking for any other connections between Hudson Lang, Asher Ministries, and violence. Over the last twenty years there are violent assaults on people who became disenchanted with Asher Ministries. Clearly not the same guys, but violence has been a factor, historically and now.'

'So, what could go wrong? Our witnesses, our complainants, whistle blowers if we have any – those on whom we rely for information, intelligence and evidence may be hurt. We need to protect them, keep them safe.'

This task was assigned to one of Zoe's teams, first items: a plan, due dates, contact details, where the plan would be posted.

An older man in a suit was ushered into the room. He was not introduced. Noopur said he'd talk with them a while, take any questions and they would all need their laptops. Five minutes later everyone was back, a login and password were screened, read-only.

The man was softly spoken, Welsh accent, chinos and a linen shirt, face scarred down one side, an angry scar, old, poorly healed.

'Now, like you I have a little to do with Intelligence, some say too little, they'd be the English for whom I'm delighted to learn from Noopur and Mick we share a common antipathy. This,' he drew a finger along his scar, 'not heroics in the field of battle, a Slade concert in Cardiff, well before you were born.'

As the laughter subsided, someone's device roared the opening to 'cum on feel the noize'. Everyone else was taken aback, this usually didn't happen at Ethics, at least with a guest.

Their guest brought his hands together and bowed, 'They couldn't spell,' he said, 'but they could play. And so, can you, I can tell I'm going to enjoy our little chat.' More laughter. He had them.

He told them of crowdsourcing used to combat crime and terrorism. The Boston bombers were identified because police appealed to the crowd for any video footage of the race, any part of the race, and especially around the bombing. The huge amount of data received, 13,000 photos and videos, was a problem, crashing the police website. Another problem was that access to crowd data, crowd footage, CCTV required analysts to access different and unrelated databases, most standalone, then find material germane to the event, download, copy, save, log. All this added a lot to the amount of time required to turn data into intelligence, and eventually evidence.

Since then, there had been two breakthroughs in sophisticated analytics software. One breakthrough was in software able to connect what had previously been unconnectable; citizens' private and public photos and videos recorded on mobile devices, dash cams, body worn cameras, CCTV, 000 and 112 calls, social media content.

The second breakthrough, 'Have I your attention still? That is so gratifying.' He beamed, he was having a lend and they knew it, the expert was human.

'If you would login, please, I'll show you the second big step forward.'

He introduced them to a practical example of data drawn from a London shooting. He took them through how to use an easily navigable search engine to select any files across the huge amount of, now connected, data. Once they had what they wanted, save it, log it, and share it – not more steps than using a word document.

In pairs they practised, played and soon they were across the first level of application. Over a late afternoon tea, their anonymous visitor was clapped, cheered, bombarded with questions. Someone opened a single malt. He stayed for 'just the one, thank you so much.'

Harriet Cooper finished up the evening now by revealing that the software would be installed overnight. One of Mick Darby's units would train a small team to begin with and then roll out more sessions.

'We're crowdsourcing to collect data as part of Operation Rose. We may yet hold public hearings. Before we do that let's see what's out there on social media, mobile devices, complaint call lines, security and CCTV footage.'

'I know we'll get much more than we're looking for – and that's where the software you now have a glimpse of, will be so useful in cutting down the analytical time required.'

More rousing cheers. It's like going to a Raider's game said one, Their guest was thanked, Harriet thanked, Mick Darby too as he whisked his anonymous guest to Alex waiting in the car.

Molly reflects.

A decade of the conservative right's powerful hold over federal politics yielded a bureaucracy where the boundaries between ministerial staff and departmental staff had been stretched beyond the point of inelasticity. None of the current crop of secretaries and agency heads could recall a time where advisors did not direct agency heads. So, it was of no surprise that three federal agency heads were summoned to the office of Molly Lavandar, Chief of Staff to the Attorney-General.

Her assistant let her know the three men had arrived. No coffee or even water he had been told; they were not expected to be in with Molly long enough for the tea to cool. Molly's eyes brightened as the men entered her office, stark in comparison to their own corner suites. No ego selfies with celebrities, no glamorous family make-over photos, no Asher Ministries' symbols. A glass topped desk, laptop, hard-backed chairs circling a table for eight. Molly was the room's centrepiece.

She welcomed and dismissed them in a couple of sentences. They were to be escorted out of the building, driven home. They were suspended pending the results of investigations which had started as they left their offices. Nothing said Monday better than a few scalps. Ethics Australia had reported all three agencies' poor information security protocols. They had been advised of this months ago and, despite assuring their ministers to the contrary, no protocol or procedure had changed.

'Your inaction,' summarised Molly, 'resulted in promoting a culture where breaches of information integrity and process were encouraged.'

Molly pressed a button on her phone. Her door opened, and three men stood there. 'Gentlemen,' she said to the department heads, 'your escorts are here.'

Over the fifty years with the federal public service Molly had been schooled in deceit. The service leadership had been mostly male until quite recently. Parliamentarians, staffers, bureaucrats, dissemblers, with soft hands and sleek, fat bodies, skilled at talking themselves up and others down. Always looking over your shoulder when they talked to you, anxiously scanning the room to make sure there was no one more important with whom they should be seen.

They sold their votes and their influence to the highest bidder, not always for money; some for sex, some for fame, others for privacy, still others for a more long-term gain. Like the current Prime Minister and ministers close to her who had sold themselves to those who promised the richest life after death, Asher Ministries. Look the other way for eternal life? Count me in. Industrial scale worship of Jesus of Avarice.

By the turn of the century Molly realised that her rise through the public service was not as rewarding as she had anticipated. She pictured her rise through the ranks as an arc with a steep curve. Sadly, she was witness to the decline of the public service which arc was also steep. She knew she was swimming up strongly in an increasingly shallow pool. The realisation brought her no comfort. Molly had assessed herself against rank, position, influence, quick promotion – all measures she now found lacked value. So, she changed measures, spurning looks, happy families, 'A' class listings, mysterious men, and settled on amassing wealth. Secretly amassing wealth through Polonius, named for all the meddling hypocrites who'd consumed her career.

Molly called her favourite gallery to follow up an email she'd sent about rotating some of her collection. With more light in her apartment as winter merged with spring, she wanted works which better complemented the blues of Lake Burley Griffin. The gallery could deliver them on Friday.

She missed her whisky with Johnny Koh, toasted him, until next time.

Operation Rose continues.

One week into Operation Rose, most of the time had been consumed with making sure the new operation protocols worked, sifting information for intelligence, checking the reliability of the triage team's decisions. One of Ethics Australia's Assistant Commissioners supervised the team analysing crowd sourced data using the UK analytics software, GUIDE, Group User Information Decision Engine.

Harriet Cooper, Mick Darby, and their senior leaders reviewed what they had. While all were competent users of the latest intelligence, machine driven data collation, forensic and investigation technology, it had to come together for people. They also saw the value of simple questions, face to face, not shy of complexity but shy of complications.

Although the invitation for information went out only to residents and family of Asher House, volumes of data were logged. Much had nothing to do with Asher House.

Mick was unimpressed, 'Harriet, I'm not sure this is working for us now, maybe we just get on with it, and play with this stuff when we're done? We're getting so much crap, even stories and photos of sick old ladies in Belgium for fuck's sake!'.

Harriet gave him her full judicial stare, penetrating Mick's, at times, obtuse skull.

The group disbanded, review finished, priorities set. Harriet motioned for Mick to stay.

'There's a lot to follow up,' said Mick, 'Will this take long?'

'As long as it takes,' said Harriet, 'Crap? Lines of text and a photo, a story sent by her daughter, of a woman's final days in a poorly run nursing home in Belgium, not crap, Mick. Not to the woman, not to her daughter, not to me, and not to you. It is not relevant to us, irrelevant does not make it crap. This is show stopping time Mick.

We don't need your insensitivity to do our job really well. These people believe in you, busting their arses for you Mick. Operation Rose, Mick. Named after a woman you met. Or have you forgotten that? Because they,' she pointed out towards the floor, 'they haven't.'

Mick brooded, sulked for a bit. He'd often thought, hoped really, his dismissive, cavalier approach to taking or ruining a life gave him focus, discipline.

'It's my way of coping, denial,' said Mick. 'Used to work. Now, it gives me nightmares.'

'You're in decay, Mick, way past denial.'

'Decay?'

'Denial for so long. Deny yourself, you betray yourself. That's decay. Would you talk to Bain about this? If you don't want to go to your inhouse counsellor?

'Yes,' he said, 'good idea.' It was important to him that Harriet should know he was taking accountability. He couldn't risk being lost to Harriet.

'Call him now, make the appointment. We're not going to be able to do all this without you.'

. . . .

The leader of the GUIDE team made a demanding task look easy. With her brilliant legal mind and background, and her logic puzzle expertise, she had won international competitions. These skills combined to provide her team with quick decisions. Her mastery of language meant she generated alternative search words more quickly than they could search, creating links between unconnected data, all the while building the case. She was the wood for their trees.

The team trawled photos, videos, text from Asher House residents, families and visitors who'd used their mobile phones apps to communicate with each other, sharing experiences. They found recordings of Australian Health Minister visits to facilities, opening them, launching new programs. They saw the facilities before and after ministerial visits, where Asher House had called in stylists from a local real estate office to dress the rooms the minister would visit. All the plants, cushions, artwork, occasional furniture pieces were retrieved the same afternoon, returning the rooms to their weary dinginess.

Armed with Medicare records of physician visits to Asher House they went looking for these doctors, physios, dentists, medicos, and found few matches between claimed and actual visits. They saw evidence of groups of residents singing and clapping to Asher Ministries music while the daily schedule showed individual physiotherapy sessions, logged, copied to investigators. They saw bowls of unrecognisable food, residents in disposable and clearly re-used lobster bibs. Over days of viewing and reading they saw few staff, the staff to resident ratios they calculated differed significantly to the information provided by Asher House facilities. The software was proving its value.

Located in the middle of the floor for Operation Rose, the triage team analysts had to make consistent decisions; it was critical that they made the same decision each time they judged an incident to be referred to another agency or pursued by Ethics Australia. They also had to be impartial to avoid flawed judgement about the weight of each incident.

Paradoxically to some, Harriet deliberately staffed triage team with analysts of different backgrounds and expertise, ensuring different opinions. They were also trained in how to work as a multidisciplinary team, structuring their discussions to mitigate the influence of the loudest voice or the highest rank.

The team's reliability was one hundred percent, which meant whichever pair at the desk conducted the triage assessment, the result was the same, this one for us, that incident to Medicare, one here for Tax Australia. If they were unsure who best to deal with a suspected offense it went to all the possible interested parties. They did their best to mitigate the risk of interagency jealousy by calling the officers sent the material and socialising the evidence, also letting each know who else had it.

· · · ·

A t the end of week four analysts were still assessing the information they had. More reports of complaints about Asher Ministries had come to Noopur, then the triage team, and majority referred to other agencies. With the all-consuming desk work, logging data, verifying, and validating, the teams were keen to be out of the office. Instead, Harriet brought them all together for an update.

She had Mick begin with a reassurance about the value of desk work, the data collection records and the checking, slow build of data into evidence.

'Remember,' he stressed, 'Darby's Law of Investigation – the art and the science of screwing around with the little things until a big one jumps out.'

Harriet stepped in, 'OK, let's start with where are we starting from this week? Noopur, would you take us through what you have please?'

'The team have finished their analysis of the data retrieved from Keith Evan's flash drive. We have compared our data against his files and clearly he has manipulated the data. In Asher nursing homes and retirement villages, you die early.'

'Noopur,' said Alex, 'we have more background on that, how people are treated in the Asher nursing homes.

'Can you take us through it?' she asked.

'We're looking at the effects of corruption when we look inside the nursing homes,' said Alex. 'We inspected one and we've desk research on the others. Food orders, laundry services, resident bank accounts, phone records, staff comings and goings.'

'What,' said Zoe, 'you've been through one of the places?'

'Discreetly, yep, ' said Alex, thumbing his iPad, 'all the material is here.'

Monitors lit up, phones and tablets vibrated, 'you'll see it's all under five headings of abuse.'

'Abuse? You are that certain?'

'Yep,' said Alex, 'it's the only polite word for it.'

'Alex,' said Harriet, 'your recommendation?'

'Two,' said Alex, 'First, we take another look at one of their nursing homes. Just to be completely certain, confirm what we know now. Second, we close them down. Not us, ACT Health will close them down.'

'Why ACT Health?'

'Well, it's their patch, their call,' said Alex, he put his hand up, 'yeah, I know, why haven't they done it before? Simply because the Lang's political connections and their lawyers made it impossible.'

'How long to organise a close down?'

'I've taken a few liberties,' said Alex.

'Some prominent people have relatives in Asher. Should we let them know in advance?'

'No,' said Alex.

Mick Darby added, 'we've met with ACT Health, they need twenty four hours' notice. There are hundreds of hospital beds around Canberra as part of an emergency response, say a terrorist attack. Seriously equipped, staff on standby, ambulances; the lot. Police will contact next of kin, explain visiting hours etc.'

'I'm sending to you this minute more details of a plan,' said Alex and screens changed again, 'the Asher House assets will be frozen. Then ACT Health do a deep clean, and reopen with their staff, and they'll take on suitable Asher people. It's all set to go, once we agree.'

'Thanks Alex, this is very thorough. Let's get back to Noopur, we can make all the decisions based on all we know.'

Harriet looked to Alex sitting low in his chair, head down, 'Alex?'

'I'm good,' he said straightening, 'bit of a relief to get it all out.'

Noopur stood, 'so, we can compare Asher House to other providers. Moving on, the forensic team have suspicious transactions, hundreds of them just under the $10,000. Dozens of accounts, layers of different banks and credit unions, all Asher Ministries, and related entities.'

'What are you thinking, 'said Mick, 'got enough to bring some of them in?'

'I'd like nothing better,' said Noopur, thinking that Darby came in about the money, not the abuse, 'especially after hearing Alex's evidence, what they're doing to people. But we need enough to make it stick, so no-one can get them out of it.'

'I'm with you in this Noopur,' said Alex, 'our guys have never seen money so heavily layered. It needs to be uncovered.'

'We have a trust fund,' said Noopur, nodding at Alex, 'where the sole beneficiary is Hudson Lang, the fund trustee is a medical group. We suspect that group are fraudulently invoicing for an impossibly high number of services, all Asher House. I'll take any questions, observations. Then it's Zoe.'

There were a few questions of detail, references to the summaries displayed on the wall monitors, tallies of amounts in the various accounts. Millions.

'While we're talking money,' said Zoe. 'Hudson Lang is chasing small change, compared to what we've just seen. It's not so much about the money here, but it's more about how the guy operates. A clinical trial of monitoring residents remotely ran in Asher House nursing homes. Called,' she checked her notes, 'Detect and Alert, all the gear supplied by the Commonwealth, free to Asher. There are complaints about residents being charged for the technology. Complainants got their money refunded and the error was excused under poor record keeping.'

'Ian Sturgess, Chief Scientist, conducted the trial. It's finished now and according to some of the complainants, the trial end supposedly added to the paperwork confusion at Asher House. We can find nothing about the clinical trial, even our hackers couldn't. No records.'

'Sturgess?' Mick said, 'we do want to know more about him.' And he told the group of the Sturgess connection to Molly Lavandar, 'there are a few coincidences about that guy. What do you think? I think the Detect and Alert thing is basically OK. Is there any trace of the next phase though, any reference to social robots?'

'Robots? No, nothing,' said Zoe.

'Keep looking,' said Mick, 'these robots are the clincher. We freeze his money, the lawyers'll have it back to him before it hurts. Medicare fraud? Double dipping? Might snare a few underlings. No, to get Lang, I want him with the robots, assistive robots; suspicion of unlawful surveillance, cybersecurity offences.'

'Ok,' said Zoe, 'we'll keep on it. We keep going with the other lines too though, right?' she looked to Harriet.

'Yes,' said Harriet, 'nothing is going on hold.'

The Hudson Lang connection to money intrigued them. Asher Ministries had been reported for numerous breaches of its not-for-profit status.

While the investigations found evidence of inadequate governance oversight, failure to manage conflict of interest and chaotic records management, the regulator's response had been to recommend Asher Ministries review their governance framework. No follow up was conducted to determine if the framework had been reviewed.

Mick Darby was scathing in his assessment of the regulator, 'What the fuck is a governance framework anyway?'

Even newcomers recognised it as a rhetorical question, if indeed it was a question. Charities Australia had lost credibility with a restructure of its own governance framework. A new position of Chair established, and the appointment of the first Chair added to the controversy. The government had ignored the unanimous recommendation of the selection panel and appointed an ex-government minister to the position. The former minister had few links to charities. Her media release cited her guest speaker roles at various Asher Ministries functions as evidence of her charitable connections.

Her most important internal structural change was to undermine the independent role of the Commissioner of Charities Australia. The Chair now had final approval of all investigations into charities, terms of reference, and of any regulatory action recommended at the conclusion of an investigation. In weeks, the Chair had unduly interfered in investigations, had authorised no telephone intercepts, required proof of criminality as the threshold for complaint investigation, and further ingratiated herself with the Prime Minister. It was another example of the reach of Asher Ministries.

Harriet's meeting concluded that their investigation would retrace some of the steps of the Charities regulator, so included the financial management of Asher Ministries in Operation Rose.

The group moved to decide their next action where more team members were put to researching Ian Sturgess and Hudson Lang. Interception warrants were approved for Sturgess and Lang's mobile phones and land lines, including the landlines at Asher Ministries.

Harriet had the investigation teams brought together. She reassured them of the value of rechecking, matching witness statements against documentation. She asked not to take rank, privilege, and political connections as anything other than that. Rank is just rank, status just status, it does not go to trust or credibility.

'We are investigating whether there are grounds to issue summons for a private examination or public hearing into the behaviour of these people, Ian Sturgess, Hudson and Phoebe Lang, Frank Riccini. Have they acted corruptly? Our, your investigations so far, give me confidence to keep going.'

'These people live conceit. We are beginning to see through it – to expose what they are concealing with money, religion, science, status. We are starting to unravel the deceit. When we get to issue summonses, assuming we get that far, we will want them to see themselves for who they are, to see their deceit. Who are they without status and money? That's what we will want to know, and that's what we want them to answer. Noopur, is that it, I've covered everything?'

Officers turned to look at Noopur, thumbing a touchpad, wall monitor scrolling through actions, 'site visit, inspection to an Asher House? Decision need on that.'

'Alex, ' asked Harriet, 'you had a recommendation.'

'Thanks,' said Alex, 'I was thinking one more visit. If it confirms, we get ACT Health to close them all, they have their plan.'

Harriet nodded to Noopur, 'thanks, write that one up; Alex, down to you.'

Harriet's thoughts.

Canberra was built on a sheep station 'a good sheep station wasted', was a line repeated by every smartarse. The buildings holding Australia's federal politicians and the accompanying bureaucracy were built on land where sheep were shorn, slaughtered, skinned. Harriet imagined the spirits of the dead sheep inhabiting the buildings, rendering the occupant's sheep – subservient – now, to the dogs of the religious right.

The image bothered her as she ran through the ethics of the Asher investigations. She felt compromised. Her mother who died in a nursing home played on her mind, her own animosity to Asher Ministries and its ubiquitous hold over craven politicians and bureaucrats, difficult to keep in check, lending a personal and political agenda to Operation Rose. She'd authorised intelligence activities, signed interception warrants, and back dated surveillance approvals, convincing herself and those around her of the necessity to break some moral conventions to expose corrupt behaviour.

She asked herself her shock-jock question. If it became public knowledge that we knew all this, no matter how we got the information, and had done nothing; how would she be judged? She decided the public view would be she had dishonoured her office.

Her husband had their dinner ready for when she was driven home, and now he joined her bes
ide the perfectly lit fire, glass of red in hand.

Harriet met him when he was Principal Trumpet for Opera Queensland, and she was new to law. Now, he's the Principal Conductor of a regional Symphony Orchestra. He'd seen her in court once years ago, performing for the jury. He thought her mastery of gesture and eye contact far superior to his.

Harriet loved the time in the theatre before the performance began. Generally, alone, she sat to the front, relaxed as the musicians wandered on stage one by one, sometimes two together. Around them the harp was wheeled out, four of the burlier players might wrestle the Imperial Bosendorfer grand piano into position for a special performance. The double bass was nearest the stage exit, players perched on stools, fitting the endpin at the last minute. All dressed in black, they sat with their instruments, played a note here, part of a scale there, adjusted the instrument, smoothed their skirts, hitched their pants, checked buttons and the noise built, bubbled into the theatre. Combination of warming up, tuning, getting the posture right, it was a tableau of the musicians of Bremen she thought.

And then first violin stood, silence, tuned to the oboe, followed by each instrument, then whole orchestra. Chaos into order. And her husband arrived on stage, bowed to the audience, turned his back, shook hands with first violin and the magic began.

Harriet turned to her husband, took the glass, 'just what I need, thanks.'

'Oh, yours is here.'

'Why do you have a first violin and I don't?'

'It's not about music is it?'

'If it is,' said Harriet, 'it'd be the music of Schoenberg.' They laughed together, dissonance a feature of both their professional lives. Harriet told him a little of everything about Operation Rose. Mostly she talked of her concerns about Mick Darby.

'Remember what that guy said about dementia, can't recall his name, ordinarily that would be unremarkable, in this context though... He said something about the purpose of the disease was to remind us to think well of each other and of our lives.'

'I do remember the conversation, not the man – an author maybe?' Harriet frowned.

'His mother was diagnosed, and in the deterioration, she would have only the one conversation, for three years or more. He thought after ninety good years, she remembered only one event, one conversation – playing out her one bad memory until her forever ended. He talked about how every illness had a purpose. With dementia, it was to only have good memories so that if the day comes and we have only one event, one experience to play over and over, then better make it a good memory, one that will make us smile.'

'Why are we talking about good memories?'

'We are talking about one,' he nudged her elbow. 'These complaints about aged care, nursing homes. You're always passionate about your work, I just wonder if there's a little more to this inquiry though, you've changed your screen saver to a photo of your mum, you're maybe a little more reticent that usual.'

'Guilty as charged, of guilt as well. It was the same when the Productivity Commission reports came out a few years ago. I remember thinking what if Mum had been treated that badly? And then I realise that I don't know that she wasn't. I didn't see her often, I didn't ask for any of her records, didn't question ...'

'Harriet.' he broke her reverie.

She put her hand on his arm, 'you don't think it's is about the music, nor about Mick, do you?'

'Not all of it.'

'Silly, isn't it? It's done,' she said. 'You know I used to hate driving over there to see her, hated being there listening to her ask when her father was coming back to get her, he said he would be here by now, and I hated leaving her. That was the memory she played out for her last four or so years, her only words with me. So, yes it plays on my mind.'

He leaned over and kissed the top of her head, got up to change the music and refill their glasses.

Harriet mulled over this conversation about her mother. Pleased that she could do this and not second guess her decision to use some ethically questionable methods. She'd called the investigation

'Operation Rose' as a reminder that the behaviours being investigated were harmful to people.

Bain interviews Mai.

Mai sat at the only table in the room. To her left and behind her, in front of a door, stood a uniformed officer, arms crossed in front of her body. Bain entered the room through another door which opened in front of Mai.

Detained for the twenty-four hours following her appearance at Keith Evan's house, Mai had been released under surveillance. Her outburst when told of Evan's injuries, and her initial reference to Judee led Alex to assume she was innocently involved with Keith, and maybe manipulated by the Asher Ministries' pastor. However, that view changed when she said nothing in the twenty-four hours. Before she was released her house was searched to reveal $15,000 cash and an unregistered firearm. Her laptop screensaver featured her photographed with a rifle, standing between two men also holding firearms. All three were wearing 'Magdalene Saves' T shirts.

Mick Darby and Alex Briggs were now open to the possibility they were dealing with a violent gang. Two men had assaulted Keith Evans, a group of men threatened police officers who responded to the tipoff about the house those two had driven to, and now Mai, who may help confirm a group.

• • • •

Mick and Alex had observed Mai's first interview where she was informed of the charges related to possession of an unlicensed firearm. She had remained defiant and curt. The gun must have been her boyfriend's as she had never seen it, same with the money.

'What money? I've never seen any money either.'

'This money. Fifteen thousand dollars.' Reaching behind and placing the money now marked as an exhibit.

'Where was that?'

'In your house.'

'Well, that's good.'

'Why?'

'Because I could do with fifteen grand.'

'So, you have seen this before.'

'No, but you said it was mine, I may as well have it then.'

'So, you could tell us how the money came to be in your house?'

'How the fuck would I know, you said it was mine, not me, but I'm happy to get it.'

At this point the record of interview features a breathless silence, followed by a scraping of chairs, '1009 hours, interview suspended.' The video shows two officers leaving the room.

'Bet they wish it were the good old days, eh? No chance of losing this video,' said Alex, 'it'll be in the interview training sessions from now on.'

'Yeah,' said Mick, 'clowns, we're fucked.'

'You don't want to interview her?' said Alex.

'Mate, we can't,' said Mick, 'we're not even supposed to be here. Feds let us in as a favour. That was their best shot, she won't talk now.'

'As soon as she asks for a lawyer, or one turns up, she'll be out. Just because the guns were in her house doesn't mean they're hers. Do we have a choice Mick?'

'Where's Bain?' said Mick.

· · · ·

Thomas,' said Mick, 'she's all we have. Let me show you her interview, see what you think?'

'You want my thoughts on that?' asked Bain as the screen showed the two officers leaving the room.

'Mate, I need you to interview her.'

'I know nothing about her,' said Bain.

'None of us do,' said Mick. 'Thing is that Alex and I are not here, she,' he pointed his thumb at the screen, 'is logged in. Alex and I are not, way out of jurisdiction and no chance of getting paperwork in time for us to talk to her. You, though, you're an expert interrogator, and I can get immediate authorisation from the Feds for you, you're a civilian. You got us this far with Evans, now with his girlfriend, you're our best shot.'

'OK, I'm in,' said Bain, 'can you play that interview again please?' Bain studied the interview four more times, took notes. Darby came back with the authorisation,

Bain prepared to spend most of this interview listening, usually at least a third of an interview was building the rapport, establishing a relationship that made it easier for participants to talk about events that may incriminate them. Mai was a player and Thomas was looking to assess whether her decisions and behaviour were influenced by social groups to which she belonged. He had two groups of interest. Asher Ministries? And were the two men with whom she'd posed for the photograph with weapons, members of a group, was she?

He had to get Mai talking before he could challenge her, as the first interview had proven, challenging her first up would probably make her more defiant.

• • • •

She greeted him with, 'are you plan A or plan B?'

'I'm Thomas Bain,' he said, smiling as he sat.

'Keith talked about you,' she said and stopped.

Thomas waited and said, 'He's not doing any talking now, day four of his coma, he is badly hurt.'

'I had nothing to do with that.'

'Others were planning to hurt him?'

'No.'

'Do you know, do you think you might know what their plan was? Maybe it didn't turn out the way it was planned, and...'

'No one told me anything about hurting him. It was those dickheads next door raided for drugs, they caused it when the cops came. It wasn't the plan.'

'So, could you tell me a little about the plan? How would you have planned it differently?'

Mai snorted, 'You think they'd let a girl do the planning? Can I get out of here now?'

'Sure,' said Thomas, 'this officer will take you out of here whenever you want.'

'So, I can go?'

'Sure. Your call - you can stay here or in your room.'

'That's not a fucking choice!' Screaming now and leaning towards Thomas, the officer took a step forward.

'He's blown it now,' said Alex to Mick, observing.

'So, what do you think you'll do?' Bain asked her.

'Well, I don't have much of a choice, do I?'

'Is that how you felt about the plan, they didn't give you much of a choice? The guys who went to Keith's house?'

'I hardly know him; he came around to the house in the morning to get Jackson. All he wanted to know was did I know where Keith would hide stuff. I didn't so they left. They were in a hurry, they had to meet Hudson Lang at the Hub and couldn't be late. Nearly hit a car coming the other way he was going so fast.'

'Jackson?'

'No, the other guy, I don't know his name, just seen him at the Hub a few times.'

'Fast cars; Lexus.'

'What?'

'They were seen driving away from Keith's after bashing him. A couple reported a speeding car, it just missed them, registration, police found it at an address in Garran. I thought Jackson may have mentioned that.'

'I haven't seen him since Friday night, I've been in here remember?'

'Did Jackson mention he was leaving the pistol at your place?'

'Jesus, the gun again, it's not mine. Maybe he left it there.'

'So, I'm a bit confused. Maybe it's confusing for you too? The pistol was found at your place, may be Jackson's may not be, and it's not yours. You don't have a license so it can't be yours, right? Nobody knows who owns it because it's not registered. Confusing right?'

'You're right, it's doing my head in,' she said.

'It's not all confusing though is it; you know the gun was found with your fingerprints on it, in your house, in your drawer with your underwear.'

'Bet you fucking loved that – a shrink with a gun in my panties! Was it smoking? Get off on that did you?'

'Well, it was helpful.'

'Helpful!' She snarled. 'Helpful! It wouda been helpful if you'd gone into the fucking Lake, like you were supposed to.' She was standing now, fists clenched, knuckles down on the table.

'Bastards,' said Alex.

'Yeah,' said Mick, 'good to get that confirmed, another charge.'

Bain sat still. Mai sat immobile with her legs straight to the floor, arms straight to the desk, Bain figured he had plenty of time to move out of her way if he needed to. He waited another ten seconds.

'Soft material,' he said, 'helps preserve fingerprints. Did you pose with the pistol? See how fast you get it out of the drawer, aim at the mirror...'

Mai stood, straightened, sat, shrugged and rested her hands beside her, on her seat.

'Not much point, it's not loaded or anything.'

'Were you thinking about hurting or harming yourself?'

'Nah, anyone would pretend...I mean when you get a gun in your hand, you know.'

'Take a few selfies with it?'

Her face crumbled; bottom lip trembled.

She looked about five years old thought Bain.

'You have my phone? Has anyone called?'

'I can find out,' he offered.

She shook her head.

'Mai, so, have you ever had thoughts about hurting or harming yourself? Maybe when you're posing with the gun?'

Again, she shook her head.

'Have you ever had thoughts about hurting or harming anybody else? Thought about it, while pointing the pistol, the rifles?'

'Well, sometimes, I mean, anyone would. It's how they train the army to shoot isn't it? Think about a target, someone to fire at, to make it real you know.'

'Army training?'

'Well, that's what Jackson reckons, that's how he was trained.'

'So, you've thought about it, tempting, with a rifle in your hands, hearing Jackson's advice. Do you want to hurt someone? Do you think you might?' Bain, still, listening, observing, focused on identifying the problems, the risks Mai posed. 'Have you hurt someone before – not with a gun?'

'Some girls in school, they deserved it.'

'Sometimes people do deserve what comes their way, how come these girls...'

'A new high school, trying to fit in, and Asian, people think Canberra is a tolerant place because people here are from everywhere, but it's not, is it?'

A little later he stopped the interview for a break. Mai was taken back to her room, lunch provided. Meanwhile Mick and Alex had fed the information about Jackson through to their team, they had names and an address now, including a 100-acre property out of Canberra.

Mick, Alex, Thomas met Harriet briefly, quickly highlighting the interview results. Mick proposed handing over everything they had including transcripts of interviews with Mai to the federal police. It was up to them to liaise with NSW as the Killimicat property was outside the ACT.

'It'll be useful to have some of Hudson's own pressure him,' said Mick, 'and he's not used to dealing with police.

He'll find them not as easy to slip away from as bureaucrats, politicians and his eager devotees.'

'And Mai,' said Alex, 'the unlicensed pistol, photos of herself with it in her house and on her laptop, fingerprints all over it – it's a big charge. Thomas what did you make of her? By the way mate, I thought you'd lost her there for a minute, but no, great work.'

'Thanks mate. My impressions, I'll prepare a report with some caveats. If it helps confirm your decision to hand her over the police, I agree. Left on her own she may be a risk to herself. Left with Jackson she may be at risk herself. Emotionally, adds to that really, you saw her in there, emotionally expressive at times where she demonstrated anger and anxiety. No empathy or concern for Keith, showing a lack emotional depth, lack of remorse for her part in the assault.'

'Mate,' said Alex, 'English, remember Mick's a Queenslander. How did you not react when she mentioned the Lake? Reckon that was the cyclist she was talking about?'

'You know, I missed it when she said that, I think I got it a few seconds later,' he grinned.'

'You showed her great respect Thomas,' said Mick, 'a lesson for us all. Mai? Your thoughts on her, before Alex interrupted you, or were you done?'

'I get the sense it's important to her to feel part of a group – two groups – the singing dancing Asher Ministries and the shooting bashing Jackson and his mates. Feeling part of a group, but not sharing their goals, She's not an organiser. All up – it speaks to her vulnerability, she's safer in custody, albeit monitored for self-harm.'

Asher Ministries' Directors.

O ne element of Operation Rose was a coordinated investigation of the directors of Asher Ministries with other agencies. Tax Australia's fraud investigators were eager players. So far, they had found irregularities in the land sold to Asher Ministries, around fifty hectares throughout Canberra and Queanbeyan, land now built on by Asher House. The owner of the real estate company was a director of Asher Ministries.

Background checks and preliminary investigations mainly desk audits, into the other directors had also commenced. All were actively involved in local and national politics, some office bearers, some on preselection panels. All prominent members of Asher Ministries. All company owners, their businesses innocent enough; a luxury car dealer, an ex-banker turned finance expert with lucrative media contracts and government advisory roles, and the owner of a labour hire company in the health care industry. The odd one out, because he lived in Sydney and had no business interests in Canberra was Frank Riccini. Riccini and his companies owned extensive property and companies in a string of proximate suburbs – Balmain, Rozelle, Five Dock, Leichhardt, and Petersham. Apartment blocks, cafes, restaurants, factories, commercial offices, warehouses, service stations – he was all over the inner west. An old-fashioned bricks and mortar businessman, struggling a little as most of his business interests ran a loss, and publicity shy – especially compared to his fellow directors of Asher Ministries.

Asher Ministries' directors rang each other, compared notes on who was showing an interest in their companies. Those who had been tempted to follow Hudson and shun Bailey now sought his advice. Some had their residences checked for surveillance equipment and found some. Their lawyers aggressively threatened exposure of government spying on the family homes of innocent and successful businessmen. Tax Australia's chief investigator asked for Mick Darby's guidance.

'Your blokes have done very well,' Mick began, 'to provoke them, a regular hornet's nest. Let's get them in and be very open with them. Those bugs are not mine and not yours. Offer to run a forensic investigation on the devices, offer to share the results with them, establish a proper evidence trail.'

'I'd go further,' he continued, 'let them know you are investigating some suspected conflicts of interest between some related entities of Asher Ministries. The agency has been investigating any involvement they might have; tell them you are interested in how they discharge their duties as directors of Asher Ministries.'

'Yes mate, let them bring in their lawyers too. It simply reinforces you have nothing to hide, just going about your business. You're gently putting them between their own interests and Hudson Lang's. Don't forget he chose them because they are venal, now, his choices may be to our advantage.'

. . . .

Frank's local business friends and associates had left the timing of their plan to him. His loss-making businesses depended on some help from Tax Australia officers, many of them now senior, and news of the agency's interest in Asher directors had reached Frank. He judged the timing was right and launched step one.

He'd arranged to meet the Asher Ministries' accountant out of Canberra. They drove to Hall separately, bought some sandwiches and sat at an ageing bench table. Frank put a cooler bag on the table and said, 'I wasn't sure what you drink so instead I came with $50,000 and an all-fees scholarship for your daughter's high school education. Most exclusive girl's school in Canberra. Think of the contacts she'll make, set her up for life, best musical coaching.'

She sat there, mouth open. She wanted to breathe, to vomit, to run and use the toilet all at the same time. Frank just sat until she was breathing more normally.

'It's like this,' he said, 'these characters at the tax office look at Hudson, see the deals he's involved in. Many of them involve you as well. They don't look at these deals the same way Hudson does.'

'What do you mean they involve me?'

'You sign all the paperwork; the papers Hudson submits, the few returns he submits, are prepared on your computer. I know he sits beside you and tells you what to enter, but they don't know that. You are listed on all Asher Ministries official documents as the company secretary. Hudson, Phoebe and their trust funds are the owners. You witnessed their dealings. You are the responsible officer.'

Her eyes widened, her hands covered her mouth. He should have arranged for someone to drive her home; he did that now while she sat trembling. A car crash – a literal one anyway, was not what he wanted.

Frank, at his most avuncular, introduced her to her future. A whistle-blower was needed, the investigators had to be stopped somewhere, and a whistle-blower with the quality information she had would see the end of the investigations. He explained how she would claim immunity for her and for him as the board Chair – for he had been deceived too. In return she would tell not quite all. He would have experts coach her in how to handle questioning, coach her in identifying and beating their tricks. The money and the scholarship were hers now.

The weather turned and they moved to Frank's car, where he went through it all again. She asked him, 'what's an investigator's trick?'

'To stay silent after you have said something, in the hope you will say something more. Most people will keep on talking because they can't handle the silence. To beat that, you just don't talk. Now, I know you can do that.'

'My ex used to tell me all the time that I didn't say anything.'

'Just pretend the investigator is your ex.'

'I hit him once!'

Frank laughed, 'when I said beat them, I didn't mean beat them.'

She laughed and opened the bag.

· · · ·

A couple of days later the accountant experienced some of what Frank talked about that day in the Hall Park. She was about ready to leave for Asher Ministries, easier as her daughter had gone already. Downing the last of her coffee, straightening her jacket, one final glance in the mirror, then keys etc. The doorbell rang, followed by loud knocking.

She opened it to two men in suits, brandishing ID wallets, 'Tax Australia, you'll let us in.'

'I don't have time for this, I'm...'

'I think you'll find you do.'

She heard only a few words, 'investigating the not-for-profit status of Asher Ministries...understand you are the accountant ...some irregularities...we're sure they won't take long to clear up.'

She was frightened. One of the documents she completed with Hudson telling her how to respond, was the self-evaluation of not-for-profit. As Frank said, her name and not Hudson's, her computer.

One of the suits, took a step back from her, 'I can see this visit may have upset you, let's come back at a time you decide. For reasons which may be obvious, and which will become more obvious, we'd rather not talk with you at your office. Anywhere else would be fine.'

They both wished her a good day, business cards on the console table beside the front door and left. Ten minutes later, far away from the accountant's regular route to the office, one of the men used his mobile.

'Yes,' said Frank. His follow up message delivered.

Frank also took a call from the accountant as she drove to her office. He was anxious on her behalf, concerned about her welfare, and delighted her account of the men's intrusion matched theirs perfectly. An accountant who may be trusted – at least when scared enough. He listened to her account, asked her to repeat some of it and congratulated her. On the phone Frank told her of the arrangements he had made for her to be coached in handling the questioning that would follow her whistleblowing. He didn't think she'd need much coaching; she had stood up to these two characters well.

'Also, as whistle-blower you'll not be bothered by this kind of interruption. They'll play very nicely because of your value to them. These characters today must be quite junior if they thought being abrasive is a useful tactic.'

The Purchase Order.

There are some warning signs of imminent threat to one's career which even the least astute employees do not ignore. But this employee wasn't astute, and it was Friday afternoon. She despatched the order. Purchase Order 350410E for forty-five million dollars of domestic sensory and monitoring technology. Paperwork accompanying the order had been amended and the total amount, not half, was to be paid upfront. The memo explained the change request curtly, as the government intended to spend around $100 million on the technology, the forty-five was in effect the fifty percent upfront fee. Both the purchase order and the change request had been initiated and approved by Ian Sturgess, Chief Scientist.

The despatch of the order triggered the transfer of the money into the Polonius account. Thus, activating the first of a series of transfers of the money until it was split, and the smaller amounts safe in more than fifty different accounts. The money was cleared by the time the procurement clerk swiped her pass out of the building. The purchase order was left to languish in an unused email account.

Excited, Hudson opened his laptop and the ElderTech online account and waited for the deposit – fifty percent of forty-five million dollars. An impressive return for his two million investment, and there was more to come. The purchase order would divert to the overseas supplier, the technology would arrive in Australia. Aged care facilities would pick up what they needed, all the installation, and maintenance handled by local providers throughout every electorate – a small and important consideration. Hudson knew the money would not be cleared right away but knew to expect the amount in the account.

Over the weekend Hudson' surprise grew to despair, then anger. Blakeley didn't have a phone that worked. He'd been surprised to see Jackson and his mate at the service. Jackson and his crazy hacker mate had sorted Keith Evans for him. Pity they didn't find the flash drive.

'Boys.' He welcomed them backstage. Surprised to see them both. 'Good to see you here.'

'Yeah, we want our money, you're a few days late, and we had to put up with your shit music.'

Hudson had a ready explanation, for which they had no time.

'No Hud – none of your bullshit, just the fucking money tomorrow night, plus fifty percent, a hundred grand. Today, we'll take what you collected in cash. And, we'll be back for the rest, from now each week as we agreed.'

Jackson divided the cash, close to $100,000 equally between the two of them and left for the Majura rifle range. Their membership and regular attendance there proving excellent cover for their own range and clubhouse on a hundred acres of bush near Killimicat.

Hudson had thought he had some grace to pay these guys, the money he was to pay them gone to Nigel Blakeley, who had assured him he'd have twenty-two million dollars in a few days. The few days were now a week, and now frantic to get hold of the bureaucrat monitoring the transfer, he drove to his house. There, complications seemed to overwhelm Hudson. The bureaucrat said the system holding procurement records and accounts could not be accessed remotely, they'd have to drive to the office, and he had his two small kids with him as his wife was at a lunch with some girlfriends, on a weekend he could not get Hudson a temporary pass. Hudson – one-minute charming the next abusive, the kids began to cry, Hudson yelled for him to shut them up, then apologised, needing forgiveness.

They decided to drive to the Commonwealth office, stopping on the way for ice creams for the children at Hudson's insistence, but they're not used to sugar, they'll spill it on the seats, their mother will find out.

'Jesus,' screamed Hudson, 'it's just a fucking ice cream.'

Hudson sat with the kids and their ice creams while their father logged into the building, logged onto the system, printed out the purchase order and the money transfer. He'd have time to get rid of Hudson now he had what he wanted, clean the car, bath the kids, all before his wife's lunch finished.

He logged out, nodded to the security, got in his car, and gave the papers to Hudson, who read them carefully, and sat, trembling until the car was turned off, the children asleep lifted out and taken inside. When their dad came back out of the house, Hudson was gone. 'Thanks for your help,' said the bureaucrat to no-one.

• • • •

Back home Hudson decided on a run, got his gear on, decided on a swim instead, changed, changed his mind again and rang Frank. Frank could not take the call he was told, Sunday lunch at the Riccini's was never interrupted. He rang again until he suspected his number was blocked. He called the Asher Ministries accountant who did come in. He told her what he needed, and she complied, transferring money from a couple of different Asher accounts into Hudson's personal account. She suggested to Hudson it would be prudent to have him email her the instructions, and an explanation for the transfer.

'Just dictate it to me,' she said, 'and I'll write it up for the record.' So out of sorts was Hudson, he agreed and dictated a story about a personal loan approved by the Board.

• • • •

With the Purchase Order emailed to Polonius, Hudson assumed the money transferred there too. He desperately wanted the hackers by Frank to find the Polonius account, owners, and company directors. Google was no help, and neither were the various company databases Hudson could access.

Hudson started on a short pile of busywork to distract himself. Chef wanted him to finalise the guest list for the trial night at the restaurant, he wanted the names of eight invitees. Hudson thought two tables of eight for the night a better arrangement, so sent sixteen names, taking a little delight in how annoyed chef would be.

He remembered he'd dictated an email to the accountant, called her, leaving a curt message to delete it. He'd check her phone tomorrow to make sure. A little distracted he took a call before checking who had rung. It was his lawyer, the managing partner of the firm he used, successfully too. He was a month in arrears to them, and they wanted their money. Like the muscle earlier that day, and in much the same language. Although more eloquently delivered the lawyer said he didn't want an assurance. He wanted money transferred this afternoon.

That fucking Nigel Blakeley, Hudson thought not for the first time today. Again the cash for the lawyers had contributed to the ElderTech purchase. He hung up and authorised the transfer. The managing partner rang back to thank Hudson and invite him for lunch next Saturday on his boat, they would sail leisurely around the lake. Hudson asked him to think about anyone who may be interested in investing in a start-up technology firm.

By the end of that call Hudson had started to relax and to believe he could strategise his way to offload ElderTech, make his two million, maybe more. He also convinced himself that he could handle the muscle for their $200,000, maybe less, as they had taken the cash that morning.

Now he went for his run. He struggled through the 'dirty thirty', that first half hour of a run where the body screams 'stop' and began to enjoy the endorphins. By the time he was cooling off and nearly back he'd decided to keep ElderTech. He might be able to convince the procurement office of the value in having more than one supplier, ElderTech involvement in the clinical trial would give him some leverage. He also thought he could sell the technology to private aged care facilities, and he had connections now in Singapore so maybe there too. The two million was starting to look like a very astute spend again.

Bain Workshop follow-up.

'No,' said Alex, 'there's been no change. I was in there last night. No-one at the hospital is giving us any kind of indication. They are playing his playlists softly; they say it won't hurt.'

Thomas and Alex were interrupted at Alex's workstation as they caught up, operators asking about Keith. As he came out of the lifts at one end of the building, Thomas had swiped his card through another security door. From there the floor stretched out through workstations clustered in groups of four, partitioned at about shoulder height if you were sitting. The triage analysts held the middle of the room, beyond them a row of four offices along the far wall, Harriet's, Noopur's, the other two fitted out for meetings.

Alex's was the first workstation inside the secure door. He sat alone, no pod and no partition. Straight-backed chair, laptop, and phone on the desktop. If he moved away from the workstation, he took them with him, chair tucked under the table, squared away. Anyone on their way to the lift, the bathrooms, or getting a coffee passed by Alex.

Thomas was there to check in with the team, find out how they were going with the agreement they had made at the workshop. He'd been phoning team members to monitor if the agreement had been followed. This was his final call; he'd decided to come in as the agreement's final item had been actioned.

Alex rolled a coin across his knuckles, long delicate hands for an otherwise burly bloke. Thomas saw that the coin had the Holden badge on one side and Ford on the other. He asked about it.

'My dad gave it to me years ago,' said Alex, 'when everyone tells me things were simpler; choose your tribe, and, there were only two. So today, you go around the people, what do you ask them? When you phoned them over the last two months, how do you follow up that agreement, what do you look for?'

'Only one thing,' said Thomas, 'I just ask if they have followed the agreement. For each item in their agreement the team nominated someone whom I could call to check in with, we called them the follow up. Usually not the person responsible for the item. So, I'd call the follow up, ask if the item was actioned, and ask them how they knew it was complete.'

'Really? That's it? No chat, no interest in how they're going? I thought there may be some hand holding, counselling stuff involved there as well, it seemed to be a highly emotional day, that workshop.'

'My only interest is the action plan, the agreement – were they keeping to it or not? If I do any more than that I'd be part of their problem. It's their plan, their workplace, they have to make it work, my follow up is really just a short-term extra hand, like most people find it easier to stick to a change – gym, diet, smoking less if they have someone to nag them a little. That's me - chief nag.' They laughed.

'Mate, I think you may be more than that, I saw how you handled Mai after those two fools stuffed it up. No-one's touched your car?'

'No, nothing after that photo.'

Alex flipped his coin, came up Ford, 'maybe you should get a Mustang? We figure it was Jackson and his mate. Also stalking Harriet. Jackson has form, intimidation and harassment, and his mate, for whom we have three names, we think is a computer genius. We figure the hacker as the stalker, used photos of damaged property, did the photo of your car too, must say, it was an improvement. They are both missing, we can't find them, just a few card transactions in one of the three names.'

Noopur left her workstation, noticed them talking and walked over.

'Our two guardian angels,' she smiled. 'We're getting together for a heads-up, please – we'd like to have you there, it's only five minutes.'

The daily heads-up had started a few weeks earlier, a suggestion coming out of a team meeting. It started by listing what had to be completed that day and if any help was needed. Zoe's final question was about bottlenecks, anyone stuck? There were a few, no solutions were provided then, but all knew they'd be resolved right after the meeting. Zoe and her teams took the stairs to their floors.

Genelle and Vic were visiting the Asher House facility at Cook and signalled they had a few questions. Noopur invited Alex and Thomas in to hear them too. Security at aged care facilities was now strengthened. The only tangible outcome of the aged care inquiries: not better care staff to resident ratios, not better food, not better treatment – just that much harder to get in. Alex suggested using the navigators on the triage team, so they invited one of them to join them. Problem resolved, Genelle and Vic left for Cook.

Noopur explained their visit was a final scout as ACT Health was ready to close all Asher House aged care facilities. Ethics' role in this was not to be divulged. Ethics' practice was to investigate, gather all and any information they required, sort it for intelligence and evidence, and only then interview in private, or hold public hearings. Ethics Australia would stay out of the operation, not visible.

Alternative aged care placements were organised, medical and care staff, transport, phone calls to resident's next of kin scripted. Whistle-blowers were in witness protection. They had evidence of poor-quality food, fraudulent Medicare claims, mismanagement, unlawful staff to resident ratios, unqualified or low qualified staff in positions requiring qualifications, Asher Ministries' dance programs substituted for secular, evidence-based therapies, medication errors. All fraudulently documented. ACT Health would look after the residents, alternative accommodation, next of kin, and medical supplies. Federal Police would take care of the paperwork, computers, hard drives, security footage and send it to Ethics Australia.

Asher House raided.

Vic and Genelle opened the door of the Asher House aged care facility in Cook. They were met there by a uniform, an ill-fitting uniform, bothering no longer to disguise the belly.

'No access, Miss,' sneered Darrell, the name on his tag,; apparently no surnames were needed for this job, 'not without authorisation.'

Genelle made a quick phone call, read off the facility's phone number, folded her mobile.

'And this number rings...?' she asked.

The guard pointed to the wall.

'It's about to ring,' she said.

Genelle had called the triage desk, set up for Operation Rose. In ten days, everyone working on this operation swore by the value of this team. The team grew by two seconded officers, valuable old hands, these were the navigators. They responded to questions about authority, status, turf ownership – helping the operators find their way through the IEDs of interagency cooperation.

It was one of the navigators who called Darrell. Is this the same guy wondered Genelle, for now Darrell could not be more helpful, opening doors, offering tea, coffee? As they signed in, Vic asked if everyone had to sign in. 'Everyone,' said Darrell pleased to prove his value.

'Bet the medicos like that,' said Vic.

'They all have to sign in sir, no exceptions, no matter how many initials after their name - physicians, pharmacists, doctors, specialists, physios, dentists. All in that register.'

As they were talking Vic moved so that Darrell's back was to the register, which Genelle slipped into her tote bag. Denied access to resident rooms Vic and Genelle made a show of inspecting the common areas, wary of cameras. In the kitchen they were unobserved and Genelle took quick photos of each page of the register on her phone. Vic took a few photos of boxes of vegetable and fruit, just delivered and yet to be stored. He took a few more photos of boxes of canned food, lentils, chickpeas, crushed tomatoes. They were interrupted by a door opening and a young woman holding a heavy box, backing into the kitchen. Vic rushed to hold the door open, explaining their visit.

He helped her with the box, she unfolded a few pages and smoothed them out.

'Just the order,' she said, 'got to sign off each item against the paperwork. Making sure we don't pinch anything,' she scoffed, 'as if, it's all past its best-by anyway.'

Genelle photographed the itemised order while Vic helped again with another box still outside the kitchen door. 'My name's Hiba,' she said, 'are you guys here for Health and Safety, oh and Wellbeing.'

'You've had a few issues there have you?'

Hiba and Vic heard Darrell in the corridor, heavy cough, and a heavy tread, Hiba's eyes fearful. As they lifted a box of fruit onto the kitchen bench together Vic passed her a card, whispered, 'call that, I'll get it.'

They'd seen enough for now and thanked the kitchenhand, were escorted out to their car by Darrell.

'Shit, my phone,' said Genelle, 'must have slipped out, be right back.'

She was back in a minute, phone in hand and minus the register.

With Vic, Darrell was anxious their time had not been wasted.

'Oh, you know what it's like, mate,' said Vic, 'spend half your time ruling things out.'

Darrell nodded sagely, 'gotta be done.'

Back in their office Genelle and Vic logged their report of the Cook facility, including the photos, Hiba's name, and their observations. It took a long phone call to the medical centre Asher

House used in Cook, but Vic managed to get the list of all the physicians, health care providers on call to Asher House. They searched Genelle's photos of the register and found a doctor's name four times, a physio twice in the past eight weeks. No other names were on the list. Vic checked again with the medical centre verifying the names on the list were the only practitioners used.

They talked over their main findings with Noopur. The kitchen order form for fresh food was to a high-quality providore, the paperwork accompanying the received order was that of a cheap, bulk-buy food supplier. A sample of the canned food delivered while they were there was past best-by dates, Vic had photos of rows of canned food past best-before dates.

At first glance the tip-off about food quality and ghost medico visits confirmed intelligence gathered during the investigation. The hypothesis was that Asher House bought poor quality food cheaply and invoiced the Commonwealth for much higher quality food. The register of visitors would be compared to Medicare claims for the facility residents, and the medical centre's records.

The register Genelle photographed was seized by two officers later that afternoon. The pretence being to check the visits made by the coroner's office against their timesheets.

'A routine compliance check, Darrell,' said the officer who signed for the document and those for the past two years.

Eager to ingratiate, Darrell rang the coroner's office. 'Thanks mate,' he was told, 'meant to give you a bell over that, didn't think they'd move that fast.'

'All kosher mate,' said Darrell, 'they'll probably find they owe me overtime I've forgotten to claim.'

The Coroner's Office had their own concerns about Asher House and the lack of any action by the Commission for Aged Care and cooperated.

Genelle and Vic went over to the navigators, thanking them and letting them know what had been found after taking care of Darrell.

• • • •

A sher House facilities were closed by ACT Health the next day. Only one unplanned event. Hiba was met by Vic and Genelle on her way to work, told of what was happening in Cook. Crying with relief she talked.

Hudson Lang and Asher Ministries' Board.

The day Asher House facilities were closed, and assets frozen, Hudson Lang received a summons for a compulsory interview with Ethics Australia, scheduled to commence in three days. The summons invited him to bring legal representation and directed Hudson to not disclose the summons to anyone, other than his lawyers.

Treating the notice of non-disclosure as a suggestion, Hudson elected not to follow it and called Frank, who when he heard what Hudson wanted to talk about hung up. Hudson's lawyers read the summons and were concerned as he was not asked to provide any documentation for his appearance. This suggested to the lawyers Ethics Australia already had any documentation they needed. They were alarmed to hear that Hudson had broken the non-disclosure by calling Frank.

Most members of the public, police and not a few from the legal fraternity thought if you chose the lawyers Hudson used you were admitting guilt of whatever charge they were defending you from. Exorbitant fees, vicious attacks on witnesses, dramatic media conferences – gave them some high-profile success, and their failures deflected by threats to mount a vigorous appeal, and overplayed protestations of client innocence. And the money rolled in.

Added to their concern over documentation, alarm over disclosure was anxiety about money. The freeze on Asher House effectively meant a freeze on Asher Ministries. The law firm knew this as they had constructed the charade where Asher House had no assets, no funds. All was held by Ministries. The firm's practice meeting agreed not to represent Hudson or any entity to which he was attached. The managing partner called Frank Riccini, chair of Asher Ministries to let him know.

Frank said he understood and thanked them for their value over the years. Privately he was delighted, as Frank was one of the many who shared the view, hiring this firm telegraphed guilt.

For a document restricting disclosure of its existence, the summons generated a spike in telephone calls and internet traffic. Frank called the Asher Ministries directors to a board meeting the next day, the day before Hudson's mandatory interview. He then arranged to meet the Asher accountant as soon as he arrived in Canberra.

Frank and the accountant met at the National Gallery, she was prepared, her daughter already staying with cousins in Melbourne.

'Use the public phone here,' he suggested, 'call Ethics Australia and ask for whistle-blower protection. Give them my name as Chair and tell them you've made your disclosures known to me, I advised you to call.'

He gave her a new phone just for calling him.

'Ask them to come and pick you up here at the taxi rank.'

The Asher board meeting started at eight am. Hudson was annoyed he hadn't been consulted, but pleased Phoebe was not here to see this. She was in Singapore for a week of services, then three weeks in Malaysia. The time difference meant he'd miss her phone call this morning, and by the time she was back in Canberra he'd have this sorted.

The early start meant the directors were not greeted by the usual slide show, music and video clips of Hudson and Phoebe. Directors responded to Hudson's high fives and hugs clumsily; there really is nothing more awkward than a poorly executed high five between middle aged men and women.

Hudson, a little put out, sat next to Frank, and prepared to talk.

Frank asked him not to. 'I'll begin shall I?'asked Frank. 'Hudson, this meeting is about one item only.'

His hand on a sheet of paper, face down on the circular table, Frank moved it halfway to Hudson.

'This is your letter of resignation, turn it over and sign, now. If not, I have notice of termination for you. Whichever, you leave your keys, and you'll be escorted out of here, driven home.'

Hudson sat, shocked mouth open, saying nothing. He looked just like the photos of victims of a surprise fiftieth birthday party, at the point of being confronted by a room full of people.

A minute, Frank nodded, and the two escorts lifted Hudson out of his chair, walked him out. Jackson was waiting beside the car. He opened the door, whispered to Hudson. 'Money. You still owe me, remember?'

· · · ·

'Now,' said Frank, 'the meeting's finished, I call the police. No doubt they'll be in touch. We found he'd embezzled money from Asher Ministries' accounts into his own name, dismissed him and now it's over to them. All true. Bailey, you've had a lot of experience, would you handle the publicity, you use a good firm, right?'

'Yeah, ex journalists, leave it with me or do you want some oversight?'

'No thanks, just keep the rest of us out of it. One contact, and that's you.'

'Acting CEO?' Asked Asher's one female director.

'Well, my thinking is,' began Frank, 'if you see a problem then you're elected. If we're all agreed?'

'Thank you' she said, 'I'll get the staff together then. If we're finished. Salary?

'You have been learning from Hudson,' said Frank, 'I would have thought you'd see less wisdom in that now. Let's give you a month, then we talk again. Preaching? Who will do that? It's key to money coming in.'

'A month? OK. There are some young preachers, pastors, we'll use them.'

'Frank? Won't the money coming in be frozen too?'

'Likely,' said Frank, 'but not forever. Plus, we keep coming, we're letting them know we're not giving in.'

• • • •

Frank rang Phoebe in Singapore, not minding at all about the time difference. Her hosts were to wake her up. Frank insisted. So, Phoebe took Frank's call still wearing her overnight facial mask, and sleep buds, Singapore was so noisy.

Crying into the phone, telling Frank she couldn't believe it, Phoebe logged in using her laptop to access Asher accounts, personal accounts, and Hudson's accounts. She found the accounts could be opened, she could see what was there, and not access any of the money. She dropped her mobile onto her bed, ignoring Frank's 'hello, Phoebe?'

Minutes later he texted her to stay overseas.

Dressing quickly, Phoebe gathered her hosts and told them of the unfounded, deeply personal, and scandalous attacks on her and her husband in Canberra. She thought she'd better support Hudson from Singapore rather than flying home, and she needed to use some of the funds held by Asher Ministries, Singapore.

'You didn't know?' Her Singapore Chief Pastor asked, 'Hudson withdrew the bulk of the money three days ago.'

She hadn't known. At her insistence, the accounts were checked again, access only and unable to withdraw or move any money, except for deposits.

Now Phoebe wailed.

In twenty-four hours, Asher Ministries went from the source of spiritual and financial hope to a religious COVID. Successful treatment included denial of any involvement, public retraction when caught out in the denial and ceasing direct debit instructions. The Prime Minister who had begun to think Phoebe Lang may be a more popular figure than her was moved to scuttle Phoebe's nomination to the Senate. Parliamentary choir practice was suspended until further notice when it was discovered the room used no longer was fit for purpose. Another venue was yet to be found.

She also had her office request Harriet Cooper's official file, and had a copy delivered to a generous, and private, party donor as background to a secret investigation of Harriet.

Politicians and bureaucrats, freed from the Lang's influence and threats, eagerly backgrounded journalists; tabloids, current affair programs, social media, and talk-back radio were populated with segments exposing Asher Ministries sub-standard aged care, and financial malpractice. If the English do parks well, the Scandinavians noir, Australians excel at schadenfreude.

Where in the very recent past, agencies were reluctant to deal with complaints about Asher Ministries and Asher House, over training records, overcharging, conflict of interest, not-for-profit status; they fell over themselves to brief the Prime Minister's office, the Attorney-General's office of their now zealous pursuit. Only the federal police, Tax Australia and Ethics Australia continued to quietly investigate and interview. Content to be out of the limelight, as if there was any to spare.

The Prime Minister too stayed out of the limelight, leaving the scandal of Asher House abuse of older people to be deflected by one of her junior Health ministers. She coached him in the classic conservative whitewash. Apologise for the perception, explain any errors as due to the highest of motives (the government is committed to providing for older people to age gracefully in their own homes), and focus on the future, as nothing much has happened, really. 'Oh, and make sure the passive voice is used. We all risk making mistakes,' she reminded the junior Health minister, 'when we choose to walk alongside Mary Magdalen.'

The Chair of Charities Australia resigned for exercising her responsibilities in a way which, until a week ago, had ingratiated her with the Prime Minister. Molly Lavandar texted Ian Sturgess and arranged to meet at Fellows, the University House bar. 'cu@8', Ian was mastering text. Seizure of assets of Asher House may mean more exposure of the clinical trial. While it had finished months ago, Australia Health auditors may be prompted to re-examine the clinical trial documentation and intensify their efforts to recover forty-five million dollars from Polonius. Ian had escaped censure over the Polonius payment, simply directed to probity training workshops, yet to be scheduled. He was removed from the chair of the Aged Care Research Board but remained a Board member. With federal police now involved, some of these investigations and outcomes may be reviewed.

Molly's phone call to Ian was intercepted, and a group of noisy post-graduate criminology students settled into Fellows around seven, leaving only a few seats vacant. Criminology students, their cover was perfect, it was a subject they knew a lot about.

Ian and Molly sat at the only free table. The criminology students had 'reserved' it for them, adding a listening device underneath it, and one in the table light. Unfortunately, both proved completely useless as the criminology students did too good a job posing as criminology students celebrating project results. Alex pointed out to Mick that all was not wasted though as we were able to pick up two team members' plans to become a couple later that night.

'Three hours at a university bar, bill to match, eight operators, two expensive devices, thousands of dollars of expensive equipment to filter background noise and isolate a conversation...' Alex thought Mick quite enjoyed it, his operators not so sure as they placed bets on the outcome of the recorded plan.

The next day Ian Sturgess PhD was issued a summons to appear before Ethics Australia in two days' time. He was advised to not disclose the summons to anyone except legal counsel he was invited to have attend with him. He was not required to bring any material to the interview.

He rang Molly that night, she listened to him, and she hung up. Molly booked a business class ticket to Vanuatu, for the next day. She packed, slept, and drove to Sydney early. She arranged an Uber to the international airport from a Starbucks two blocks from her apartment at Circular Quay, left her car with the valet. Five hours later Molly stepped out of a private chartered jet at Baurfield International Airport.

Vic and Genelle did their final preparation for interviewing Ian Sturgess, discussed how to open the interview, scripted, and rewrote their lines. The striking insights each had in the shower, in the car, anywhere they couldn't note them, eluded them. They felt dull, and he was due the next morning. If anything, they were over-prepared.

They had sat with Noopur and Alex and selected the evidence they would use with Sturgess: the phone recordings, the paperwork, the witness statements from his research meetings, Purchase Orders for the domestic sensors. They had the printout of incel sites he had visited, every screen he'd accessed, account details, statements from his plumber in Dalmeny.

Unusual artefacts sometimes find their way into corruption investigations. Operation Rose was no exception. They had a box of steel magnets same diameter as a one-dollar coin and five times as thick, a box of sturdy metal bracelets, and a box of glass cylinders the same size as the magnets. Embedded in the cylinders appeared to be tiny, printed circuit boards, or parts of, about half the size of sim cards. Decorative, not functional. All from fridges, microwave ovens and ovens in residents' rooms at Asher House in Cook.

Noopur knocked at their meeting room door, 'Ready for us?' She walked in with Alex. Noopur and Alex had spent the last thirty minutes talking through how to approach Vic and Genelle. They were not there to tell them what to do. They saw their task as opening them to consider approaches they may not have developed, affirming the choices they had made. Noopur had seen them in the meeting room and was concerned at their body language, she saw them flat, overwhelmed maybe.

'You're on the right track,' said Alex, 'it's tempting to focus on the questions to ask, and to concentrate on the evidence. You have that under control, the hard part, the critical part is the bit you two have identified. That is, in the first few minutes, your relationship with this guy; marathon kayaker, Chief Scientist, university professor, public service medal, more degrees than a compass! It's not so much about rapport, it's about getting him to talk so you can listen, remember you can't do both at once.'

'I didn't know he had a public service medal. Where is that referenced?'

'Poetic licence. No, he has one,' laughed Alex, 'The thing is if you think of those degrees, recognition, status as an outfit for a special occasion – like the language he uses when he makes a speech differs from how he talks in the office. What's that like, and who can tell us that now?'

Genelle said, 'We have the language analyses we had his staff complete for us, let me get it up.'

The screen showed results of language style surveys Sturgess's staff, Board members, colleagues had completed. It listed items like 'shows support for work effort' and asked respondents to indicate if this behaviour occurred and how often.

The results summary indicated Sturgess rarely encouraged, behaved defensively when questioned; dominant and aloof. He was disinterested in developing his research staff, and talked about his own achievements, contribution most of the time, arrogant.

'The original fig jam,' said Alex.

'Fig jam?' Noopur quizzed him.

'Yeah,' said Alex, 'acronym, Fuck I'm Good Just Ask Me.'

This went up on the whiteboard, under the heading Alex's Major Finding.

They figured to get Sturgess talking, Vic and Genelle would be keen to show him they were interested in what he had to say, and not so much interested in asking their questions. Noopur thought it vital to let him talk, 'give him the floor, he's the main act - your questions a support act.'

'Like the comedians at a strip show,' said Alex, 'no-one's there to see them.'

As Alex told Mick later, 'that didn't make it to the whiteboard.'

'It's a wonder they let you back in,' Mick said.

They elected to inform Sturgess of their allegations grouped around his status, experience, and financial acumen. His response would determine which of these to pursue first.

Ian sat across from Vic and Genelle. He was impassive as Vic, for the record, read his name, titles, and the agency for which he worked. When that concluded and Genelle was readying to present the allegations, Sturgess corrected Vic, 'It's Professor, not, Adjunct Professor. Surprisingly, all your other details are correct.'

Genelle, 'Professor at Shanghai Therapeutic Institute?'

Sturgess barely hid his displeasure, 'Yes.'

Genelle knew there wasn't one, Shanghai boasted the Shanghai Pharmaceutical School, they had never heard of Dr Ian Sturgess, and had no professors on their staff.

'Professor of...?'

'Professor.'

'Dr Sturgess,' Genelle began, 'Ethics Australia issues a summons to appear following extensive research and investigation into suspected corrupt conduct. The purpose of the examination commencing today is to inform you of our allegations and the evidence summary, and to seek your response. You were invited to bring legal counsel, you choose not to, and we may give you leave to seek counsel should you change your mind.' Genelle and Vic knew from his peers Sturgess prided himself on never changing his mind, a view contrary to what's generally expected of scientists, so they were confident that the offer to change his mind would not be accepted.

Genelle presented the allegations, and as she spoke windows appeared on the electronic whiteboard, opening from left to right.

'Allegations concerning your role as Chief Scientist.' A window appeared, opened to read 'Domestic sensors, clinical trial'. Followed by a picture of the view of Montague Island from Ian's house at Dalmeny, opening to read 'Personal Finances', and finally 'International Reputation' and a photograph of Shanghai Pharmaceutical School.

Sturgess opted for Chief Scientist.

'Chief Scientist, one of four in Australia. You have summoned me. Questioning my role as Chief Scientist, Aged Care? I had no idea Ethics Australia is anti-science, where is the ethics in that? Your ethics, your personal ethics? You think the world would be a better place if we did not use evidence to make decisions?'

Vic said, 'maybe we don't appreciate the contribution to aged care made by you as Chief Scientist...the health economics of aged care for example?'

Sturgess started his lecture, part professional history, part personal motivation, part interesting. Vic and Genelle listened closely, especially to the material between the lines, fact checkers were also listening to him talk, comparing what he said to the extensive records. Sturgess's PhD developed an algorithm for allocating money and resources in health care. Scientific, devoid of emotion, rational, the algorithm worked by loading a 'black box' with health data, health factors, life expectancy variables and produced a number. The higher the number the better the chances of a longer, and healthier life. Multiply the number by the costs of treatment and you have an unbiased way to allocate scarce capital in healthcare.

Sturgess made no reference to the university investigations into plagiarism, investigations which delayed the award of his doctorate. Nor did he mention the generous scholarship he won from the insurance industry association which had an undisguised interest in his work.

Sturgess continued, 'My early research in deciding where to allocate capital, both human and financial, in aged care focused on trying to predict the best returns. I found doctors, nurses, psychologists less than useful, simply not smart enough to make reliable decisions about life expectancy. So, my research shifted to designing an approach which took the human factor out of the decision. I started working on an expert system taking the best of what we knew, simplifying it and automating it.'

Between Ian's lines they heard no mention of any colleagues he may have had, no reference to his hiring only of those who advocated an actuarial approach to resource allocation, and continued consultancy with life insurance companies.

Now, as the interview got to the clinical trial Mick Darby wanted to be there, to question Sturgess about the social robots. He looked through the window to the interview room.

'What's in that white box?'

'We're all about to find out,' said Alex, 'Vic brought it in here first thing this morning. Logged it in as part of the raid.'

Genelle asked about the clinical trial into sensors on domestic appliances, monitored by bracelets.

'AI, or to give its full name, Artificial Intelligence, is an extension of my research on expert systems, automated decision making. I put it through the algorithm, and for the cost per consumer, it was a no-brainer to trial, and now it's a proven success, for implementing more broadly across the sector.'

'How did you come up with the idea?' Genelle, 'such an innovation?'

'That's my expertise.' said the Chief Scientist.

Ian was left alone to eat his lunch. He spent time reading through, scanning the documents neatly piled on the table. Ian also opened a polystyrene box, not unlike a box used to transport broccoli, saw bracelets, magnets, and glass buttons.

Darby stood on his toes, face against the observation window, peering, what's in that fucking box, he wondered?

Vic and Genelle came back into the interview room, Vic cleared away Ian's lunch plate, asked if there was anything else he could get for him. Sturgess shook his head and cried out.

'Your paperwork is incomplete...'

'Incomplete? Tell me how...,' began Vic.

Sturgess interrupted, waving the paperwork, 'there is no reference here to ElderTech.'

'ElderTech? We didn't see it relevant to your interview,' began Vic. 'ElderTech is a company registered with Australian Securities, owned by Hudson Lang, for two years now, the company's annual review is outstanding, and the business address may be incorrect. ElderTech, maybe we missed something?'

'No, well yes. It's owned by Nigel Blakeley, not Hudson Lang.'

'The only reference we find to a Nigel Blakeley is in your diary. We have no record of a Nigel Blakeley anywhere else in any government records; no birth certificate, no drivers licence, no passport, no Medicare card, no credit card, no bank loan, no tax assessment, nothing, anywhere. Except in your diaries.'

'Well, you're wrong.' Sturgess bit his lip, pressed his hands to his forehead.

'OK, we're wrong, 'said Vic, 'what have we missed?'

'Not what, said Sturgess, 'who. Blakeley, that's who you've missed.'

Harriet joined Mick and Alex in the observation room, all standing now around the window.

They could see that the box disturbed Sturgess. The magnets and trinkets looked remarkably like what Blakeley had called sensors at Dalmeny so many months ago. Nigel Blakeley's role in the clinical trial came out, Sturgess focusing on the polystyrene box, looking like he expected a snake to slither out of it.

Vic slapped the box, Sturgess leapt, paled. 'You mean you, Chief Scientist, knew these were ornaments, trinkets,' slapped the box again.

Mick felt as if he'd been slapped.

'No, don't touch it. They came from Blakeley, there're his.' Sturgess in agony, pushing his chair away from the table.

Vic again, 'as Chief Scientist, these ornaments, you authorised a Purchase Order for one hundred at $7000 each, sourced by a firm called Polonius?'

Vic stood, picked up the box and emptied it onto the table. Glass buttons, magnets, cheap bracelets, anklets glittered and spilled, some to the floor, some into Sturgess' lap.

Sturgess was up on his feet now; the trinkets in his lap clattering, he swept the ones in front of him off the desk. He trod on a few, crushing them into the floor; uncontrolled.

'The clinical trial,' Sturgess said, 'the clinical trial was a success. None of the sensors signalled; none of the sensors on the domestic appliances triggered. The old people remembered to use them, closed them because they wanted to avoid the alarms sounding. They are cost-effective, acceptable to old people, and they reduce the staff to resident ratio – huge cost savings.'

Vic and Genelle each took a sip of water, not game to look at each other, desperate not to look at Sturgess, who calmed as quickly as he had erupted.

'Passionate people scientists, that's what I looked for in recruiting, passion,' he said.

'The passion required to run a clinical trial on fake devices.' asked Genelle.

'I didn't know they were fake, and then the results were so positive, I mean, this is way beyond the halo effect, isn't it? This is a real scientific advance.'

Genelle said, 'The devices are fake, we agree with you there. Let's put to one side for now the value of the scientific advance. There are some things I'm a little confused by though. ElderTech's role? Nigel Blakeley's role?'

'Nigel came to me with a clinical trial proposal, suggested I redraft it and present it to the Research Oversight Committee for consideration.'

'A committee you chair?'

'Yes.'

'So, you draft a research proposal, submit it to a committee chaired by you, and it's endorsed by that same committee.'

'Yes.'

'And then Asher House facilities were selected for the trials?'

'Yes, my research budget paid for the trials, the devices, the research assistants. Field work is costly.'

'Ian, thank you,' said Vic, 'can you tell us a little about the second phase of the trial, the socially assistive robots.'

'Sure,' said Ian, 'be happy to. There's not much to tell though. Socially assistive robots, knowns in the literature as SARs...'

''I am sorry to interrupt you there,' said Vic, 'I have a junior who could look that up for me, I'm really interested in what you only, what only you may know as Chief Scientist. Could you tell me when you plan to introduce them into nursing homes?'

Sturgess laughed, 'shit, I mean, who knows?'

Darby recoiled, recovered, slipped his hands into his pockets; hiding clenched fists.

Vic again, 'you have a project approved to trial them?'

'Yeah, well that's if they get them built. The project,' said Sturgess, 'is an approval to research their feasibility. I'm going to Italy next week to see a company there who might be able to build them. They are yet to build a prototype. They don't even have a 3D model. I reckon they'll hit me up for money that's why they've invited me to a private dinner with their Board. Really, I don't know what you're getting at.'

• • • •

Ian's interviews extended for three more days, covering his personal finances, the payments made to him by Blakeley through the fictitious Shanghai university college, and finally on day three, his use of incel websites. He'd subscribed to two of these sites, directly funding violent misogynists, suspected terrorist attacks. For his own safety Sturgess remained in custody that night, on watch.

The next morning Ian Sturgess was a different man, seemingly unburdened by the weight of evidence and his own admissions over the past three days.

His conceit held.

On day four Noopur joined Vic. Genelle didn't trust herself with Sturgess, she just wanted to challenge him, not to listen to him.

'The subcontinent' said Sturgess, 'huge interest in my algorithms and in Artificial Intelligence applied to health care.'

'We're nearly there,' said Noopur, 'I have just a few things to put to you.'

'Let's start at the end. You authorised a Purchase Order for twenty-two million dollars of these,' she indicated the polystyrene box, 'to be procured by Polonius?'

'I made it forty-five million dollars,' said Sturgess, 'the PO was for half of our requirements and since the eventual orders would total nearly 100 million, I acted on our intention and made the first payment forty-five.'

'An upfront sum?'

'Of course, not unusual where sole providers are involved.'

'So, Ian, maybe you can help us out here. The forty-five million is missing, the money transferred to an account, and so far, untraceable from there. No supplies have arrived, nothing has been procured.'

'You think I have the forty-five million?'

'Well, your department doesn't have it. There is no Nigel Blakeley. ElderTech has lodged a formal complaint stating they are the preferred supplier, so they don't have it.'

Noopur pressed on, 'You are the Chief Scientist, Aged Care, let me ask you. How would you justify your decision to spend forty-five million dollars on fake devices, money which is now missing? Fake devices which we don't have – without losing credibility in your evidence-based decision process?'

'Would your colleagues, students, the Health Minister, be disappointed if they knew what we've been talking about here the past four days, if they knew what websites, what terrorist activity, you've been funding?'

'How would they know?' Asked Sturgess.

'Let's assume they find out. Just for now between us, what do you think they would feel? How might they react? Your close friend Molly Lavandar, what would she say to you, if she heard about this?'

'Molly could never know,' he whispered. Noopur and Vic said nothing, even the listeners stopped any noise.

'She's the only one who ever believed me, right from the start, she got those vicious rumours about plagiarism stopped. She, she must never know, it wasn't my algorithm alone, and it's all been wrong since then. Molly even told me how to handle Nigel.'

Noopur, 'Ian, you have been very helpful. I want to thank you for your willingness to tell us what has been going on. Let's put this all past us,' she swept her files aside, 'where to now Ian, from here, for you?'

Ian could not move, hands flat on the desk, chin on chest, he started to tremble.

'Ian, any thoughts?'

Ethics Australia was satisfied Sturgess had engaged in serious corrupt conduct. The opinion was also formed to obtain advice from Prosecution Australia in relation to other criminal allegations, including manslaughter.

Darby gets sprung.

H arriet turned to Mick, 'let's talk about this in my office.'
'The interview's not finished,' said Mick. 'We need to pressure Sturgess about the robots. He's hiding something.'

'We've seen enough,' said Harriet, opening the door.

They got to Harriet's office without another word, she opened the door, ushered him inside and left. Darby's boss was waiting for him.

Darby took his hands from his pockets, reached out to shake hands and was ignored; decided to see his boss's cards.

'Can't this wait? I've got to get back down there. We don't know anything about the robots yet. I can get it out of him. Harriet's people, they're playing too nice.'

Darby's boss sat, gestured to a seat.

'Sturgess, he's just a fucking scientist,' said Darby, 'the only pressure he's had is for a deadline. I know I can crack him. The robots.' Darby took the seat, sat, elbows on his knees, 'the robots...it's all over isn't it?'

Darby's boss waited.

'Was I set up?' Darby's voice thin, shocked, Adams Apple blocking his throat.

'I was, at best, agnostic about the robots. While you,' his boss sipped water, 'you though, leapt for the faith; altar boy, acolyte, deacon. Tell me,' he said, 'was yours a Damascene conversion or did you at least play hard to get, a reluctant convert to the world of the Jetsons?'

'I don't know where to start,' said Darby, his words still choked, mind desperate for clues to his betrayal.

'Or when to stop,' said his boss, seeing shock in Darby's wide eyes, open mouth, wild Adams Apple, and pressed on. 'And the result, a perfect own goal. Set up? Yes, by you.'

'I thought.'

'We know what thought did.'

'I'm drowning,' said Darby clutching at his throat, 'I feel like I'm drowning.'

'There may be another explanation,' said Darby's boss. 'The world is not a blank canvas, there for you to draw those images you want to see. If you are drowning, it's in a puddle of your own making, your image.'

'There were no robots to be found,' said Darby, 'I've fucked up. Made a terrible mistake.' Darby looked up, 'out of order boss, I'll go now, leave you my letter.'

'Three mistakes,' said his boss, emphasising the numbers. 'One, you, missed the trinkets, directed us away from them. Two, you, missed the money, let forty-five million dollars loose. Three, missed the robots, you, steered us towards robots which do not exist.'

'You'll miss me,' said Darby, his mind already turning to payback.

'Unlikely,' said his boss.

Mick, confused, the fingers of his right hand slipped to his shirt sleeve, tracing the circle and the square on his cufflink.

'You owe me,' said his boss.

Darby stared, as his boss opened his hand to reveal a Viking USB.

'You don't believe me?' His boss smiled.

'Your laptop recognises this USB, Darby.'

'So fucking what?' said Darby, 'it worked didn't it. It was the circuit breaker we needed. Hudson Lang opened his front door, welcomed us in. It's how we got them.'

'And that's enough for you is it? The boy who squared the circle? You don't fuck with geometry son. And you don't fuck with me.'

Darby in his humiliation, mumbled, 'what about Harriet? What does she say?'

'Ha!' His boss sneered, 'that goody two shoes? You betrayed her, fractured her trust, misplaced as it was. She'd have you arrested. Me, I want you working for me, owing, me.'

Mick Darby couldn't breathe, couldn't stop blinking, couldn't stop the blood leaving his face. He wiped his face to stop himself crying. He didn't notice his boss leaving. He didn't notice Harriet back in her office, sitting behind her desk.

He looked up to see her, 'too focused,' he said.

'Try, narrow minded,' said Harriet.

'Narrow minded,' he repeated, savouring the image, looking down a sniper's scope, wilfully oblivious. Mick knew he was as defenceless as he was dependent on Harriet's regard. Uncertain; he needed her, needed to look good in her eyes, and he needed to deny it.

Darby saw things others didn't, joined dots others were convinced were random. He wasn't always sure what he was seeing, but others had learnt to trust his insight. For Darby the standard of proof of wrongdoing was his assessment of the balance of probabilities. This time though, he'd been convinced of what he saw, and there had been nothing to see.

'Mick, you distracted us. My question is, from what? Your right hand waving at robots. What're you hiding?'

Darby sniffed, just the once. Heard his mother talk of the Vatican, saw her in the kitchen, washing up already spotless cups and saucers. Thought of his father; choosing to be broken by the trip of his lifetime. Not me, not Mick though. And Harriet. Harriet thinks all this deliberate. Well, OK, best not disappoint.

Looked up, smiled, and said, 'Above your pay grade, Harriet.'

'Mick,' said Harriet, 'you've had ten minutes, your ration of self-pity. It's done. We need you here in the morning. Let Alex take you home.'

She reached for her phone. 'And, Alex, stay with him for the afternoon, okay?'

Darby was disoriented enough to take her advice. Shame about the robots, relief Harriet didn't know it all, his defensiveness, the discomfort from not being in control, his clumsy boss revealing all he had, sudden images of his humble parents; too much.

Asher Ministries' accountant.

Genelle and Vic drove to the National Gallery, parked on Queen Victoria Terrace. They were second to arrive, and they waited. Two of their team had coffees from the café outside the gallery entrance and sat chatting in the morning sun, opposite the taxi rank.

A tall, well dressed, older man walked between them and a woman standing beside the 'taxi' sign. She checked her watch constantly, checked her phone, folded, and unfolded her arms and checked her watch again. She looked to the man walking just to her side and shrugged, the WTF shrug.

He whispered, 'they'll be here,' and climbed stiffly into the back of a BMW Uber which pulled in just as he reached the kerb. The woman with the coffee again fiddled with her watch. Genelle started her car.

They drove Lorraine to the Gillard Building. Parked underground and led her to an unmemorable reception room.

Genelle asked her if she was comfortable. 'There is some paperwork and two of our specialists will be here soon to start that; name, address details, where you fit in at Asher Ministries. It'll be a few minutes, so can we make you more comfortable here, tea, water?'

Lorraine said she as fine, and immediately departed from the script Frank had carefully planned and rehearsed with her, 'I'll be comfortable as long as those two tax men are not here.'

'Tax men?'

Lorry, now, to Vic. 'Describe them? I can do better than that.'

Genelle asked if she might copy the photos from her phone, 'Of course, if it helps.'

Leaving Lorraine with Vic, Genelle took the stairs and printed the photos. She was distracted by some noise at the triage team and walked over. The coffee drinking couple from the art gallery, and Zoe were talking animatedly.

'Genelle, the tall guy who spoke to your witness outside the gallery is Frank Riccini, chair of Asher Ministries.'

'Talking to a woman who said she wants to inform on him?'

Since the start of Operation Rose the teams had investigated all the Asher directors. They knew of the tax inquiries, they had directors, business associates and families under surveillance for some months now. It was simple to find a match between the photos taken this morning and their files. Genelle showed them the photos from Lorraine's (she would never be Lorry to Genelle) phone.

Ten minutes later they knew, the bogus tax agents were two of Frank Riccini's grandsons.

Lorraine abandoned the plan hatched by Frank when she was told who the tax agents were.

Genelle and Vic had talked to Noopur about where to begin with Lorraine. They had decided to let Lorraine know the identity of the tax agents; leave her for half an hour with a notebook, just in case anything else about these two occurs to her, a memory triggered? A uniformed officer stood inside the door.

Noopur's counsel was to let Lorraine decide what she would talk about when Vic and Genelle joined her. 'We've shocked her with the identities, given her time to mull it over. She's bound to lose the money and the scholarship if Riccini is prosecuted, so we have that up our sleeves. Let's see if she'll let you know what's on her mind now?'

When they walked back in Lorraine had made a few notes of that morning. She started to talk as soon as they walked in.

'We can record this,' said Vic, and signalled.

'I want it recorded. Don't want to memorise this!'

Lorraine took them through the phone call from Frank, meeting at the gallery, her instructions to phone from a public phone, and to wait at the taxi stand. Genelle and Vic, like Frank before them, were impressed with her credibility, she was honest. She hadn't noticed the couple eating ice cream, but she did accurately talk about Frank passing her, accurately repeated what he'd said and knew the car he'd been driven away in.

Then she produced the phone Frank had given her, and his instructions for when to use it. This was the second phone he had given her she told them.

'Could you tell us more about the first phone, do you have it with you now?'

'It's at my house, you can go and get it, as long as you don't mind the mess.' A minute later the officer, now outside the door, came in collected Lorraine's keys, and left.

'Thank you,' said Genelle, 'where were you when Frank handed you the first phone?'

'In a park at Hall, it was freezing too, I remember thinking he doesn't need a cooler bag, the drinks'll be kept cold enough on the table.'

So began the story of Frank's attempt to set up the whistle blower. At that evening's go-through of the day's highlights, Mick Darby sat enthralled by Lorraine's information, 'now that is a story I've not heard before.'

The phone Lorraine called the 'first phone' was recovered from her house, she identified it as the one Frank had provided at Hall, logged, and data from it retrieved. Lorraine had deleted nothing from that phone she said.

Interviews with Lorraine were conducted in the mornings. She was introduced to different interviewers, yet she felt familiar with them all. Some of the questions she found a bit strange; was she comfortable, where would she like to sit while being interviewed. Interviews followed much the same pattern, she was informed of the purpose of that day's interview, the documents they wanted to discuss were set out, some files opened on a laptop screened onto an electronic whiteboard. They would ask her if other document or files from Asher Ministries would be relevant to include, Board minutes perhaps.

She dismissed that, 'There are none,' she said, 'Hudson claimed that fixed structures destroyed the human spiritual, proof positive, he would say, is the Catholic church, in ruins because it clings to formal structures, we need to be fluid, flexible.'

Fluid, flexible, fucked, thought Vic.

Sometimes they played recordings of telephone conversations, asking where a call may have been taken, who else may have been in the room or the car at that time.

In the afternoons, the analysts spent double checking Lorraine's accounts against documentation, statement from other witnesses, constantly verifying and validating her testimony. There was some talk that Lorraine was too good to be true as a whistle-blower.

'OK,' said Noopur, 'let's assume Frank's plan is working perfectly and Lorraine is doing exactly what was asked of her for fifty grand and a school scholarship, what would we do?'

'I'll tell you what we would do, we would do exactly what we're doing now, spending hours, ten of us all day, every day, rechecking, verifying, validating every piece of information.'

'What else would we do?'

Silence.

'Good, let's move on then. Enough distraction.'

Vic nodded his appreciation to Noopur. He thought Lorraine a little naïve. But she was taking a huge risk, and with her daughter, he felt she deserved all their support.

Hudson Lang interviews.

A fter five days, Harriet, Alex and their senior teams debated whether Ethics Australia had jurisdiction to further investigate Asher Ministries' directors. Hudson was the managing director of a registered not-for-profit and therefore was he a public official? Similarly, the other Board members, Riccini included, directors of a not-for-profit, not public officials? There were other matters uncovered in the investigation to be referred to other agencies; not acting as responsible company directors to ASIC, tax matters to be referred to the ongoing tax investigation, questions about the status of Asher as a charity for Charities Australia to review, impersonating tax officers to be referred to the police.

Harriet ended any debate, 'Let me use a sailor's expression,' began Harriet as the others held their breath, 'we've been around the buoy a few times over this and getting not far. Let's get a legal opinion. If we find it easy to question our jurisdiction, we must assume others will when we have our findings. So, a submission on jurisdiction from counsel assisting us will be useful now for us, and later, should our jurisdiction be contested.'

Ethics Australia accepted the submission by counsel assisting it about the jurisdictional issues Harriet and assistant commissioners had discussed.

Harriet summed it up, 'Asher Ministries, through its ownership of Asher House, is funded by the government to provide aged care facilities and services. The government funding ties Hudson Lang, Phoebe Lang, Frank Riccini and the directors to acting in the public interest as they perform their duties.'

'For our purposes they are public officers, so we may investigate allegations of corrupt conduct in their performance, and stewardship of public money.'

The advice helped further narrow Ethics Australia's investigation task to corrupt conduct allegations. However, Harriet made it clear not all interviews, examinations and investigations had to relate to corrupt conduct allegations, they would explore any matter to investigate allegations of corrupt conduct.

This walking the fine line between matters relevant to corrupt conduct findings and those relevant to other criminal allegations was done by the triage team, who now met with the team leaders daily. The robust discussions gave everyone confidence in their decisions.

The discussions resolving jurisdictional questions would influence the structure of the Hudson Lang examination. Vic and Noopur planned the interview sequence, involving Harriet and Alex initially and again when they had a draft.

Alex's final thoughts, 'once you get him talking, he won't stop. That's suits us, we have the time. We've all seen him talk, he talks himself up, he's always on when he's talking. He'll talk himself right into you. Relax, look interested, you don't really have to pay attention to what he says, probably better off not, you'll never follow his train of thought!' Alex had spent hours on YouTube, taking notes on Hudson's clips. He figured once they got him off script, he was theirs.

Hudson had been interviewed formally, just covering name, address, occupation, reasons for being held, the legislation under which he'd been detained. He'd answered the questions; not eager, not defiant, voice flat, body still. He'd been left an unopened bottle of water, had declined the bathroom.

The interview room was bare except for one table in the middle of the room and two chairs against one wall. When Vic walked in Hudson was standing in a corner facing the door, shoulders touching both walls of the corner.

'My name's Vic.' He had two bottles of water with him.

'Sure.'

'Would you like to sit?'

'Sure.'

Vic held the back of one chair, 'where would you like to sit,' he asked.

'I'll sit here,' said Hudson, taking the chair from Vic, putting it by the side of the table closest to Vic.

Vic picked up the other chair, moved it all the way around the room, while Hudson watched.

'Can I ask,' said Vic, 'have you been treated well this morning while you've been here? Respectfully?'

'Are you asking if I've been strip searched, beaten, water boarded? Then, no. I haven't.'

'Would you like water?'

'Thanks, no.'

'You don't mind,' said Vic unscrewing a bottle, 'only I'm a little dry?'

'Be my guest,' said Hudson, trace of a smirk, 'is there anything else I can get you? Only, I may have to go out if it's not in this room,' he looked about him.

'So,' said Vic, 'Petersham to Canberra. Would you mind telling me why? Quite a move?'

'Why would I mind?'

'It's more of a personal question,' said Vic.

'I don't do personal,' said Hudson, 'everything I do, every day, is for Jesus. He is the god of everyday.'

'You moved for Jesus?'

Noopur, Zoe, Genelle and Alex in the observation room, absorbed.

Genelle covered her mouth, spoke through her hand, 'Vic!'

'Not afraid to mix it is he,' said Alex.

Hudson bent towards Vic, sat back and looked away, then turned to face Vic.

'Vic, you live here? Canberra right? You know the place?'

'I do,' said Vic, 'Canberra native.'

'Then, let's see if you understand. You see, when I saw Canberra. When I saw this town, the people here. The arrogance and aspiration to provide the homeless with your architect-designed bus shelters to seek refuge in at night. I knew this was my kinda town.'

'And, what kind of town would that be?'

'The kinda town that needs me, to help the people see Jesus.'

'And you've done that?'

'Well,' said Hudson, 'God's work is done when God says it's done.'

'You'd have some indications though,' said Vic, 'God would be pleased; attendance numbers, music charts, book sales, tithes, Asher House nursing homes, your house, the cars, A lister, Phoebe's political ambition, talk of a gong for you in the new year.'

Hadn't heard about the gong thought Hudson, hooking his thumbs on his belt, 'I can't say we're not very proud of the progress, just the beginnings though.'

'Just the beginnings?'

'You know, I'm surprised at what's happening here, not what I expected,' said Hudson leaning across the table.

'Surprised?'

'I expected the garden of Gethsemane.'

'One night?'

'A bad night too,' said Hudson.

'Oh, I think you'll be here for longer than that.' Vic stood, picked up the two water bottles and left the room.

• • • •

Harriet, Alex, Vic, Noopur and Zoe watched Hudson unfold. The sound had to be turned down as he paced the room, slapping walls, stamping his feet. He did his trick with jumbled phonemes, head back, jerking body.

'Not a bad Peter Garrett impersonation,' said Alex. 'Vic, you've set him up nicely. He's doing this to himself.'

'Tunce uwon a pime,' said Genelle, 'wer thas a litty pittle lerl called Prindallera. Prindallera tad hwo sisty uglers and a sittle mepstother.'

They all turned, mouths open as wide as the laughing clowns, staring at Genelle.

She blushed at the confusion she'd caused, 'my sister and I ...when we were kids, say it as fast as you can and you sound like him,' she tilted her head at Hudson through the window, 'talking in tongues, it's not that hard, helps if you're pissed. So I'm told'.

'Cinderella,' said Vic, 'Prindrella?'

'Nearly,' said Genelle, 'Prindallera and the Cince.'

'Holy shit,' said Alex, 'I'm going in there and talk to him like that. Ponce a won...'

'No,' said Genelle, 'maybe for later.'

'Much later,' said Harriet laughing, 'Genelle, how funny. How did you learn this?'

'I think from an aunt, she heard it on the radio, thought my sister and I would like it, and we did.'

'Must try it in Hindi,' said Noopur, 'the mystery of speaking in tongues, revealed.'

'We better move on,' said Harriet, 'I could do with coffee though. Let's get two officers in here and we'll come back in half an hour, it's not every day a mystery is revealed.'

Noopur began. 'Hudson, we are going to show you two lists of allegations, the first list is of criminal allegations in which we have no interest, and which will be investigated by other agencies, including, federal police, NSW police, Tax Australia, Charities Commission, Health Australia, Securities Commission, and Medicare. The second list comprises allegations of corrupt conduct as a public officer, and we do have an interest in these allegations, and we are continuing our investigations with this interview.'

'So, you can see how serious this is, and perhaps better understand the significance of the restrictions on disclosing to anyone that you were issued the summons.'

Hudson, who had seemed uncomfortable, relaxed at this last statement, leaning back in his chair, 'Well, you can note for the record, you take yourselves very seriously, and who am I to disclose anything about you when I don't even know you?'

'Help me out here Hudson,' asked Vic, 'You have not disclosed to anyone the summons? That's a great start to our work together.'

'Well,' he snorted, 'I won't be working with you, but I didn't tell anyone, no.'

Vic, earnest, 'So, to be clear, right at the very beginning, you told no-one of the summons?'

Hudson, singsong, 'I've told you once, I've told you twice. I know, let me say it again. No.'

Noopur, 'I'm going to play you a recording of a telephone call from your mobile phone to Frank Riccini, intercepted on...' The sheet of paper with the transcript of the call, time, date, and phone numbers, she passed to Hudson.

He protested it was forged, the whole thing.

In all there were ten sheets of paper, separate transcript, and call data for each attempt to get through to Riccini. Showing Hudson leaving increasingly desperate calls, then an angry call to Riccini to pick up and talk to him, then a threat in call eight, followed by begging for Riccini's forgiveness in the final two calls.

'What was going on here?' Vic asked.

'Let me help you figure it out,' he said, played a recording of Hudson's accountant talking about the role Frank had outlined for her.

'So, now he's sacked you, and left you, alone. They all have.'

The electronic whiteboard filled with images of happier times for Hudson, Hudson with Frank, Hudson with each of the directors, in pairs, groups, Hudson with the Prime Minister.

'Take that last image Hudson, you, Phoebe and the Prime Minister. She has now ended Phoebe's chances of becoming a senator.'

Noopur took over, 'And as I explained earlier, Hudson, these are matters in which we are not interested, and other agencies will be.'

'Well, I am interested in these bastards,' thundered Hudson, a fury of impatience in a room of deliberation. 'It's not easy making God real, you know,' pitch rising, 'it's exhausting. I worked very hard to make the invisible come to life. Why would they spread this gossip. This is so disappointing.'

· · · ·

There followed weeks of Hudson providing testimony, searches for documentary evidence to either support or deny his allegations centred on the involvement of others, and further interviews. Ethics Australia found that Hudson had engaged in serious corrupt conduct, and advice was sought from Prosecutions Australia about criminal charges.

Evidence provided by Hudson and Lorraine was marshalled by Mick Darby who invited senior NSW police leading fraud and criminal gang investigations to Canberra. Their meetings concluded that publicity about criminal charges laid against Frank Riccini would likely trigger interest by other crime networks in the activities he controlled. They considered dealing with Riccini in three broad strategies.

Weakening his family bonds was the first stage. Sacred, Sunday, family lunch at the Riccini's was rudely interrupted by the incessant ringing of the doorbell. Riccini unplugged it. The patriarch restored order to the extended family temporarily. Police used a battering ram. In front of family, Riccini and two of his grandsons were arrested for impersonating tax officers. The cousins' arrest charges also included impersonating police officers, customs officers, and undercover police. An earlier search of the flat shared by them revealed false name tags, false warrant cards, and false identity cards.

Second stage was the fraud and tax evasion charges centred on Riccini's role as chair of the Asher Ministries board, and, sweeping up the other board members.

Third, and more troublesome were the investigations of the Riccini business interests in Sydney's inner west. Frank's corrupt tax office contacts turned informant and proceedings commenced to freeze the Riccini family assets. Here the decision to weaken the family bonds paid off as a few, followed by more, family members – aided by their lawyers - sought immunity for information.

News of the threats to Frank's businesses was of interest to other criminal networks. A dry-cleaning shop and an empty warehouse were firebombed two days after the last extended family Sunday lunch. Frank's 1968 Mercedes 280, bought new, stolen, found abandoned at St Peters, stripped, but the parts left lying around – a message.

Ethics Australia was satisfied, Hudson, Phoebe and all Board members of Asher Ministries had engaged in serious corrupt conduct. Ethics also provided briefs of evidence for Prosecution Australia to decide whether criminal charges, including manslaughter, could be laid.

Chasing Molly.

In the months since Alex had warned Mick that Molly Lavandar's record was too well orchestrated her life had been thoroughly scrutinised. Her files were now thickened. Mick had sent investigators to Vanuatu to research her family connections and her trips. They found she had extensive property interests there, no family, and, no one willing to talk about her. Her portfolio comprised luxury villas, luxury town houses, luxury homes on carefully tended estates, never singly, always in clusters of three or four.

Visitors and guests were rare; accompanied by security teams, arriving, and leaving the country by private jet. Indonesian and local security officers were excluded from the estates and adjoining properties. Over a few beers at a local bar, Darby's men found out the locals were pissed at this arrangement because if they weren't working, they weren't paid. Almost as bad they said was being dismissed as second class by the Indonesians. The locals said the Indonesian security boasted of being serving military, there to protect their clients with links to the Indonesian taipan.

Two operators posed as potential buyers of luxury villas, and were turned away, then when they persisted, warned off. The team returned to Australia as their cover would not survive hostile research.

At the time of the forty-five-million-dollar Polonius payment, Darby's financial team found evidence of transactions moving money in and out of accounts linked to Molly. Intelligence, yes; evidence, no. His investigators were convinced there was money hidden. They were searching for black and white, money either in an account or not, what they were seeing though was coloured glitter, confusing transactions, comingled accounts. Most of the properties in Vanuatu were bought by trust funds, sold to other trusts or companies controlled by trusts of which Lavandar was sole beneficiary, and leased back.

'We can see her hiding stuff. We don't know what she's hiding, and hiding's not a crime.'

'OK,' said Mick, 'Alex's take on her resume, her record is that she is really smart, no errors there, no life there. Alex's reasoning therefore is she is obsessive and not street smart. If she were street smart, she'd create a resume like we would – showing a few tears in the fabric, hiccups, in other words, believable.'

'So where would a person obsessed with getting it perfect make an error? If the error is not with moving and accounting for money, then where do we look? Maybe when she was younger, or something dumb, like vehicle registration, certainly not with a bank account or a transaction. Not street smart so what might she overlook?'

It took a month and some luck, and they identified a potential weakness. A month spent hunched over computers, running financial intelligence (FINT) programs, and related party analysis. The piece of luck was a New Zealand Professor of Finance reviewing Vanuatu's Financial Intelligence Unit. He was encouraged to have a research assistant use the list of entities controlled by Molly Lavandar as his sample of reporting entities. In Vanuatu trustees and managers of unit trusts are reporting entities and complete records would be expected in the registered list of entities. These records would also show the lawyers and accountants used in the buying and selling of real estate. Mick's thinking was that these data would yield some intelligence.

When the researcher pulled the records, she found there were none. The names and details of the entities concerning Molly Lavandar had been removed from the register in 2011. This was legal, the director of the unit may remove the details at the request of the entity. What was less legal was a reporting entity not to trade if its name and details are not on the register of reporting entities.

Businesses controlled eventually by Molly had continued trading after removal from the register.

Mick Darby wanted Molly. He saw her head on a plate, a gruesome twist on Salome's lust for John.

He flew to Vanuatu to meet Vanuatu Financial Intelligence Unit's director. Molly was currently in Vanuatu on extended leave. It was suspected her financial arrangements in Vanuatu were compromised, leaving her open to blackmail and extortion of her authority in the Australian Attorney-General's office. Would the Director see her way clear to detain Ms Lavandar, and allow Australian Security officers interview her on Vanuatu?

The director talked about the difficulty of a modest republic maintaining the surveillance and investigation standards required as a signatory to the United Nations Financial Sanctions Act. She had limited access to intelligence gathering techniques and software, to the extensive network of experts maintained by Australia, even the latest training initiatives. Mick moved immediately, he and the Director signed a formal MOU, for a collaborative working relationship between Mick's unit and hers. Mick flew to Sydney. Molly was confined to her residence, her passports confiscated, her assets frozen, pending investigation by a joint operation with Australian security.

Twenty seconds later it was over.

The NSW police officer pointed her 'Police Stop' sign at a dark blue Mercedes and a black Hummer. The Mercedes driver debated himself for a second or so, and, followed by the Hummer, pulled into the left lane alongside the traffic cones, just outside Cooma.

The police database of suspect vehicles sounded no alarm as the roof-mounted cameras fed the registrations of each vehicle to the recognition software. The drivers were asked for their license, breath-tested, thanked and wished a good day.

They drove away sedately, waiting until out of sight to call each other and boast, 'Man, I was so close to flooring it.'

'I'd of been right behind you, up your arse if you hadn't moved fast enough!'

Due to a feud between a federal police officer and an NSW police officer the urgent despatch from the ACT was listed last in the series of messages scrolling on laptop computers. It was read, along with reports of stock on the road, other suspect vehicles, and missing persons when the roadside operation was closed thirty minutes later.

Details of this sighting of the vehicles, and the drivers' licenses were circulated, rank pulled, and constables dressed down. None of it helped. The Mercedes was found abandoned in a shopping centre two kilometres away from Hudson Lang's rented flat, the Hummer in the Mt Pleasant nature reserve carpark, closer to Lang in Campbell.

Mick Darby's team was alerted. Alex, Ahmed, and Danny were in the long room when the call came, organising teams and equipment to fulfil the first scheduled task of the MOU Mick had signed. Mick was about halfway to Sydney from Vanuatu. Alex and his two operators checked their firearms and grabbed armour, their belts holding tasers, capsicum spray, portable radios. They weren't far from Lang's flat. As Danny drove to the address, they heard sirens.

Outside the block of flats Danny stopped on the grass, sirens filled the air now and lights reflected in the tower's windows. There was no one around. While still registering the lights, the noise, and scanning for people, a black SUV sideswiped Danny's side of their vehicle, scattering Otto bins over the courtyard at the front of the block, then braking, destroying the glass door of the block.

Waving firearms, two men fled inside and reappeared a minute later, holding pistols to Hudson Lang's head. Police cars filled the street and the courtyard. Lang, held between the two men, was screaming. The two holding him screamed at him to stop. The taller of the two, now identified as Jackson, struck him in the head and he slumped forward, blood pouring from his head. He was dragged through the broken door.

Twenty seconds later it was over.

Jackson wrenched Hudson off the ground, shoved his pistol into his chest and fired. Hudson fell back into the second man who stumbled firing wildly, as Alex and his men rushed them.

Jackson, screaming with rage, howling, beating his chest with one hand, and raising the pistol with the other was shot by an officer.

Someone took charge. Ambulances wailed, more lights flashed, more police arrived to take statements from those first there. Hudson Lang died from his wounds in the ambulance. Jackson in the operating theatre soon after admission. Alex Briggs hung on.

I never could call it.

Mick Darby's plane landed on time at Sydney International Airport. He cut a strange figure as he left the plane in a loud island shirt over dark suit pants, carrying his jacket over the shoulder, bag in the other hand. Customs lead him to one of the rooms reserved for officials where Harriet Cooper was waiting.

He put his bag down, pointed to his chest saying, 'It was a gift.'

'Oh Mick, 'she said and reached for him.

'It's not my colour, is it?'

Harriet told Mick the story. Two security officers guided them outside to Harriet's car, her husband driving. She would have it no other way.

They headed to Canberra, followed by the car carrying the two officers.

Mick sat in the back, on the phone to the hospital, to Alex's sons, also to Ahmed and Danny. He would be silent for kilometres, then garrulous with Harriet and her husband, asking about the music playing, if Paul'd conducted it, then asking for the music to be turned off. They didn't know what he would want next – music on, off, softer, louder, once he demanded more bass. Again, calling the hospital. Now sleeping, restless. He wanted to be left alone at the hospital, out of place in a dark suit and loud island shirt, colours exaggerated by the harsh lights.

The next morning Mick had Danny collect him from the hospital, drop him near Old Parliament House and he walked to the Gillard Building, oblivious to the bus loads of tourists marking off their first landmark of the day in their tour books. Ahmed wasn't oblivious to them though, ever watchful, as he followed Mick's walk. Danny had parked and was ahead of Mick, although Mick may not have noticed today.

Harriet had told him last night of winding up Operation Rose. Its tasks completed with findings of corrupt conduct against Hudson Lang, Phoebe Lang (awaiting extradition), Frank Riccini and all directors of Asher Ministries, Ian Sturgess. Briefs were drafted for Prosecutions Australia to consider prosecution. Some political fallout; the Attorney-General, and the Minister for Aged Care resigned, together on the back bench, scheming now against a common enemy. Investigations conducted by agencies other than Ethics Australia also resulted in criminal charges for fraud, tax evasion, money laundering. It was a long list.

· · · ·

Mick had a sense it was half time. He'd played the first half with Ethics, their game over now. He had to continue with another team on other, some related, investigations, Lavandar for example. Tracking the elusive Nigel Blakeley. And his own boss; we'll see about this debt he thought.

His sombre mood swept him through security, shadowed him as he swiped his card onto the floor occupied by Harriet and her offices. Danny and Ahmed observed from inside the security doors, as Mick walked to the right of the floor, approaching the analysts and operators. A quiet word with one, a smile, a remark shared with the triage team, a hand briefly resting on a shoulder, an elbow.

Harriet came out of the lift, through the doors and stood beside Danny. She stood very straight and very still. She had in her hand the day's national foreign-owned newspaper, folded to try and hide the front page. 'Time for a reckoning', shrieked the headline. 'PM questions Chief Commissioner's ethics', the strapline clarified. The lead story underneath described Ethics Australia's tactics as unethical (the lazy journalist revelling in the word play), brutal interrogations causing the death of a prominent Australian religious pastor and the exile of his wife; God-fearing people condemned for their faith.

Harriet studied Mick working the office, acknowledging each one's contribution. Noopur and Zoe in their offices, came out, hugged him. Turning away, walking along the other side of the floor, moving on to acknowledge those around their pods. Those to whom Mick had spoken remained standing as he continued his walk alone to where Alex had had his temporary workstation – bare, chair tucked under – exactly in the middle, squared away.

Mick stood, flipped what looked like a penny into the air, called, 'Ford', caught the coin, put it on the desk. He removed his hand to reveal 'Holden'.

'I never could call it,' he said, leaving the coin in the middle of the desktop, exactly.

Don't miss out!

Visit the website below and you can sign up to receive emails whenever Joe Moore publishes a new book. There's no charge and no obligation.

https://books2read.com/r/B-A-TAIY-FPBNC

BOOKS 2 READ

Connecting independent readers to independent writers.

About the Author

Joe Moore draws on his eclectic career including as MD of an international conflict and violence management company to write fiction about characters immersed in the anxieties and ambiguities exposed by violence and conflicted ethics. Joe lives with his wife in the Blue Mountains researching and writing his next piece of fiction on the corrupt management of Australia's Murray-Darling Basin.